LAST RITES

David Wishart studied Classics at Edinburgh University. He then taught Latin and Greek in school for four years and after this retrained as a teacher of EFL. He lived and worked abroad for eleven years, working in Kuwait, Greece and Saudi Arabia, and now lives with his family in Scotland.

Praise for David Wishart:

'As ever, Wishart takes true historical events and blends them into a concoction so pacy that you hardly notice all those facts and interesting details of Roman life being slipped in there ... Salve! To this latest from the top toga-wearing 'tec of Roman times!' *Highland News Group*

'[I]t is evident that Wishart is a fine scholar and perfectly at home in the period' *Sunday Times*

LAST RITES

David Wishart

NEW ENGLISH LIBRARY
Hodder & Stoughton

Copyright © 2001 by David Wishart

First published in 2001 by Hodder & Stoughton
First published in paperback in 2002 by Hodder & Stoughton
A division of Hodder Headline

The right of David Wishart to be identified as the Author of
the Work has been asserted by him in accordance with the
Copyright, Designs and Patents Act 1988.

A New English Library paperback

10 9 8 7 6 5 4

A CIP catalogue record for this title is available from the British Library

ISBN 0 340 76886 X

Typeset in Centaur by Palimpsest Book Production Limited,
Polmont, Stirlingshire
Printed and bound in Great Britain by
Clays Ltd, St Ives plc

Hodder & Stoughton
A division of Hodder Headline
338 Euston Road
London NW1 3BH

DRAMATIS PERSONAE
(Historical characters' names appear in upper case)

CORVINUS'S FAMILY AND HOUSEHOLD

Alexis: the smart-as-paint gardener
Bathyllus: Corvinus's head slave
Lysias: the coachman
Meton: the chef
PERILLA, Rufia: Corvinus's wife

IMPERIALS ETC

AGRIPPINA: Gaius's mother, now dead
DRUSUS: Gaius's elder brother, now dead
GAIUS: Tiberius's 'crown prince', the later emperor Caligula ('Caligula' – 'Little Army Boot' – was a nickname). Currently with Tiberius on Capri
MACRO, Sertorius: commander of Praetorians and Tiberius's de facto representative at Rome
SEJANUS, Aelius: Macro's predecessor, now dead (executed for treason AD 31)
TIBERIUS ('The Wart'): the emperor, currently in retirement on Capri

PURPLE-STRIPERS

AEMILIA: Galba's wife
ARRUNTIUS, Lucius: a prominent member of the Senate
CAMILLUS, Marcus Furius: the deputy chief priest. (The actual chief priest was the emperor)
Cornelia: the dead Vestal
GALBA, Servius Sulpicius: the current senior consul and later emperor

Gemella, Furia: Secundus's wife

LEPIDA: Lepidus Senior's daughter, formerly the wife of Drusus Caesar

LEPIDUS, Marcus Aemilius (Senior): a prominent (and wealthy) member of the Senate

LEPIDUS, Marcus Aemilius (Junior): his son

Murena, Gaius Licinius: a junior finance officer ('quaestor')

Nomentanus, Sextius: a city judge ('praetor')

PROCULUS, Gaius Considius: Myrrhine's former owner

Secundus, Gaius: an old friend of Corvinus's, currently city judge in charge of the Treasury

Servilia: a Vestal

TORQUATA, Junia: the chief Vestal

OTHER RANKS
Aegle
Harmodia ('Harmy') } flutegirls
Thalia

Antistius, Titus: Crocodile customer

Aquillia: Harmodia's neighbour

'archigallus, the': title of the chief priest of the Great Mother (Cybele). The holder was traditionally given the name Attis after Cybele's divine (or semi-divine) lover

Celer: expediter at the fluteplayers' guildhouse

Chilo: with Faustus, a member of the Public Ponds Watch

Crispus, Caelius: a rumour-merchant, currently on the city judges' staff

Hippo, the: owner of the Crocodile

Lippillus, Decimus Flavonius: commander of the Public Ponds district Watch

Melissa: Lepida's maid

Myrrhine: a runaway slave

Niobe: Cornelia's maid
Perdicca: a slave in the House of the Vestals
Phoebe: employee at the Crocodile
Phrixus: Thalia's brother
Scorpus: a second-hand furniture dealer
Valgius, Publius: a clerk in the citizen births registration office

Corvinus's Rome

——— Line of Servian Wall

0 — 500 — 1000
metres

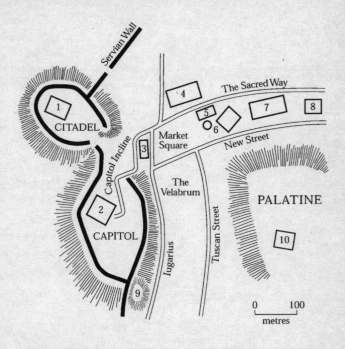

1. The Mint (Temple of Juno the Warner ['Juno Moneta'])
2. Temple of Jupiter Capitolinus
3. Temple of Saturn
4. The Aemilian Hall
5. The King's House ('Regia')
6. Temple of Vesta, House of the Vestals and chief priest's residence
7. Pearlsellers' Porch
8. Temple of Jupiter Stayer of the Host
9. The (Tarpeian) Rock
10. Temple of the Great Mother (Cybele)

I

Even without the bundle of rods that he carried when he was on active duty, the guy interrupting our breakfast was something: six foot six high by four wide, muscles like boulders and all the facial delicacy of an Alp. Jupiter knows where they find these buggers. They must breed them special and feed them on gravel.

'Marcus Valerius Caecinus?' he growled.

Bathyllus was doing his scandalised Greek chorus act in the doorway, and I could feel the waves of disapproval all the way across the room. Bathyllus's waves would've reduced any ordinary mortal to a cringing, apologetic wreck, but then Axemen aren't your ordinary mortals. These bastards have skins like rhinos. Tempers, too.

'I told him he had the name wrong, sir,' he said, 'but he wouldn't listen.'

'That's okay, Bathyllus.' I'd set down my roll and honey. 'No harm done. Go and count the statues, sunshine.' He left, fizzing. I looked back at the Axeman. Shit, this didn't look good. Axemen worked as gophers for the top brass, and they were bad news; especially these days with Macro running things as Praetorian commander. Less than a month in Rome and I was in trouble already. Worse, I'd no idea why. 'You made two out of three, friend. The name's Corvinus.'

That got me a scowl and ten flexed fingers.

'The mistress told me Caecinus.'

Yeah, well, I'd give him full marks for persistence. Speed

of uptake was something else, but then smart isn't an adjective that figures very highly in the job description. With these muscle-bound hulks the thought process is so straight and narrow you could use it for an aqueduct. You don't contradict them, either. I shrugged. 'Fine. We won't argue. Uh ... "mistress"?'

'The Lady Junia Torquata. She said find Marcus Valerius Caecinus, Rufia Perilla's husband, just moved in to the old Apronius place on the Caelian. This is the place so you must be him, right?'

There ain't no arguing with logic like that. I glanced at Perilla, lying on the other couch. Her eyes were wide and there was a crust of bread she seemed to have forgotten about poised halfway to her mouth. Well, that explained the confusion, anyway. I'd met Junia Torquata a couple of years back, when we'd had her round to dinner and she'd put a hole in my wine cellar you could drive a marble-cart through and still managed to walk out the door straight as a legion's First Spear. She hadn't been able to hold my name in her head then, either. I grinned and relaxed; if the guy was Torquata's then unsociable hour or not maybe I wasn't going to be hauled off to the Mamertine after all.

'Right,' I said. 'So what can I do for the chief Vestal, pal?'

The Axeman was flexing his hands like he was squeezing a couple of those wooden balls wrestlers use to strengthen their grip. 'I'm to take you to the Galba place,' he said.

'Is that so, now? And why would you do that?'

'Because there's been a death.'

I stared at him. Jupiter, not again! Five minutes back in residence at the Hub of the World and we were already hitting corpses. At breakfast-time, too. Maybe I was the thanaturgic equivalent of one of those screwy stones from Magnesia that snatch iron pins from your hands.

'Yeah?' I said. 'What kind of death?'

The guy hesitated and the squeezing went up a notch. Axemen aren't particularly known for showing their feelings, but if he'd been human I'd've said he was nervous. And where an Axeman's concerned that takes a hell of a lot of doing.

'Just a death,' he said.

This was getting silly. 'Fine,' I said. 'You care to tell me whose, at least? Or is that a secret too?'

His eyes rolled: personal initiative is another quality that isn't a prime requirement for Axemen, and we were obviously working right on the edge here.

'One of the Ladies.'

Shit. I sat back and heard Perilla draw in her breath. One of the Ladies, eh? For Torquata's Axeman that could mean only one thing.

The dead woman was a Vestal.

He'd brought a litter. Usually I've no time for litters, but an hour after dawn on a raw December morning with the rain gusting in from the north it beat walking hands down, especially where a trip across town to the Sacred Way was involved. Besides, I needed space to think.

Bubbling George hadn't been exactly forthcoming: ask as I might while Bathyllus had helped me into my formal mantle and thick cloak, the guy had zipped up tighter than a constipated clam. Still, certain things were clear enough. First off, we were moving in exalted circles here. Sulpicius Galba was the current senior consul, at the tail end of his year of office. I'd never met him, and from what I'd heard that was no loss because he was a first-rate, twenty-four-carat bastard; an arch-snob, tight-fisted as an Aventine landlord and with a sadistic streak you'd need a yardstick to measure. He was also (which went a long way to explaining how the guy had made

consul) a close crony of Prince Gaius, currently strutting his
stuff with the Wart on Capri, and – if you believed wineshop
rumour, which I always do – queer as a five-legged cat.

His wife, on the other hand, I didn't know at all, not
even her name; and if I didn't miss my guess it was his wife
who'd be relevant here because that was where the Vestals
came in. Early December is when the nocturnal rite of the
Good Goddess is held at the senior consul's house, with
the guy's wife playing hostess, and last night had been the
night. The ceremony involves only women, and only those
at the top of the social tree. Galba, along with every other
male and male animal in the house, would've been thrown
out on his ear while his wife, the Vestals and a pretty large
slice of Rome's female beautiful and good did whatever the
hell they do that evening after dark and then partied until
dawn with not a man in the place.

Only this year, obviously, they hadn't. Something had
gone wrong, and in the morning when the barriers came up
Junia Torquata had sent Bubbling George to look for me.

That last bit was what really bugged. 'A death', Bubbling
George had said, and he'd said it very carefully, which
implied that that was the word Torquata had told him to
use. A death, not a murder. Murder I could've understood
as the reason for hauling me away from my porridge, but
there again Vestals don't get murdered: they're about as
sacred as you can get in Rome, and you don't mess with
them, nohow, no way, never. Oh, sure, when they go out –
and Vestals are as free to come and go as anyone – they have
complimentary Axeman bodyguards, but that's only because
of who they are, not for protection. A Vestal could walk
through the Subura end to end alone with a purse stuffed
with gold pieces any time of the day or night and not a
mugger would touch a single hair of her six-tressed head.

He wouldn't dare. Just the thought of murdering a Vestal made my scalp crawl.

Also, Torquata wasn't the sort of person to call a spade a digging implement. If she said a death, then that was what she'd meant.

It just didn't make sense.

The other question, of course, was why me?

I settled back against the cushions. I had the feeling I wasn't going to enjoy this at all.

2

The Galba house was one of these big old rambling patrician mansions you get near Market Square, taking up a whole corner just short of the Temple of Jupiter Stayer of the Host, and it had half a dozen of Bubbling George's colleagues round the door leaning on their rods and dripping stoically on to the pavement. I noticed there were none of the ghouls hanging around that you usually find when someone's been hustled into an urn before their time, but that didn't surprise me: even ghouls have a healthy respect for Axemen, and with six of the buggers standing guard that pavement would not be a healthy place to be. I climbed out of the litter and went inside, past a door-slave whose grey face you could've used as a dish-rag: deaths in the family, especially suspicious ones, are always bad news for slaves. Sometimes fatally bad.

Junia Torquata was waiting for me in the atrium. The place was still rigged out for the ceremony, with the goddess's couch — empty, now, of course: they'd've taken her back to the Aventine — at the far end where the screens and curtains had been pulled back from the family rooms beyond to give more space. The walls and ceiling were hung with greenery and some of the statues still had sheets over them; these would be the male ones, too heavy to lug out but decently covered over, because not even male statues are allowed to see the rites of the Good Goddess. There was a gaggle of people clustered in the middle of the room, and they looked round when I came in. I recognised old Lucius Arruntius, the pal of my father who I'd last seen at Dad's funeral two or three years back, the time when he and Aelius Lamia had asked me to dig the dirt on Sejanus.

'Ah, Caecinus.' The lady came over nose first, like a trireme heading for the kill. Junia Torquata might be pushing sixty but she was built like a Suburan bruiser and you could've used her voice to warn shipping. Given the choice of meeting a *qef*-stoned gorilla head-on down a dark alley and Rome's chief Vestal I'd've taken the monkey any time. 'Decimus found you, then.'

'Uh ... yeah,' I said. 'And the name's Corvinus, by the way.'

'Indeed.' Well, that disposed of that one nicely. 'How's your wife? Thriving, I trust?'

'Uh, yeah, Perilla's—'

'Excellent. Well done. Now take your cloak off, young man, the weather is exceptionally mild for the time of year and it isn't a bit cold in here.'

Jupiter! I found my fingers going automatically for the pin and another grey-faced slave was at my elbow to catch the falling cloak.

'You know everyone, I assume?' The trireme's ram nose turned towards the group. Maybe it was my imagination, but the huddle seemed to tighten. Probably a self-protective herd instinct.

'No, I can't say I—'

'The consul Servius Sulpicius Galba and his wife Aemilia. Terrible for them, of course, the whole house will have to be purified top to bottom, and that is such a chore you can't imagine.'

'Corvinus.' Rome's current brightest and best gave me a stiff nod. He was a fattish, balding man with a hooked nose and quick, shifty eyes. Aemilia was short and on the plain side, but a snappy dresser: tight-fisted as the guy was rumoured to be, that mantle and the jewellery that went with it must've set him back a couple of months' income. Her perfume – it had to be hers, because she was the only other woman in the room except for Torquata, and that lady just smelled scrubbed – was four-figures too, and despite the fact she'd been up all night she was made up like a doll. All I got from her was a scared flutter of eyelashes.

'The deputy chief priest, Marcus Furius Camillus.' The trireme's ram pointed to a big old guy with white hair who wore his broad-striper mantle like it was a military uniform. Yeah; I'd heard of Furius Camillus. As governor of Africa twenty-odd years back he'd been the guy who finally put the skids under that bastard Tacfarinas. Camillus was no puffball: the bulk under that mantle was muscle, not fat, and there was a mean brain behind the pair of ice-grey eyes that turned in my direction.

'Delighted to meet you, Valerius Corvinus,' he said. 'Even under these sad circumstances. I knew your father well. A good man.'

'No introduction in my case, Torquata.' Arruntius had stepped forward. 'Corvinus here did me – and Rome – an inestimable favour two years back.' He held out his hand. I hesitated, then took it. Broad-striper to the bone though he was, and not my type at all, I'd always respected Lucius Arruntius. He might be one of that shifty bunch of hypocritical self-servers in the Senate House down the road, but he was a lion among jackals and he stuck by his principles, politically correct or not. 'Also, Corvinus, I should admit here and now that I'm the reason for dragging you away from your family at such an ungodly hour.'

Well, that was one question answered, anyway. 'Is that so?' I said.

'Unfortunately, yes.' He hesitated. 'I did it because you possess a flair for this sort of business which I felt we should avail ourselves of. Also a commendable degree of tact.' Hah! Perilla would love that! 'The latter is important because we would prefer any investigation to be conducted privately rather than involve the usual authorities.'

'Uh-huh.' In other words, whatever was going on here stank like a cat's-meat factory in high summer and he was just about to land me with the whole boiling. Thank you, Lucius bloody Arruntius and the gods bless and keep you. However, it wouldn't do to come out with any sarky comments at this juncture. I kept my lips buttoned.

'Myself, I have a double interest in the matter.' The smile was gone now and Arruntius looked grave. Clearly we'd come to — or were coming to — the nitty-gritty. 'First of all the dead woman is the daughter of Cornelius Lentulus, a cousin of mine currently abroad; second, Aemilia here is my wife's niece.'

Right; in other words, the old blue-blood network in operation. Well, at least I had a name now if nothing else: the dead Vestal must be a Cornelia, one of *the* Cornelii if her father's surname was anything to go by. And the mention of Aemilia had got me another eyelid-bat. I had the impression that physically exhausted or not, stressed out or not, the lady enjoyed making up to any presentable male within range. Although given her husband's rumoured predilections maybe that wasn't so surprising.

Not that it left me any further forward understanding the situation here. I was beginning to think this crowd was giving me the run-around on purpose; like no one wanted to be the first to put the thing into words. 'Uh, that's all very interesting, pal,' I said. 'But maybe you could just tell me what—'

Arruntius laid a hand on my arm. 'All in good time,' he said. 'I am asking you formally, Valerius Corvinus: will you help us?'

I've never been happy with the cold, clinical way that the Roman upper classes go about things. Even an invitation to dinner can end up sounding like a treaty of alliance complete with oaths before the Fetial priests. Still, it was how the guy was made. 'Sure,' I said. 'No problem. If I can. Now I'd really like to know——'

'Excellent. You'll be liaising with Camillus, naturally, but he has an appointment shortly so with his permission I'll deputise.' He glanced at Camillus, who frowned and nodded. 'Very well. The body, I think. Torquata? If you'd care to do the honours?'

We went to see the Vestal. Or what was left of her, anyway.

Torquata led us down a long marble-floored corridor with doors along its right-hand side. At the far end I could see a window with a grille set high in the wall, but there were still lamps burning in the embrasures, and most of the light came from them. Also in the embrasures – bagged, so they must've been male – were a line of what from their shapes had to be portrait busts. Oh, yeah: Galba's ancestor kick. I'd just bet that what we were passing was a roll of honour. It was a big place, though. These old patrician families didn't skimp themselves.

'She's down here, Caecinus.' Torquata turned sharp left down a side passage and into a small hallway with a staircase in the middle. 'In one of the spare bedrooms.'

She pushed open the third door along. The room was bare, apart from a bed in the centre and a clothes chest against one wall with a single oil lamp perched on top of it. On the bed lay a small sheeted figure. Torquata crossed the room and picked up the lamp.

'Watch your feet,' she said.

I looked down. Between the door and the bed, splashed like spilled wine across the white marble flooring, was a red stain. I edged carefully round it and Arruntius followed me.

Torquata had pulled back the sheet and was gazing down at the body beneath it.

'The silly girl,' she said softly. 'The silly, silly girl!'

They'd left her flame-coloured veil covering her face, but these things are light as gossamer and almost as transparent. Girl she wasn't, although she didn't miss by much: I'd reckon early twenties, twenty-five max. And she'd been beautiful; even the axe-blade nose jutting straight up at the ceiling added to the beauty, giving it character. Her face was all strong lines, the features clear-cut with no blurring flab. I'd guess that when she'd been alive this lady had had a mind of her own.

How she'd died was obvious at the first glance. The throat just beneath her chin was nothing but a gaping hole.

'I took the knife out myself,' Torquata said. She looked and sounded old, now, and not hard at all. 'Her hands were still round the hilt.'

My stomach went cold. Dear sweet Jupiter! So that was what all the reticence had been in aid of. 'She killed herself?'

'That's the question we need you to answer, Corvinus,' Arruntius said. 'You see how it looks, but the truth may be otherwise. We have to know, either way.'

'She was lying beside the door. Where the blood is.' Torquata laid her hand, very gently, on the woman's head, above where the six tresses lay beneath the veil. 'There was no sign of any struggle. I put her on the bed when I'd removed the knife.'

'You'll want to see that too, of course.' Arruntius crossed to the clothes chest and brought back a small bloodstained bundle. I unwrapped it – they'd used a napkin from the dining-room – to reveal a cheap double-edged knife with a broad blade fitted into a wooden handle and bound in place with a strip of undyed leather: the sort of thing you could pick up anywhere in Rome with change out of a silver piece. I wiped it on the napkin and tested the edge with my thumb. It'd been ground and then carefully whetted until it was razor-sharp; you could've shaved with it, easy.

'This belong to Cornelia?' I asked Torquata.

'I don't know, young man. I certainly hadn't seen it in her possession before, but that means nothing.'

'Uh-huh.' I wrapped the knife up again and gave it to Arruntius. Then I turned back to the corpse. Beyond the veil's edge I could see the line of a leather thong that disappeared under the neck of the woman's mantle. Carefully, very carefully, I lifted the veil a little and pulled at the thong. Beside me I felt Torquata stiffen, but she made no move to stop me.

At the thong's end, threaded like the pendant of a necklace, was a man's signet ring. Arruntius grunted but he said nothing; nor did Torquata. The silence was almost deafening. Oh, hell, no: cat's-meat factory was right. I held the ring up as far as I could without disturbing the veil so they could see it clearly. The stone was a garnet, and it showed two clasped hands.

'You recognise this, Junia Torquata?' I said.

She was quiet for a long time. Then she shook her head. 'No,' she said firmly. 'I do not.'

Deliberately, I shrugged and kept my eyes away from

hers and my hand steady as I laid the ring down on the dead woman's chest. Torquata knew, we all did, what the implications were of a Vestal carrying a man's ring in her bodice. Or at least the possible implications. I didn't have to spell them out, nor did I want to: some things are best left unsaid, in case saying them makes them true.

'You've seen enough?' Arruntius said. His voice was strained and very formal.

'Yeah.' I turned away while Torquata pulled the sheet back up. 'Yeah. I've seen enough.'

I was feeling cold and sick and empty. Oh, Jupiter! Dear holy Jupiter!

I knew now why Torquata had called it simply 'a death'. Murder was bad, sure, and a Vestal's murder was worse; but the responsibility – and the penalty – for it would lie squarely on the killer. Suicide in itself was no crime, not even for a Vestal. The crime lay in the cause, and in the case of a young woman who carried a man's ring next to her heart there could only be one crime that leaped immediately to mind. Vestals, like I say, were the most sacred things in Rome. They were sacred because the whole spiritual and physical health of the state depended – literally – on their chastity. A Vestal who broke her vows was a danger and an abomination, and there was only one penalty, mandatory even in these enlightened days. An unchaste Vestal was buried alive.

Torquata had to know, however much it hurt; Rome had to know. And the chief Vestal was hoping against all the evidence, against the evidence of her own eyes, that Cornelia's death had been murder.

Murder, at least, was clean.

3

We left the room and Torquata closed the door gently behind us.

'Okay,' I said. Gods, I hated this. 'You want to fill me in on the background before we rejoin the others?'

Torquata drew herself up like a battle-weary centurion getting ready to give an unpleasant report.

'It happened after the rites were over,' she said. 'The ceremonial meal also, if only just. Some time during the sixth hour.'

'Uh-huh.' Halfway to dawn, in other words. 'How many people are we talking about?'

'Present in the house? Six Vestals. Thirty invited celebrants, plus the servants and the musicians. In all, sixty. All women, of course.'

'Right.' While she was speaking I was having a look round the far side of the staircase at the screened section of wall. Immediately behind it was a solid, no-nonsense door that looked like it'd been there since the house was built a dozen generations back. There was no keyhole but it was fitted top, bottom and middle with heavy iron bolts that would've kept out anything short of a battering ram. The bolts were firmly shot home. 'This the back door?'

'Yes. It opens on to an alleyway.' That was Arruntius. 'It's the only other way into the house apart from the front door itself. That was bolted too, naturally, while the ceremony was in progress.'

There was a lamp set into an embrasure just to the left, and its light glistened on the marble at my feet. I bent down and brushed the tip of my finger against the floor. It came away damp; not wet, just damp. It could've been condensation or seepage, sure, but on the other hand . . .

'What's upstairs?' I said.

'Mostly family rooms, with storage space above that. The slaves sleep in the attics.'

'And the corridor we came along?'

'A private bath suite with a WC attached. On the atrium side there's the kitchen and a couple of storerooms.'

'Uh-huh.' I pointed to the second passageway, opposite the one we'd come through. 'Where does that lead?'

'To the garden. There's a door at the far end but it's unlocked. The garden's an enclosed one.'

'You mind if I take a look?'

'Go ahead, Corvinus.' Arruntius's lips twisted. 'You're in charge.' *And I don't envy you*, his tone said. Right. I didn't envy myself: we were going through the motions here, and all of us knew it.

I went down the passage. Sure enough, there was an open door at the end. Beyond was a big walled garden, formally laid out with statues, walks and rosebeds. It would've been beautiful in summer, I'd've guessed, but in December it just looked bleak. The walls, what I could see of them, were ten foot high, easy.

Arruntius was standing behind me. 'The only other way in is from the atrium, through that covered porch there to your left.'

I nodded. This didn't look good. Including the other staircase at the far end of the corridor off the atrium itself that'd connect with the upper floors there were plenty of access points to the bedroom where Cornelia had died, but they were all internal; and if both doors, front and back, had been bolted then sixty women – or fifty-nine, rather – was all we'd got. Scratch the disturbed burglar who'd panicked, stabbed first and asked questions later; he didn't exist.

I led the way back to the hall and opened the remaining doors. Most of them were storerooms. The two either side of where Cornelia lay were bedrooms, bare and anonymous as the one with the corpse.

So much for the floor plan. 'Okay,' I said. 'So what about the lady herself? Who was she, exactly?'

'As I told you, the daughter of Publius Cornelius Lentulus, currently in Asia,' Arruntius said. 'An only child. Her mother is the sister of my friend the ex-consul Marcus Lepidus. They divorced many years ago and both have remarried. Lepida Calvina and her new husband moved to Tarentum.'

'Uh-huh.' All that, I knew, was incidental: Vestals are selected by the chief priest from a list of eligible girls between the ages of six and ten, and when they're appointed the old family ties are cut completely. Cornelia's 'family' would've been the other five Vestals living with her in the House of the Vestals just down the road next to the temple itself. I turned to Torquata. 'She, uh, show any signs of odd behaviour recently? Seem worried, out of sorts, that kind of thing?'

I'd kept my voice neutral, but it was clear what I was asking. Also that Torquata wasn't happy about the answer. Her big bruiser's face reddened. 'Yes, young man,' she said. 'As a matter of fact she did.'

'Did she tell you why?'

The old girl's lips were tight, and she was still holding herself like a soldier. 'No. I didn't ask. I don't pry, Valerius Corvinus. I believe the best policy, especially with young girls, is to make oneself approachable and let them come forward themselves when they feel ready to do so. I've always been a great one for trust, and in an artificial environment such as ours — and it *is* artificial, I acknowledge that — one must be very careful not to infringe on the private space of others.'

There was a quietness to her voice, and I knew why; it'd been there since she'd touched the dead girl's forehead. The chief Vestal was crucifying herself, wondering if things might've been different if she had interfered for once, knowing that it was too late now for anything but regret. I felt sorry as hell for Junia Torquata. Still, this had to be done.

I hadn't missed that 'Corvinus', either. That was significant, too.

'What about the other sisters?' I said. 'Would she talk to any of them?'

'I doubt it. Cornelia wasn't ...' Torquata hesitated. 'Cornelia was a very private person, and although we get on well enough generally as a group there is still the occasional friction and the petty jealousies that exist in every family. Especially a family wholly composed of women.' The corners of her mouth turned down. 'You being a man would not understand, or you would find the details trivial, so I won't be more explicit. However you may take it from me that had Cornelia approached any of her colleagues it would have been myself. I knew her from birth, and we were always close.'

'There's Niobe, of course,' Arruntius murmured.

That got him a look that would've skewered a rhino, and Torquata's voice took on its old sharpness. 'Lucius Arruntius,' she snapped, 'I am fully aware that we have not yet come to Niobe, and I also possess a perfectly serviceable pair of ears. Caecinus was asking about the sisterhood, not the servants. Or do you think that I am prevaricating intentionally?' Arruntius winced and said nothing. Jupiter! Well, at least the old warhorse was showing signs of pulling herself out of her slump. And I noticed that I was Caecinus again.

'Niobe?' I said.

'Cornelia's maid.' Torquata was still glaring at Arruntius. 'You can interview her shortly, young man. Lucius here is quite correct, they were extremely close; in fact they were brought up together.'

I nodded; yeah, that made sense. It happens all the time, especially in the old traditional families. A kid barely past the toddling stage will be matched with another of the same sex and about the same age belonging to one of the house slaves. From then on the two'll be inseparable, with the slave kid naturally filling the role of personal maid or valet. 'She was here last night?'

'It was Niobe who found the body.' Arruntius cleared his throat; the poor guy still looked chewed. 'If anyone can help you with time or any other details like that she's the most likely.'

'Uh-huh.' I paused, gathering my courage. Hell, we'd gone round the houses long enough. We all knew the vital question had to be asked and answered sooner or later, and however I phrased it it had to sound brutal. 'Junia Torquata, I'm sorry, but is there any possibility that Cornelia had been seeing a man? That she committed suicide because she was pregnant?'

The silence was total. I expected a glare like the one that had frozen Lucius Arruntius's balls for him, but all I got was the sort of look a doctor might expect when he told a patient she had only a month to live. Arruntius, too, said nothing, but his lips tightened and he looked away.

Finally, Torquata drew in her breath and let it out. When

she did speak, her voice was low and careful, with more than a touch of steel to it. 'I have told you, Valerius Corvinus, that I knew Cornelia from the moment she was born to the day of her death. She was a lovely girl, full of life, but she was a true Vestal. I would as soon suspect myself of breaking the vow of chastity as I would her. Your answer is no. Categorically no. Suicide or not, Cornelia lived and died a virgin, and I would swear to that by Vesta's fire itself. Whatever proofs or indications to the contrary there might be.'

'I agree,' Arruntius said quietly.

Well, that was that. I sighed. 'Fine,' I said. 'Let's go and join the others.'

When we got back to the atrium we found that the gaggle had lost one and gained one. Camillus had left and in his place was a smart-looking guy in his mid-thirties with a broad purple stripe to his mantle and the go-getting air of the professional politician. He came over and held out his hand.

'Gaius Sextius Nomentanus,' he said as I took it. 'City judge.'

Uh-oh; the top legal brass had arrived. Yeah, well, I supposed that was inevitable: not just because of the death but because the city judges, as a corporate group, foot the bill for the December rite. Nomentanus, or if not him one of his colleagues, would have a vested interest in the proceedings.

'You've seen everything you need to, Valerius Corvinus?' That was the consul, Galba. The guy had a jaw like a pike's, and his skin had a pasty, sweaty sheen.

I nodded.

His eyes slid away from me. 'It's a bad business,' he said. 'A very bad business.'

'Yeah.' I had the distinct impression that he meant it

was bad *for* business: sure, he hadn't been around when the girl had died but a Vestal's death in your back bedroom under suspicious circumstances wasn't exactly a plus where a political career was concerned. I hadn't expected to like Galba, and first-hand experience confirmed it. 'I'll want to talk to whoever was in charge of the servants last night, of course. The dead woman's maid as well.' I looked at Nomentanus. 'If that's okay with you, sir.'

Nomentanus had sat back down on one of the couches. He was a good-looking guy, and I noticed Aemilia was giving him sidelong glances from her own couch next door. 'Don't mind me, Corvinus,' he said. 'I'm not here in any official capacity, at any rate not in these terms. I think Arruntius explained that to you.'

Well, he couldn't say fairer than that. Since we'd come back in I'd been letting my eyes wander round the room. There was a long wooden screen across part of the opposite wall, with a low platform in front of it, and I could feel cold air blowing from that direction. Arruntius had said you could get into the garden from the atrium via the covered porch. No doubt that was how. 'Uh, why the platform?' I said.

'Oh, that was for the musicians.' I'd thought Aemilia would have a mousey voice, but she sounded brassy if anything, and she drawled her vowels like some of these top-class patricians do.

'Musicians?'

Bat-bat, flutter-flutter. Jupiter! 'The rite needs music. Flutes mostly. Especially at the point when—' Aemilia stopped, and her eyes slid nervously towards Junia Torquata, who frowned and pursed her lips.

'*Euphemeite*,' she murmured.

Keep holy silence: a rap over the knuckles because of the men present; only women are allowed to know the details of the Good Goddess's rites. Aemilia coloured up and looked away. Yeah, well. I turned to Torquata.

'I told you about the musicians myself, young man,' she snapped. 'We ordered a dozen from the guildhouse near the Temple of Juno Lucina.'

'They've gone?'

'Naturally they've gone. Their contract was only until dawn. They left with the other celebrants.'

'Guild policy, Valerius Corvinus.' Nomentanus was smiling. 'You pay extra for overtime.' There spoke the guy who held the purse-strings: the state gave a grant for official ceremonies, but it never went all the way towards covering costs and the balance would have to come out of the appropriate magistrates' own pockets. Meaning, in this case, Nomentanus's. 'Besides, they're working girls, they have other engagements.'

Well, it couldn't be helped, and I could always call in at the guildhouse later for a list of names. Although it was unlikely that one of the musicians was involved. 'You think I could talk to the maid now?' I asked Galba. 'Uh . . . Niobe, wasn't it? And to your head female slave.'

'Certainly. Certainly.' The consul was frowning: I had the impression that he thought all this rigmarole was a waste of time and the sooner we all stopped cluttering up his living-room and went home the better. Maybe he was right. 'I told them to wait in the kitchen. You, there.' He beckoned over one of the slaves standing against the wall. 'Fetch Niobe and Pythia.'

'No, that's okay.' I didn't fancy conducting an interrogation with a fair slice of Rome's beautiful and good breathing down neck. Besides, I'd bet the girls would be more talkative on home ground. 'I'll go to them.'

Galba just looked at me, then turned away with a sniff.

Par for the course. I wondered if the bastard even knew where his own kitchen was.

They were sitting together side by side at the kitchen table, although I got the impression that there hadn't been much talking going on. When I came in they jumped to their feet like someone had yanked on a string. Home ground or not, they looked nervous as hell; understandable, because like I say under the strict letter of the law with a suspicious death in the house all the slaves could be killed out of hand just on the off-chance they might've been in on it. It was obvious which was which: Pythia was a grey-haired old biddy seriously handicapped in the teeth department, while Niobe was a dark-haired, dark-skinned little stunner the same age as the dead girl.

There was a stool in the corner by the sink. I pulled it over and perched on it while they watched me like rabbits watching a snake.

'Hey, that's all right,' I said quietly. 'Sit down. No one's going to bite you.'

They looked at each other. Pythia sat but the girl didn't.

'You're Niobe?' I said to her. She nodded. Her eyes were big and scared. 'I was told you found the body.'

Another nod. Moisture gathered under her right eye and crept down her cheek, but her expression didn't change.

'You care to tell me about it? From the beginning?' The girl swallowed, tried to speak and swallowed again. I waited patiently. 'Take your time. There's no hurry.'

'We'd finished eating. After the rite.' Her voice was low and husky, and the accent was good for a slave's. Of course; she'd been brought up outside the slave quarters, as one of the family. 'The mistress had been sitting on her own in the corner and I'd been serving her. She got up. I was going to follow, but she said not to bother, she was only going to the toilet, she wouldn't be long. I waited fifteen minutes, maybe twenty, and she didn't come back.'

'So you went to see if there was anything wrong.'

She nodded. 'She wasn't in the WC. I thought maybe she'd been taken ill and gone to lie down somewhere, so I went looking for her. The door to one of the spare bedrooms was open and I saw ... I ...' She stopped.

'That's okay,' I said gently. 'Take your time.'

'She was lying on the floor with a knife in her throat. There was ... there was blood ... all over ...' The tears were running freely now, but she paid them no attention. Another gulp. 'I'm sorry, sir. That's all I can tell you. Except that I fetched the Lady Junia Torquata right away.'

'Was it your mistress's knife?' I kept my voice neutral.

She brought the back of her hand across her eyes, wiping away the moisture; a single, sharp gesture as if she were ashamed of it. 'No, sir. At least, I hadn't seen it before. Any knife, I mean, not just that one. What would the mistress want with a knife?'

'But she could've had it without your knowing?'

The girl was quiet for a long time. Then she said, in a voice like a ghost's, 'Yes. Yes, she could.'

Just that. 'Okay.' I shifted on the stool. 'You sure you don't want to sit down?' She shook her head. 'The Lady Torquata said your mistress seemed worried, that she had something on her mind. You know anything about that?'

'No, sir.'

'She didn't talk to you about it? Give any sort of hint?'

'No, sir.'

The lips were tight and her eyes never moved from mine. She was lying, sure she was; however, short of turning her over to the torturers I wasn't going to get much further, and I didn't want to do that. I sighed. 'Was your mistress pregnant?'

'*No*, sir!' Her chin went up, and I thought for a moment she was going to hit me. 'The Lady Cornelia was a Vestal!'

'But you've just told me she didn't confide in you. It's possible.'

'It is *not* possible! The Lady Cornelia would've—' She stopped, then went on carefully. 'My mistress would have died first. If that's what they're saying out there then—'

'Okay, okay.' I held up my hand. 'Is there anything else you can tell me? Anything at all?'

Was that hesitation? I wasn't sure. In any case, she shook her head.

'No, sir. Nothing.'

'The lady was wearing a ring. A man's ring, on a cord round her neck. You know where she got it?'

The lips tightened again. If looks could have killed I'd've been a grease spot. 'No, sir.'

Well, that was that. She knew, I'd've bet a year's income on it, but short of dragging the information out of her with red-hot pincers I was stuck. Probably I wouldn't get it even then. I turned to the other woman, Pythia. 'Who opened the back door?' I said.

I thought she was going to faint. 'Pardon, sir?'

'The tiles were wet. Someone must've opened the door and let the rain in.'

She was dish-rag grey and shaking. 'The back door's bolted, sir.'

'Sure. It is now. But the floor was still wet. Damp, rather. It'd been mopped. My guess is whoever bolted the door, or rebolted it, maybe, cleaned up first.'

Niobe was staring at her. 'Pythia . . .' she said.

Pythia didn't look at her. 'I swear to the Lady Diana, sir—'

'Pythia, this is important.' The old woman was obviously terrified, but I couldn't let up now. 'I need the truth, okay?'

'The back door was open?' That was Niobe. She was still staring at Pythia.

The other slave's eyes flicked between us. Her mouth opened and closed.

'I didn't mean any harm, sir,' she whispered finally. 'I swear I didn't. Sir, if you tell the master he'll—'

'I won't tell anyone.' Shit! If the back door had been open all the time then this was a whole new ball game! 'All I want is the truth. Was the door open or not?'

'It was bolted at the start of the evening, sir, I swear!' The old woman was mumbling so hard it was difficult to pick out the words. 'I made sure myself.'

'But not later?'

'After the lady was found I saw the bolts had been slipped. I put them back, sir, just that, and I cleaned up like you said. The door was closed, there wasn't much water. By the sweet Mother, sir, I swear I didn't mean any harm!'

I turned away. Dear holy Jupiter, it'd been murder after all! Or at least it could have been murder.

We were getting somewhere at last. Now I needed time to think.

4

I walked back to the Caelian despite the rain. It felt funny not turning up Victory Incline to the old house on the Palatine, but we were settling in nicely to the new place on Fabricius Street. It must've been the fastest sale on record. Three months back we'd been twiddling our thumbs in Brindisi waiting for a favourable wind to take the ship we'd booked passage on back to Athens when a messenger had arrived hotfoot from my stepfather Priscus to say that one of his antiquities-nut cronies had fallen off his perch unexpectedly (the guy was ninety) and his house was being put on to the market. Perilla had talked me round and that was that. Half our stuff was still the other side of the Adriatic, mind, and it would stay there until the sea lanes opened again in two months' time, but, hell, we could rough it. The only slug in the salad was that the new place was within shouting distance of Mother's. Staving off dinner invitations without starting a major family feud was going to be much trickier in future. Not just dinner invitations, either: our compost heap was already the richer for a couple of Phormio's more outré efforts that Mother had sent round to make sure we were eating properly. If *properly*'s the word. I'm not too sure about *eating*, either.

Bathyllus was waiting as usual with the obligatory jug when I pushed past the door-slave and got rid of my sopping cloak and mantle. The wine was steaming hot with a touch of cinnamon, just the thing after a wet, chilly walk all the way from Market Square; freshly hot, too, not a reheat. I've given up wondering how the little guy knows I'm coming home. Maybe he keeps a tame augur in the cupboard.

'The mistress around, Bathyllus?' I sipped the wine carefully as the cup thawed my hands out.

'Yes, sir. And the new water clock's arrived.'

'Oh. Oh, yeah.' I'd forgotten they were delivering the brute this morning. Perilla had seen it on one of her forays to the chichi shops in the Saepta, and she'd been immediately captivated. Me, I had my doubts. Machinery of any kind isn't my bag, and some of those Greek gizmos are too clever for their own good. Or anyone else's. Well, we'd just have to hope for the best. I picked up the jug from the tray and carried it with the cup through to the atrium.

'Ah, you're back, Marcus.' The lady was supervising four beefy slaves who'd obviously just finished setting the thing up against the wall in the corner. They were looking pretty chewed; when Perilla supervises, she supervises. 'How did it go?'

'Tell you later.' I set the jug down on a side table and laid the customary smacker between her chin and nose. 'Jupiter! That's a *clock*?'

The thing was at least five foot high by three broad, with a reservoir at the top and a maze of bronze piping beneath. Halfway up, a winged Victory with a simpering grin and a tutu held a pointer against a vertical scale with the numbers one to twelve marked on it, on the other side of which stood a titan with his hammer raised above an anvil. At the bottom two chubby-cheeked-and-buttocked cherubs were poised over a basin.

'Right, Zosimus, fill her up!' snapped one of the delivery-men; obviously the foreman, because he was standing well back with his hands through the belt of his tunic.

I watched fascinated as another guy shinned up a ladder with a bucket and emptied it into the reservoir.

The foreman stepped forward and cleared his throat. 'These are the calibration valves, madam.' He touched two eggbound ducks in bronze part the way down two central pipes. 'They're in the off position at present. The one on the left is for day, the one on the right for night. If one is open, the other must be closed. You understand?'

Jupiter! Complications already! I didn't like the sound of this, but Perilla was nodding.

'The calibration is simple. As the days lengthen during the first half of the year the left-hand duck's beak is advanced at the rate of one notch on the kalends and ides of each month, while the right-hand duck – the night-duck, that is – is rotated in the opposite direction by a similar amount, thus matching the water flow for each pipe to the corresponding lengthening and shortening of the daylight and night-time hours. At the equinox the procedure is of course reversed for each duck. No messing around with wax to be added and removed to control the flow, you see.' He smiled a superior smile. 'This is a *very* sophisticated model.'

The lady was beaming. 'But that's absolutely marvellous! Most ingenious! Isn't it, Marcus?'

I grinned at her weakly. Yeah, well, I'd take her word for it. One thing was sure: I wasn't going to touch this bastard machine with a bargepole. Sophisticated was right; it sounded smarter than I was, for a start.

'The Victory figure, of course, indicates the hour, and at its commencement the titan will strike his anvil bell. The water in the lower part of the system empties automatically at the close of the twelfth daytime and night-time hours respectively' – the guy indicated the basin with the cherubs – 'bringing the indicator back to its starting point. Your slaves then return the voided water to the reservoir by draining the basin into a bucket via the spigot which you will see at its base, and reset the valves for the appropriate upcoming time period, whereupon the cycle is repeated.' He smiled. 'Is all that clear, madam? Or do you have any questions?'

Gods! My brain had gone numb. What was wrong with an old-fashioned sundial? Sure, this superintelligent bugger told you every hour out of the twenty-four but personally I had better things to do with my sleeping hours than pad downstairs to a freezing atrium and check what the time was. And Bathyllus and the lads were going to just love it to bits.

Besides, I had a bad feeling about this. A very bad feeling.

'Perfectly clear, thank you.' Perilla was looking like the cat that got the sturgeon. 'And, as I said, most ingenious. Would you set it going for us, please?'

'Of course, madam.' He turned to the guy with the bucket. 'What's the time, Zosimus?'

There was a terrible silence while the bucket-slave shuffled his feet and looked uncomfortable.

'Uh ...' he said finally, and blushed to his ears.

I grinned; so much for the cutting edge of engineering science. 'The garden's out that way, pal,' I said. 'Only it's overcast at present, so I wouldn't bother. Why don't you just set the thing for the sixth hour and we'll make allowances?'

'Right. Right.' The foreman's smile had slipped: I had the impression Archimedes here felt his professional integrity was being compromised, but there wasn't a lot he could do about it. 'Advancing the daytime duck to the limit of its screw opens the system completely. I would advise you, madam, never to try this yourself or allow your slaves to do so. The mechanism is extremely delicate and although the operation is completely safe in competent hands it is best left to a trained hydraulics engineer such as myself.' Yeah; and I'd bet consultation fees were sky-high into the bargain. This looked like costing me an arm and a leg.

He twisted the valve. Water gurgled alarmingly in the pipes, wheels spun, the winged figure lurched upwards on its pole and the titan suddenly went crazy.

Tingtingtingtingting . . .

When the pointer touched the six the guy turned the valve back and it stopped. Well, so far so good. Maybe the thing worked after all.

The gurgling changed to a steady drip . . . drip . . . drip.

'You, uh, wouldn't have a silent model, would you, friend?' I said.

He glared at me. 'No, sir, I wouldn't. This clepsydra is the most advanced of its kind.'

Yeah, right. Even so, the drips were getting on my nerves already. 'Fine. Fine,' I said. 'Just asking.'

'Indeed.' He turned back to Perilla. 'As you can see, madam, it is now in the standard operating mode. I have set the duck for the kalends of December. This notch here' – he pointed – 'represents the corresponding night-duck position. The instrument is now fully functional and should require no further attention apart from the ongoing procedures I have outlined. However in the unlikely event that you have any problems, please don't hesitate to get in touch. Zosimus, the ladder.'

They left.

Perilla lay down on the reading couch. 'Well, Marcus,' she said. 'Tell me about your morning.'

I told her. The basics, anyway.

'But that's dreadful! The poor girl! You think it was suicide?'

'It's a prime possibility, sure.' The jug of wine was beside me, at the edge of my own couch. I topped up the cup and took a slug. The clock went drip ... drip ... drip in its corner while I tried to ignore it. 'There's the way she died, for a start. And there was no sign of a struggle. The main problem with suicide is why.'

'Pregnancy?' Perilla's no fool; given the shocking fact that a Vestal had killed herself, pregnancy's the obvious reason. After all, there's no way of hiding it and as I say the girl'd end up dead in any case. Added to which, a knife in the throat's a lot cleaner than having to climb down into a pit and wait while they pile the earth on top of you.

'Torquata says no. Absolutely no. Lucius Arruntius agrees, and they're both very smart cookies who've known the girl all her life. Her maid said the same and almost scratched my eyes out for suggesting it. Still, there's the ring.'

'The ring?'

I told her about the man's signet ring Cornelia had been wearing round her neck.

'It could be an innocent keepsake, Marcus. Her father's, perhaps.'

'Her father's still alive. Besides, Torquata denied all knowledge. She may've been covering up, sure, but if the thing had been innocent and she'd known it was she wouldn't've had any reason to. That ring bugs me. Also there was the girl's state of mind. Something was worrying her the last few days, even Torquata had to admit that.'

'You know Junia Torquata's niece is engaged to Prince Gaius, incidentally?' Perilla had poured herself something from a jug on her own side table. It'd be some whacky fruit juice or other; she was working through everything on offer in Delicatessen Market off the Sacred Way. What they had for December I just didn't like to think. 'Junia Claudilla. Her brother Marcus's girl.'

'Yeah?' Marcus Junius Silanus was the only one of that family I hadn't run foul of, and if he was anything like his brothers and had passed it on to his daughter then maybe I was wasting my sympathy. Still, I wouldn't wish marriage to that loopy egocentric bastard on anyone. 'Since when?'

'Official word has just come from Capri.' Perilla sipped at her cup. 'Bathyllus told me.' Oh. Right. That put the news up in the death and taxes bracket as far as reliability went. The slave grapevine is shit-hot, and Bathyllus is never wrong. Never. 'So. Suicide is a distinct possibility, whatever the motive. Death while the balance of the mind was disturbed. Have you any reason to think otherwise?'

I scowled into my wine. 'All I've got's a door, lady, with three pulled bolts. And a half-gaga slavewoman's word that it was originally locked.'

Perilla sat up. 'Explain.'

I explained. 'The thing is,' I finished, 'it could all be wishful thinking. Torquata wants the girl to have been murdered so bad that it hurts, because then she needn't ask herself why she committed suicide. The problem is, who the hell would murder a Vestal? And everything else points to a self-killing, which — granted we don't know the reason — makes perfect sense otherwise.'

'All right. Take murder as a working theory. Where does it get you?'

I drained the cup and poured myself some more wine from the jug. I was still trying to ignore the drip ... drip ... drip from the corner. Hell, maybe I wouldn't notice it after a few days. If I was still sane enough to notice anything, that was. 'Okay,' I said, 'let's think about the door. It wasn't locked, it was bolted, so it had to have been opened from the inside. That means either someone let themselves out after killing the girl or someone on the inside let another person in. Which do you want to start with?'

'The first.'

'Fine. In that case it's an inside job, because the house was sealed for the rite. We've got fifty-nine suspects, all women. Five of them are Vestals, thirty are the cream of Roman society and the rest are professional flutegirls and assorted household slaves. You want to pick a category?'

'Ah.'

'"Ah" is right, lady.'

She sniffed. 'You're not helping, Marcus. Very well. I may not have to choose. If the killer let herself out then ipso facto she wouldn't be in the house after the murder, would she?'

'Perilla, the rite was over. What we have is a free-for-all party with sixty guests and the food and booze running free. I'd say, barring the Vestals and maybe the flutegirls who came as a group, any given woman could've slipped away and no one would be any the wiser. And by the time I arrived they'd all gone home in any case, so there was no way of checking.'

'Oh.' Perilla turned the cup in her hands. 'Then again, an additional complication is that the murderess needn't have slipped away at all, need she? She could simply have pulled the bolts on the back door as a blind and gone back to where she came from. Is that a possibility?'

Rats; I hadn't thought of that particular twist. This was a real bugger. 'Yeah, it's possible,' I said. 'In fact there were three ways of getting to and from the atrium that I could see: one along the bath suite corridor, one through the garden and the third via the upper floors.'

'Hmm.' Perilla frowned. 'All right. Let's leave it and try your second option. That someone inside the house opened the door to the girl's killer.'

'Okay.' I settled back against the cushions. 'That theory's more promising because it means the suspect field is wide open; the actual killer could've been anyone, male or female, from any background. The problem is, who opened the door?'

'Could it have been left unbolted from the beginning?'

'The head slavewoman Pythia said no.'

'She could've been mistaken. Or lying.'

I shook my head. 'Uh-uh. I know I said the woman was past it, but making sure the doors are locked at night, especially the back door, is the slave in charge's prime duty. They don't delegate, and they check and double-check, particularly when the master's a punctilious bastard like Galba. That door was bolted, Perilla, at least at the start of the evening. Which meant that someone unbolted it deliberately later and left it unbolted. And if that had nothing to do with the murder then I'm a blue-arsed Briton.'

'Very well, then. We're back to our list of suspects. On the other hand, of course, it could have been Cornelia herself.'

I stared at her. '*What?*'

'The very fact that the door was left *un*bolted subsequent to the girl's death implies that the killer had no means of relocking it behind them. An accomplice – a live accomplice – would surely have done that. The obvious alternative implication is that the person who opened the door was no longer able to bolt it; indeed, that she was dead.'

I sat back. 'Lady, I'm sorry, but that doesn't make sense. Why should Cornelia open the door at all?'

'I don't know. Unless it was by prearrangement and she knew the person on the other side.'

I took a swallow of the wine. It added up; even the timing added up. The rite's over, technically the ban's lifted, so although the house is still sealed for practical purposes the religious prohibition, strictly speaking, no longer holds; and the religious aspect would weigh with Cornelia, sure it would. She agrees to an arrangement with whoever the visitor is, then when the time comes she makes an excuse to her maid, goes to the back door and slips the bolts ...

Only I couldn't see Cornelia doing that, no way, nohow, never; not after what Torquata had told me about her. She hadn't been the kind of girl who would take advantage of a technicality just because it suited her. Besides, who could the 'visitor' who turned out to be her murderer have been? A man? The man who belonged to the ring? That made the theory even more unlikely, because it meant the girl's actions had been really underhand. And what would the purpose have been? Not an assignation, that was sure, not in a strange house full of people on one of the holiest nights in the year. Cornelia the Vestal would never have connived at that ...

'Lunch is served, sir.'

I blinked. Bathyllus had crept in and was doing his perfect butler act. When he saw he'd got my attention he cast a disapproving eye on the clock dripping away against the wall and sniffed. Bathyllus is no machine-nut, either. He can't even operate a corn mill without grinding his fingers.

Hell, theorising could wait: I'd missed out on breakfast,

I'd had a hard morning and I was starving. Food first. Then this afternoon I'd go across to the fluteplayers' guildhouse and check out the girls who'd been playing last night.

There was the question of the knife, too. That I hadn't mentioned to Perilla; and the knife was interesting.

5

The fluteplayers' guildhouse was near the Temple of Juno Lucina, at the Esquiline end of the Subura. I cut up Head of Africa (keeping my own head carefully covered as I passed Mother's house) and made for the Carinae, skirting the Oppian Mount to the right. The weather had improved, but it was still blowing through rain: the worst kind of day to be walking. Heat and dry cold I don't mind, but I really hate the wet.

That knife had got me puzzled. If Cornelia's death had been suicide — which was still on the strong side of possible — then it needed explaining. Sure, you could pick up a weapon like that anywhere in Rome no questions asked, but it was the cheapest of the cheap: all you got was the basics. And that meant, in its original condition, the blade wouldn't've cut porridge; the metal was poor and the manufacturer wouldn't've spent good time and money giving it a proper edge. So the first thing any normal purchaser would do was take it somewhere to be sharpened, or do it themselves. That was the first point: stress the word *normal*. Like Niobe had said, Vestals don't buy knives as a rule, and I'd've bet if I gave one of the cheapos to Torquata the idea of sharpening it wouldn't've entered her head. To most women — let alone Vestals — a knife is a knife is a knife.

Point two: the knife Arruntius had shown me wasn't just sharp, it was *sharp*. That edge had been a labour of love, with not a nick or a missing flake marring its line. Putting it on a cheap bit of metal must've taken hours and a great deal of care and skill. No blacksmith or cutler in Rome worth his salt would've taken the bother to get the thing into that condition; at best he'd've told the person who brought it in to chuck it over the side of Sublician Bridge and buy something he could really work on, or more likely sold them a replacement himself. No; whoever had sharpened it had done it personally, very carefully and very skilfully; and that couldn't've been a Vestal. No way. It was a small glitch, sure, and there might be a dozen valid explanations, but like I say it bugged me.

I reached the fluteplayers' guildhouse, a crumbling old two-storey property that looked like it might've reverted to rubble if you sneezed too close. Flutegirls aren't all that well paid, apart from sometimes in kind when they perform services over and above the call of duty at private dinner parties, and the few copper coins creamed off the top of their wages to pay for a professional and social base wouldn't rent or buy much, even in aggregate. I pushed the door open and went in.

'Yes, sir, can I help you?' A fat, fussy little guy with baggy jowls busied out of one of the doors in the tiny hallway. The expediter, obviously: musicians, like any fragmented group of professional individuals, need a front man who's always around to take customer bookings and manage the timetables. 'A private function, would it be? Dinner party? Wedding?' I shook my head and his jowls dropped into pious respect position. 'Funeral?'

'Not that either, pal,' I said. 'Just some information.'

'Ah.' The jowls retracted, and he lost a lot of his eagerness. I pulled out a silver piece and the eagerness came back. 'Yes, sir. Certainly. What can I do to help?'

'I'm looking into the death at the senior consul's house

last night. You heard about that?' A rhetorical question: sure he would. Probably half of Rome had by now, one way or the other.

'Yes, sir. A tragic business. Tragic. For a Vestal to kill herself . . .'

'I was hoping you might be able to give me a list of the girls who were playing.'

'Nothing easier, sir.' He palmed the silver piece. 'But I tell you now, none of my girls was involved. I can vouch for them all personally.'

Yeah; I'd thought that might be the case. The musicians'd been an outside bet anyway. 'That's understood, friend,' I said. 'No hassle. I'm just checking the angles.'

'Of course.' He looked relieved. 'Then if you'll come into my office I'll show you the relevant tablet.' I followed him into the room he'd come out of. There was a piled desk and two chairs in as good a shape as the building itself, with a set of filing shelves on each of the three facing walls. 'Have a seat, sir. I won't keep you a moment.'

I sat down. He raked through the wax tablets lying on the desk, picked up one, checked the heading and handed it over.

'There we are, sir. A dozen ordered, a dozen sent.'

I looked at the names. There were twelve, like he'd said, but one was scored through and another written beside it.

'There's a change here,' I said.

'Yes, sir. The girl called in a few days ago with a persistent cough. It happens, especially this time of year, and of course it makes playing impossible.'

'The replacement, Thalia. She a regular?'

'Oh, yes, sir. All our girls are, been with us for years. And she's an excellent fluteplayer, one of our best, or she wouldn't have been eligible.'

'So how come she wasn't on the original list?' The rite of the Good Goddess is a top-notch gig. Torquata – or Aemilia or the city judges or whoever made the arrangements – would insist on quality; get it, too. And from the flutegirls' side inclusion in one of the biggest society events of the year would go a long way professionally to netting them future bookings.

The jowls wobbled. 'We try to be fair, sir. The ceremony being an annual one and so prestigious, arrangements are made well in advance. The girls – the most suitable, anyway – draw lots for inclusion among the twelve. Thalia was unlucky this year, initially. When the vacancy occurred, however, we held a second ballot and Thalia drew the lucky straw.'

'Uh-huh.' Well, nothing there, then, especially with the element of chance involved. Still, I had to start somewhere, and this Thalia was as good a place as any. 'You have her address?'

'No, sir, unfortunately not.' The guy coughed delicately. 'Most of our girls are, shall we say, migrant. They move around on a temporary basis, and although many do have rooms the odds are that they won't be found there. Certainly any records we tried to keep would be very unreliable. Hence this guildhouse. The girls call in here on a regular basis to check their upcoming engagements and compare notes on customers.'

Shit. I needed to talk to someone now. 'Okay. Is there anyone on this list you can put me in touch with immediately?'

He took it from me and frowned at it for a bit. Then he pointed to a name halfway down. 'Aegle's your best bet for that, sir,' he said. 'She's . . . not so much in demand as some of the other girls. I'm not speaking professionally, you understand. And she does have her own place, not far from here as a matter of fact. In the tenement on Suburan Street opposite the Shrine of Picus, although the floor I can't help you with.'

I stood up. 'Thanks a lot, pal. You've been very helpful.'

'Don't mention it, sir. I hope to have your custom in the future.'

The rain was coming down in buckets as I left the guildhouse, and I was glad of my hooded cloak. Like the guy had said, the tenement wasn't far, only a few hundred yards. The entrance was sandwiched between a second-hand clothes shop and a very suspect-looking pork-butcher's. Not a good area.

There was a round-shouldered guy leaning against the wall outside chewing on a sausage. I went up to him.

'You happen to know which floor Aegle the flutegirl lives on, pal?' I said.

His eyes took in the quality of the cloak: it was covering my narrow-striper mantle, but that and the upper-class vowels were enough. 'You don't want Aegle, sir,' he said. 'I can recommend a much better—'

'Just tell me the floor, friend.'

He shrugged and bit into his sausage. 'Top,' he said. 'Under the tiles.'

I brushed off the sprayed bits of gristle and went inside. The entrance passage and the stairs beyond smelled of piss, and the local artists had done their melancholy best with the walls. Under the tiles, right? The cheapest flat, six floors from anything and cold as hell. Damp, too, probably, if the landlord didn't lose sleep over the condition of the roof. Fluteplaying certainly didn't pay.

It was a long way up. There were four doors at the top, so I chose one at random and hammered on it. No reply. I tried the next one.

Footsteps, finally. Well, at least I could ask again. The door opened.

The girl looked tousled, like she'd just got up; but then maybe she had. She was young enough — twenty-five at most — and she'd a dancer's figure, but half her face was covered with a strawberry birthmark. Right. That explained the comment about her not being as popular with the punters as her colleagues.

'Uh ... you Aegle?' I said.

'Yeah.'

Well, I'd heard friendlier voices. 'My name's Marcus Valerius Corvinus. I got your address from the guy at the guildhouse.'

'Celer?'

'Probably. Can I come in? It's about the business last night.'

She gave me a measuring stare. Then she shrugged and turned. 'Suit yourself. I'm sorry about the mess but I don't usually entertain purple-stripers. Not at home, anyway.'

I followed her in and closed the door behind me. There was a small entrance hall, just big enough for a few pegs. I hung my wet cloak on an unoccupied one and went through. Beyond was a single room with an unmade mattress on the floor, a few sticks of furniture and a flute-case propped against the wall. Aegle pulled up a stool for me and sat down opposite on a rickety clothes chest. She yawned.

'I'm sorry,' I said. 'You were asleep?'

Another shrug. Jupiter! Despite her name the girl was no sparkler. 'It doesn't matter,' she said. 'So what can I do for you, Marcus Valerius Corvinus?'

I ignored the tone. 'I'm not sure. Maybe nothing, I'm just doing the rounds. I wanted to talk to one of the musicians at the rite. Ask them if they noticed anything unusual in the course of the evening.'

'How do you mean, "unusual"?'

'Out of the ordinary.'

'Look, I know what *unusual* means.' For a moment her face lit in a smile that changed it completely: she'd've been pretty if it hadn't been for the birthmark. 'Just what kind of unusual?'

It was my turn to shrug. 'You tell me.'

'Nothing to tell. We played. The rite finished. Then we ate. The food's one of the pluses at the Good Goddess ceremony: we're given our share of the real stuff, because we're celebrants too. Then the lady's body was found and we were sent home early. That's all I know. There was no difference from other years, if that's what you're asking. Apart from the suicide itself, of course, which sort of marked the evening out a little.' No smile this time; clearly one was all I got.

'You've played at the rite before?'

'Sure. A couple of times, anyway. Most of the girls there had.'

'Only most?'

'For some it was the first time. Especially the younger ones.'

'Celer said all twelve of you were experienced fluteplayers. That you'd been working together for years.'

'Uh-huh. But he'll also have told you that we draw straws for the rite. Some of the girls just hadn't been lucky before.'

'So you knew them all? You'd worked with them all before?'

'Yeah.'

There was something there. I couldn't put my finger on

it, but I had the feeling that she had hesitated for the barest fraction of a second before she'd answered.

'You sure?' I said.

'Sure I'm sure. Why shouldn't I be?'

'What about Thalia?'

'Thalia wasn't—' She stopped and looked away. 'Yeah. Yeah, I've worked with Thalia. Lots of times.'

'You said Thalia wasn't.' The back of my neck was prickling. 'Wasn't what?'

She stood up suddenly and moved in the direction of the door. 'Look, do you mind if we leave it, Corvinus?' she said. 'I'm tired and it was a long night. Also I've got a dinner party this evening so I've got to practise. I've told you all I know, which isn't much but then that's life, isn't it?'

'Thalia wasn't there, was she?' Jupiter! I was on to something after all! 'But there were a dozen of you. So who was the twelfth girl?' Silence. 'Aegle, do you want me to go back to Celer? Tell him one of his team didn't show and ask him to find out who took her place?' Still silence, but her teeth snaggled at her lower lip and she was watching me like I was going to jump up and bite her. 'Look, I don't want to cause trouble, right? All I want's the girl's name and where to find her.'

She strode over to the bed, bent down with her back to me and began pulling the blankets straight with short, sharp jerks. 'I don't know her name,' she snapped. 'I'd never seen her before, had I? Nor had the rest of us.'

'She was a stranger?' Oh, dear sweet Jupiter! 'So where did she come from?'

'Thalia sent her. Something had come up at the last minute, she couldn't make it. It was too late to contact Celer, and this girl was a friend.' The bed looked even worse than it had done. Aegle gave the top blanket a last vicious tug and turned to face me. 'Don't tell Celer, Corvinus. That little rat handles the bookings and unless someone asks for one of us by name he can pick who he likes to send out. Get a reputation for being unreliable and you don't work too often.'

I hadn't moved. 'Is Thalia unreliable?'

'No! I told you, she just couldn't make it. It happens now and again to all of us; not often, but enough. The rest cover, and Celer's none the wiser.'

'But this time you didn't cover. The girl was an outsider.'

'She could play the flute. Well, too, good as me, and I'm good, Corvinus, very good. That was all that mattered. And Thalia was off the hook.'

'Okay.' I held up my hand. 'Relax. I won't tell Celer, I promise. Now why don't you sit down?'

She did. We faced each other. She was glowering, the birthmark red and angry.

'Fine,' I said. 'Okay. Now what did this girl look like?'

'Tall, well-built. Muscular, even. Husky voice. Not old but older than me, maybe late twenties. Very dark hair. Wore a lot of make-up.'

'That usual?'

There was that fleeting smile again, breaking through the scowl. I wondered how much of the attitude was just hard shell or if there was a soft centre somewhere. 'Sometimes. Depends what's underneath you want covered. Me, for obvious reasons I lay it on with a trowel. Maybe she had the same problem.'

'Maybe.' And maybe not; my brain was buzzing. 'She leave with the rest of you?'

Aegle was silent for a long time. Then she said, 'I don't know.'

The prickling was back with a vengeance. 'You don't know?'

'She could've done. I just didn't notice. When the dead Vestal was found things got pretty confused. Then the Lady Junia bundled us all out together. I didn't see her around, but then I wasn't looking.'

'When was the last time you saw her?'

'That's easy. She was sitting on the floor next me at the meal. She said she was going out into the garden for a crap and a breath of fresh air.'

The garden. My stomach went cold. 'And she didn't come back?'

Aegle shrugged. 'Maybe she did, maybe she didn't, I don't know. Maybe her business took longer than she thought it would and she was still out there. Anyway, then the Vestal's maid found that the lady had killed herself in one of the back bedrooms and all hell broke loose. And that was that.'

That was that. Sweet merciful gods. I stood up. 'One more thing. You happen to know where Thalia lives?'

'Sure. In Public Ponds near the Capenan Gate. First tenement on the gate side of the wineshop, fourth floor. She probably won't be there, though. She has a better social life than me.' That came out naturally, without rancour.

I put a half gold piece on the stool as I left. She'd earned it.

6

It was a long hike over to Public Ponds, but at least once I was there I'd have a shorter walk home. I called in at Watch headquarters on the off-chance that my pal the local commander Flavonius Lippillus was around to split a jar of wine, but he was out on a society burglary and the guy on the desk didn't know when he'd be back, so I just left my regards and headed for the Capenan Gate.

I found the tenement. It was slightly more upmarket than Aegle's, but not much; meaning you could see what colour the shops fronting it had been painted a dozen years or so back and the graffiti on the entrance walls was better spelled. Same smell, though: public latrines aren't too plentiful in the Ponds, and bladders are the same size everywhere. I walked up to the fourth floor and knocked on the first door I came to.

It was opened by an old woman in a tattered dressing-gown. Behind her a kid of indeterminate sex stood chewing on a bread-ring.

'What d'you want?' the old woman snapped. Ouch; as far as friendly greetings went this obviously wasn't my day. Yeah, well; at least it told me a second career as an itinerant brush-seller wasn't really a viable proposition.

'Uh, I'm looking for a flutegirl,' I said. 'Name of Thalia.'

She nodded at the door opposite. 'That's hers.'

'Right. Thanks, mother.' I crossed to the door and knocked. No answer. I tried again, louder. Not a cheep.

The woman was still watching me. 'She's out,' she said.

Gods; I'd pulled the sharpest analytical mind in the empire here. 'Yeah,' I said. 'So it would seem. You know where she might be, by any chance?'

'No idea, son. I hardly see her one month's end to the next. You tried the guildhouse?'

'Yeah.' I hadn't, not again, but saying so would've complicated matters. Maybe I should've called back there first when I left Aegle's and left a message for Thalia to get in touch with me, but you can't think of everything and I wasn't traipsing all the way back over to the Subura now. 'You sure you don't know where she might've gone?'

She bridled. 'I've got better things to do than watch out for sluts,' she said. 'Decimus, stop picking your nose.' The kid behind her had inserted a grubby finger in his left nostril. He was staring at me like I had three heads. 'Them musicians is all alike. If they aren't bringing boyfriends back all hours they're bed-hopping elsewhere. Now I've work to do, and so should you. You're too old to be chasing flutegirls. Why don't you go home to your wife?' She pushed the nose-picking kid inside and slammed the door behind her.

I grinned; neighbours like that are a joy perennial. Well, there was nothing more to be done here for the moment, that was sure, although certainly Thalia was one person I had to talk to before much longer. It'd have to be the guildhouse, or maybe Aegle again, but it had been a long hard day already and that could wait until tomorrow.

I took the old woman's advice and went home.

Perilla was in the atrium, curled up on the couch with a book. Surprise.

'Hey, lady.' I kissed her. 'How are things?'

'All right.' She set the roll aside. I didn't even look at the title: it would only have made my eyes water. 'How was your afternoon?'

'Not bad.' I put the jug and cup Bathyllus had given me on the side table and lay down next to her. 'The new clock behaving itself?' I could hear the drip ... drip ... drip clearly all the way across the room. Well, as I say maybe you got used to it but if that was an example of cutting-edge technology then give me a marked candle any time.

'Oh, it's going perfectly. I'm quite looking forward to the first changeover. That should be in about an hour's time, at sunset.' As if on cue, a bell went *ting!* as the titan belted his anvil. 'There we are, you see. The start of the twelfth hour. It's quite exciting, really.' She beamed.

Jupiter! I'd never seen Perilla like this; she was like a kid with a new toy. But then the lady always did have a scientific bent to match her literary talents. Me, I think some things are best left alone. Start monkeying around harnessing the power of complex, elemental forces like wind and water and the gods knew where it would end.

'There've been developments,' I said. I told her about the visit to Aegle and the phantom flutegirl. 'And we've got a good description. Seemingly our spurious musician was youngish with very dark hair. She was also tall, well-built and muscular, and she had a husky voice and three inches of make-up.' I paused. 'All these things suggest anything to you, lady?'

Perilla was staring at me open-mouthed, horror-struck; obviously it did. 'Oh, Marcus!' she said.

'Yeah. Yeah, right. That's exactly what I thought.'

'Clodius Pulcher!'

Trust Perilla to go for the historical parallel straight off, even if it was the obvious one; so obvious that even

I'd drawn it. Young Clodius Pulcher had been a well-born dandy about a hundred years back. He'd had the hots for Julius Caesar's wife — some people said it was mutual — and he'd dressed up as a flutegirl to gatecrash the rites of the Good Goddess held that year at Caesar's house. Pulcher had been caught, sure, but although he'd got off the subsequent sacrilege rap by bribing the jury the scandal had stunk so much you could still smell it four generations down the road. One got you ten history had just repeated itself; at least partly so. I'd bet a jar of imperial Caecuban to a used bunion plaster that our phantom flutegirl — and so the murderer — had been a man.

'But this is appalling!' Perilla was still in shock. 'It means the rites were profaned! Does Torquata know yet?'

I blinked. Damn; that aspect of things I hadn't thought of. The chief Vestal would burst a blood vessel. 'No. That's a pleasure in store, lady,' I said. 'And as far as the murder's concerned it opens up a whole new can of worms. Like who was he and what the hell was going on.'

'So what was going on, do you think?'

'The gods only know.' I took a swallow of wine. 'Okay. Let's consider the angles. The whys first. What was the guy doing gatecrashing the rites to begin with?'

'But that's obvious. He came to murder Cornelia. Why we may not know, but—'

'Hang on. It's not that simple. Maybe he did, but there are other possibilities. For a start, what's wrong with taking the Clodius Pulcher line to its logical conclusion?'

Perilla sat up. 'You're saying he had an assignation with the senior consul's wife? In her own house, during one of the most sacred ceremonies of the religious year? Corvinus, have you taken leave of your senses? This isn't—'

'With her or one of the other ladies, sure. But Aemilia's

a prime candidate. That sweet little bubblehead's got an itch
in her girdle, take my word for it. And from all accounts
Galba's no Hercules. Maybe she's not scratching yet but
it isn't for the want of trying.'

'*That* is wineshop bilge! You have absolutely no grounds
for accusing Sulpicius Galba's wife of infidelity!'

I shrugged. 'Okay. True. But it would explain a lot. It'd
get Cornelia off the hook, for one thing.'

'Quite.' Perilla sniffed. 'Cornelia. She was the one who
was murdered, after all. Or has that slipped what I can
only loosely term your mind?'

Jupiter on a seesaw! 'Lady, if you'll just get off your
high horse for one minute and shut up so I can explain
then maybe we'll get somewhere, okay? I'm as much in
the dark as you are, but we won't solve this thing by
ignoring possibilities. Or calling each other names, for
that matter.'

Perilla coloured up, then ducked her head. 'Very well,
Marcus. You're quite correct. I'm sorry. Carry on.'

'Right.' I took an inspirationary belt of Setinian. 'Let's
say the guy — call him X — has made an arrangement with
Aemilia to scratch the lady's itch for her. Despite what you
said, Perilla, if you ignore the sacrilege aspect the situation's
ideal. She's in her own home and she's her own boss, on the
one night of the year when she can be sure her husband's
not going to walk in at an embarrassing moment waving
a horsewhip and demanding a divorce. More, the thought
that his wife might be using her evening off to press the
sheets with some young stud who has more under his belt
than he does doesn't even cross Galba's tiny mind, because
it's an all-women shindig.'

'Corvinus, don't be crude, please; it isn't necessary. Just
give me the theory.'

I grinned. 'Yeah. Okay. Sorry, lady. Anyway, that's the other thing. When the rite itself is finished and the eating and drinking start, not to mention the sleep-over, no one's going to notice where anyone else is, and no one's going to care, either, because what's the point? The house is sealed until dawn, they're all girls together and the chances for an extramarital tumble upstairs are zero because there ain't no men around to fill the other half of the bed.'

'You're beginning to convince me,' Perilla said slowly. 'Stop it.'

I grinned again and kissed her nose. 'Yeah. Fine. So X has planned a rendezvous with Mrs Galba. He's inside, he's off and running. At the prearranged hour he slips out into the garden and round to the hall door. Either they're going to slake their burning passion in one of the spare bedrooms off the hall or — more likely — he's going to use the back staircase and nip up to Aemilia's own room while the lady herself takes the corridor stairs when her duties allow her to retire gracefully to bed. Only at that point something screws up.'

'Cornelia sees him,' Perilla said. 'Marcus, this really is beginning to sound rather plausible.'

'Right. It'd mean she came the wrong way out of the WC, sure, but maybe she heard him moving around and got curious. Or maybe she was just curious anyway and was taking a look round the back reaches of the property. In any event she sees X climbing the stairs, or about to, and—'

'Wait a moment. Why doesn't she give the alarm? Or run back to the atrium?'

'Why should she, lady? What she sees is only a flutegirl, remember. Maybe the girl's lost, maybe she's been sent on an errand. In any case all the situation demands is for Cornelia to order her back and send her down the corridor to where she belongs. There's no need to go overboard.'

'Very well. So what happened next?'

'Now we come to the tricky bit. I don't know; I honestly don't know. Maybe from that close range she saw through his disguise. She may even have known the man's name, if he was out of the top social drawer. Anyway, the upshot is that X panics. He grabs Cornelia and hustles her into the nearest bedroom which is only a step or two away opposite the staircase. Then he draws his knife and stabs her. He's——'

'Wait a moment. Why would he be carrying a knife?'

I frowned. 'What?'

'X is on a romantic assignment. Also, he's disguised as a flutegirl, and as you are well aware flutegirls' costumes are on the skimpy side. Why should he have provided himself from the outset with a weapon he didn't envisage using?'

'Shit, Perilla, I don't know! Maybe he took it in case there was trouble.'

'In a household full of women? Who would he be planning to use it against?' She sniffed. 'Hardly chivalrous behaviour, is it?'

'Jupiter, the guy's a murderer!'

'Not yet he isn't.'

'Added to which, lady, some men are unchivalrous by nature. While others have unchivalry thrust upon them by their smartass bloody wives raising smartass bloody objections to a perfectly good theory.'

'There's no such word as unchivalry, Corvinus; the objection is a valid one; and don't swear just because you're losing an argument.'

Hell; she had a point. The knife – particularly *that* knife – was a major stumbling-block. Not that there mightn't be an explanation; it was just I hadn't got it yet. 'Okay,' I said. 'Let's call a truce on the knife and finish the scenario.'

'Very well.' Perilla settled back against the cushions.

'X is stymied. Sure, Cornelia hasn't had a chance to yell, but it's only a matter of time before someone finds the body. There's no point, of course, in going through with the original plan of meeting up with Aemilia, and for equally obvious reasons he'd be a fool to go back to the party. Besides, judging by the amount of blood on the bedroom floor he must be covered with the stuff. So X doesn't stick around. He pulls the bolts on the back door and slips off into the night.' I took a satisfied swallow of wine. 'So. There you are. Theory number one. What do you think?'

'It hangs together, certainly, although there are problems besides the large one of the murder weapon . . .'

'Yeah? Like what, for example?'

'. . . which we won't go into for the present.'

'Gee, thanks, lady!'

'So. What's theory two?'

'Theory two has X's assignation with Cornelia.'

'Oh, Corvinus!'

'Hang on! The difference is that it may not have anything to do with sex. Or not on that occasion, anyway.'

'You told me that both Junia Torquata and Lucius Arruntius were convinced that Cornelia died a virgin. Not to mention the girl's maid.'

'Look, I'm just covering the possibilities here, right? And the chance that X was her lover is one of them.'

'Very well.'

'Actually, there're two major differences between theories one and two. The reason for the assignation is one.'

'And the other?'

'That the meeting wasn't prearranged. Which is why Cornelia died.'

7

'All right, Marcus. Carry on.' It wasn't often I had Perilla's full attention, but I'd got it now. 'This is fascinating.'

'Okay. First of all I admit theory two is more unlikely because, as you say, Torquata, Arruntius and Niobe are all against the pregnancy angle. However, it does explain the knife, and so far as I can see it fits all the known facts.'

Perilla's lips twitched. 'You're hedging,' she said.

'Sure I'm hedging, lady! I've been mauled often enough to know when hedging's called for!'

'Don't snap. There's no need for it.'

'Right. Fine.' I downed another mouthful of the Setinian and filled the cup. 'So. Cornelia is pregnant and X is the guy responsible. He knows the score because she's told him, and he also knows that when the fact becomes apparent he's in trouble up to his eyebrows. Sure, she might do the noble thing and refuse to divulge his name, but he can't depend on that. Pregnant women don't always act rationally, especially if they're Vestals and all they've got to look forward to when the happy news breaks is a pit near the Colline Gate. And just as there's only one penalty for her there's only one for him: to be flogged to death publicly in Cattlemarket Square. So X has no option but to cover his tracks.

'He chooses the night of the Good Goddess ceremony for the reasons I've already given: getting into the house initially may be difficult, but once he *is* in everything's comparatively easy-peasy. He dresses up as a flutegirl—'

I stopped: Perilla was frowning. 'You got a comment, lady?'

'Not at the moment, Marcus. Go on, please.'

'Uh-huh. Okay. He dresses up as a flutegirl and takes part in the rite. Cornelia — and this is important — doesn't know he's there; probably he stays well in the background, keeps his head down and his face hidden. When the rite's over he watches and waits his chance; sooner or later, if he's lucky, Cornelia's going to leave the room to take care of the demands of nature. When that happens he slips out into the porch, runs round to the garden door and lies in wait for her in the hall passage near the WC. When she comes out he attracts her attention and calls her over. Now he's got no reason to carry on with the charade; in fact for the next bit of the plan to work she has to recognise him. Which she does. Cornelia isn't going to give the alarm; he's her lover, after all, and she wouldn't want him caught. Besides, she trusts him. He takes her into one of the bedrooms. Okay. Now the scenario can go two ways. Either he kills her straight off with the knife he's brought with him for the purpose or he persuades her to kill herself. The end result's the same. And once Cornelia is dead he pulls the bolts and does a runner.' I paused and looked at Perilla. 'So, lady, what do you think?'

She was winding a lock of her hair round her finger. A good sign; she does that either when she's tired or when she can't think of a comeback. Great! It seemed I wasn't going to be vapourised with sarcasm this time after all.

'It works, Marcus,' she said finally. 'Certainly it explains the knife. The main difficulty, as you say, is the pregnancy.'

'Yeah. Only I can't get round that.'

'What if X had another reason for seeing Cornelia alive as a threat to him?'

Hey! 'Go on,' I said.

'You say Torquata told you that the girl had had something on her mind the last few days. What if she'd ... I don't know; seen something, heard something involving X that put it in her power to harm him in some way. And she was swithering over whether or not to report it.'

'It'd have to be something pretty big, Perilla. Whoever X is, he'd think twice about killing a Vestal in cold blood. More than twice, for all sorts of reasons. Unless he's totally out of his tree, and that sort of thing gets you noticed in other ways.'

'Admitted. We can't even begin to guess the nature of the reason itself. But it is possible in general terms, would you say?'

'Yeah. Yeah, it's possible.'

'Very well. Taking that as a modification to your theory, where does it lead us? The first part's fine: X insinuates himself into the rite, waits for Cornelia to leave the room and takes the back way into the hall. He watches for the girl to come out of the WC and—' She stopped. 'No. No, that's a problem. If X isn't Cornelia's lover then he can't just lure her into the bedroom on the pretext that they have to talk. She'd be at the least suspicious and, if she did see through his disguise, she would certainly have given the alarm.'

'What about the original idea? That he made a noise, intentionally this time, that brought her within grabbing distance? It'd be risky, sure, but again it's possible. From the look of the girl I'd say she was no shrinking violet, and if she thought the house was sealed the likelihood that she'd be facing a male intruder wouldn't've entered her head.'

'Hmm. All right. And being a man he would have the physical strength to overpower her, plus the advantage of surprise. Very well, Marcus; we'll accept that with reservations. Having decoyed the girl into the hall, he grabs her, covers her mouth, pulls her into the bedroom and stabs her, being careful to choose the throat to give the impression of suicide. He then straightens the body to ensure there's no suggestion of a struggle, places the girl's hands round the hilt of the knife and leaves through the back door.'

Yeah; it would work. It would work very well. And the big plus was that it got us over the pregnancy question. Sure, it left the matter of the guy's reasons wide open, but like Perilla said we couldn't even begin to guess at these anyway. And the hairs on the back of my neck were prickling. That was always a good sign. I reached for the jug and topped up my cup.

'Fine,' I said. 'Okay. Let's move on to who X is.'

Perilla frowned. 'That's the real puzzle,' she said. 'Oh, not his name, just *who* he is. The murderer doesn't make sense.'

'Run that past me again, lady. In simple Latin this time.'

'It's a matter of class. Whichever of the theories you choose X had to belong to the same social stratum as the women. Neither Vestals nor senior consuls' wives mix with the lower classes, so there would be no opportunity for . . . *connection*, if you like.'

'I see. Okay. Agreed.'

'Also, he knew the layout of the house; he had to, to be able to plan his movements in advance. That again argues a certain inside knowledge that could only be gained by social intimacy, which in itself would entail parity of social standing. Of course, the house slaves themselves would have the information, but I think we can safely rule them out on grounds of motive.'

'Yeah.' Jupiter! What had happened to the simple Latin?

'So what you're saying is that the murderer was a friend of the family. Or at least he was familiar enough with the house to know the floor plan in detail.' That was looking good for the Aemilia angle; it was her house, and if the guy were her lover he'd've orchestrated his movements herself. On the other hand, if Cornelia had been the target he'd've had to get his information some other way, and sorting that problem out would be a real bummer. 'Okay. So our X is a top-drawer nobleman with an in to the Galba household, young enough and pretty enough to be able to pass for a woman at close range. Great! That should—'

'Wait a moment, Marcus. I haven't finished. On the other hand, he shows features which definitely do not fit the average upper-class gentleman.'

'Such as?'

'To begin with, how many of your acquaintances can play the flute? Or any other instrument, for that matter? Not just adequately, but well enough to be accepted by professionals as an equal?'

'Uh ...' Hell's teeth! I hadn't thought of that! And the lady was right; sure, some families – especially the ones with strong Greek connections and artistic leanings – encourage their sprogs to play a musical instrument or sing, but for the Roman aristocracy in general there's always been something very suspect about the performing arts. If I'd ever told Dad I wanted to learn the harp the guy'd've started checking my clothes chests for bras.

'Together with that, how did X know so much about the fluteplayers' booking arrangements? Enough to ensure that he would be able to take the place of one of the girls who was herself a last-minute appointment and be accepted as such by the others? And not only take the girl's place but convince them that he was a close friend of the actual girl in question?'

Thalia! Bugger! We kept going back to Thalia! That lady I just had to meet. If anyone held the key to all this it was her. 'You got anything else to throw into the pot, lady?' I said sourly. 'Or should I just give the case up now?'

She ignored me. 'Third and last — although it's a very small point in comparison — there's that knife of yours. You're right; it is not a high-class Roman's weapon. Oh, I'm not saying that a nobleman would have used a blade from Toletum with gold studs and an amethyst in the hilt but, as you remarked, that particular knife combines cheapness with careful and laborious attention. As a murder weapon for someone of the same social standing as the victim it just doesn't fit.'

Jupiter on wheels! 'You finished now, Perilla?'

'I think so. Unless you can think of anything further.'

'Uh, no. No, lady, I'd say that about covered it for the time being.' I cleared my throat. One of my cardinal rules is never, *never*, to let Perilla know how smart she is; the lady can be really insufferable, especially when she's right. Which is ninety-nine per cent of the time. I've found the best tactic is simply to change the subject. 'Did, uh, Bathyllus say anything about dinner, by the way?'

'I asked him to wait until sunset. I want to watch the clock.'

'Oh. Right.' I was beginning to have serious doubts about that thing where Perilla was concerned. It was the fruit juice cocktails all over again; when the lady gets an obsession you can't shift it, and this obsession wasn't healthy. I got up from the couch and walked over to the mass of gleaming bronze piping in the corner. The little Victory's pointer was about halfway between the twelve and the very top of the scale. Half an hour to go, then. My stomach rumbled. 'You think we could maybe just have the starters to be going on with?'

'Don't be silly, Marcus. If we go into the dining-room now by the time we've settled down and Bathyllus has brought them it'll be so close to sunset that we'll miss the changeover. Which reminds me: we'll need a stepladder and a bucket to transfer the water back up to the cistern. Bathyllus can do that while I operate the ducks.'

Oh, bugger. Double bugger. I went over to the passageway that led to the kitchen and yelled, '*Bathyllus!*'

He was there in two drips of a clepsydra. 'Yes, sir.'

'You're on bucket duty tonight, little guy. One bucket, one stepladder front and centre spit-spot. Got it?'

Bathyllus glanced at the water clock and gave the thing his best sniff. 'I'll send Alexis immediately, sir,' he said.

'Not Alexis, pal. You.'

'But sir, as your head slave it's not my place to—'

I held up my hand. He stopped. 'Listen, sunshine. We're all in this together, right? If I have to put off dinner until a little fucking bronze titan taps his little ditto anvil with his little ditto hammer then the whole world suffers with me. Which prompts a thought. When you bring the bucket and the ladder have the rest of the staff up here too. We may as well all watch this scientific marvel together.'

Bathyllus was fizzing quietly. 'Meton's going to be very upset, sir,' he said. 'He's serving rissoles of wild boar marinated in cumin, wine must and juniper and they need to be—'

'Tell Meton from me he can take the very largest and most succulent of his rissoles and—'

'*Marcus!*' Perilla snapped.

'Yeah, well.' Jupiter in rompers! I just hoped these bloody all-singing-all-dancing clepsydras didn't catch on. If we had to do everything on the ting of a titan Rome and the civilised world would grind to a halt.

We waited. And we waited. And we waited. Lysias the coach driver, impregnating the air of the room with the smell of wet horse, looked as bored as I felt. Alexis – the smartest of the bunch – looked interested. Bathyllus, clutching his bucket, looked pained and put-upon. And Meton, flexing his great size-ten hands and muttering darkly to himself, looked like he was mentally weighing the comparative merits of aconite and ground death's-cap mushroom as an additive to the rissole seasoning. Yeah, maybe insisting on Meton showing up had been a mistake after all.

Behind them a Greek chorus of five or six minions, skivvies and assorted Other Ranks were having trouble enough just looking human.

The little Victory at the top of its pole suddenly trembled. A collective breath was drawn. One of the female skivvies was sick with excitement and had to be removed.

Perilla clapped her hands. 'Oh, Marcus!' she said. 'I think it's starting!'

'Yeah.' I had to admit, the excitement was getting to me, too. It was like the bit at the races just before the president drops the napkin.

Then everything happened at once. The little titan raised his hammer and brought it down with a *ting!* on the anvil. The drip ... drip ... drip became an intestinal gurgle and the Victory figure plummeted towards the bottom of her pole. And at the base of the whole contraption ...

Tinkletinkletinklepssss ...

At the base of the whole contraption the two flying cherubs were pissing into the basin. I grinned. Yeah, well, I supposed if you wanted the voiding of the water to look natural then that would be the obvious way to arrange things.

There was a terrible silence. Finally one of the minions sniggered and got a look from Bathyllus that made me wince just from the side-burn.

Perilla had gone red. She was glaring at the cherubs like they were doing it on purpose.

'Marcus,' she said, 'that is *gross!*'

I straightened my face. 'Don't blame me, lady. You bought it, it's your clock. You should've inspected the plumbing arrangements in the shop.'

'Listen, Corvinus, when I go shopping for statuary I am not in the habit of minutely examining the figure's—' She stopped and bit her lower lip. I waited. I knew what was going to happen next; it was just a matter of time. 'However it is rather ... I mean ... if you think of ...'

Which was as far as the lady got before the giggles took her. We sat down on the nearest couch and hugged each other until our sides stopped hurting.

Finally I looked up. The atrium was empty except for Bathyllus, the bucket and the stepladder, and every hair in the little guy's nostrils was quivering with disapproval. Bad sign; *bad* sign. Bathyllus has a list of many heinous social gaffes and outright crimes in that card index that he calls a brain, but we'd just committed the worst of the lot, for which there was no forgiveness: we had abandoned our seigneurial *gravitas* before the entire assembled staff.

This was going to take us months to live down.

'Uh, they've gone,' I said.

Silence. Finally, Bathyllus said, 'Yes, sir.' You could've used his tone to pickle mummies.

'I'm, ah, sorry about that, little guy.' Perilla started

giggling again and I elbowed her in the ribs. 'It was just, uh, unexpected, you know?'

'Yes, sir. Quite, sir.' Ice was beginning to glister in the ornamental pool.

I indicated the bucket. 'You, ah, can get Alexis to handle that, pal. Or maybe one of the skivvies. The mistress'll see to the ducks when she's feeling more herself.' I clapped a hand over Perilla's mouth just in time and held it there while she gave way to another spasm. 'Which had better be pretty damn soon if she wants to make the Winter Festival with her wedding ring still in place.'

Bathyllus's grade-A glare can freeze the balls off an imperial legate at twenty yards. The one we got now might've managed thirty. 'Thank you, sir. Madam. Will that be all?'

'Yeah. Tell Meton we're ready to eat.'

'Certainly, sir.' He stalked off.

Ouch.

8

Bathyllus was still pretty sniffy next morning. He wasn't having anything to do with the clock, either, so I made a unilateral decision and handed control of the thing – under Perilla – to Alexis. There isn't much gardening to be done in December (the garden's Alexis's province; his choice, not mine) and like I say he's the smartest of the Corvinus ménage with a genuine interest in what's going on outside his own narrow world.

Me, I'd a busy schedule lined up. First was another trip to the fluteplayers' guildhouse to arrange a meeting with Thalia. Second, over to the House of the Vestals – or rather to the chief priest's house next door, because rough uncouth men weren't allowed across that hallowed threshold – to give Junia Torquata an update on the latest developments; that I wasn't looking forward to. Third ...

Third was Caelius Crispus. That little encounter wasn't going to be a barrel of laughs either. Crispus and I went way back, and he'd loathed my and Perilla's corporate guts ever since the lady had got him thrown out of Rome's premier bachelor club on the Pincian. Threatening to slit his throat, losing him his Treasury job and putting the screws on him three months back when he was the praetor's rep for the Caere district hadn't helped much, either. Still, Crispus was my best bet when it came to the Aemilia angle, because when it came to rooting through the dirty linen basket Caelius Crispus was a greasy neck ahead of the field. He might be on his way up — repping for an out-of-city judge was a pretty prestigious job for someone with his antecedents, or lack of them — but the reason was still who he knew. Or more to the point what he knew about who that they'd rather he didn't and were willing to pay in money or position for the privilege of keeping the lid on.

Celer, the little fussy expediter, was in residence when I got to the guildhouse.

'Ah, Valerius Corvinus,' he beamed. 'Did you find Aegle?'

'Sure. No problem.'

'Oh, that *is* good!'

I rubbed the side of my nose with a silver piece. 'Actually, I've got another favour to ask you. That Thalia girl. She been around since we last spoke?'

The smile slipped. 'What would you want with Thalia in particular, sir? I understood that—'

'Just a few questions,' I said smoothly. 'Aegle told me the girl might be the best one to answer them. You seen her yesterday or today?'

'To tell the truth, no I haven't.' Now the guy was looking slightly peeved. 'Which is very annoying, really, because she has a booking tonight and there've been some changes to the original arrangements.'

A feather of cold brushed my spine. 'Is she, uh, usually conscientious about checking in?' I said.

'Of course.' He sniffed. 'All the girls are. It's in their own interests if they want to eat. But I've seen nothing of Thalia since before the ceremony at the consul's house.'

Damn. Well, there was no point in worrying until I had to. From what Aegle had said the girl was probably shacked up with a client somewhere working her embouchure off. 'If

I gave you my address could you send her round as soon as she turns up?'

The beam came back. 'No problem whatsoever, sir. This would be a professional engagement, I take it?'

'Uh, yeah.' Bugger. Well, it might simplify the issue. 'Yeah, okay. If you like.'

'Good.' He took the pen and stylus from his belt. The Alexandrian port authorities could've used the beam now to power their lighthouse. 'In that case standard last-minute guild rates would apply. Payable in advance, of course.' He named a figure and I blanched. Jupiter! That explained Aegle's opinion of the guy: if I were making that much of a rake-off from my clients I'd be able to underwrite the Treasury. I slipped the silver piece back where it came from; who needs chicken-feed when you can eat caviar? 'I'll send her right over. Previous commitments permitting, naturally.'

'You do that, sunshine.' I gave him the address, sourly, together with a large proportion of the coins in my purse. 'Tell her to wait until I get back. Oh, and have a nice day.'

'You too, sir.'

Bastard. I set off through the Subura towards Market Square. At least the weather had improved.

The House of the Vestals and the chief priest's official residence are part of the same building, fronting on New Street next to Vesta's temple itself. Like I say, there was no point in knocking on the Vestals' door because I'd just have got the bum's rush, so I went round to the other entrance and asked for Camillus who in the absence of the Wart in his chief-priestly capacity was currently in occupation.

The slave who opened up could've deputised for the high priest of Jupiter himself, if you'd given him the fancy hat and the right togs. Scratch that: give the guy an electrum thunderbolt and a gold-wire beard and he could've done the god.

'Yes, sir?' he said. Uttered. Enunciated.

'The master in, sunshine?'

'I will enquire. Your name?' I told him. He let me in and waited until I'd wiped my feet carefully on the mat. 'If you will be kind enough to follow me?'

I dogged his august footsteps into the hall where he left me communing with the fancy artwork the state had filched over the years to decorate the surroundings allocated to the holder of its principal religious office. Actually – this was the first time I'd been in the place – it was pretty seedy. I'd guess from the chewed look of some of the woodwork the deputy chief priest had rodent problems.

'Good morning, Valerius Corvinus.' Furius Camillus was coming towards me in an old tunic and slippers. 'How pleasant to see you again, my dear fellow. You have some news?'

'Uh, yeah.' I cleared my throat. 'But if it's all the same to you, sir, I'd like Junia Torquata to be present before I tell you.'

Camillus raised his eyebrows. 'Oh. Oh, dear. As bad as that, eh?' I didn't answer. 'Well, come through to the study and I'll send someone round to see if the lady's free. Lucius!' The Jupiter look-alike manifested himself. 'Send next door, will you? My compliments to the chief Vestal, and would she favour us with a visit at her very earliest convenience.' He turned back to me. 'Now, Corvinus, this way. I won't bother to change if it's all the same to you. Fortunately I have no official engagements myself this morning, and Junia won't mind in the slightest, we're old friends. You're a fast worker, I'll give you that, my boy.'

The study was a lot more comfortable than the hall, and

I got the impression it was where Camillus spent most of his time. There were a lot of books. There was also something I'd never seen before: a big side table with a plain, hills and a river sculpted on it in clay. Groups of toy soldiers and horsemen were drawn up in ranks like they were just about to beat the hell out of each other. In front of one army was a line of miniature elephants.

The deputy chief priest blushed when he saw me looking. 'A small hobby; refighting battles. That one's Zama. Cornelius Scipio Africanus has always been rather a hero of mine.' He lifted half a dozen book-rolls off one of the two reading couches and dumped them on the desk. 'Make yourself comfortable. Junia shouldn't be long. I know it's early, but some wine while we're waiting?'

'Yeah. Yeah, great. Thanks.' He poured it for me himself but left the second of the three cups empty. It was an excellent Falernian. I was beginning to warm to Furius Camillus. 'Did you know the dead girl well yourself, sir?'

'No, not really. Oh, I saw her occasionally as a child, of course — Lepidus was and is one of my closest friends — but apart from formal occasions since then when she was only one of six I haven't seen much of her. A pleasant girl, though, Cornelia, I always thought. Very quiet, very serious, but strong. Good Vestal material.'

'Not the, uh, hysterical type, then?' While I'd got Camillus on his own I might as well get another informed reaction to the death. 'You think she would ever commit suicide? Given the, uh, appropriate circumstances, I mean?'

'Certainly not. It would be completely out of character.' Camillus had stretched his long length — he'd been a big man in his day, big as me, easy — on the other reading couch. 'If Cornelia was not one thing, that thing was hysterical.' His lips twisted. 'If that isn't tortuously phrased. I mean she was an extremely well-balanced young lady. Also, she had a good mind, especially for a woman. And although she didn't make friends easily those she did make she kept. Furthermore, I can think of no "appropriate circumstances" in which she would find suicide a viable option.' His eyes held mine; they were level, clear and very, very smart, and he'd stressed the phrase carefully. 'None whatsoever, Valerius Corvinus. Does that answer your question?'

'Yes. Yes, it does. Thank you, sir.' Well, I hadn't been expecting anything different, but it was nice to get confirmation. If I'd needed it. 'Still, if you don't mind my saying so, that's a pretty categorical encomium from someone who didn't know her all that well.'

'It's the chief priest's job to choose from among prospective Vestals, which naturally means the emperor. However, I was deputy when Cornelia joined the sorority, and Tiberius did me the honour of leaving the choice to my judgment. And if I flatter myself on one thing, Corvinus, it's judging people, even if they're as young as eight. I vetted the girl myself and, as I say, Cornelia was natural Vestal material. There is no way — no way at all — that she would have brought disgrace either upon herself or the office she held.'

'So what—' I stopped. Jupiter was back.

'The chief Vestal, sir,' he said, and withdrew. Evanesced.

'Good morning, Marcus.' Junia Torquata swept in. 'And to you, Caecinus.'

'What kept you, Junia?' Camillus said drily.

'I was on my way round in any case.' Torquata pulled up a chair. 'The door-slave — a most reliable girl — said you had a visitor, and when she described Caecinus here I put two and two together. Ah.' Her eyes lighted on the wine jug. 'Fruit juice. How nice. I do believe I'll have a small cup of that.'

Jupiter! I'd been through this before! However, Camillus

didn't bat an eyelid. He filled the cup and handed it over.

'More for you, Corvinus?' he said.

'Uh, yeah. Yeah, thanks.' I held my own cup out for a refill.

'Now.' Torquata took a belt of the Falernian and then fixed me with an eye steady as a prizefighter's. 'Come on, young man. No shilly-shallying.'

'Cornelia was murdered,' I said. 'At least I think she was.'

The chief Vestal sagged slightly. 'Thank the gods!' she murmured. 'Thank all the holy gods!'

'Hold on, Torquata. That's the, uh, good news.' Jupiter! So much for the reservations! And after that reaction I wasn't even going to *hint* that pregnancy was still an option. 'If I don't miss my guess, the murderer was a man.'

They both stared at me. Camillus was the first to speak.

'But, my dear fellow,' he said gently, 'that's impossible. The house was—'

'Sealed. Yeah. I know. Only one of the flutegirls was a man in disguise.'

Torquata set her cup down. 'You're sure?' she said.

'I'm sure. What his reasons for being there were exactly I don't know, but I'd bet a year's income on that, at least. He slipped out into the garden just after Cornelia left the room, went round to the hall, murdered the girl and escaped through the back door.'

'But how could he expect to get away with it?' Camillus was still looking like someone had belted him from behind with a sacrificial stunner's hammer. 'The imposture, I mean. Although obviously he did, or we wouldn't be having this conversation.'

'As far as physical appearance was concerned he must've

been soft-featured enough to pass for a woman,' I said. 'For the rest, he could play the flute. Not just pretend to play; *play*. How he managed actually to get himself included among the twelve musicians I don't know yet – there's a woman called Thalia who might have the answer – but he did.'

'Clodius Pulcher all over again.' Camillus filled himself a cup of wine and took a sip. 'I'm impressed, Corvinus; most certainly I am. My congratulations, young man. You confirm Lucius Arruntius's predictions.' He turned to Torquata. 'You realise, Junia, that if what Valerius Corvinus says is true – even if there's a possibility of it being true – you'll have to repeat the rite.' He paused. 'Junia? Did you hear what I said?'

The chief Vestal blinked and shook herself. 'My apologies, Marcus; I was wool-gathering. Yes; yes, of course we will. A nuisance, of course, but it has to be done.'

Camillus chuckled. 'Nomentanus isn't going to be pleased either, not when he's had to fork out more from his own pocket than he can afford already. If I were you, Corvinus, I'd keep clear of the city judges' offices for the foreseeable future, because you are not going to be popular in that quarter, not popular at all. You're absolutely sure of your facts, I suppose?'

'Yeah. Certain.' Hell! I'd forgotten about Nomentanus! Sure, I'd got a special commission, but technically as a city judge – or one of the college, at least – the case lay in his province. I could do without stepping on sensitive toes. Also, forget avoiding the city judges' offices because I'd be going over there later to see Caelius Crispus . . .

'Well, that's that, then,' Camillus said. 'Junia, you'll just have to . . . Junia? What on earth is wrong with you, woman?'

I glanced at Torquata. She still looked fazed. 'Nothing,

Marcus,' she said quietly. She emptied her cup and set it down. 'I'm sorry, it's just . . . the thought of a man at the rites is shocking, that's all. I've had too many shocks recently, and I'm too old for them. Of course we'll repeat the ceremony, that goes without saying. And we owe Corvinus here our thanks. The gods know what the repercussions might have been if the goddess had been slighted and we hadn't found out in time.' She stood up. 'I'll go and make the arrangements at once.'

She left. Camillus stared at the closing door for a moment, frowning. Then he turned back to me. 'And I,' he said, 'will have to give some thought to the appointment of a sixth Vestal. No doubt the emperor will be asking for suggestions, at the least. Corvinus, my dear fellow, I'm afraid I'll have to throw you out. Most inhospitable. My apologies.'

'Hey, that's okay,' I said. 'I'm used to being thrown out.'

I did my obeisance to Jupiter at the door and set off for the Capitol. All the way up the hill my brain was buzzing.

Shock, nothing, nor old age neither; that lady was as hard-boiled as they come. Camillus had seen it too, although he'd been too much the gentleman to give her the lie in her teeth. Something had thrown her, and I'd missed it . . .

What the hell was biting Junia Torquata?

9

I thought, when Caelius Crispus saw me, he was going to call in the half-dozen Axemen that city and out-of-town judges rate. Either that or die from a stroke on the spot.

'Hey, Crispus,' I said, sitting down uninvited on the chair in front of his desk. 'How's the lad?'

'You ...' He was pointing at me, eyes goggling. 'You ...'

'Yeah. Me. I've come because I need some help. A favour. Some information.'

'Get the hell out of my office!'

'On the private life and passions of Aemilia, the senior consul's wife.'

'Corvinus, I swear to you if you're not out that door in five seconds flat I'll—'

When in doubt, ask for more. 'Also, I wouldn't mind an inside edge on the senior consul himself. If you're feeling generous.'

He gagged. Interesting; I wouldn't've said, personally, that a face could match exactly the colour of a windfall plum that's slightly gone off, but Crispus's was doing its best. And I could've sworn the hairs in his ears were smouldering.

'Screw you, Corvinus! Screw you and your whole family, twice, and six times on the kalends! Especially that bitch of a wife of yours!'

'Perilla sends her regards. She still talks about the visit we made to the Pincian all those happy years ago. In fact, she was just saying we should meet up again soon, now we've moved back to Rome.'

That one always gets him. It did this time, too. He blanched like an almond. 'Keep her away from me! You hear me? Just keep that woman—'

'In fact, as soon as I find out where you spend your free time these days, which shouldn't be all that difficult, we intend to drop in one evening. Unexpectedly. With no prior warning whatsoever.' I gave him my best smile. 'Won't that be nice?'

Crispus stared at me, his mouth working. Then he drew a long breath and shuddered. 'All right,' he said quietly. 'What exactly do you want this time?'

'That's better. I told you, but you weren't listening. I want to know about Aemilia.'

'Know what?'

'Does she have a lover?'

'Jupiter's balls, Corvinus!'

'And if so what's his name and where can I find him?'

'Corvinus, watch my lips, right? We are talking about the consul's wife. The *senior* consul's wife. Consul as in "consul". You understand me?'

'Sure. I told you that myself, pal. Twice. Of course I understand.' I waited. Nothing. I stood up. 'Well, Crispus, it's been really nice talking to you again. We'll see each other again very soon, and—'

'Sit down,' he growled. I did. He breathed deeply for a while with his eyes shut then leaned over the desk, close enough to whisper. His breath smelled of violet comfits. 'All right, you bastard. The man's name's Gaius Licinius Murena. He's a junior finance officer at the Mint.'

'Your old stamping ground,' I said. 'No pun intended.'

'Hah-hah. Right. Now get the hell out of here. Go for a swim in the Tiber. I'll lend you the bricks.'

I didn't move. 'What about Galba?' Then when he hesitated: 'Come on, Crispus! Give! We're all alone, the door's closed and you know you'll have to tell me eventually.'

He grinned evilly. 'Oh, you are pushing it, aren't you? You want his lovers as well?'

'Plural?'

'Sure, plural. Our senior consul likes variety. But no one important. Actors. Fluteplayers. Freedmen. Even the occasional slave, if he's hosed down first.'

Something with lots of legs was strolling up my spine. 'Fluteplayers?'

'Why not? There's nothing like a good fluteplayer.' Crispus sniggered. 'They've got the lips for it.'

'You have any names?'

The snigger died. 'No. And if I had I wouldn't give you them. You can push only so hard, Corvinus, and pleasant though it'd be to see you tangling with Galba and getting your long patrician nose lopped off he might trace the information back to me. Whatever the Wart might think of him, Galba's a close pal of the prince, and you don't mix with Gaius. Especially now with his mother and brother dead he's Tiberius's blue-eyed boy.'

Yeah, I'd heard about that: Agrippina and Drusus Caesar, both in exile, had committed suicide by starving themselves a couple of months back. Or that was the official version, anyway. 'Galba and the Wart don't get on, you say?' I was fishing here, sure, but you never know what you might catch. And to give Crispus his due, he had the true professional's interest in his job, even if that job was raking over muckheaps.

He shrugged. 'You know the senior consul. If he spotted

a copper piece in a latrine he'd have it out no matter what he had to grope through to get it. And he's close enough to skin a flint. He's had his knife into Tiberius for years, ever since the old empress's bequest. And it's quite mutual.'

'The empress's bequest?'

'Sure. You don't know that story?' Now we'd moved — I assumed — on to the safe ground of old gossip Crispus was beginning to relax like a Suburan grandmother swapping scandal with a crony over the shelled peas. Sickening to watch, but then that was Crispus for you, and I wasn't complaining. There was just the chance that he might come across with something useful.

'Uh-uh,' I said. 'Tell me.'

'Seemingly the two were related through Galba's step-mother, and they were as thick as beets and fish sauce.' Crispus had leaned forward and dropped his voice to a conspiratorial whisper. Gods, Suburan grandmother was right; all the guy needed was the shawl and a few less teeth. 'Anyhow, when the will's opened it turns out that she's left him a cool half-million. Gold, not silver.'

I whistled; half a million gold pieces was a lot of gravy.

'The Wart, as executor, turns several shades of grey and says there must be some mistake: his mother meant five hundred, not five hundred thousand. The emperor's the emperor, so Galba has to grit his teeth and nod. In the end it doesn't matter because the Wart never pays him a plugged copper.' Crispus grinned. 'Oh, Galba doesn't like Tiberius. He doesn't like him at all.'

'So how come the guy made consul? Surely the Wart has to approve the appointments?'

'I told you, him and the prince are like this.' Crispus held up two interlocking fingers. 'And we're not just talking Damon and Pytheas here, either.' Shit; classical allusions now.

Crispus certainly had come on. 'What Gaius wants these days he gets, and if he doesn't get it he takes. And if he doesn't take it himself his pal Macro takes it for him. All the Wart's interested in is screwing fancy boys alfresco on that island of his. Not that I blame him, because this time next year he'll be dead anyway and Gaius'll be our new emperor.'

Well, I knew the truth or lack of it in the first little nugget of scandal, and the Wart had four years yet before he was due to pop his clogs. But I wasn't going to let Crispus in on the secret. Oh, no. Still, that bit about the fluteplayers had been interesting. It could be coincidence, sure, and there wasn't an ounce of reason to link Galba with Cornelia's death, but taken along with the fact that she'd died in his house it was certainly something to think about. And I didn't like Galba's smell; I didn't like it at all.

I stood up. 'Thanks, pal. You've been very helpful. I owe you one.'

Crispus grunted. 'Just stay out of my life. That's all I ask.'

I left. On the steps of the building I saw Sextius Nomentanus coming up, but I pretended I hadn't seen him. He wouldn't've known about Torquata having to repeat the rite, sure, but I wasn't taking any chances: bad news travels fast.

The Temple of Juno Moneta, where the Mint is, was only a comparative step or two away. At least today I was saving on shoe leather: Murena could just as easily have been attached to the grain supply offices in Ostia, which would've been a real bugger. If finding the guy was easy, though, getting to talk to him was going to prove a bummer because I couldn't just walk up and say, 'Hey, my name's Valerius Corvinus, I understand you're screwing the senior consul's wife and I was wondering if you played the flute.' I needed an in, and an in I hadn't got. I was still desperately trying to think of one when I reached the temple steps.

Which was when I saw Gaius Secundus limping towards me. Secundus and I had practically grown up together, and until our paths had split in our late teens he'd been my best friend. Then as one of the Wart's son Drusus's aides in Pannonia he'd taken a bad tumble from his horse and wrecked his right leg and with it a blossoming military career. Not that it had soured him. Nothing could sour Secundus; he was too nice a guy.

I waved. 'Hey, Gaius!'

He looked up, did a double-take, beamed and came over. We shook hands and grinned at each other. He'd aged, of course, since I'd last seen him a few months after the accident, but then that happens to us all, and he was still the good-looking bastard who'd had half the unattached females in Rome twittering round him.

'So, Marcus,' he said. 'You're back.'

'Yeah.'

'Permanently?'

'I think so. For the foreseeable future, anyway.'

'How's Perilla?'

'She's well.' Then, before he could ask: 'We've an adopted daughter. She's living up in the Alban hills with Perilla's Aunt Marcia. You?'

'Married too, now.' His grin widened. 'Very much so. You remember Furia Gemella?'

'Oh, yeah.' I did: the little stunner with the soup, the earrings and the matrimonial gleam in her eye. So she'd got him in the end. 'She any relation to the current deputy chief priest?'

'The daughter of a cousin.' Well, us old families did

tend to marry into each other, and relationships were so involved sometimes it'd need an Alexander to cut through the tangle. Marrying Perilla had made me unusual. Not that I was complaining. 'We've three kids. All boys.'

'Congratulations.' Hell; Murena could wait. 'You have time to split a jug of wine?'

He shook his head. 'Can't, unfortunately. Not now, anyway. I'm working.'

'As what?'

'A city judge, believe it or not. Only I drew one of the short straws for the Mint.'

Yeah; that made sense. The two chief Mint officers were praetors. So the gods did reward those who led a blameless, upright life after all. I sent up a small prayer of thanks to Mercury, guardian god of snoops; the duplicitous old reprobate was obviously on my side, and he was working his winged sandals off. 'Really?' I said.

'Really. If you've business, though, we could meet up later. Name the place and I'll be there when the office closes.'

'You've got a deal. Ah . . .' I hesitated. 'You happen to know a guy called Murena, by the way? Gaius Licinius Murena?'

'Sure. He's one of my finance officers.'

Better and better! Oh, thank you, Mercury! 'Could you describe him? Physically, I mean?'

Secundus frowned. Intellectually gifted he wasn't, but he was no fool either. 'What's this about?'

'Maybe nothing. But I have to know what he looks like.'

'Young. Twenty-something. Good-looking, eye for the girls.'

Yes! 'He, uh, play the flute at all?'

The frown deepened. 'Not that I know of, but I'd be surprised if he did. Marcus, you involved in something?'

'Yeah. Only it's complicated.'

Secundus's face cleared and he laughed. 'Meaning you don't want to tell me, right?'

'Right.' I grinned back. 'Not at the moment, anyway. Look, pal, I need a favour. A big favour.'

'You only have to ask. You know that.'

'Could you bring us together? I don't want an introduction, in fact I'd rather not have one, but it'd help if I saw the guy myself. Is that possible?'

'Sure. Nothing easier.' He shrugged. 'If he's around he should be in the clerks' room. I'll take you there now.'

'That'd be great.'

We went into the Mint building. One thing about tagging along with the boss, you aren't asked any questions and you don't have to answer any. Secundus led me along a maze of corridors and opened the door of a long room stacked with shelves and smelling of ink and parchment. The dozen or so scribes sitting at desks took one look and began to be very busy indeed. One of them, an old guy with buck teeth and ink-stained fingers, came over.

'Morning, Sestus,' Secundus said. 'Is Gaius Licinius here?'

'Yes, sir.' The slave's eyes went to me briefly and slid off incurious. 'In his office.'

'Fine.' He turned to me. 'Excuse me, Marcus, this won't take a minute. Do you want to wait or will you come as well?'

'Oh, I'll come,' I said.

Murena was at his desk. As we came in he looked up and set the tablet he'd been reading aside. Yeah, he fitted. He fitted very well.

'Ah, Gaius,' Secundus said. 'I wanted to have a brief word with you about the die stamp for the new issue.' He glanced over his shoulder at me. 'I'm sorry, Marcus. A little business, I'm afraid. You're sure you don't mind waiting?'

It was beautifully done. I hadn't known Secundus had any acting talents, but he could've given old Roscius lessons. 'No, I'm fine,' I said. I leaned against the doorpost and did my best to look bored while Secundus talked technicalities.

The guy was perfect: twenty-four, twenty-five max, slim and muscular as a Games net-and-trident man and with a face like a Greek Apollo. Good voice, too: 'husky', like Aegle had said. I could just imagine women curling up when he whispered sweet nothings in their ears. No wonder Aemilia had lost her heart and her pants. The fluteplaying side of things was a problem, sure, but that was something I could check up on along with the guy's movements on the evening in question.

Secundus gave it a good ten minutes then got us out. He didn't relax the pose until we were back outside the building itself.

'Well?' he said. 'You get what you wanted?'

'Yeah. Thanks, pal.' I grinned. 'In spades. I owe you one.'

He grinned back. 'You owe me one jug of the best Caecuban in Gorgio's cellar. Or half a jug, anyway, this time of day. I'm not greedy and Gemella doesn't like me going home pissed and reeking of strong drink.'

'You too?' I laughed. 'Okay, you've got it. So when are you free?'

We arranged a time and I left him to do whatever praetors in charge of Rome's mobile wealth do between sunrise and noon. Probably rest their feet on top of a desk and let the minions do the work. Then I went back down the hill towards Market Square and Tuscan Street to put myself a cup or two ahead while I waited. I reckoned I deserved the break. It'd been a busy and largely successful morning, and there ain't no better way to unwind than in a good wineshop with a saucer of cheese and olives and a decent belt of Caecuban.

Also to think. How the hell did I go about finding out more about Gaius Licinius Murena?

10

It was late afternoon before I got back home, slightly the worse for wear: we'd a lot to catch up on, and the one jug had turned into two after all. Perilla was upstairs in her study working on a poem, but she came back down to the atrium in any case. That suited me: being in Perilla's study with all these books and not a wine cup in sight makes me nervous as hell. Some people's ideas about what constitutes necessary furnishings are weird.

I slipped off my sandals, we settled on to the couches and Bathyllus wheeled in the Setinian.

'So, lady, how was your day?' I asked.

'All right. That is, if you except the arrival of a note from your mother asking us round for a meal over the Winter Festival.'

I groaned. Jupiter! 'Can we get out of it?'

'Marcus, dear, I am no more keen to be poisoned by suspect cooking than you are, nor do I relish the prospect of your stepfather covering one of my best mantles with sauce as he usually does; but no, we cannot get out of it. This is our first year back, and naturally Vipsania expects us. We'll just have to grit our teeth.'

'I'm more worried about what we'll be gritting our teeth on, lady.' I scowled into my wine. This was going to be a bad one, I could tell that now: Phormio, Mother's hyperinventive chef, went into overdrive on big occasions like the Winter Festival, and he didn't take prisoners. 'You think she and Priscus'd consider coming to us instead?'

'I asked. Vipsania said Meton was fine in his way but his menus were pedestrian.'

Ouch. I winced. If Meton ever got to hear that little squib he'd blow every gasket in his tiny food-fixated brain and go looking for Phormio with a cleaver. Well, there was nothing we could do; we were committed. Maybe if we were very lucky there'd be a plague or a major fire between now and the Festival that'd give us the chance to cancel. Failing that the only defence was to eat before we left.

The clock went *ting!* That'd be the tenth hour. Strange, I hadn't noticed the drips. Maybe I was getting used to them after all.

'How's the clepsydra behaving?' I said.

'Perfectly. It's an absolutely marvellous machine, and so useful I don't know what we did without it. I can't understand Bathyllus's attitude. He doesn't like it at all.'

Surprise, surprise. 'Yeah, well, he's a traditionalist, our Bathyllus. And I don't think the pissing cherubs went down a bomb with him either.'

Perilla settled back on her couch. 'So,' she said. 'How is the case going?'

I told her about the various visits. 'That guy Murena is a perfect fit, physically, anyway. It looks like the Aemilia theory is working out. All I've got to do now is check on whether he plays the flute and what he was doing two nights ago. That's going to be difficult but not impossible, thanks to having Gaius Secundus on the strength.' I took a swallow of Setinian. 'We'll have to have Gaius and his wife round, by the way. They're practically neighbours.'

'Perhaps we should ask your friend Caelius Crispus as well,' Perilla said demurely. 'Since he's been so helpful.'

I laughed. 'Jupiter, lady, the guy'd have apoplexy! But you're right, he's been a great help. That angle on Sulpicius Galba was interesting, too.'

'You think that's a possibility, Marcus? That the senior consul was involved?'

'No. Not really. He'd have no motive, for a start. But he's the only person we've come across so far with fluteplayer connections, and since it's his place the mechanics of the thing wouldn't be a problem. If we could find a reason why he'd introduce one of his fancy boys into the house on the night of the ceremony, then—'

I stopped. The clock had gone *ting!*

Perilla's brow wrinkled. 'But it can't be nearly that time already!' she said.

I got up and went over to check. The Victory's pointer was on the eleven. 'Wrong, lady. At least, your bronze pal in the tutu says it is.'

'But that's absolute nonsense!'

'Come over and see for yourself.'

She did. We stared at it together.

'The drips are too fast,' Perilla said finally. 'The valve needs adjusting.'

'Where to? This is December. One more notch and we're at the end of the scale.'

'Do it anyway.'

I turned the duck so its beak pointed to the last notch. The drips speeded up.

Perilla said, 'Hmm.'

'You got any other bright ideas, lady?'

'Try it the other way.'

I did as she'd told me. The drips speeded up some more. I turned the duck back, or tried to, and there was a dry metallic *tunk!* as it came free. The drips became a single trickle, then a rush, and the Victory lurched upwards on her pole like a dog after a rabbit.

'Oh, shit,' I murmured.

'*Marcus!*'

'Yeah, well.'

The little titan raised his hammer and brought it down with a sharp *ting!* The Victory kept on going.

Perilla rounded on me. 'Corvinus,' she snapped, 'if you've broken that clock . . . !'

'I hardly touched the thing!'

'Then what's that duck doing in your hand?'

Jupiter! Suddenly everything was my fault: typical bloody woman's logic. 'Look, Perilla,' I said, 'the bugger's sentient, right? It's got a mind of its own.'

'Nonsense! Here, let me—'

Ting!

Gurglegurglegurgle.

We both stared in horror as the pointer clanged against the top of its scale.

Tinkletinkletinklepsssss.

Silence. *Long* silence.

Perilla let her breath out. 'There, now,' she said brightly. 'Crisis over. It's reached the end of the cycle. All we have to do is leave it switched off until the engineer comes.'

I looked at the titan. I swear the little bastard had a sneer on his face. 'Listen, lady,' I said. 'Trust me. Forget the engineer, okay? The thing's only biding its time until it gets the chance to really let rip. Send it back while you still can.'

'Don't be silly, Marcus. Honestly, sometimes I think you—'

Knock knock knock.

The front door. Oh, hell. That was all we needed:

visitors, and the door-slave had gone walkabout. I yelled for Bathyllus, but he was obviously sulking or keeping a low profile or both: where domestic crises are concerned the little guy has a psychic streak that's positively uncanny.

Knock knock knock.

'Are we expecting anyone?' Perilla said.

'Uh-uh. Unless it's that flutegirl Thalia. I told the guy at the guildhouse to send her straight round if she showed up.'

'Really?' A sniff: the lady was clearly peeved. 'Then perhaps you should let her in.'

Barefoot, in only my tunic – I always get rid of my mantle, whenever I have to wear the thing, as soon as I get inside – I went through to the lobby and opened the door.

It wasn't Thalia. It was another Axeman, fist raised to knock again, glaring down at me in silent outrage like I hadn't even bothered with the tunic. Standing on the pavement behind him, bristling, was a Vestal virgin.

She was tall, thin and angular as a cloakstand, yellow-faced and ugly as sin. I didn't know if Vestals conformed to any dietary rules, but this one looked like she lived on dry bread and vinegar.

'Marcus Valerius Corvinus?' she snapped. 'Marcus Valerius *Messalla* Corvinus?'

'Uh, yeah.' She'd said the extra handle to my name like she was making sure another MVC wasn't pulling a fast one on her. 'Yeah, that's me.'

'My name is Servilia.' Her nose went up. 'May I come in?'

'Uh . . . yeah. Yeah, sure.' I stepped aside quickly.

She brushed past me like a homing wasp. 'Quintus,' she said to the Axeman, 'stay here, please. I'll call if I need you.'

Still glaring at me, the guy lumbered inside and set his solid back against the wall. I swear the stonework creaked. I closed the door.

Servilia looked me up and down. 'The atrium is this way?' she said.

'Yeah.' I was beginning to feel slightly steam-rollered here. 'Just go straight through.'

She cleared her throat. 'Do you normally answer your own door, young man? Just out of interest?'

'Uh, no.' Jupiter on wheels! 'I'm, uh, sorry about that. We've – ah – had a slight domestic crisis.'

'Really.' She made the word sound like she'd caught me in the middle of a full-blown orgy and the atrium was packed wall to wall with naked dancing girls. 'Never mind. I am prepared to make allowances.' Another freezing stare. '*Some* allowances.'

'That's great.' I edged across the lobby. Servilia didn't move, and the freezing stare dropped another couple of temperature points. 'Uh ... is there a problem?'

'Naturally,' she said, 'you will want to make yourself respectable before we talk. You have my leave.'

Ouch. The mantle. Or lack of one, rather. 'Got you,' I said, nodding. 'Right. Right. Fine. Just follow me, then, and my wife'll look after you while I change.'

Perilla was reclining sedately on the couch in her receiving visitors pose. Thank the gods for a wife with social graces. I made the introductions and bolted upstairs to comply with the decencies.

When I came down Servilia was sitting stiff as a ramrod on the most upright, least comfortable chair we'd got. She fixed me with a disapproving eye, and I noticed that Perilla was smiling brightly and looking ragged at the edges. Obviously a little of this lady went a long way.

I lay down on my usual couch. 'Now, Servilia,' I said. 'What can I do for you?'

'It is more a question, Valerius Corvinus, of what I can do for you. I have some information regarding my deceased colleague Cornelia which, painful though it is for me to pass on, I consider relevant to your enquiries.'

Uh-huh. I perked up; maybe letting the old sour-face over our threshold hadn't been such a mistake after all. 'Does – ah – Junia Torquata know you're here?' I said.

Her thin lips set. 'As a matter of fact, no. I have not consulted the chief Vestal, partly because the information is mine alone to give and partly because I am not at all sure that she would—' She stopped.

'That she would what?' I prompted.

Servilia gave me a long slow stare. 'My reasons, Valerius Corvinus,' she said, 'are immaterial, and none of your concern. I would be grateful if you would simply allow me to provide you with the information and refrain from asking irrelevant questions. Is that agreed?'

I was beginning to take a real dislike to Servilia. 'Yeah. Yeah, okay,' I said. 'It's agreed.'

'Good.' She glanced at Perilla. 'Perhaps your wife could leave us. My Axeman is in call, so the proprieties would be observed. And I would prefer for the sake of the sisterhood that the fewer people who know of this the better.'

I felt myself flushing. 'Now just a minute, lady!'

'That's all right, Marcus.' Perilla got up quickly. 'I have some work to do anyway. A pleasure to meet you, Servilia.'

The Vestal sniffed.

When Perilla had gone I turned back to her. 'Now,' I said.

'Cornelia was seeing a man. A young man. Clearly on

a regular basis. And they were on terms of considerable intimacy.'

A cold knot formed in my stomach. 'You're sure of that?'

'I saw them together myself.' There was no mistaking the quiet satisfaction in Servilia's voice. I felt my fist bunch. 'Three days ago, the day before the girl's death. The circumstances of the meeting were quite clandestine and completely unambiguous.'

'Uh-huh.' I kept my voice neutral. 'You want to tell me the whole story?' Sure she did; I couldn't've stopped her with a blackjack. The sour old cat was enjoying every minute of this.

'It was, as I said, three days ago. I was in my sitting-room, which opens on to a corridor off which Cornelia's own set of rooms lay. I had occasion to . . .' She hesitated. 'That is, I decided to leave the room for a few moments. On opening my door I glimpsed a figure hurrying down the corridor ahead of me, wearing a heavy cloak and hood. Naturally I was suspicious.'

'Naturally,' I said.

Her eye went into me like a gimlet. 'Valerius Corvinus,' she said, 'I do not find this either easy or pleasant. However, I would be failing in my duty if I withheld important evidence merely because it pained me personally to give it. Do you understand me?'

'Yeah.' I cleared my throat. 'Yeah, I understand you.' I did, too: the woman was a nosy, self-righteous, interfering bitch. Unfortunately, she was a nosy, self-righteous, interfering bitch with information vital to the case. 'My apologies. Carry on, Servilia.'

'I fetched my own cloak and followed, being careful, of course, to avoid being seen. By this time I knew who the

woman was: Cornelia was a very ... well-proportioned girl'
– a genteel cough– 'and quite recognisable, even in that garb.
She went straight to the side door of the house, which isn't
often used, and slipped outside.'

'And you followed her.'

'I did. As I say, at a discreet distance, which was just
as well because the girl was obviously concerned that she
should *not* be observed. However, since this occurred at
mid-morning there were plenty of people about, and I
was able to escape her notice. Also, the distance involved
was comparatively short; less than a hundred yards, in fact.
To Pearlsellers' Porch. There was a young man waiting near
one of the pillars. She went straight up to him and they ...
embraced.'

'"Embraced"? You mean they kissed each other?'

Servilia's colour rose. 'It was more of a hug, Valerius
Corvinus, but still very indecorous behaviour for a Vestal;
indeed, blasphemously indecorous. I ... waited and watched
under cover of a trinket stall while they talked, I would
say for upwards of twenty minutes. Their heads were
very close together as if they were whispering; Cornelia,
of course, was hooded but the man was not. They became
quite animated.'

'"Animated"?'

'Excited. But not pleasantly so. I could not see Cornelia's
expression, naturally, but I had the impression that the man
was pleading with her about something. Several times he
touched her arm.'

'And that was all you saw?'

'That was all. They embraced again and Cornelia ran down
the steps and back, I presume, to the House of the Vestals,
since she was there when I returned. The young man went
off in the other direction.'

My scalp was prickling. Forget the obvious let-out clause of a long-lost brother and a fraternal hug: Cornelia, I knew, had been an only child. So the next question was the crucial one. 'You, uh, you'd recognise the guy again if you saw him?'

She smiled; not a nice smile. 'Oh, yes. Valerius Corvinus. Of course I would. His name is Marcus Aemilius Lepidus.'

II

It was too late to do anything about it that day, but I was down at the chief priest's house early next morning interviewing Junia Torquata. I was pretty angry.

'You knew!' I said.

She was watching me calmly. Furius Camillus was out on priestly business and we were on our own in the chilly atrium, but the affront to propriety didn't seem to worry her and I was past caring.

'I did *not* know,' she said quietly. 'Servilia did not think fit to tell me.'

'I don't mean about the meeting.' I'd been pacing around the room. Now I pulled up a chair that looked two hundred years older than Cleopatra and sat down facing her. 'You knew the guy existed and they'd been friends for years, yet you never mentioned him. I'll bet you recognised the ring, for a start.'

'Yes, the ring was young Marcus Lepidus's. Although I hadn't seen it for a long time. How Cornelia got it, or why she was wearing it round her neck, I have no idea.'

'Right.' I took a deep breath. 'Let's start at the beginning with the basic facts. When her parents split up, remarried and moved away from Rome, Cornelia went to live with Marcus Lepidus Senior's family. True?'

'She was only four at the time. Neither parent particularly wanted her in their new ménage, and Lepidus Senior was her uncle. It was a natural arrangement.'

Shit. I'd been *told* about the Lepidus connection! When I'd asked Furius Camillus about Cornelia he'd mentioned Lepidus himself, only I'd assumed it was just a slip of the tongue and he'd meant the girl's actual father Lentulus. Fool! 'Lepidus had — or has, rather, because the guy's still alive — two children of his own, a daughter and a son. The son, Marcus, was two years younger than Cornelia. They grew up together.'

'Only for the next four years. Cornelia became a Vestal when she was eight. Marcus, of course, would be six. At which point, naturally, the tie was severed and Cornelia moved to the House of the Vestals. Four years, Corvinus, hardly justifies the term "growing up together".'

'Don't split hairs, lady! Obviously the two were very close. They kept up the friendship, only any one-to-one meetings had to be secret because they weren't brother and sister by blood, or even stepbrother and stepsister. They kept it up until practically the day the girl died. What I want to know is exactly how close they got to each other.'

Torquata sat up. *'Corvinus!'*

But I'd had enough; certainly too much to be frozen out. 'Come on, Torquata!' I snapped. 'Up to now largely thanks to you I've been working on the assumption either that Cornelia was killed by a stranger or, if she did know the man, a sexual connection between the two of them was unlikely. Now I find out, no thanks to you, that there's a prime candidate who's been seeing her regularly since they were kids together.'

'In public, certainly, and perhaps even as a fellow guest at the more respectable private dinner parties. I don't deny that. Vestals, as you know, are not cloistered. However—'

'Junia Torquata, I'm not talking about those sorts of

meetings and well you know it! I'm talking about the sort of rendezvous Servilia witnessed.'

'Servilia is a—' Torquata stopped and bit her lip, then went on more carefully. 'Servilia did not like Cornelia, Valerius Corvinus. A product of one of those petty jealousies I mentioned. The meeting may have been an isolated incident and the rest the result of my sister-in-Vesta's overheated imagination. Certainly I knew nothing of any unaccompanied trysts, or I would naturally have put a stop to them.'

'What Servilia saw doesn't sound like an isolated incident to me, lady. And if it wasn't, that makes a big difference. Sure, the girl was a Vestal, but Lepidus Junior was no direct blood relation, and the two obviously liked each other a lot or they wouldn't've got together. The meeting could've been on the innocent brother–sister level but it could equally be an assignation between lovers. Whether you like it or not sex is back on the cards, and the pregnancy angle with it.'

'Corvinus, I have already told you that under no circumstances would Cornelia have broken her vows. And young Marcus Lepidus is neither a seducer nor a murderer, especially of a girl who was both his cousin and a Vestal virgin. I have known him from birth and I can assure you of that fact categorically.'

There was something wrong. Maybe it was something in her eye or in her tone, I didn't know, but it was false as hell. However certain her words sounded, I'd bet a sturgeon to a pickled mussel that Torquata wasn't as hundred-per-cent convinced of the truth of them as she wanted me to think she was. And the reason was she still knew something that I didn't and was terrified that I'd find it out. So what the hell was it?

Then I remembered her shock the last time I'd been here with Camillus, and what exactly it had been that we'd been discussing; and the hairs stirred on my neck as the answer hit me.

Oh, Jupiter! Jupiter best and greatest! We'd got our murderer!

'Marcus Lepidus can play the flute, can't he?' I said quietly.

Torquata stiffened. She closed her eyes and I thought she was going to faint, but then she opened them again and stared straight at me without blinking, her face expressionless. She was a fighter, the chief Vestal, I'd give her that. Even when she was beaten.

'Yes,' she said. 'As a matter of fact he can. Very well indeed. The Aemilii Lepidi have always had strong musical interests. And of course the Cornelii connection was an added incentive. The Cornelii were Graecophiles from the first.'

I stood up. Well, that put the lid on it: Marcus Lepidus was our man. The why and the how were details that could be cleared up later by the chief city judge. Sure, there'd be the question of alibi or lack of it and maybe a few small loose ends no one would ever tie in, but the simple fact that Lepidus was the killer was plain enough. 'Okay,' I said. 'Thanks for your help, Junia Torquata. I'll see you—'

She reached out and gripped my wrist. Gods, the lady was strong! I could almost feel the bones grating.

'Wait,' she said.

'Torquata,' I said gently, not moving, 'it's finished.' I felt sorry as hell for her, but there was no more to be said. 'The guy's guilty six ways from nothing. He has to be.'

'Marcus Lepidus did not kill Cornelia.'

'Fine. Give me firm proof – give me any proof at all to weigh against what we've got – and I'll scratch him off the

list.' Silence. 'Yeah. Right. Now if you'll let me have my
arm back I'll—'

'Talk to him. Let him put his side of the story.'

'You admit there is a story?'

She hesitated. 'Marcus was . . . very fond of Cornelia, yes.
As a sister, I mean. He's a very weak boy in many ways,
sensitive and easily dominated, which perhaps explains his
reputation.' Jupiter! I wondered whether the chief Vestal
wasn't showing unexpected pseudo-maternal astigmatism
here. Sure, I'd never met young Marcus Lepidus, but I'd
heard of him, and 'reputation' was right in spades. The
kid was neck and neck with the fastest set in the city, and
whatever Torquata said he was no sweet little cowslip. 'I
won't beg you, Corvinus, because I'm acting in the interests
of truth. Also I admit that the facts would all seem to be
pointing to one conclusion. However, I think it would be
very, very foolish to condemn the boy without a hearing.
Go and see him. See him now.'

I sighed. Yeah, well; it wouldn't serve any useful purpose,
I knew, but what can you say?

The Lepidus place was a big, old, rambling house with a
big, old, rambling garden that took up a sizeable slice of
the Quirinal; which figured, because the Aemilii Lepidi were
one of the oldest, richest and most aristocratic families in
Rome. Not to mention exclusive. Like I say, I'd never met
the son but I knew the father slightly. Certainly I knew
of him: Marcus Aemilius Lepidus Senior had been on the
defence bench at the Piso trial – in fact he'd been the only
straight-shooter involved in that fiasco – and before that his
name had been one of the ones Augustus had suggested was
fit to have the title 'emperor' tacked in front of it. Mind
you, the sharp old bugger had added the footnote that he

wouldn't've touched the job wearing three sets of gloves. Which tells you something about Lepidus Senior.

I knocked on the door – a huge slab of ancient oak banded with iron – and the door-slave opened up. Not your usual cheeky type; the guy was solid oak like the door itself, and he obviously took his job seriously. I introduced myself.

'The master at home?' I said. 'The young master?'

'He's in mourning, sir. I doubt if he's receiving visitors.'

'Give him my apologies, but say it's important. Very important.'

'Very well, sir. If you'd care to wait.' The door-slave led me through and left me in a gleaming marble atrium the size of a racetrack. There were statues there that wouldn't've looked out of place in the Wart's villa on Capri, and the ornamental pool was big enough to stage a mock sea fight. Rich was right.

The slave reappeared. 'Would you follow me, sir?'

We went down an expensively panelled corridor paved with coloured marble that ended up at what was in effect a separate self-contained suite facing on to the garden. The slave stopped at a door, knocked and opened it. We were in a small reading-room.

'Marcus Valerius Corvinus, sir,' he said gently.

The guy lying on the couch looked terrible. The mourning didn't help, mind – that much stubble doesn't lend anyone an air of sharpness and insouciance – but his tunic was creased and rumpled like he'd slept in it and his face was red and puffy. I could see what Torquata had meant: he had soft, almost feminine features, long eyelashes and a weak mouth and chin. Not one of life's forceful characters, that was sure. A follower, not a leader. He'd've made a good flutegirl, though.

He got up. The slave left, closing the door behind him.

'What can I do for you, Corvinus?' His voice was flat and dead. 'Venustus said it was important.'

I cleared my throat. Hell, the guy might be guilty, but he was obviously also suffering. I wasn't going to enjoy this. 'It's about Cornelia. I'm ... looking into her death. As a favour to the chief Vestal.'

'Looking into her death?' Something shifted in his eyes. He waved me to another couch, then sat down again on his own one, his movements jerky. 'But it was suicide, wasn't it? They told me it was suicide.'

I hadn't moved. 'The Vestal Servilia said she'd seen you talking to her the day before she died. Outside Pearlsellers' Porch.'

His mouth went slack with shock. 'She said *what*?'

'You deny it?'

I thought he wasn't going to answer, but finally, quietly, he said, 'No. I don't deny it. But—'

'Or that you'd been seeing her regularly over a period of years?'

Another pause, even longer. 'No.' His voice was a ghost's. 'Not that either.'

'Cornelia was wearing a ring on a cord round her neck. Was it yours?'

'A ring?'

'With two clasped hands.'

He swallowed. His eyes were glittering. 'Yes. That was mine. I gave it to her years ago, a keepsake. I didn't ... didn't know she ... carried it around with her ... but certainly—' He broke off and took a deep breath. 'I'm sorry, Valerius Corvinus, but I'm very tired and very upset and I really don't know what you want of me. I'd like you to go.'

'Not yet.' I tried to make the words as unthreatening as possible. Maybe he didn't know, but in that case he was one

of the poorest guessers I'd ever come across. 'I have to ask
you what exactly your relationship with Cornelia was.'

'But that's simple.' He half smiled. Or maybe that was
what he tried to do but it didn't come out right; maybe he
was the one who was simple. 'I loved her, of course.'

I loved her, of course. Jupiter best and greatest! My stomach
went cold. I crossed over to the other couch and sat down.
'The girl was a Vestal,' I said quietly.

'Yes, I know that. Of course I do.' The half-smile was
still there, and it just looked . . . wrong. My skin crawled.
'That was the problem. She came when I was two. She was
chosen to be a Vestal when I was six. That's all I had of
her, Corvinus, four years, before I was left alone with the
Bitch. I can't even remember half of them.'

'"The Bitch"?'

'Lepida.' Uh-huh. The elder sister. She'd be the Lepida
who'd been married to Drusus Caesar before the marriage
was dissolved and Sejanus took her over as his mistress.
She was in her late twenties now, still single and one of
the hottest, fastest ladies in Rome. 'That's a joke, by the
way. You can laugh if you like.'

'Uh . . . what's a joke, friend?' He hadn't laughed himself;
hadn't even sounded amused. I shifted on the couch. The
lack of expression in his voice was getting to me seriously;
it wasn't natural, and it wasn't healthy, no more than his
lack of resentment at what anyone else would've seen as a
covert accusation. This guy was Weird with a capital 'W',
and he was making me nervous as a cat at a dog-breeders'
convention. More than anything else I wanted out of that
room, out of that house . . .

But I couldn't go yet. Not now that he was talking.

'Lepida. It means pleasant, agreeable. Lepida was a bitch
when we were young, she's still a bitch. *The* Bitch. Cornelia

was the only sister I had. I couldn't let her go, could I?'

I said nothing.

'We didn't meet for almost five years. I saw her in the street sometimes. Sometimes by accident, sometimes on purpose. Then I saw her maid one day, buying a scarf in the Velabrum. I gave her a message, she brought one back. That was how it started. Then two months later Cornelia managed to slip away herself. We've been seeing each other ever since, whenever we can. I gave her the ring six years ago. When I came of age. She didn't want to take it, but I insisted.'

The question had to be asked, and the straighter the better. 'Did you sleep with her?'

He looked directly at me for the first time, his eyes wide.

'No,' he said. 'Of course not.' But there was no surprise in his tone, or shock.

'Cornelia was murdered. By a man disguised as one of the flutegirls attending the rites.' I paused. He was staring at me now, but he didn't speak. 'You play the flute, don't you, Marcus Lepidus?'

Silence. Then, suddenly, his face changed as the penny dropped and he was on his feet and headed for my throat, so fast that I only had time to stand up and raise my arms to catch him as he hit. He was heavier than he looked, in good condition, and more to the point he was angry as hell. It took me all my time and all my strength to prise his thumbs free of my windpipe, spin him round and get an arm-lock on him. He struggled for a bit then went limp against me like a sack of grain. I let go and he slid to the ground, then I stepped back and waited. He sat at my feet, his head in his hands.

Minutes passed. Jupiter knew where the slaves had got to — we'd made enough noise to bring the whole household running — but no one came. Finally he looked up.

'You think I murdered her.' There was no anger left in his voice. It was chillingly calm like before, and it sent a shiver up my spine.

There was no point playing games. 'Yeah,' I said. 'That's what I think.'

He scrambled to his feet. 'Then you can go and fuck yourself.'

Ouch. He meant it, too. Well, perhaps it was for the best. For a minute there I'd actually felt sorry for the guy.

'Maybe you didn't do the actual killing, Lepidus,' I said. 'The girl could've killed herself. But you were directly responsible.'

He looked at me like he was seeing me for the first time; didn't speak, just looked. And his expression was sheer blank horror. Then he began to move his head slowly, numbly, back and forward, back and forward . . .

'No,' he said. 'No.'

The change was so sudden it was shocking. I had the weird feeling he was talking to himself, trying to convince himself, not me, and not doing too well. The hairs crawled on my scalp. What had I said to Perilla? *Anyone crazy enough to kill a Vestal would show it in other ways . . .*

Maybe it was grief and lack of food, but from where I was standing and my experience of the guy so far Marcus Lepidus was short of a watertight roof by all the tiles and half the joists. And if ever I saw guilt written plain on a face, Lepidus's was the one.

At least there was no fight left in him now. I steered him gently to his couch and pushed him down on to it. He didn't resist, just stared past me at nothing; or rather at something I couldn't see and probably wouldn't want to.

'Okay.' I moved gently on to the really shaky ground. 'So what were you talking about, you and Cornelia? The day Servilia saw you?' I waited. Nothing. His eyes had gone blank, like twin coin dies. 'Come on, Lepidus! You were with the girl for a good twenty minutes. Servilia said you were asking her something; "pleading" was the word she used. So what was it?' Nothing. I could've been talking to the fancy bronze statue in the corner. I sighed. 'All right. We'll leave it and move on. Second: why did you gatecrash the rites? And what exactly happened that evening?'

I waited. And waited. Even a refusal to tell or another brawl would've been better than what was happening. He'd simply frozen up on me. His face was set like a wax death-mask and he was staring into nothing, completely immobile. I leaned over and waved my hand in front of his eyes. He neither moved nor blinked. My spine went cold.

Jupiter!

Well, there was nothing more I could do, I was beginning to shake, and all I wanted was out. I stood up. No reaction. None. I moved to the door.

With that open, I felt better. I took several deep breaths and turned round. Lepidus was still staring.

'Did you kill her?' I asked quietly.

But he didn't answer. I closed the door gently behind me.

12

I left word with the slave to look after him and made my way down from the Quirinal. There wasn't much I could do now except make my report to Camillus, who as acting chief priest was technically responsible for putting any prosecution into gear. I didn't envy him. On the one hand, the murder of a Vestal was unheard of and it'd call, if anything did, for the guy responsible to be chopped; on the other hand Lepidus came from one of the top families in Rome and his father was one of the biggest wheels in the Senate. Also, Lepidus was clearly two buns short of a baker's dozen to begin with. Both of these facts might well make a difference, and I was glad that whoever ended up fielding the mess and deciding how to deal with it, it wouldn't be me.

Camillus wasn't in, either at home or at the King's House where he had his office, so I left a message at both places asking him to get in touch as soon as he could and set off back to the Caelian. Mid-morning or not, I felt washed out: sure, we'd got our murderer, but it hadn't exactly been a satisfying case. 'Mess' was right; there were too many loose ends flapping around for my liking, and that wasn't good at all. Besides, I had an uncomfortable feeling that we'd screwed up somewhere along the line. Where precisely I wasn't sure, but the feeling wouldn't go away.

Perilla was in the atrium. I planted a kiss on her upturned mouth and slumped down on to the couch opposite her.

'Marcus?' she said. 'Are you all right?'

'Yeah.' I lay back and rubbed my eyes. They felt like someone had thrown sand in them. 'Yeah, I'm fine, lady.'

'Really? Then why do you look like something the cat dragged in?'

'The investigation's over.'

'Oh.' A pause; Perilla sounded as let down as I was. 'Lepidus admitted killing the girl?'

'No. But he was responsible, all right, I'd take my oath on that. The guy had "guilty" written all over him.'

'Very well. So why did he do it?'

'Jupiter knows. It must've been the pregnancy angle, although he denied it. They were close enough, and on his side he was head over heels in love with her.'

'But?'

'Why the hell should there be a "but"?'

'Don't snap. Because if there isn't then you'd sound more convinced. And convincing.'

True. 'Okay. Pregnancy just doesn't fit, nohow, nowhere, never. He's the wrong type, she's the wrong type and everybody who knew them says it's impossible.'

'Then Lepidus must have had another reason.'

'Perilla, there isn't one, or none that I can see. Anyway, it doesn't matter any more. The case is out of my hands and working out the whys and wherefores is up to Furius Camillus and the head city judge.'

Perilla was quiet for a long time. Then she said softly, 'You don't think it was Lepidus after all, do you?'

'Gods, lady, he has to be the killer! Nothing else fits! He's the right age and class, the right physical type with the right skills, he was seeing her in secret, he gatecrashed the ceremony, he left the room the same time she did and if there was something between them, sexual or not, it explains how she could be decoyed into the back bedroom without giving the alarm. Also the guy's a total fruitcake with as much grip on reality as a Minturnian prawn. What more do you want?'

'I should have thought that was obvious. If Lepidus did kill the girl then I want to know why. And so do you.'

Yeah. She was right; that was the bummer. Everything made sense bar that. Or a kind of sense, anyway. I shrugged. 'Okay,' I said, 'let's work it out. Forget the pregnancy and the affair, they won't wash. What else is there?'

'For a start, what he was doing at the rites in the first place.'

I poured myself a cup of Setinian from the jug beside me. 'Lady, we're going round in circles. He went to kill Cornelia. It's the—'

'Assume for a moment that he didn't. Kill Cornelia, that is. Where would that idea take us?'

'But—'

'Let's go over the facts, Marcus. First of all, Servilia saw Cornelia talking to Lepidus in Pearlsellers' Porch. Lepidus admits to this, and also to the existence of a long-term relationship. Second, Junia Torquata tells us that she has been preoccupied and moody for some time. Third, the day after the meeting Lepidus disguises himself as a flutegirl and attends the rites at the Galba house. Fourth, in the course of the evening, Cornelia makes an excuse and leaves the room. Shortly afterwards Lepidus also slips out via the garden porch. He does not reappear. Shortly after *that*, Cornelia is found dead in the back bedroom. The natural assumption is that Lepidus killed her, but that is all it is, an assumption. He had the opportunity, certainly; but, equally certainly if we discount a sexual link between the two, he had no obvious motive, especially since from what you say he was strongly attached to the girl. And if he had no motive then the means, too, is problematical at best.'

I frowned. 'Uh . . . run that last one past me again.'

'Marcus, if Lepidus *didn't* attend the rites with the express purpose of killing Cornelia, then where did the knife come from?'

I sat back. Shit; she was right! I'd forgotten the knife! Without a pre-existing motive, the reason for that being there went down the tubes as well. And as the basis for a murder charge one out of three just wasn't good enough. 'Okay, lady,' I said. 'You've got the ball. Where do you want to play it?'

'Let's imagine that on the night of the ceremony – for some reason – Lepidus needs to talk to Cornelia urgently. I doubt that the meeting was prearranged, because Cornelia would have realised that it involved profanation of the rites and refused to agree. So the decision was his, and he took it unilaterally.'

'Hang on, Perilla. They'd talked only the day before. And it would've taken Lepidus time to set the scam up, assuming he had the contacts to do it.' Hell; that was another thing. How did Thalia fit into all this? 'Twenty-four hours just isn't enough notice.'

'That is a problem, I grant you.' The lady had on her prim expression. 'However, we'll leave it for the present. Very well. Cornelia goes out and Lepidus follows. She could, of course, still be unaware of his presence in the house but there is a possibility that by this stage she knows he's there. In any event, they meet and talk. Lepidus leaves by the back door and Cornelia is murdered.'

I shifted on the couch. 'No. That wouldn't work. She would've bolted the door behind him. Unless—' I stopped.

'Unless?'

'Unless they didn't talk. Because Cornelia was already dead when Lepidus got to her.'

'Hmm.' Perilla looked thoughtful. 'Would the murderer have had enough time?'

'I don't know. The two were seen leaving the room by different people. There could've been a gap, sure. But timing wouldn't've been an issue. Remember, whoever the murderer was they wouldn't know Lepidus was on his way.' I took a swallow of wine. 'Or rather I'm assuming they wouldn't. Still, the theory would fit the facts. Also why Lepidus didn't catch on right away when I said I was looking into the girl's death. As far as he was concerned, there wouldn't've been any murder; Cornelia had committed suicide. It'd explain his reaction when I accused him of being responsible for her death, too.'

'What?'

'Look at it from his side. Jupiter knows what the secret was that they shared, but it was obviously major league, and one gets you ten it was the reason why Lepidus gatecrashed the party. Maybe there'd been some last-minute development, something that couldn't wait and he had to talk to her straight away. Only the murderer got in first. Sure the guy would feel responsible; he'd saddled her with the problem in the first place. And—'

'Marcus, dear, you can't have it both ways. You've just said that Lepidus thought Cornelia had committed suicide. Now you're telling me he knew murder was a possibility.'

I sighed and rubbed my eyes again. 'Perilla, I don't know what I'm telling you, okay? This is all top-of-the-head stuff, and it may be a mare's-nest anyway.'

'There's another thing.'

'Yeah?'

'We're back to the problem of the murderer. If it wasn't Lepidus – the "flutegirl!" – then who was it?'

'Someone in the house, obviously, who was at the party and—' I stopped as the implication hit me. 'Oh, Jupiter!'

'Jupiter is right. One man in disguise at the ceremony is enough. If Lepidus wasn't the killer then it must have been a woman after all.'

Someone coughed. I turned round. Bathyllus had oiled in on my blind side.

'Yeah, little guy,' I said. 'What is it?'

'The clock repairers are here, sir.'

Bugger; I'd forgotten about the clock. In the midst of life we are in domestic crisis.

'Oh, good.' Perilla got up. 'Send them in, Bathyllus.'

'Them' was right, just: the smoothie foreman and Zosimus the Water-Carrier. Evidently call-out after installation didn't rate the full five-star treatment.

'Good morning, madam.' The foreman ignored me and beamed at Perilla. 'What seems to be the trouble?'

'Your fancy clock decided to restructure the calendar and bypass half of yesterday,' I said.

The smile wavered and I detected the slight gritting of professional teeth. He turned to me slowly. 'That's most unlikely, sir,' he said. 'Spontaneously, I mean.'

Uh-huh. This guy was beginning to annoy me. 'Are you calling me a liar, friend?'

'*Marcus!*' That was Perilla.

'Not at all, sir.' Beam. 'All I'm saying is that there are built-in safeguards to the mechanism which are normally idiot-proof, although of course they may be overridden should the id ...' – he coughed – 'ah, should the owner be misguided enough to choose so to do. Sir.'

Hell. I didn't need this; none of it. 'Just fix the clock, pal, okay?' I said.

'Certainly. Zosimus?' The other guy hefted the huge bag

of tools he was carrying and followed him over to the clepsydra. 'Ah. I see. As I thought. Tchtchtch. Well, sir, I would say the problem was obvious.' He picked up the broken duck which I'd left on the pedestal. 'Naturally you can't expect a sensitive instrument like this to function if you go breaking bits off it. Aha-ha-ha.'

'It wasn't fucking functioning in the first place, sunshine! And if the fucking duck had been properly—'

'Marcus, let me handle this, please.' Perilla gave the man a brilliant smile. 'What my husband means is that the malfunction preceded the damage to the valve and was quite unconnected to it. The clock certainly seemed to be going faster than it ought to have done. Considerably faster.'

'Mmm. How fast is fast, madam?'

Perilla told him while I glowered.

'Strange. Most unusual. It definitely sounds like a hardware problem.'

'"Hardware"?' Perilla said.

'Forgive me, madam. A professional term. I meant a problem with the component parts of the machine as opposed to the hydraulics per se. Machine parts, being metal, are hard while water is – ah—'

'Soft,' I said. 'Yeah. Got you.' Hell! Engineers!

'Quite, sir.' He bent down to examine the valve. 'Zosimus, the Number Four probe, please.'

The hairy member of the team furkled around in his bag and brought out a small bronze instrument with a sickle-shaped end. His boss inserted it into the gap the duck had left and rotated it gently, then grunted.

'There's your trouble, madam,' he said. 'They've fitted an ASD valve instead of an Anaximandrian one.'

'Really?'

'Yes. Can you believe that? Bloody Greek cowboys, eh, Zosimus? Forgive my language.'

'And that makes a difference, does it?'

The guy exchanged a quick look with Zosimus which involved two sets of raised eyes, a shrug and a quivering mouth.

'Oh, yes, madam. Quite definitely. Aha-ha-ha. I'm not – aha-ha-ha – surprised you had problems. Wouldn't you agree, Zosimus?'

'Bound to, ma'am. An ASD valve in a clock like this is just asking for trouble.'

'Oh-ha-ha-ha!'

'Hoo-hoo-hoo!'

Jupiter! Whatever the joke was, it was a good one; they were both practically rolling. I gave them time for another few thigh-slaps then said, 'Uh ... you care to compose yourself and explain, pal?'

'Of course, sir. I'm – oh-ha-ha-ha – I'm sorry. My sincere apologies.' The foreman cleared his throat, wiped his eyes and straightened his face. Zosimus was still sniggering. 'It's quite straightforward. Your Athenian standard-day valve – ASD, that is, sir – is geared to the older six-hour day/night cycle instead of the Anaximandrian twelve. Accordingly it has a different thread ratio and input-output torque, so is not compatible with this machine, which was designed for the Roman market. Throws the whole delicate system out of kilter. Like one bit of the clock's talking Greek while the rest speaks Latin. You understand?'

'So all you have to do is change the valve?' Perilla smiled. 'Well, that is splendid!'

'Er ... it's not that simple, madam, I'm afraid.'

Snigger from Zosimus.

'Ah.'

'We're talking cutting-edge technology here. The valve will have to be made specially. Normally that would not present a problem, but unfortunately our horological engineer is indisposed at present and won't be back at work until after the Winter Festival.'

'Oh.'

'A poke in the eye with a breadstick at a niece's fifth birthday party, I understand.'

'I see.'

'However I can do a patch job for the time being.' He held out his hand. 'Zosimus, the pliers.'

Oh, hell.

13

A message having arrived from Camillus to say he'd be free to see me first thing, next morning I grabbed a quick breakfast and headed across town to the chief priest's residence.

This was going to be a tough one. Young Marcus Lepidus might not be the murderer after all, but all the circumstantial evidence still pointed his way and the guy certainly had questions to answer. If he would answer them. That was the bummer. Not having any official standing, I couldn't put any pressure on, especially since the kid was top-drawer patrician, but maybe Camillus could. He was a friend of the family, for a start, and the old-boy network has ways of dealing with scandals involving their own that have nothing to do with the due processes of law. They have to have. Over the last five hundred years they've had plenty of practice.

The other problem was a nagging one that wouldn't go away, and it wasn't connected with the actual murder; at least, not directly. Lepidus was broad-striper class, like the victim and, presumably, Cornelia's killer. We were moving in high circles here. Only, if so, there were parts of the case that didn't square up because they didn't belong in the broad-striper world at all. The knife, for a start. Like Perilla had said, in the context it didn't make sense; a knife like that wasn't a broad-striper tool, even as a once-off murder weapon. It was the sort of cheap rubbish you'd find in the belt of a punter from the Aventine slums who queued every day for his grain dole and used the thing for slicing cookshop sausage. If it had been brought specially to do the killing, which seemed more than likely, then squaring the whys and wherefores was a real bugger.

Second was the whole fluteplayer business. For it to work, for Lepidus to be able to bluff his way into the Galba house, he needed an in with the fluteplayers' guild at grass-roots level. He'd have to know how the booking system worked and which particular girls would be playing at the rites. More, even if he knew the names he'd have to have some sort of personal contact with the girl whose place he was taking because otherwise he couldn't have squared it with her, especially if the thing had been arranged at such short notice. None of that was broad-striper country; yet it had to have been possible for the whole scam to work. All of which meant that even with the phantom flutegirl angle stitched up firm from the other end I still needed to talk to Thalia. Which was yet another bugger: where the hell was she? Fluteplayers can't afford to pass up invitations from well-heeled clients, especially when they pay in advance, but it seemed that that was just what the girl was doing. And that smelled. After my visit to Camillus I'd have to drop in at the guildhouse for a third word with Celer.

I knocked on Camillus's door and the slave let me in, looking more Jupiter-like than ever. Camillus was in his study. The guy looked tired.

'Good morning, Corvinus,' he said. 'You wanted to see me?'

'Yeah.' I pulled up a stool.

'There have been developments, I take it.'

'Yeah. I can put a name to our fluteplayer friend.'

'Really?' His eyes sharpened. 'Who was he?'

This was the tricky bit. 'You've talked to Junia Torquata?' I said.

'No. Not since we last spoke. I've been very busy. So has she, arranging a repeat of the rites.'

Damn, I was hoping Torquata might've softened the old guy up. Lepidus was a big name, and, like I say, Camillus and the kid's father were friends. I had to take this slowly. 'Seemingly Cornelia was seeing someone on a regular basis.'

He stiffened. '"Seeing" someone?'

'Not in the sexual sense. Or at least I don't think so. But there was definitely a ... friendship. Going back a long way. The man took the place of one of the flutegirls at the ceremony so he could talk to her.'

Camillus's mouth was a hard line. 'Go on.'

'I'm not sure what happened next. Sure, the guy could be the killer, but I've talked to him and I think profaning the rites is all he's really guilty of.'

'That is bad enough, Corvinus. His name, please.'

I hesitated. 'If you don't mind, sir, I won't tell you that yet. Bear with me, okay?'

His brows came down. I thought he was going to object but he just said, 'Very well. Cornelia knew that this man was in the house? During the ceremony?'

'No. At least, again I don't think so. The whole idea was his, and like I say he only wanted to talk. When she left the room he followed her, using the outside route to the back hall.'

'Talk about what?'

'That's what I don't know, sir, and what I'm hoping you can find out for me because you know the man's family. In the event, the conversation never happened. When he found her Cornelia was already dead and the murderer had left by the back door. I think then he probably panicked and slipped out himself.'

'I see.' There was a wax tablet on the desk beside Camillus's hand. His fingers played with the laces. He wasn't looking at me. 'Now. The man's name, please.'

There wasn't any reason not to tell him. Not now the preliminary spadework was finished. 'Marcus Aemilius Lepidus,' I said.

I'd been expecting a reaction, but Camillus just grunted and nodded. He stood up, slowly and painfully, like he was closer to seventy than sixty.

'Yes,' he said. 'I thought that might be who you meant. You truly, honestly believe he did not commit the murder?'

'Like I say, it's possible, sure, but I doubt it.' I felt uneasy; there was something screwy here, and I didn't know what it was. The guy was taking this far too well. Or, no, that wasn't it; he'd gone ... *quiet* was the right word. Quiet and gentle. 'Lepidus was fond of Cornelia. More than fond. He had no reason to murder her.'

Another nod; Camillus had his back to me. He was inspecting the titles of the books on the rack behind the desk. 'No,' he said. 'Marcus Lepidus wouldn't have harmed the girl. That's only my personal belief, of course, but I'm glad to hear you confirm it.'

I cleared my throat. 'He won't talk to me,' I said. 'All the same, I think he knows who the killer is. Or if not at least whatever the secret he shared with Cornelia was it'd give us a lead. If you can get him to tell you we might be able to wrap this thing up. Sure, he'll be in trouble over the sacrilege, but—'

'The sacrilege is academic now, Corvinus.' Camillus spoke very softly. 'And I'm afraid I can't help you with the secret, and nor can he. You see, yesterday evening Marcus Lepidus killed himself.'

Oh, gods. Sweet, immortal gods.

*   *   *

Bad time or not, bad form or not, it had to be the Quirinal next. The front of the Aemilius Lepidus house had as many cypress branches hung up on it as would've equipped a decent-sized forest, but I knocked on the door anyway. It was opened by the same slave as before, only this time he had a chunk of his forelock missing.

'Uh, I'm sorry for the intrusion,' I said, 'but would it be possible to have a word with Marcus Aemilius Lepidus? Senior, that is.' I bit my tongue as soon as the words were out. Gods, how crass can you get?

The guy just looked at me. I had the distinct impression that he wanted to spit in my face, but instead he turned and went back inside without a word, leaving the door open. I kicked my heels by the marble pillars for a good five minutes before he came back.

'The master will see you, Valerius Corvinus,' he said. 'He's in his study. Follow me, please.'

The atrium was a shock. I should've expected it, sure — the Aemilii Lepidi do these things properly, in the traditional way — but it was still a shock. They'd put him on a couch with his feet to the door, covered with an embroidered cloth to the chin so there was no sign of how he'd died. The slave stopped and handed me a pair of shears, then waited while I cut off the obligatory lock of hair, laid it in the basket beside the corpse and burned a pinch of incense on the brazier. Then he went on.

We walked along a different maze of corridors from last time until we came to a cedar-panelled door with brass hinges. The guy knocked, opened it, then stepped back to let me through and closed it behind me. Not a word throughout, but I reckoned if he'd had to go through the same routine with a cockroach as far as being shown due friendliness and respect went the bastard with the feelers would've had the edge, easy. Ouch. Obviously as far as the Aemilius Lepidus household was concerned Corvinus was not flavour of the month, or even in the last five. Mind you, I didn't blame him; when a visitor leaves the young master ready to commit suicide the family aren't exactly going to put out the welcome mat a second time round.

If it was suicide, of course . . .

Marcus Lepidus Senior was sitting at his desk. He looked haggard as hell, sure, but even in that condition he was an impressive man, poker-backed, crag-faced and silver-haired, with a nose you could've fitted to a fighting trireme and skipped the extra bronze plating. And on the reading couch to his right lay one of the most stunning women I'd ever set eyes on.

'Marcus Valerius Corvinus,' he said. Just that. Not hostile, but a long way from friendly. And no 'Please sit down' tacked on, either.

I went into my prepared speech. 'I, uh, I'm sorry to intrude, sir, I know how you'll be feeling, but I—'

He cut through me. 'This is my daughter Lepida.' The woman didn't even nod. Jupiter! Curves like that shouldn't be allowed! 'Now. What can we do for you, Corvinus? Don't bother with the politenesses, but I would ask you to be brief. If it's of any help, I know your business. And what crime you suspect my late son of.'

I swallowed. Maybe I shouldn't've come; I could've done this through Camillus. Still, it was too late now. 'Very well, sir,' I said. 'Could you tell me what happened? Exactly?'

'Exactly.' Lepidus rolled the word around in his mouth like a sour grape. 'Exactly, Marcus killed himself. Last night, just after sunset, with his own sword. He had come previously to tell me that such was his intention.'

I stared at him. Sweet holy gods! 'And you didn't try to stop him?'

'No.' I don't think I've ever seen a face more lacking in expression. 'Of course not. The decision was his, consciously made and logically reached. I tried to change his mind, naturally, but it was his right and in the end I accepted it as such. He died with great bravery, as I would have expected a son of mine to do.'

I glanced at the woman. She didn't say anything, but her lip curled. I remembered what young Lepidus had said about her. 'Did he tell you why?' I asked.

'He felt responsible for my niece Cornelia's death.'

'Uh-huh.'

'Also, he had a message for you.'

'For me?'

'"Tell Valerius Corvinus that there are worse crimes than murder."'

My brain had gone numb. 'What?'

He repeated it. 'That, Corvinus, is all I know. He said nothing else, either about the events of that night or his involvement in them.'

'Nothing? Nothing at all?'

'Nothing whatsoever.' Lepidus Senior's mouth set. 'I will swear to that, by the way. If you require it.'

'No.' My brain was whirling. *Worse crimes than murder* ... 'No, that won't be necessary. Uh ... I don't suppose your son confided in you about anything that'd been worrying him recently? Something he'd heard or seen, maybe, that was preying on his mind?'

'Marcus and I were not close.' His eyes rested on the woman, then shifted back to me. She didn't react in any way. In fact, apart from that one lip-curl I doubt if her expression had changed since I'd come into the room. I might as well not have existed, or her father either. 'Neither of my children has ever been close, to me or to each other. Certainly not close enough to take me into their confidence. That may sound odd to you, Corvinus, but I ask you to accept it as I accept it. As a simple fact. The situation has worsened in recent years, with Marcus leading a life that I—' He stopped. 'Well, shall I merely say that it was one I did not approve of, although unfortunately I was not in a position to forbid the associations he entered into. The same goes for my daughter here. This is a large house, easily big enough for all of us to lead our separate existences without impinging on one another. Which is what we have done for some time now.' The mouth twisted into something that wasn't quite a smile. In fact, I wondered if Lepidus Senior could smile. 'I trust that I do not shock you too much.'

Holy gods! I turned to the woman. She'd sat through that spiel with a face like a bored cat's. 'How about you, lady?' I said. 'Did your brother mention anything – anything at all – that he seemed concerned about?' Going through the motions, sure, but this was the only chance at the family I'd get. If you could call them family.

'Marcus and I didn't talk,' she said. She had a long patrician drawl that set my teeth on edge.

I waited, but it seemed that that monolithic statement was all I was going to get. Yeah. Right. Well, scratch that angle for a non-starter. 'Uh-huh,' I said. 'What about the Vestal who died? Cornelia?'

'What about her?'

'Did you know her well? As an adult, I mean?'

'I'd met her. Here and there, at parties and dinners.'

'But you hadn't kept up the relationship?'

'What relationship? We never liked each other, Valerius Corvinus. Even as children. She was born a virgin and she

died one, and I don't just mean physically. I have no time
for bred-in-the-bone virgins. The way my brother mooned
after her was positively sickening. And if he expected to get
anywhere by doing a Clodius Pulcher on the night of the
rite then he knew women even less well than I thought he
did. Which was not at all, the sad little pathic.'

I winced, and I noticed that Lepidus Senior did too,
although he didn't say anything. What had happened to
'Of the dead, nothing but good'? Especially with the corpse
still lying out there in the atrium. 'Did he know the Galba
house, incidentally?' I said.

'He took me there once, to see Aemilia.' I looked at
her. 'Corvinus, Rome may be the capital of the world, but
it's still in many ways a small provincial town. Unmarried
ladies are more smiled on if they do their visiting decently
chaperoned.'

'Aemilia's a friend of yours?'

The corner of her beautiful mouth lifted. 'Hardly a
friend. She's a distant cousin, of course, from another
branch of the family. More of a twig, really. Her father
was a consular but poor as a Suburan sparrow. Oh, and
she thinks she's the gods' gift to men, which may be why
she cultivates me. That sort are always so grateful for a
tip or two.'

Jupiter! Well, I supposed if you ignored the size of the
lady's ego it was a fair comment. Even in a mourning mantle
Lepida had every competitor in Rome beat six ways from
nothing, and she oozed sex like a pedigree cat in heat. 'You
were at the rites yourself, of course, lady,' I said. 'You didn't
notice anything unusual?'

Her eyes opened wide. 'Actually,' she said, 'I wasn't. I
had other commitments that evening and I find the rites
of the Good Goddess *so* boring. All that all-girls-together

nonsense, chanting and dancing around waving bits of greenery, really it's—'

'*Lepida!*' Marcus Lepidus Senior snapped.

She turned to him with a dazzling smile. 'Oh, Father, I am *so* sorry!' she said. 'Have I offended you, darling?'

But Lepidus hadn't even glanced at her. He was still watching me. 'If you've asked all your questions, Corvinus,' he said, his voice level again, 'then perhaps you would go. I wish I could help you more but I am afraid I cannot. And that is *cannot*, young man, not *will not*; please understand that very clearly. Venustus will show you out.'

So that was that; all I was getting, seemingly, from either of these two beauties. Gods! What a family!

Skin crawling, I made my goodbyes and left.

14

I went back via the fluteplayers' guildhouse. Thalia hadn't been in.

'It's most provoking.' Celer was shuffling wax tablets in his office. 'She missed her engagement two nights ago, the day you were in last. Not a word, sir, not a dicky-bird, and with all these bookings to fill I'm short-handed as it is. Luckily I managed to get Aegle to cover, but the client was most disappointed. One of the Domitii, too; I mean *the* Domitii, you understand. Good paying customers, and you can't afford to offend them. I shall be having very strong words with that young lady, sir, you may be assured.'

I was beginning to get a bad feeling about this. A very bad feeling. 'You, uh, don't think something might have happened to her?' I said.

'What, Thalia?' Celar chuckled. 'Why should anything happen to Thalia? She's as strong as a horse, she can take care of herself and anyone after her virtue would have a hard time finding it. She certainly wouldn't bother putting up a struggle. No, sir, rest assured she's hooked herself a fancy boyfriend and he's waltzed her off somewhere for the Winter Festival.'

'She's done this before, then?'

'No. I can't say that she has.' Celer banged the wax tablets down hard. 'But I tell you this, she won't do it again, either. Not after I've finished with her.'

'Yeah. Right.' Well, there was no point hanging around

this little ray of sympathy, that was sure. I might drop in
on Aegle again, though, while I was in the neighbourhood,
see if she had any information she wasn't passing on to head
office. 'The arrangement stands, okay? She turns up, you
send her along.'

'Of course.'

'Good.' My hand was on the door when another thought
hit me. 'By the way, Celer, you haven't had anyone else asking
about the girls, have you? Especially what girls were playing
at the Good Goddess rite?'

'We have enquiries all the time, sir. Naturally enough.
Although I can say categorically that no one — apart from
the consul's wife herself, of course — asked about which had
been selected for the ceremony.'

'The consul's wife? Aemilia?'

'Naturally. She organised the non-religious side, sir, as the
hostess of the rites always does. I provided her with a list of
names in advance. Simply a matter of form, of course, since
they would mean nothing to her.'

'Is that so, now?' We could be on to something here; my
scalp was tingling. 'Would that include the update? With
Thalia's name on it?'

'Oh, yes. In fact that would be the only one she'd have.
I don't send it until the day before the ceremony, unless of
course the lady requires it.'

'Uh-huh.' Interesting. So; Aemilia had had a list of
flutegirls ahead of time, had she? That little nugget of
information might not be particularly significant at the
moment, but you never knew what the future would bring.
I filed it away for future use. 'One last thing. One of your
general questioners wouldn't be a Marcus Aemilius Lepidus,
would he? Young guy, early twenties—'

Celer was smiling. 'Oh, yes, sir. You needn't go on.

I know the young gentleman very well. He's a regular customer, in fact.'

'Is that right?' Yeah, well, I suppose it was inevitable, given the kid's lifestyle. And I didn't take Lepida's jibe about him being a pathic too seriously; that had been dislike speaking, to put it at its mildest. 'Did he ever ask for Thalia, incidentally? By name, I mean?'

Celer's smile broadened. 'Most of the young men ask for Thalia, sir, at one time or another. Aemilius Lepidus is no different.'

'Uh-huh.' Well, that was that; the missing link, so obvious it was laughable. In its circumstantial details the case was falling into place like the stones in a good mosaic. Maybe Lepidus had been the killer after all. 'Thanks, Celer,' I said. 'If Thalia shows up send her round, okay?'

Aegle wasn't at home either but a neighbour pointed me to a cookshop where she often went for lunch, and there she was, sitting in a corner, tucking into a couple of small rissoles and a big plate of winter greens. She glanced up as I caught her eye, then looked away quickly. It would seem that I wasn't flavour of the month today with flutegirls, either.

Breakfast had been a long time ago and I was starving. I ran an assessing eye over the place; always a good idea with cookshops you don't know, especially in areas like the Subura. This one looked okay. It was full, for a start, and that was a plus: establishments where customers are carried out green and groaning tend to lose their regular clientèle pretty rapidly, one way or another. The food looked the right side of edible, too, and none of it had that telltale crust you get when the dish of the day was also the dish of yesterday and, if you're really unlucky, special offer of the month. I ordered a sausage, a bowl of beans and bread and a cup of their best wine and carried it over to Aegle's table.

'Hi,' I said, sitting down opposite her.

Her eyes were fixed on her plate; rabbit food, but I supposed she'd need to think about her figure. She didn't look up. 'What do you want now, Corvinus?'

Well, at least she remembered my name. 'I'm still looking for Thalia. You know where she could be?'

'No. Ask Celer.'

'I've asked. He's chewing the tiles because she hasn't reported in for days.'

'I know.' She'd condescended to make eye contact now. I noticed she hadn't put any make-up over the strawberry birthmark. Probably because make-up was too expensive to use off duty. Or maybe she just couldn't be bothered. 'I did a slot for her a couple of days back. Celer's just lucky it's the slow season.'

I started in on the bread and beans and sausage. 'Slow season?' I said. 'That wasn't the impression he gave me, sister.'

'He wouldn't. Celer's a natural moaner. First half of December there isn't much happening religion-wise barring the Good Goddess and the Agonalia. The wedding and dinner party market's pretty quiet as well.'

'What about funerals?'

That got me the almost-half-smile. 'Oh, there're always funerals. Death's a nice steady earner. What's your business with Thalia, anyway?'

Good question. At the start I'd been looking for an elusive flutegirl, but now apart from the mechanics of how Lepidus had worked things there couldn't be much she could tell me that I didn't know. Maybe it was just the fact that I *couldn't* talk with her that kept me looking. Also a touch of coldness in the pit of my stomach when I wondered about why that was. 'I just want a few words,' I said. 'Check up on the information I've already got. And I must admit I'm curious about where she's disappeared to.'

'Yeah.' Aegle frowned and spooned in some of the chopped-up winter greens. 'It's not like her, I'll give you that. Apart from losing out on the work she isn't exactly making herself popular with the other girls. No one minds covering, but if you know you'll miss a slot you're careful to give notice.'

'You don't think she could be in some kind of trouble?'

Aegle hesitated, then set down her spoon. 'This time yesterday I'd've said no; but four days, that's a long time. Now I'd have to say maybe.'

'Uh-huh.' The cold feeling got worse. I took a careful sip of the wine. 'Okay. So where else do we look before we blow the whistle?'

'Her flat, certainly. Then there's Valgius.'

'Valgius?'

'Her boyfriend. Or at least her fallback boyfriend. He's a clerk at the citizen births registration office.'

That was in the Temple of Saturn, across Capitol Incline from the Treasury and a stone's throw from the House of the Vestals. Back where I'd started out from this morning, in other words. And Thalia's flat, of course, was down beyond the Circus, the far side of Public Ponds, near the Capenan Gate. Well, I was certainly getting my share of walking today. If this was lunch then I'd better finish it. I took a bite of the sausage and chewed. Not bad, but they'd overdone the cumin. 'You ever play for a client called Marcus Aemilius Lepidus, by the way?' I asked.

'The son or the father?'

'The son.'

She picked up her spoon and began eating again. 'Yes. Just the once. A dinner party in the Lepidus house.'

'Just the once?'

'My face didn't fit. Literally. Or almost literally.' Like it had been the last time she'd referred to her birthmark her voice was matter-of-fact. '"Dinner party"'s the wrong phrase. There wasn't much food; not much conversation, either. Aemilius Lepidus's friends aren't the talking type.' She shrugged. 'It paid well, though.'

'When was this?'

'Three months ago? Four? I can't remember.'

'Was Thalia there?'

She gave me a suspicious look over her rissole. 'What's this about, Corvinus? I mean, seriously.'

'Nothing. Just making conversation.' I was; I already knew Lepidus had a connection with Thalia, and I've never enjoyed eating in silence.

'Uh-huh.' She bit into the rissole. 'Okay, yes, Thalia was there. She went with young Lepidus, in fact. We were one for each of them. Only mine decided he'd have one of the servants instead.'

'Girl?'

'Boy.'

'Ah.' I took a spoonful of beans. 'You know Lepidus played the flute?'

She spat out a fragment of stone. You have to be careful with cookshop rissoles; the silicate content tends to be pretty high and an incautious chew can lose you half a molar. 'Yeah. He favoured us with a tootle or two before he and his pals got stuck in. To coin a phrase.'

'"Tootle"?'

'That's the word. Oh, don't get me wrong; he wasn't bad for an amateur, especially a purple-striper amateur. Not bad at all. You could see he'd been well taught. But he was a counter, not a natural. He could hold a tune but he'd no real flair.'

Something cold was brushing the nape of my neck. 'You're sure?'

'Sure I'm sure. The guy was drunk at the time, but that wouldn't've mattered, it would've made for a bum note or two, that's all. His phrasing was rubbish, and I don't just mean now and again. Any professional would've curled up and died.' She frowned. 'Hold on. You said "played".'

'What?' My brain had gone numb and taken my ears with it.

'"Played." Past tense, not present. You asked if Lepidus *played* the flute. You mean he's dead?'

Jupiter! The girl was smart! 'Yeah,' I said. 'He's dead. As of last night. He killed himself.'

She set down her spoon again. 'But that's terrible! Why?'

I hesitated. 'He thought he was responsible for the death of the Vestal.'

'Why should he think that?'

'He'd arranged to meet her. In the Galba house, after the rite.'

She was staring at me. 'But that's impossible! He wouldn't've been allowed in! The house was sealed until dawn!'

'Lepidus was your substitute flutegirl. The one who took Thalia's place.'

Aegle's mouth opened. Then she laughed. 'You think ... Flora, Corvinus, you're serious? You're actually *serious*?'

'Sure I'm serious.'

'But that's crazy! I told you before, that girl could *play*! And you think I could sit next to Aemilius Lepidus and not recognise him?'

'Uh ...' Oh, Jupiter best and greatest!

'Corvinus, you are really something, you know that? I'm not blind. The girl could've been a man, sure, easy, no problem at all, she was butch enough. But whoever the guy was, he wasn't Aemilius Lepidus.'

15

I left the cookshop and headed down Suburan Street towards the Argiletum and Market Square. It was beginning to rain, and the city looked as miserable as I felt. So. We were back almost where we'd started, with X being both the phoney flutegirl and the murderer. I didn't doubt what Aegle had said: she might've missed Lepidus under all that make-up, sure, especially if she wasn't expecting a man in disguise and she'd only seen him once, but she wouldn't've made a mistake about the playing. When a real professional gives you their opinion, you listen, and the girl was professional to her henna'd fingertips.

So where did that leave us? As far as I could see, up the creek without a paddle. If the guy had been the killer but hadn't been Aemilius Lepidus then who the hell was he? *Why* the hell was he? And why, if he hadn't gatecrashed the rites, did Lepidus still feel responsible enough for Cornelia's death to stick a sword between his ribs? The 'secret', sure, but I was no further forward with finding out what that had been than I was with anything else. Two things were certain: one, the murderer was as much a professional as Aegle, which meant scratch the disguised purple-striper theory; and two, Thalia was still the key. Our fluteplayer had used her name, and the two had obviously been connected in some way. And I had a bad feeling about Thalia.

There are some crimes worse than murder. That was something to think about as well.

I ran up the steps of the Temple of Saturn and went into the citizens registration office adjoining it. The place was pretty quiet that time of day, and in the entrance hall I stopped a thin clerk with an armful of wax tablets and a preoccupied expression.

'Where can I find Valgius, pal?' I said.

'Publius Valgius?' The clerk nodded towards one of the side rooms. 'He's H to N. In there.'

The room had half a dozen clerks. The first pointed me towards a tubby little plain-mantler in the corner who was busy transferring names from tablet to roll. I went over and he looked up.

'You Publius Valgius?' I said.

'Yes. That's me. How can I help you, sir?' Jupiter! Standby boyfriend was right; the guy must've been forty if he was a day, and he could've doubled for an ink-stained pigeon in moult.

'You know a flutegirl called Thalia?'

His eyes took on a guarded look. 'We see each other on and off, yes.'

'That include the last few days?'

'Wait a moment, sir.' He set his pen down on the desk. 'Exactly who are you, and what's this about?'

I gave him my name; all four bits, because that might distract him from pushing too hard for an answer to his second question. 'I've been trying to get in touch with her, that's all. One of her colleagues said you might be able to help me.'

'Uh-huh.' The guarded look increased. 'This would be a – uh – professional matter, would it? In which case, I'd suggest you call in at the guildhouse and talk to Celer. There're plenty of other girls on his books.'

'Not professional.' I was grinning internally; I recognised

jealousy when I saw it, and the guy was practically green. I'd the distinct impression that I wasn't the first to make enquiries about sweet little Thalia, and that Valgius wasn't too keen on agenting, especially with purple-striper clients. 'Not in any sense. No hassle, pal. I just want some information about the night of the Good Goddess rite.'

He relaxed. 'Then I can't help you, Valerius Corvinus. I don't know anything about Thalia's professional life. Try Celer.'

'I've already done that. She hasn't been around recently.'

'But if she was at the Good Goddess rite then—'

'She didn't turn up. I was hoping you might be able to tell me why.'

He looked blank. 'She didn't? But that's—' He stopped. 'She was looking forward to it. It's the slot of the year. You're sure?'

'She sent a substitute. You didn't know?'

'I haven't seen Thalia since the end of last month. What substitute?'

'That's what I'm trying to find out. Not one of the usual girls. Someone she knew.' I hesitated. 'Maybe a man.'

'At the *rites*?' His eyes opened in shock.

'Yeah. You wouldn't have any notion who he could be, would you?'

He shook his head numbly. 'No. But Thalia wouldn't do that. It'd be more than her reputation was worth, and if anyone found out it'd finish her.'

'Uh-huh.' That made sense, and it didn't leave me feeling any happier, either. 'Okay. So what about in general terms. She have any fluteplayer friends – male friends – that you know of?'

'One or two.' He pigeon-pouted; either he didn't see the 'friends' as being much of a threat in the sexual sense or he dismissed them as competition. Which was fair enough: for a girl like Thalia even a plain-mantle clerk as a regular boyfriend was quite a catch.

'You have any names?'

'No. Celer might know. He doesn't have anything to do with the male members of the profession himself, but he may be able to lay his hands on a few for you.'

Not a very felicitous way of putting it, but the guy didn't seem to notice and I didn't bat an eyelid. 'Yeah. Right.' Well, that was something I could check later. 'What about Thalia herself? You any idea where she may have got to?'

The guarded look came back. 'She's a popular girl. We ... go out together now and again, but she's very independent. Not to say close-mouthed. We have what you might call a flexible relationship.'

Someone sniggered behind me. I looked round. The other five clerks had stopped work and were following the conversation with interest. Valgius glared at the nearest and he bent back over his tablets.

'So you can't give me any names there either?' I said.

'I'm afraid not.' He was on his dignity now, and he lowered his voice. 'Also I have a considerable amount of work to get through today, so unless I can help you further ...'

The standard brush-off. We were flogging a dead horse here, obviously. 'Okay, friend,' I said. 'One last question. You been to the girl's flat recently, checked if she's around there?'

'Certainly not. Public Ponds is a most undesirable district. We meet at a friend's house in the Argiletum.'

'Not at your own house?'

He stared at me. 'Why would I do that? She's only a flutegirl. Besides, my wife wouldn't like it at all.'

*   *   *

I left him to his cross-referencing. Okay; so it had to be the flat, for what that was worth. The rain was coming down in sheets by the time I reached it, and Public Ponds was living up to its name. I thought of calling in at Watch headquarters to see if Lippillus was around and waiting for the weather to clear, but after walking half across Rome I was soaked in any case, and it would've meant a detour. Sure, I could've taken a litter, but I don't like these things, and anyway the ranks were empty.

I climbed the stairs to Thalia's floor. Someone was boiling cabbage, and the smell got stronger all the way up. Probably Thalia's domestic neighbour: tenement dwellers don't go in for home cooking much, braziers being braziers and these places being regular firetraps. Like the last time I'd been there the door looked seriously closed, but I knocked anyway. No answer.

Not from the Thalia side of the hall, at least. As I thought it might, old Grandma Charybdis's door opened and there she was, with the same kid in attendance. This time he'd got a boiled pig's trotter in his fist and he was sucking on it. I'd been right about the cabbage, too; if the smell had been bad on the staircase now it practically knocked me down.

'Oh.' She sniffed. 'It's you again, is it?'

'Yeah.' I winked at the kid, who pulled himself round the old woman's tunic like I'd just turned into an ogre with designs on his trotter. 'Thalia hasn't been back?'

'No.' Categorical. Uh-huh, so that was that, then. For a self-professedly incurious neighbour she seemed to be doing pretty well in the observation stakes. 'You're persistent, I'll give you that.'

Just for something to do, I beat another tattoo on the door and listened. Silence. Shit, this was hopeless. Still, I wasn't going to go away a second time without having a look inside, even if it meant breaking in. I took a hold of the knob and pushed hard ...

No resistance. The door creaked open.

'Here! You can't do that!' The old girl was bridling again. 'That's private property!'

I ignored her. The ice was forming on my spine. Even with someone like Charybdis here standing guard, you didn't leave doors unlocked in a Public Ponds tenement if you were spending a few days away from home. This looked bad. The worst.

She was right at my shoulder, craning her neck to see past.

'Take the kid back inside,' I said.

Maybe it was something in my voice, but she didn't argue. The door closed behind them. I went in. The first room was empty, and no tidier than Aegle's. I stepped over the remains of a meal and a bundle of clothes that was possibly the girl's dirty washing. Beyond was a small bedroom, and on the bed ...

Yeah, well, at least it was winter and there were no flies. Not even, with the window being open, much of a smell. What there was was blood and plenty of it, dried now, but all over the pillow, the blanket and the floor. Where it'd come from was obvious. Thalia had certainly been a looker; even under the circumstances I noticed that. Her head was pulled back and her throat had been slit ear to ear like a pig's.

My stomach heaved. Quickly, I went back outside and closed the door behind me. She'd be safe enough left for the next half-hour or so. And it looked like I'd have to go round to Lippillus's after all.

16

'I'd reckon she's been dead for four days, Corvinus.'

I watched as Lippillus poked around the room, lifting bits of discarded clothing and setting them down again. 'That's quite a precise guess, pal,' I said. 'Why four exactly?'

'Your sharp-eared old girl in the flat opposite's the local midwife. She was out four days ago at a difficult birth, which means she wouldn't be around to hear any visitor arrive.'

Uh-huh. Four days; that'd put the murder the same day as the Good Goddess rites. It fitted. 'Anything else you can tell me?' I said.

'Not a lot. At the moment, anyway. I'll talk to the other residents, see if anyone noticed anything, but it's not likely. Or at least not likely they'd tell me if they did. Tenement folk don't have much time for the Watch.' He moved over to the body and turned the head sideways. It lolled half off the pillow so that the empty eyes were looking straight at me. My stomach gave a lurch.

'Jupiter, Lippillus!'

He grinned. 'You want to come next door? I've seen all I have to here, and the lads with the stretcher will be along soon.'

'Yeah.' We went into the other room. I opened the window – this one was shuttered – and took a few breaths of fresh air while he sat on the only chair and swung his legs. He was looking even more like an evil-minded dwarf than ever. Smart, though; vertically challenged or not, Lippillus is one of the best Watch commanders in the city.

'So,' he said. 'What's this all about?'

I told him; the basics, anyway. He listened in silence.

'I'll tell you this much,' he said when I'd finished. 'The murderer's no amateur. Whoever killed her did a good job. Very neat, very professional. And if you're looking for someone who can play the flute as well as he can slice throats then the field's pretty limited. Fluteplaying knifemen aren't exactly thick on the ground.'

Yeah; I'd worked that out for myself. But it still left us with a stack of unanswered questions. The guy could be a know-nothing hireling in the pay of someone who did have a motive, sure: that would make a lot of sense and solve a lot of problems with the theory at the same time. The fly in the ointment was you don't hire fluteplaying killers just by painting an ad on a wall in Cattlemarket Square, and like Lippillus had said they don't exactly form a significant percentage of Rome's criminal classes. If our bogus fluteplayer hadn't been acting for himself then the man behind him needed to have pre-existing connections, especially if – as it had to have been – the killing was set up at short notice. And in that case then one name led all the rest.

Forget actual motive for the moment, because we couldn't even guess at that anyway. Who did we know who moved in high circles, who knew the geography of the Galba house, who had access through his wife to the musicians' list for the evening and who, according to rumour as reported by sleazeball Caelius Crispus, fraternised with male fluteplayers?

Right. The senior consul, Servius Sulpicius Galba.

'Corvinus?' Lippillus was looking at me. 'You okay?'

'Sure.' I could hear bumping and shuffling on the landing outside; the guys arriving with the stretcher, no doubt. I glanced out of the window. The sun was almost on the horizon; far too late now to hike halfway across Rome for another talk with Celer — or maybe Aegle would be a better bet — and there was nothing more I could do here. The next stage was to scare up a few male proponents of the fluteplayers' guild and ask them some very pointed questions. 'I'll catch you later, Lippillus, right? Any news, you know where to find me.'

'You don't want to split a jug?'

'Sorry. Not today, pal. It's too near dinner, and if you don't give Meton three days' warning in advance that you'll be late for the rissoles you're talking serious repercussions.'

If I could eat anything after finally tracking Thalia down, of course. But the walk to the Caelian might bring my appetite back.

At least when I got outside the rain had stopped.

'But, Marcus, *why*?' Perilla shelled a quail's egg. 'Why on earth should Galba want the girl dead? It makes no sense whatsoever.'

I shrugged and reached for a stuffed olive. 'I don't know, lady. But if the killer was a proper fluteplayer then Galba's a better proposition than most.'

'Surely that very much depends on who your "most" are.'

True, unfortunately. 'Yeah. That's the problem. We've got no suspects, or rather no actual names. None that's better than another, anyway. Sure, we know why Cornelia died, or at least we think we do: Lepidus told her something which presumably seriously compromised whoever arranged the killing, and she was on the point of letting the cat out of the bag. Okay. So now with our fluteplayer just a hired killer and the murder done by proxy the field's wide open. Completely so. The guy – or the woman – responsible didn't even have to be at the ceremony themselves any more.'

'All right.' Perilla dipped the egg in fish sauce. 'In that case why not start at the other end, with Lepidus. What could the secret have been?'

I put the olive down. 'Jupiter, lady! The guy was running around with half the blue-bloods in Rome! You like to guess how many skeletons there are currently propped against the inside of upper-crust cupboard doors waiting to fall out?'

'Emaciated enough to kill for?'

'Maybe. How do you decide that?'

Perilla frowned and bit into her egg. 'Yes. Yes, I suppose you're right. Very well. If not what, then who. Who did it concern?'

'Same problem. These guys aren't lily-white innocents, and some of the things they get up to would make your hair curl. It could be anyone.'

'Not quite. Murdering a Vestal – or arranging to have one murdered – does argue considerable ... desperation. And very strong character. In fact, the young man's own family would be the logical starting place. The sister, I've heard, has quite a reputation.'

I'd been lifting my cup for a slug of Setinian. I put it down slowly.

'Lepida?' I said.

'Why not? She would certainly be a better candidate than Sulpicius Galba, wouldn't she?'

'Yeah, but—' I stopped. I'd been going to say that Lepida hadn't been at the rites, but of course that wouldn't matter now; in fact, if she'd known there was going to be trouble she might well have stayed away intentionally. She had the nerve for murder, too, at first- or second-hand; and I'd bet a dozen of Caecuban to a bunion plaster that there were enough skeletons locked away in her closet to stock an ossuary. So all being equal, character-wise, Lepida was a reasonable bet. More than reasonable. Motive, however, was another matter. 'Okay, lady,' I said. 'Go on. Why should it be Lepida?'

'For one thing, she's the common factor linking her brother and Cornelia. He'd be more likely to pass on something concerning her than anyone else. And, naturally, there would be no problem about how he came upon the information.'

I shook my head. 'Uh-uh. Wrong; that won't work. They hated each other's guts, or at least that was the impression I got, from both sides. The Lepidi don't exactly share their little hopes and fears over the breakfast porridge, Perilla. Marcus Lepidus wouldn't necessarily have known any more about his sister's private life than she knew about his. He probably wouldn't've cared, either.'

'Mmm.' Perilla wiped her fingers carefully on her napkin. The lady didn't look happy, but then she's never liked having her own pet theories squashed. 'Still, they were brother and sister. That would explain, wouldn't it, why both Lepidus and Cornelia hesitated about making the matter public. Whatever it was.'

Family loyalty. Yeah, I'd believe that. These big names might fight tooth and nail among themselves but when there was a danger of the lid coming off the dirty linen basket they tended to close ranks and mouths pretty smartly. And it would explain Lepidus's message to me, too: *There are some things worse than murder.* Like blowing the whistle publicly on another member of the clan, for example. The old family code. Still, he hadn't told his father, either:

Lepidus Senior hadn't known the secret, of that I was sure. At least – hold that – he'd said, and been ready to swear to the fact, that his son hadn't told him anything, which didn't necessarily mean he didn't know already off his own bat ...

Or did it? I couldn't remember the old guy's actual words, but I had the distinct impression Lepidus Senior had denied all knowledge, from whatever source. Categorically. And if the secret concerned his sister, then why should Lepidus tell Cornelia but not his father? Unless, of course, he'd done just that, for reasons of his own that I couldn't begin to guess at ...

Hell; we were in a maze here. Leave it.

'There's one other problem, Perilla,' I said. 'Our flute-player. If Lepida was behind this, then where did she get him from? Fast lady or not, she's still broad-striper class and he's specialist low-level merchandise. Added to which, how did she know enough about the arrangements for the musicians to fix the swap with Thalia?'

'Assuming she did recruit him somehow, he could have found out for himself. He may even have known Thalia already. Or perhaps Lepida got the list from Aemilia. You say they were friends. Acquaintances, rather.'

'Yeah.' I was frowning. Sure, it was all possible, but there were too many grey areas. Still, Lepida was someone to think about.

I picked up the stuffed olive just as Bathyllus soft-shoed in.

'I'm sorry to disturb you, sir,' he said, 'but a message has arrived from the deputy chief priest.'

Uh-oh. This looked bad: the little guy had his serious face on. 'Yeah?' I said. 'What sort of message?'

'It concerns the dead Vestal's maid, sir.'

'Niobe?' Oh, hell. I knew what was coming next; I just knew it. I put the olive down again.

'Yes, sir. She's been found in an alley off the Sacred Way. Her throat has been cut.'

17

So it wasn't going to be a quiet evening after all. Still, at least the sun was down and wheels were allowed in the streets, so we had time for an abbreviated dinner while Lysias got the carriage ready and then set off for Market Square. This time Perilla came too.

The Jupiter look-alike Lucius brought us through the chilly, formal atrium to a small well-lit sitting-room where Torquata and Furius Camillus were waiting.

'Corvinus. I'm sorry to drag you here, especially at such short notice, but I thought you'd rather be told immediately.' Camillus had stood up. He looked at Perilla. 'Ah. Your wife, yes? Rufia Perilla. I'm delighted to meet you, my dear, even under such unfortunate circumstances. Have a seat, please. Some' – he glanced at Torquata – 'some liquid refreshment. Lucius?'

'Not for me,' Perilla said. 'Good evening, Junia Torquata.'

Camillus was watching his major-domo pour wine into one of the two empty cups. 'Also,' he said, 'I'm afraid I must apologise yet again for having to leave shortly. A dinner party this time, and rather an important one, although not one I'm particularly looking forward to since our new commander of Praetorians will be present.' His mouth twisted. 'I never thought that I would regret the demise of Aelius Sejanus, but Macro I find almost equally objectionable, and unfortunately my absence would be noticed adversely. However, I can let you have the salient points before I go, such as they are, and I've asked Junia Torquata if she will be kind enough to handle any questions or requirements you may have in my absence.'

'Uh-huh.' I tasted the wine. It was Caecuban this time; Camillus was doing us proud. Lucius poured a belt into Torquata's cup, put the jug down on the nearby table and withdrew, closing the door behind him. 'So. What happened exactly?'

Camillus glanced at Torquata. 'The girl was found huddled against the wall of an alley by one of my own slaves some two hours ago,' he said. 'Luckily, he recognised her and informed me immediately.'

Torquata grunted as if someone had run a needle into her arm. 'She'd left the House of the Vestals an hour or so before, Corvinus. She asked leave to go to the old market off the Argiletum.'

I took another sip of the Caecuban: that stuff you don't gulp. It went down like liquid velvet. 'And this would be her first time out since the ... since her mistress died, right?' I said.

Torquata's eyes rested on me speculatively. 'Yes,' she said. 'As a matter of fact it was. Apart from the funeral.'

Hell. We should have thought of that angle and had her watched. But it was too late now. 'No one saw anything?'

'The alleyway is a short cut leading from the Sacred Way to the rear of this building.' That was Camillus again. 'It isn't much frequented.'

'You think there was a connection, of course, young man,' Torquata said. 'Between Cornelia's death and Niobe's.'

'Yeah,' I said carefully. 'I think we can assume that. The girl knew something that Cornelia's murderer didn't want made public, and the guy knew she knew. Only until she left the House of the Vestals he couldn't do anything about it. I'd guess that since Cornelia died he's been watching and waiting for his chance to make sure she didn't blab.'

Torquata closed her eyes. 'That,' she said, 'is horrible.'

'Niobe didn't say anything over the past few days about what had been troubling her mistress, Junia Torquata?' Perilla asked gently. 'She gave no clue or hint? None at all?'

'No.' The chief Vestal's eyes were still closed. 'Not to me, at any rate.'

'Would she have confided in anyone else? Had she a close friend among the servants, perhaps?'

Torquata hesitated. 'I have seen her with one of the kitchen slaves, a woman called Perdicca. Niobe may have spoken to her. Certainly it's worth asking.'

I glanced at Camillus.

'All right, Corvinus,' he said, getting up. 'I'll see to it.' He went to the door and opened it. 'Lucius!' The slave appeared. 'Send round to next door's kitchen and tell the slave Perdicca that Valerius Corvinus here would like a word with her. Now, please.' He came back and sat down. 'So. Who is this killer of yours? Are you any further forward?'

'I think so, sir, yes.' I gave him a run-down of the case so far, including Thalia and the fluteplayer. 'He's a professional. But the one we really want is whoever hired him.'

'Indeed.' Camillus looked grave. 'You honestly think the man's a purple-striper? One of us?' There was total distaste in his voice. That I could understand: to someone like Camillus only one thing could be worse than the murder of a Vestal, and that was that the murderer should be someone he knew personally. 'I thought perhaps after young Marcus Lepidus was cleared that the person responsible would turn out to be ... well, not a gentleman. I realise that sounds naïve, but there you are. You couldn't be mistaken?'

'No, sir. At least, I don't think so.'

'And you have no idea at all who he might be?'

'No. Not yet.'

He grunted and stood up. 'You will. And when you do find out, you make sure that I'm the first to know. Remember that, please. In return I guarantee that the ba—' – he glanced at Torquata – 'that the fellow will get the Rock, even if I have to drag him up there and push him off myself. That, or death by flogging. The emperor will agree, I'm sure.' He set his empty cup down on the tray. 'And now unfortunately I really must be going if I'm to avoid insulting his new lieutenant by arriving late. My apologies again.'

After he had gone we waited in silence. Finally there was a knock on the door and Lucius came back in.

'Perdicca, sir,' he said.

From what Torquata had said I'd expected someone about Niobe's own age, but her best pal was a nondescript little woman in her sixties with mousey-grey hair and a moustache. She didn't look too happy; in fact, she was nervous as hell.

'Come on, girl!' Torquata snapped as Lucius closed the door behind him. 'Stand up straight and no mumbling!'

I winced. Ouch.

'Perhaps, Torquata,' Perilla said, 'I should ask the questions.'

'Yeah.' I gave a sigh of relief. 'Yeah, good idea. Go ahead, lady.'

She turned to the old woman. 'You know that Niobe is dead, Perdicca? That she has been murdered?'

'Yes, madam.' The voice was barely a whisper. I'd heard noisier mice.

'You were a friend of hers? A close friend?'

'Yes, madam.'

'You want to find her killer?'

No answer this time, but her head nodded.

'Very well. In that case you must answer my questions as best you can. Will you do that?'

'Yes, madam.'

Torquata opened her mouth, but I held out my hand and she closed it again. Perilla ignored both of us.

'Has Niobe said anything these past few days about something her mistress told her before she died?' she said.

Perdicca glanced quickly at Torquata, then away again. Her lips tightened.

'No, madam,' she said.

'Nothing at all?' Silence. 'Perdicca, Niobe is dead and we are only trying to help. If she did tell you anything then we need to know what it was.'

'She said it wasn't her secret to share, madam. She would've gone to the' – again her eyes flicked nervously towards Torquata – 'to the Lady Junia, but she decided she couldn't. It wasn't her secret, see. Or that's what she said.'

'But she told you?'

'*No*, madam!' That came out sharp. Uh-huh. So there was spunk there after all.

'You're sure?' Silence again. 'Perdicca, we are only trying to help. I give you my word that if Niobe did tell you anything then whatever it was you need not be afraid to repeat it, for her sake or your own.'

The old woman raised her eyes. 'I swear, madam,' she said. 'I swear by Vesta herself. She didn't tell me nothing. Like she said, it wasn't her secret. She didn't tell me nor no one else, neither. And that's *my* word, madam.'

Perilla sighed. 'Very well. Let's leave it. Now. About what happened today. The Lady Junia Torquata says that Niobe asked permission to go to the market. Do you know why that was?'

I'd been watching the old slave carefully and I saw her freeze. I shot Perilla a look and she nodded imperceptibly.

'No, madam.' We were back to the whispers and the lowered eyes.

'Perdicca, I'm sorry,' Perilla said softly, 'but that's just not true, is it?'

Silence.

'All right. So why did she go? To meet someone?'

A long pause. Perdicca was trembling now, but I'd bet it wasn't through fear: despite appearances I'd reckon they didn't come much tougher than this old bird. All she was doing was deciding which way to jump. Finally, she made up her mind.

'Yes, madam,' she said.

Shit. I sat up. Perilla didn't move.

'Do you know who?'

Instead of answering, Perdicca reached inside her tunic and brought out a scrap of paper. Perilla took it, smoothed it out and looked at it. Her breath caught.

'How did you get this?' she said.

'She asked me to keep it for her, madam.'

'You know what it says?'

'No, madam. I can't read. But Niobe told me.'

'And how did Niobe get it?'

Another nervous glance at Torquata. 'One of the other slaves found it behind the side door yesterday morning, madam. It had her name writ on the back.' Torquata stiffened but she said nothing.

Perilla handed the scrap of paper over to me without a word. There were only a few lines. It was a note asking for a meeting by the Aemilian Hall on the market side of the Sacred Way, and it was signed Marcus Lepidus.

*   *   *

'Is it genuine, do you think?' Perilla asked when we were back in the carriage and on our way home.

'It could be, sure,' I said. 'Good quality paper, virgin, not a reused offcut. Good hand, well spelled. And the timing would fit as well.'

'So? You don't sound convinced.'

I wasn't. 'It smells, Perilla. When I saw the guy he was in no condition to write notes, let alone neat ones, even given that he'd a reason for sending it. And why the hell sign his name?'

'He might have had no option. Not if he wanted to be sure that Niobe would come.'

'She went and she was murdered, lady. By which time Lepidus was already dead. I think that's a fairly strong argument in itself for the thing being a fake, don't you?'

'Unless, as you said, the murder had no connection with the note and the killer was watching the building in any case.' Perilla sighed. 'No. I'm sorry, Marcus; I'm only playing devil's advocate. You're quite right. Of course it's a fake.'

'Okay.' I settled back against the cushions. 'So if it was sent by the killer to winkle Niobe outside, then what does it tell us?'

'What we already know: that the girl knew something and had to be silenced. Also, naturally, that her secret involved Marcus Lepidus.'

'Yeah, right. But we can do better than that. It also confirms the fact that there're two people involved, a brains and a brawn. Whoever wrote that note it wasn't our pal the fluteplayer, not unless the guy includes a good Roman education among all his other talents. He was given it, or it was delivered for him, by someone who could write and spell.'

'There's another thing, Marcus.'

'Yeah?'

'It's only a feeling, but if the note were genuine then I would have expected more of an air of secrecy in the message itself. Unless the young man was an absolute fool he must have known that signing his name, unavoidable under the circumstances though that might be, was unwise in the extreme. And it doesn't sit well at all with the method of delivery, which was definitely clandestine.'

'Uh, yeah.' Sometimes Perilla's way of putting things makes my head hurt, but I'd caught her general drift and she was right. 'You mean that if Lepidus had really wanted to make sure the meeting stayed secret he'd've said so.'

'Exactly. Or included an instruction to Niobe to tell no one or destroy the note on reading, perhaps. It's as though whoever wrote the letter didn't care whether anyone knew of its existence or not.'

'Or that they actually wanted it to be found after the girl was dead so Lepidus would be nicely set up to take the rap. Yeah; that fits, lady. And that way it would kill two birds with one stone, Niobe and Lepidus both, because when the delivery was made Lepidus himself was still alive.'

Perilla was quiet for a long time. Then she said: 'There is one further point. Whoever wrote the note knew the girl quite well; Niobe herself, I mean, not just the fact that she was Cornelia's maid.'

'You've lost me, lady.'

'You don't assume literacy in a slave, Marcus, not unless they've been trained as a clerk or a secretary. To send a personal note in the first place implies the knowledge that the recipient can read it. So the killer, or the brains behind him, rather, had to know that Niobe had been schooled with Cornelia.'

'That's no big deal. It wasn't a secret, surely.'

'Perhaps not, but it is a further indication. Lepidus himself would know, certainly, but there's no reason for anyone else to. Not outside the family or the sisterhood itself, anyway.'

'Fair enough. We'll just have to—' Suddenly my jaw stiffened and I found myself yawning. Jupiter, I was whacked! Although it wasn't especially late I'd had a heavy day even before Camillus had called us out. 'Lady, let's pack it in for the night, okay? I haven't got the mental energy for puzzles any more.'

Perilla smiled. 'If you like,' she said. She leaned over and kissed me.

I glanced out of the window. We'd turned down the long drag between the Circus and the southern slopes of the Palatine. More than halfway home, in other words, and just in time because the weather was getting worse. Gods, but I was tired! Well, Camillus, Arruntius and company couldn't complain they weren't getting value for money.

I pulled my cloak round my ears and settled down into the cushions.

18

I was down pretty late the next morning, although earlier than Perilla who was still flat out. I checked our smug piece of cutting-edge technology for glitches in passing, but whatever the hydraulics whizz-kid had done to its insides seemed to be holding. Not that I trusted the bugger an inch. It was probably busy working out third-level scenarios in its master plan to take over the empire.

Bathyllus was setting the breakfast table. Extensively. Me, I don't go much beyond a crust or two first thing, but Perilla scours the market for exotic dried fruits, cheese wrapped in straw and those fancy pots of Greek honey with herbs in. Or what I hope and trust are herbs.

'Morning, little guy.' I stretched out on the couch and reached for one of Meton's poppyseed rolls. 'Sleep well?'

'Yes, sir.' He set down a bowl of what looked like yoghurt with jam through it. Uh-huh; I'd have to watch that lady. The last thing I wanted was another Mother on my hands. 'You had another message, by the way, sir. Delivered shortly after you and the mistress left yesterday evening.'

There was a ghost of a sniff in the little guy's voice. I'd been tearing off a scrap of the bread. I stopped. 'Yeah?' I said. 'What kind of message?'

'An invitation to call at the Lepidus mansion, sir.' Bathyllus had on his prim expression. 'The sender being the ex-consul's daughter.'

Well, that explained the disapproval: as a guardian of

morals Bathyllus had old Cato beat six ways from nothing.
I put the roll to one side. An invitation, right? Jupiter! That I
hadn't expected, especially since last time I'd been practically
thrown out of the house on my metaphorical ear. And from
Lepida, not the father; interestinger and interestinger. 'She
give any sort of reason?' I asked.

'No, sir.' The little bald-head treated me to a full-scale
sniff this time. According to the tenets of the Bathyllus moral
code invitations from unattached females with reputations
like Lepida's were the equivalent of being hit by a bra
from a balcony. I'd just bet he'd chosen to tell me now
on purpose, rather than pass on the news last night while
Perilla was around. 'She did, however, stress that the matter
was of some urgency.'

'Yeah, okay. Thanks, Bathyllus.' While he finished laying
out the goodies I settled back, tore a bit off the roll and
dipped it in oil. My brain was buzzing. *Some urgency*, right?
What the hell did ice-bitch Lepida have for me that was so
urgent she would send a skivvy round at an ungodly hour
and yank me up the Quirinal before the cypress branches
round the family door had even dried out? It had to have
something to do with her brother, sure; but I'd as much idea
of the whys and the wherefores as I had of basket-weaving.
Still, I wasn't going to pass up the opportunity, and the
invite would give me a chance to check the lady out. But
to do that properly I needed intelligent help.

Bathyllus had unloaded his last plate of prunes and
was heading for the kitchen, his back still radiating disapproval.

'Hey, little guy,' I said. He turned. 'Alexis around?'

'I expect so, sir.'

'Fine. Send him through, would you? I've got a job for
him.' I kept my face straight. 'Oh, and when the mistress

surfaces you can tell her I've gone to the Market Square for
a shave.'

Bathyllus gave another sniff, and his mouth looked like
he'd just taken a swig from the pickle barrel. 'A shave in
Market Square, sir.' He eyed my already stubble-free chin.
'Yes, sir. Certainly, sir.'

I didn't smile until he'd gone. Yeah, well, maybe I
shouldn't wind the prissy little so-and-so up, but he couldn't
get much fun out of life and the whiff of vicarious scandal
would keep him sniffing happily until dinner-time.

The weather had turned nasty again and it was chucking it
down like there was no tomorrow, so I stilled my prejudices
and went by chair. Litters I hate – they make me feel queasy,
even when they're carried by a good team – but it being
daylight the ban on wheels was in force and Lysias and
the coach weren't an option. Besides, the Lepidus ménage
was no place to turn up looking like a half-drowned rat. I'd
been careful to put on my best mantle, for a start.

We got there. Eventually. Sure, Perilla uses the litter on
occasion, but she's not a honey-wine-and-tartlets socialiser
by nature so the litter guys aren't exactly lean, mean and
speedy; with the result that when I do take them out they
tend to breathe heavy, move slow and arrive knackered.
Especially when the target destination is the Quirinal with
its chichi panoramic views and one-in-three gradients. Alexis
ran alongside; he doesn't mind the rain, and an extra body
to tote would've finished those lardballs off when we hit the
first slope. Embarrassing, really.

We left them heaving their lungs out against the Lepidus
family's streetside wall. Alexis worked the door knocker,
and while my old pal the Faithful Retainer showed me
through to the lady's private apartments he went off,

suitably instructed, to mix with the other ranks in the servants' quarters. I was beginning to get the feel of the place now, so I wasn't surprised when I was led down half a mile of snazzy marbled corridor to a self-contained wing that for elegance wouldn't've disgraced one of Tiberius's villas on Capri; only I'd seen a couple of these, and the decorators Lepida patronised were clearly guys of much more robust taste. Forget the usual fruit-and-pheasant tat or Perseus holding up the head of Medusa; this artwork would've had Perilla reaching for the whitewash and Bathyllus slipping his hernia support. I noticed that my still none too friendly Mercury kept his eyes front and centre; but then perhaps he was used to it.

We reached a door with a simple pastoral scene carved into the panelling. I didn't have much time to check out the details, but from a cursory glance I'd reckon that it didn't have a lot to do with milking goats. The slave rapped sharply and waited.

'Yes, Venustus.'

Old Faithful turned the knob so the door opened a crack, then stepped back. Uh-huh. I recognised standing orders in operation when I saw them: no peeking on the part of the bought help at what the mistress currently had on offer, evidently. Bathyllus could be right. I put my hand against the unlikely opulence of the courting swain's girlfriend's bosom and pushed.

No, she wasn't lying naked on a bed of rose petals stroking a cat; not even close. She was sitting at a desk going through what looked like a set of accounts.

'Ah, Valerius Corvinus. You got my message.' Cool enough, but, lack of the traditional encouragements to seduction or not, the lady was something. No mourning now, despite the cypresses outside; her mantle was pure silk — Indian, not Coan, from the sheen — and whoever had done her make-up could've given Dioscorides a run for his pigments. Added to which, like I said before, she was a grade-A stunner with bells on. 'Come in, please. Sit down. Make yourself comfortable.'

Not a boudoir or a study; something halfway between, with a definite air of business to it. Centre stage was a reading couch that looked suspiciously wide — maybe the decoration on the outside of the door wasn't so out of place after all — but I ignored it in favour of a folding stool.

Lepida smiled and put the wax tablets away.

'I don't bite, Corvinus,' she said. There was a final-sounding click as the door closed behind me.

'You want me to take a second opinion on that, lady?' I said.

'Actually, no.' The smile broadened; long and slow. 'Second opinion might not back me up. But then perhaps the concomitant circumstances might not be quite as unpleasant as you seem to imagine.' Uh-huh. 'Now. Would you like some wine?'

'Yeah. Thanks. Wine would be great.'

There was a tray on a side table. She stood up, poured for both of us and passed me the cup. Her fingertips brushed my hand. It could've been accidental, but I wouldn't've taken any bets.

'Before we go on,' she said, 'I'd like to apologise. When you were here last I froze you out. It wasn't anything personal.'

'That's okay.' I took a sip of the wine. It was Caecuban; good Caecuban. 'No problem. I hardly even noticed.'

That got me a brief glare: evidently in Lepida's book not noticing how she reacted to you was a first-magnitude crime. 'Father's so stuffy, you see,' she said. 'I find myself playing up to him. And with Marcus dead . . .' She left the sentence hanging and sat down on the couch, so close to me we were almost touching. The couch's covering was blue velvet, and the nap looked well worn. Her perfume was grade A too.

'My head slave told me it was urgent,' I said.

'But an apology is urgent, Corvinus.' She took a sip of her own wine, her eyes on mine above the rim of the cup. 'Very urgent. I couldn't let you go on thinking badly of me, could I? I had to bring you round and say sorry face to face.' She smiled. 'If that's the position you prefer, naturally.'

Game, set and match to Bathyllus. I stood up. 'Look, thanks for the wine,' I said, 'but—'

'You mean you don't want to make love to me?'

I almost dropped the cup. 'Uh . . .'

Her smile hadn't wavered. She raised one elegant shoulder and turned away. 'Oh, well,' she said. 'It was just a thought. Don't let it worry you.'

Suddenly I felt angry. 'Was that it, lady?' I said. 'The reason for bringing me all the way up here?'

'But of course it was.' Her voice was matter-of-fact. 'What other reason could there be? If you want to change your mind, naturally, now or at any future date, then—'

'Jupiter, cut it out!'

She laughed. 'You're as stuffy as my father, Corvinus, deep down, aren't you? I told you, it was only a thought. It doesn't matter to me one way or the other, not one bit.' Her hand smoothed the velvet. The nails were long and carefully manicured. 'Very well, we'll talk about something else, just so your journey isn't completely wasted. Or my time. How is the investigation going?'

She had flair, I'd give her that. A minute before she'd been propositioning me, now she could've been a dowager making polite conversation over the cakes and honey wine.

Despite my anger – flair or not, I still didn't like or trust her
– I found myself grinning. And sitting down again. 'Yeah.
Yeah, okay,' I said. 'You know Niobe's dead?' The girl had
been with Cornelia before she'd gone for a Vestal. Maybe
she'd even been a Lepidi slave. Certainly Lepida would've
known her.

If she had it didn't show; not in the form of sympathy,
anyway. Mind you, I doubt if anything would faze this lady.
'Murdered?' she said. She might've been asking the price
of meat.

'Yeah. She was found yesterday in an alleyway behind the
House of the Vestals. Her throat had been cut.'

We were neither of us ready for a refill, but Lepida got
up to fetch the wine jug and poured a little into each of
our cups. The jade pendant on her necklace that had been
snuggling inside her cleavage swung free and brushed my
wrist. She didn't seem to notice.

'Really?' she said cheerfully. 'Well, it doesn't surprise
me.'

Maybe it was her tone, but something cold touched the
back of my neck. 'Is that so, now?' I said. 'You care to tell
me why not?'

'It was bound to happen sooner or later, that or something
similar.' Her shoulder lifted again. 'She probably brought it
on herself; Niobe always was a self-sacrificer, especially on
Cornelia's altar. One of nature's victims.'

Not much of an obituary, but I reckoned that was about
all the kid could expect from that quarter. 'She died because
she knew the secret Cornelia shared with your brother,' I
said. 'You happen to know what that might've been?'

'No. I told you before.' Another shrug. 'Or my father
said he didn't, I can't remember which now and it doesn't
matter anyway because neither of us does. As you may have

noticed, Corvinus, we're not a togetherness family. Dear Marcus would've torn out his tongue before he confided in either Father or me, and the reticence was quite mutual. Common. Whatever the appropriate term is.'

I was within an inch of really losing my temper: this total callousness and all these shrugs, physical and metaphorical, were beginning to get to me. 'Does anything really interest you, Lepida?' I said. Anger or not, it was a genuine question. 'What do you think is important?' She was staring at me like I was talking Babylonian. Maybe in her view I was. 'What would you kill for?'

Jupiter knew where that last question came from, but she laughed. 'Oh, dear, how terribly serious! Very well. Your answers are, in order, nothing for very long, except perhaps fucking; nothing very much, except, again, fucking; and nothing, full stop. Unless for the fun of it, just once, to see what it felt like and for no other reason whatsoever. Will those do you or do you want me to make some up so you don't feel quite so shocked?'

I took a mouthful of wine and swallowed it slowly. 'No, lady,' I said quietly. 'They'll do fine. If they're genuine.'

'Oh, they're quite genuine, I guarantee it.' She was watching me with a slight, crooked smile. 'Absolutely. So, now. You think the same person who killed Cornelia killed Niobe?'

'It's a logical assumption, yeah. Especially since there's another corpse. A flutegirl called Thalia.'

'Her throat was slit as well?' She hadn't even blinked. I didn't answer. 'And all three deaths had something to do with my brother?'

'Something he knew, certainly. And shared with Cornelia, who shared it with her maid.'

'What was Niobe doing in the alleyway?'

The question was a non sequitur, except if you looked at it in a certain way in which case it made perfect sense. Uh-huh; so she did have some curiosity after all. I wondered how much the lady's studied boredom was real and how much was put on. There was a brain behind those carefully made-up eyes, that was sure, and brains need to work. 'She was on her way to meet someone,' I said. 'Or at least she thought she was.'

'Do you know who?'

I'd been waiting for that particular question. I put my hand inside my mantle and took out the note I'd brought with me. 'Your brother,' I said.

That got through; she gave a little gasp. 'My *brother*? But Marcus was dead!'

It could've been acting, sure, but the surprise in her voice sounded genuine. 'She didn't know that at the time,' I said. 'And this was delivered the day before, while he was still alive.'

'It was found with Niobe's body?'

'No. She left it with a friend.' I passed the note over. 'The killer forged your brother's signature to bring the girl outside. At least, that's what I think.'

Lepida unfolded the slip of paper and read it. Her brow creased, and then she laughed. 'Well, now, Valerius Corvinus,' she said softly. 'Do you really? How very interesting.'

The last word was drawled: conscious irony. The hairs at the nape of my neck stirred. 'Hold on, lady,' I said. 'You mean the signature's genuine?'

'Quite genuine.' She handed the note back. 'It isn't my brother's, though.'

I frowned. 'You've lost me. Who else's would it be?'

'My father's, of course.'

19

Gods ...

Yeah, sure, when you thought about it it made perfect sense: father and son shared the same name. I just hadn't thought of the alternative explanation, that was all. But why would Marcus Lepidus Senior, aristo and one of Rome's most respected ex-consuls, fix up a clandestine meeting with Niobe?

Apart from the obvious reason, of course. But there again if he'd signed his own name in his own hand and then murdered the kid, or had her murdered, while leaving the note undestroyed, or at least unaccounted for, then the man was a fool. And Marcus Aemilius Lepidus Senior, the guy Augustus himself had tipped as prime emperor material, was no fool.

Unless of course he was clever enough and desperate enough to risk a double bluff ...

I must still have been glazed over because Lepida laughed as she leaned across and patted me on the cheek.

'Well,' she said, 'I never thought Father had it in him. Making illicit trysts in back alleys with slavegirls and then slitting their throats. How very plebean. Does this mean he murdered the others, too? Cornelia and this flutegirl of yours?'

It was a question I'd've liked to know the answer to myself, but I wasn't biting.

'Is he in at the moment?' I said.

'I've really no idea.' She stood up, took a sip of wine and refilled the cup from the jug. I noticed she didn't offer me any more. Not that I'd finished what I'd got, mind; I'd had other things to worry about.

'You think you could find out, maybe?' I said carefully.

She looked at me, eyes wide. Her mouth made an 'O' and she smiled. Then, still holding the jug, she sauntered over to the door, opened it and yelled, '*Venustus!*'

He must've been hanging around within earshot because he came padding along the corridor like a tame mastiff. I caught the shift of his eye to the wine jug and then to the drape of my mantle, but his face was expressionless.

'Yes, madam,' he said.

'Is my father at home?'

'He was out earlier but he's just arrived back, madam. I believe he's in his study.'

'Good. Tell him Marcus Corvinus here would like a word.' Before the slave could acknowledge the order she'd shut the door in his face and walked back over to the couch. 'Do you mind if I watch?'

'Watch what, lady?'

'You confronting Father, of course. It ought to be fun.' She set the jug down on the floor and stretched out on the blue velvet. 'You're sure you don't want to fuck? It'd pass the time while we wait, and Venustus won't come in when he gets back. He has strict orders not to.'

'No.'

'Does that mean you're not sure? Or that you're not interested?'

'Tell me about Aemilia and Galba.'

She sat up. 'What?'

'You wanted to pass the time. Let's do it my way. When I was here last you said you were a friend of Aemilia's.'

'I said she was a distant cousin and that she'd tried to strike up a friendship.' That was sharp. 'Aemilia's an empty-headed pain and a social crawler. She'd like to be a femme fatale but she hasn't even the working talents of a common whore.'

Ouch. 'You don't like her, then?'

Lepida laughed. 'No. Not a great deal. She has appalling taste; positively crude at times. She was lucky to get Licinius Murena for a lover, even if he is only using her as an in with her husband. I've had him myself, on this very couch, in fact, and he's not bad.'

'Is that right, now?'

'I'd give him seven out of ten. With perhaps another point for effort. It won't last, naturally, not now Galba's reached the end of his consular year.' She ducked her head to hide a smile. 'And you're being stuffy again, Corvinus. Oh, don't mistake me; I do have some sympathy for the poor dear. It isn't easy to be married to a man who ignores you. I speak from experience. My own brief marriage to Drusus Caesar was no bed of roses either, but at least in his case it was other women.'

'And the senior consul prefers other men.'

'If and when he can get them. Boys would be easier, but Galba doesn't like boys. He's not a very nice person, Corvinus. He's vain, he's cruel and he may be rich but he's mean with money. That puts men off as well as women. At least, except those of a certain type or slaves who have no say in the matter.'

'Uh-huh.' Yeah, well; in for a penny. And I might not get a better chance. 'You happen to know anything about one of his exes? At least, he's probably an ex. A male fluteplayer.'

She gave me a long cool stare. 'No,' she said. 'I don't.'

I blinked; the lady was palpably lying, and she didn't care whether I knew it or not. And was I imagining things, or had there been a touch of amusement in her voice?

'You sure about that?' I said.

'Quite sure.' There was a soft knock on the door and she turned away. 'That will be Venustus. I think we'd better go. My father hates to be kept waiting.'

Lepidus was sitting at his desk as he had been on the last occasion; in fact, he looked like he'd never moved. The two fixtures, animate and inanimate, could've been made for each other, and there wasn't much visible difference anyway in as much as animation was concerned. If he was surprised to see his daughter with me it didn't register, and she didn't offer any explanation. As I crossed the threshold she pushed in ahead of me and draped herself on the reading couch, smoothing her mantle like someone settling to a show. Lepidus ignored her completely.

'Sit down, Valerius Corvinus,' he said. 'You wanted to see me?'

I pulled up a chair. There was no point beating about the bush here. Reaching into my mantle, I took out the note and handed it to him without a word.

He unfolded it and read. I was watching his face closely. Not a muscle twitched. He looked up.

'So?' he said.

No inflection; polite interest, no more. Jupiter! Cool was right! No wonder guys like him ruled the world. 'You know the maid Niobe is dead, sir?' I said.

'Yes. I understand she was found yesterday with her throat cut.'

'You mind my asking how? How you know, I mean?'

'Yes, I do, actually. Very much so.' His voice was still level, matter-of-fact. 'Indeed I find the question in its implications extremely offensive. However, I will tell you anyway. I serve on the same senatorial committee as Fabius Camillus. We had a short meeting earlier this morning, from which I have just returned. Niobe was originally one of our house slaves, and Camillus quite rightly thought I should be informed of her death.' He laid the note down flat in front of him. 'Does that satisfy you?'

I swallowed. 'Yeah. Yeah, that would seem to be in order.' I indicated the scrap of paper. 'You admit you wrote that, sir?'

'You can see my signature at the bottom for yourself. And I'm sure my daughter' – he didn't so much as glance in Lepida's direction – 'has authenticated it for you.'

'You care to tell me why?'

'Why what?'

'Why you asked for a meeting in the first place. Why you chose the Aemilian Hall as a venue instead of going to the House of the Vestals yourself or having Niobe brought here. Why the note was slipped under the side door rather than being brought round to the front and delivered properly.'

He was looking at me like I'd just crawled out of the woodwork. 'No,' he said slowly. 'I don't believe I do care to tell you any of that, young man, because it's none of your damned business.'

I glanced at Lepida. She was smiling to herself, clearly keen on not missing a word. Jupiter, the bitch was enjoying this! All she needed were the oranges and the nuts. 'Sir, listen to me,' I said. 'Whether you like it or not I was asked officially to look into the death of the Vestal Cornelia. Niobe's murder is connected with that death, and the person responsible for one was very likely responsible for the other. The reason Niobe died where and when she did' – I stopped myself – 'the *probable* reason, is that the killer had finally managed to get her out of the House of the Vestals where she couldn't be touched. Your note served that end. You must see that unless you offer some sort of explanation I can come to only one conclusion.'

'That is your privilege, Valerius Corvinus.' His lips formed a hard line. 'I repeat: the purpose of the meeting and the arrangements I made for it are none of your business.'

I'd had enough of this; more than enough, especially after a session with Lepida. My temper broke. I stood up and set my hands on the desk in front of him to stop myself from grabbing the front of his mantle. 'Look, you pig-headed bastard!' I snapped. 'There are three people dead already, plus your son, and Jupiter knows he's a victim as much as the others are. I don't want a fourth body and I want their killer nailed. So why don't you just come off your fucking high horse and answer the fucking questions?'

Silence. Complete silence. Out of the corner of my eye I could see Lepida shifting on her couch, but her father hadn't moved. Not a finger, not a muscle. You could've set a couple of the family busts next to him and if you hadn't known which the real, living man was there would've been nothing to tell you. We stared at each other for a good minute. Then I straightened. 'Ah, the hell!'

I was halfway out the door when he spoke. Even now he didn't raise his voice.

'Corvinus.'

I turned. 'Yeah?'

'You're quite right. I apologise.'

Just that. Jupiter! Not so much as a batted eyelid! I'll never understand these lord-of-the-world bastards; me, I'd've punched my lights out, or tried to, anyway. Still, I'd got what I wanted. I sat down again. 'Okay, sir,' I said. 'You want to tell it in your own time?'

'Very well.' Still that calm, controlled tone of voice that made me want to thump him, but at least he was talking. 'You asked me to answer your questions. That is what I shall do. If I remember correctly, they were: why did I want a meeting in the first place; why did I choose what one might call neutral territory; and why was the note not delivered in the normal way.'

'Yeah.' I kept my fists bunched below desk-level. 'Right.'

'Indeed.' He cleared his throat. I had the distinct feeling that, poised aristo or not, the guy was nervous or ashamed; maybe both. 'The first question, then. I've known for several years, Valerius Corvinus, that my son harboured an affection for my former ward which was not wholly fraternal. Forbidding him to see her under any circumstances early in the course of things might have been wise; however, I doubt if it would have done much good, and I have never tried to control my children's lives or curb their inclinations. Perhaps I have been at fault in this' — I noticed that he was very careful not to let his eyes stray to Lepida — 'but that is another matter. However distant we became, however wild *he* became, I trusted Marcus to keep his feelings in bounds. When Cornelia was found dead that trust was ... strained.'

'You thought he might have raped her and she'd committed suicide as a result.'

He nodded. 'I didn't believe for a moment Marcus would have killed the girl, whatever the consequences discovery would have brought on himself. But suicide — yes, suicide was very possible. I couldn't ask Marcus himself, of course. He would only have denied it, whether it was true or not, and even my asking of the question might have precipitated a rupture which has been threatening for some years. Besides, as you saw yourself he was too distraught to be rational.'

'Uh-huh.' I glanced at Lepida. She was still sitting smiling, quite at ease, like she was watching a play. 'So you decided to ask Niobe.'

'She would have known, if anyone did. I'm not wholly in favour of friendships between slave and master or mistress, but when they are genuine they can be very strong. That between Niobe and my former ward was an instance of the latter case, and the two girls were extremely close. Certainly close enough for a frank exchange of confidences. In the event, of course, I learned nothing since for obvious reasons Niobe failed to appear at the appointed hour. Does that, Valerius Corvinus, answer your first question?'

'Yeah. Yeah, it makes sense.'

'Good.' He half smiled. 'Now the second: why not meet the girl here or at the House of the Vestals? Or at least, naturally, in Camillus's apartments next door. The first location, in the light of what I've already said, was obviously impossible: Marcus was still alive, of course, and although we lived our separate lives we did so under one roof. I could not afford the risk of having Marcus find Niobe and myself together since that would have necessitated either a frank admission of the reason for her presence or an outright lie. The first would, for the reasons I gave you, have been impossible; the second would have been repugnant to me in the extreme. As for interviewing her at the chief priest's residence, no, that I could not do either. It would have meant admitting to Camillus – as I would have felt obliged to do – that I suspected my own son, on very flimsy evidence, of the worst of crimes. Camillus and I have been friends for many years, and he had known Marcus since the boy's birth. He would have found the thought as painful as I did myself. As far as choosing the Aemilian Hall specifically as a venue went, I had no special reason, except of course that it has family connections, is fairly well-frequented and was not at any great distance. So much, Corvinus, for your second question.'

I said nothing.

'The third, pertaining to the matter of the clandestine delivery of the note, was the result, I confess, of a mistake. Or rather of a misinterpretation. I asked Venustus to carry it round to the House of the Vestals and hand it in with as little fuss as possible, again for reasons of preserving secrecy; or at least of preserving anonymity. Venustus, as you may have gathered, is one of my oldest and most trustworthy slaves, but he is somewhat' – the half-smile again – 'literal-minded. Instead of knocking on the front door and handing the letter in as I expected him to do he chose the method which you already know. Not that that mattered, or at least I did not think it did at the time. It was only subsequent events which rendered it . . . unfortunate.' He stopped. 'There. That is all I have to say. Have I answered your questions now to your satisfaction?'

I stood up. 'Yeah. Yeah, thanks.'

'I'm glad.' He stood up as well. He was a big man, or had been in his time, and we were almost on a level. 'My apologies again for my earlier rudeness. If you've quite finished your business here' – this time he did look at his daughter; a considering stare, none too friendly. I glanced at her myself and saw her eyes drop – 'then I'll have Venustus show you out.'

The air of the Quirinal felt sweet, even with the rain. Alexis had left earlier, and he was shooting the breeze with the now-recovered litter-louts. I climbed aboard and we set off at a lumbering trot for the Caelian, via Market Square: I wasn't too worried that Perilla would sniff my tunic for perfume or check my shoulder for stray strands of women's hair, but I might as well keep my street cred with Bathyllus by having that second shave after all. If nothing else, a duly scraped and powdered chin would put the little bastard's scandal-sensitive nose out of joint and earn me a point or two in the ongoing battle. Besides, I'd got Alexis to debrief, and we might as well do it with a jug of wine and a plate of bread and sausage in front of us. Added to which, I reckoned I needed a drink to get the taste of the Lepidus place out of my mouth. Sure, everything had worked out in the end, but I couldn't say I'd enjoyed myself. Even if the lady had been a stunner she had the feel of a hungry arena cat about her, and old Marcus Lepidus, nice as pie as he'd been latterly, made my fists bunch with every plummy vowel. If I never saw either of them again it'd be too soon.

Still, they'd given me a lot to think about.

20

The rain had slackened off to an icy drizzle. I left Alexis and the lads kicking their heels in a cookshop I knew near the meat market and walked the last few hundred yards to Market Square itself, where Philemon the Syrian barber I sometimes used had his booth. I had my eyes closed and was halfway through the pumice stage and drifting nicely when I felt a hand on my shoulder. I came awake and turned.

'How are things going, Valerius Corvinus?'

I didn't place the guy at first; then I did: Sextius Nomentanus, the city judge who was footing the bill for the rites of the Good Goddess. Footing it again, rather, thanks to me. Shit, this could be embarrassing.

'Uh, okay, thanks,' I said. 'We're getting there.'

'That's good.' He sat down in the chair next to mine and Philemon's second-stringer put the napkin round his neck. 'I don't envy you your job. It's a messy business, but the bastard has to be caught. The gods know where it would leave the state if the killer of a Vestal went unpunished.'

I glanced sideways at him while Philemon tutted and fished his slip of pumice off my lap where the movement had sent it. Nomentanus hadn't struck me as a particularly religious guy, which was what the comment implied, but then the Vestals are something special: feelings about them go deep, and even your hardened modern religious sceptic is leery of the consequences if things involving them get out of kilter. 'Yeah,' I said; then, because I knew the thought was bound to be in his mind: 'Hey, I'm sorry about the rites.'

He shrugged. 'It can't be helped. Best to be safe than sorry. The Senate's making an extra allowance under the circumstances, and the emperor might chip in with an ex-gratia. I won't lose all that much.' Well, I was glad he didn't seem too cut up: the next step on the ladder from city judge is the consulship itself, and running for that's pricey, even in these supposedly egalitarian days. Nomentanus obviously wasn't too badly strapped for cash. 'You have any leads on the man who did it? The bogus flutegirl?'

'Some.' I was cautious: you don't mention outright to one of Rome's serving elite that you're delving through a current consul's dirty laundry. The beautiful and good are a tight-knit club, and one indication that you're sniffing for scandal makes them close ranks faster than a virgin crossing her legs at an out-of-hand party. 'Uh, incidentally, how's Sulpicius Galba taking it?'

'Galba?' He faced front as the guy with the razor got to work. 'I don't think he's too concerned. Apart from being disgruntled at the upheaval, of course. That and the extra expense.' His voice was dry. 'The house had to be purified, naturally, and although technically a recelebration of the rites is the state's concern – and mine – it means his wife will have to play the hostess again. Coming on top of this latest business with the loans that doesn't altogether make him a very happy man. If you knew our present consul you'd understand what I mean.'

Yeah, well; I knew enough about close-as-a-clam Galba to grasp the basic concept, anyway. I'd reckon getting so much as a bent copper coin out of that guy voluntarily would need a surgical operation. 'The loans?' I said.

I had to wait while Nomentanus raised his chin for the barber to scrape its underside. When he'd finished the guy chuckled. 'You really don't keep abreast of Market Square matters, do you, Corvinus? You haven't heard of the emperor's latest directive? It's setting half the Senate by the ears.'

He definitely sounded smug. I'd met this attitude before in smart-as-a-whip go-getters like Nomentanus, and it always rubbed me up the wrong way. It was the tone that meant 'I'm okay personally but the other bastards are being screwed.'

'Is that right, now?' I said.

'Tiberius has been getting complaints for some time about loan-shark profiteering.' Another chuckle, while the lad with the razor shortened a sideburn. 'He's finally clamping down and my colleagues are sweating blood.'

Uh-huh. I was beginning to get his drift. Broad-stripers are forbidden by law to go in for trade, but the money for the daily crust has to come from somewhere, and over the years Rome's conscript fathers have found that loan-farming is a natty little earner; or rather, not just the loan-farming itself but its spin-off as well. Under the old Julian law, interest rates are fixed at five per cent max, with compound loans forbidden. What the beautiful and good – who had their hands on a large slice of the circulating currency – had been doing was to ignore this. They'd been advancing loans at ten, fifteen per cent compound, sometimes even higher, on security of the debtor's property; then when the guy defaulted, as he naturally did, foreclosing at their own valuation and padding their estate books with the result. Sneaky and totally illegal, sure, but when it's your spoon in the gravy and you enforce the laws then the system ain't going to change in a hurry. Only evidently from what Nomentanus was saying the Wart had decided to step in and pull the plug personally. No wonder the fat-cat bastards were losing sweat.

'The emperor's given them eighteen months to regularise matters and pay any surplus profits they may already have made into the Treasury.' Nomentanus grunted as the bronze razor slid down his cheek. 'After that the prosecutions start. Meanwhile the interest rates – and consequently the incomes – have been cut at a stroke and my less well-heeled colleagues – plus the rich but parsimonious souls like Galba – are frantically trying to liquidise their investments by calling in the debts themselves. Oh, it's all fun in the Senate House at the moment, Corvinus, believe me.'

I did. I whistled. Jupiter on a seesaw, the shit had hit the fan with a vengeance! Not before time, though. And the Wart was a braver man than I was: it takes guts to mix with Rome's finest, especially when you aim for their pockets. 'You're all right yourself, then?' I said sourly.

'Oh, I'm fine.' The smugness went up a notch. 'And if I may give you a tip' – he leaned over – 'ready money's going to be in short supply soon. You could pick up a few good bargains on the property market if you keep your eyes open. You understand?'

But Philemon had got to the talc stage and now wasn't exactly the time to take the guy's advice; not literally, anyway. Five minutes later, smooth and sweet-smelling again, I nodded to my new whizz-kid financial adviser and headed off for the wine and sausage.

So Galba had his balls in the mangle, did he? And things were going to get a hell of a lot worse. I didn't know if what Nomentanus had told me was relevant, but it was certainly something to bear in mind.

Alexis was ensconced in the cookshop's warmest corner, right by the oven: he must've fought off half the eighth district to keep the table for us, because the place was full and it was beginning to sleet outside. I noticed that my four litter lardballs were happily blowing the pocket money I'd given them a few tables off on pigs' trotters in gravy, and I tried not to think about cannibalism. Alexis stood up, but I waved him down and put my order in at the counter. I took the jug and a couple of cups with me while the cookshop owner put the food together and went to join him.

The first cup went down without a whimper — it was Massic, not all that bad — and I poured a refill. Then the waiter brought the sliced sausage, cheese, olives and bread. Me, I was happy with the wine, plus maybe a nibble or two, but Alexis dug in like he hadn't seen food for a month. Unaccustomed sleuthing obviously did wonders for the appetite. I caught the waiter's eye and got him to add a wedge of onion tart to the bill.

Finally, when the pace began to slow, I sat back.

'Okay, so how did it go?' I said.

'Not bad at all, sir.' Alexis was wiping his fingers on a napkin: the guy may be a slave, but he's more fastidious than a lot of broad-stripers I've met. Smarter, too, although that wouldn't be so difficult. 'I talked to Lady Lepida's maid.'

'Yeah?' I poured myself some more wine and held up the jug. Alexis shook his head, which was par for the course: my smart-as-paint garden slave's a clean-living boy, and no proper drinker. 'Nice work.'

'Her name's Melissa.' Jupiter! Was that a blush? 'She's a very nice girl. Spanish.'

I took a swallow of Massic to cover a grin. I'd a lot of time for young Alexis. For a start, he was the most unslavelike slave I'd ever come across. A thinker, too serious for his own good, but with a fair saving slice of the poet grafted on, plus a sense of humour. Articulate, too. From front-of-house slaves like Bathyllus you expect that sort of thing, but not from gardeners: manuring doesn't demand all that much in the way of conversational skills, and most of these guys are hard put to it even to grunt. Mind you, taking on the garden had been Alexis's own choice, right from the start: he got on better with plants than people. Which made this turn of events even more surprising.

'Uh ... she good-looking?' I said.

His Adam's apple bobbed painfully. 'Yes, sir,' he said. 'I suppose you could call her that.'

Oh, Cupid in rompers! What had I unleashed? The kid was definitely smitten. This Melissa must be quite something; although there again she could just as well have a wall-eye, chronic halitosis and a limp. Where women were concerned Alexis's opinion was about as valuable as a beetle's on metaphysics.

'Is that so?' I said. 'You, uh, think you could prise your lecherous thoughts away from her body long enough to tell me what you found out, sunshine?' I said mildly.

Now that was *definitely* a blush. I could see it spreading up from his neck to the roots of his hair, taking in the ears on the way and making them stand out like crimson pot-lids. 'I wasn't ...' he began. 'I didn't ... that is, I wouldn't ...'

'Alexis. Watch my lips. Joke, pal. Okay?'

The blush slowly subsided. 'Yes, sir. I'm sorry, sir.'

'Go ahead, then.'

He took a deep breath. 'The lady certainly wasn't at the rites, sir. She spent the night with a friend.' The blush made a brief reappearance. Obviously sex was a sensitive topic with Alexis at present. 'And before you ask, sir, no, I don't know his name. Melissa wouldn't be drawn on the details of the lady's love life, not as far as names were concerned at any rate.'

'Uh-huh.' I sipped my wine. 'She give you anything on that angle, then? Anything at all?'

'Not much, sir. I doubt if she would've in any case, even if — as she did — her mistress hadn't expressly warned her against it. As I told you, Melissa is a—'

'Nice girl,' I finished drily. 'Right. Got you.'

'She did let out, however, that the lady ... spreads her favours rather indiscriminately, sir.'

Surprise, surprise. 'She happen to mention anyone current?'

'Again no names, sir. She does have a steady, which was where she spent the night of the rites, but he isn't exclusive. Although I understand that he'd like to be.'

Bigger the fool him, I thought. Long term, that lady would be poison. 'Any other details?'

'No, sir. I'm afraid not.'

Well, I couldn't expect much more given the time I'd allowed him anyway, and considering his mind couldn't've been more than half on the job the kid had done marvels. 'Fine. Now what about the Aemilia angle?'

'I was a bit more successful there.' Alexis topped up my cup. 'The lady Lepida called on the lady Aemilia at the end of last month. Precisely three days before the kalends, in fact. Melissa remembered the date exactly because on the day previous when she was sent to ask whether the lady was receiving visitors she used the excuse to visit a friend in the Subura. It was the other girl's birthday and—'

I'd sat up sharply. 'Hang on, sunshine. Run that past me again. And leave out the ladies to save time. Also the birthday girl, okay?'

Alexis half smiled. 'Certainly, sir. The l ... Lepida first visited the consul's wife some eleven days ago. She was invited again two days later but had other commitments, since when—'

'What was that about Melissa going round on her own?'

'Her mistress sent her to check whether Aemilia would be at home the next day, sir. It's standard practice.'

'Yeah, I know that.' My neck was prickling. 'That's not the point. Alexis, you're saying *Lepida* made the running? She asked for the visit, not Aemilia?'

'Yes, sir.' Alexis's brow furrowed. 'I suppose so, anyway. Although Melissa didn't actually say—'

I waved him to silence. Shit! For Lepida to make the first move rather than Aemilia didn't add up; not given her claim that Aemilia had initiated the acquaintance for reasons of social cachet. Of course, if Lepida was casing the joint to plan the murder ...

This needed thinking about. If Lepida had lied to me about Aemilia being the driving force behind the acquaint-anceship, then the chances of her being involved in Cornelia's death had just taken a considerable hike. Especially given the time factor: three days before the kalends was only five before the murder. And if Lepida couldn't stand Aemilia, as she obviously couldn't, and as weaselling out of a second invite indicated, then why the hell, if she didn't have an ulterior motive, had she made overtures of friendship in the first place?

Alexis was staring at me. 'Sorry, sunshine,' I said. 'Carry on. What about the visit itself? Did Melissa give you any details?'

'There wasn't much to tell. It was just the usual society chit-chat. Oh, except that Aemilia had another visitor, but

Melissa had known he'd be there already. In fact, her mistress had asked her specifically to check that he'd be present before confirming the arrangements.'

'Yeah? And who was that, now?'

'One of the consul's finance officers. Licinius Murena.'

Aemilia's boyfriend. I almost laughed. Hell; there went that theory in spades. If Lepida knew Murena would be filling the third couch that day I didn't need to look any further for a motive: the lady was poaching. And although she hadn't given me an exact date when she'd told me she'd had the guy on her own couch I could make a pretty good guess: given the speed she operated, some time in the three days between Aemilia's cake-and-honey-wine klatch and the kalends. Certainly no later. Sure, he could be the steady Alexis had mentioned, in which case the liaison still had its potentially sinister side, but I doubted it. Despite what Lepida had said, Galba was no has-been; that was just the cat talking. The guy was a firm favourite of our next emperor, and from what I'd seen of Murena himself he wasn't the sort of man who'd give up the security of being the one and only of a complaisant aristo's sex-starved wife for a more precarious existence as the far from exclusive lover of that hell-cat. And as far as Lepida herself was concerned, I doubted if the lady looked very far beyond her next lay. She certainly wouldn't bother exerting herself to perpetrate anything as far removed from that as murder. Mind you, I could be wrong, of course.

Well, some you win, some you lose, and there's no use crying.

'You get anything else, pal?' I said. 'About young Marcus, say, or the father?'

Alexis shook his head. 'The households are kept pretty much separate.' Surprise! 'Melissa wasn't too cut up about

Lepidus Junior's death, either.' I caught a flash of embarrassment. 'I understand he ... er ... made rather free with
the younger slaves. Female and male.' He paused. 'I didn't
ask about Melissa herself, sir.'

'Uh-huh.'

'The father's a hard master, but he's fair. Old-fashioned,
sir, if you like. He's not a well man, despite appearances. The
rumour in the slaves' quarters is he might not last another
year.' Another hesitation. 'The girl did let drop one more
piece of information, by the way. About the consul's wife.'

'Yeah?'

The blush was back. 'It seems she has a liking at times
for rougher partners, sir. Slaves and freedmen.'

I whistled softly. That would explain Lepida's crack
about Aemilia's tastes being crude, and why the lady had
been uncharacteristically reticent in elaborating the point:
in the circles Lepida and Aemilia moved in purple-striper
lovers were one thing, but slaves and freedmen were a
whole different ball game. Fooling around like that could
get you into serious trouble, of the legal variety, and even
Lepida would think twice before splitting on a caste sister
to a comparative stranger. Alexis was seeing his girlfriend
through a rose-tinted haze right enough; Jupiter knew how
she'd come by the information, but for a sugar-and-spice
goodie-goodie who wouldn't be drawn Melissa had been
pretty free with her mouth. I'd guess Alexis wasn't the only
one who was smitten here and wanted to impress; he was
better at chatting up the talent than he thought he was.

'Is that right, now?' I said. 'Slaves and freedmen, eh? She,
ah, vouchsafe any details?'

'She mentioned one freedman in particular, sir. A second-
hand furniture dealer. The affair seems to be a comparatively
long-standing one.'

I had to stop myself from groaning. A second-hand furniture dealer. All of that. Bugger: small as the knife-wielding-cum-fluteplaying population of Rome might be, I was willing to bet that the number of homicidal second-hand furniture dealers currently for hire in the city was even smaller. The boy had done good, certainly as well as I could've expected; still, none of what we'd put together between us that morning amounted to a row of beans. Apart, maybe, from what I'd got on Lepidus Senior. At least he was worth considering. I emptied my wine cup, poured in the last of the jug and swigged it down. The Fantastic Four had finished their pigs' feet and licked the plates clean of gravy. It was time to be making tracks. If they could lug their carcases — and mine — the length of the Caelian.

I needed to talk to Perilla.

21

I noticed that Bathyllus had a careful look at my chin when I got back, but he sniffed and said nothing, just got on with his polishing. Perilla was in the atrium having her hair done: it seemed to be a day for primping and powdering all round. I planted a small smacker on her lips without getting too much in the maid Phryne's way and stretched out on the couch with wine jug and cup.

'Well, Marcus, how did it go? Your visit to Lepida's?'

I laughed. 'You know about that after all?'

'Bathyllus did drop some very heavy hints. Entirely unsolicited, I may add.'

'Uh-huh.' Shave excuse, nothing; if I ever did consider tomcatting I'd leave the sanctimonious little bastard tied up and gagged in the cellar. Not that I'd get away with cheating on Perilla in any case. 'Let's just say it wasn't all that productive.'

'As bad as that?' Perilla smiled. 'You're losing your touch, Corvinus. Phryne, dear, we'll finish off later, if you don't mind.' The maid padded off. 'Have you eaten?'

'Yeah. We had something in a cookshop on the way back.' I poured a cup of wine. 'The plot thickens, lady. That note Perdicca gave us wasn't a fake after all.'

Perilla sat up. 'Marcus Lepidus actually wrote it?'

'Not the son. The father.' I told her the story. 'So. What do you think?'

'His explanation seems plausible enough.'

'Sure it does. Maybe even too plausible. And he's a very smart cookie.'

'You're *not* saying, I hope, that you suspect Marcus Lepidus Senior of being behind the deaths?'

'Why not? In theory, anyway. I was mulling it over on the way home. At least he makes some sort of sense.'

'No he doesn't. None whatsoever. You know, Corvinus, sometimes I wonder your skull doesn't rattle when your head nods.'

I winced. Ouch; whatever happened to the good old-fashioned wifely virtue of automatic deference to the husband's opinion? 'Don't knock it, lady. Like I say, it's only a possibility. But I could make a prima facie case.'

'Really?' She didn't sound convinced, to put it mildly. 'Now that I would just love to hear.'

I took a swig of wine. 'Okay. You said yourself whatever the secret Cornelia and Lepidus Junior shared there was a better than even chance it affected the Lepidus family. We assumed that meant the sister, because that wildcat's the most likely candidate to have skeletons in her closet, but that was no reason to rule out the old guy himself. Everything else about protecting the family honour would still apply, in fact even more so: Lepidus Junior wouldn't want to blow the whistle on his own father, and he might be even more reticent in facing him privately with the nasty details if he were the guilty party rather than Lepida. Which would explain why Lepidus Senior was ready and able to swear that his son hadn't told him anything in their last interview.'

'Accepted.' That was grudging as hell, but at least the lady was scowling, which meant she'd taken the point and couldn't think of an answer. 'But what possible reason could Lepidus have for killing anyone? He's one of the most respectable and respected men in Rome.'

'Reason I don't know. Or not as such, anyway. But there's nothing wrong with the theoretical scenario.'

'Which is, in detail?'

Uh-oh; that had the waspish snap which meant that she was just dying for me to slip up so she could put the boot in. I'd have to go careful here. 'Okay. Paragon or not, old Lepidus has stepped out of line in some way; how, we don't know, but whatever it is it's pretty major. His son finds out about it. Lepidus Junior's in a quandary: it's his civic duty to spill the beans, but he can't bring himself to do it. So he goes to his long-term confidante Cornelia, who he still counts as family, and cries on her shoulder. Unfortunately, his father gets to know about this and—'

'How?'

Oh, hell! 'How what?'

'How exactly does Lepidus Senior learn that his son has told Cornelia?'

'Jupiter, Perilla, give me a chance, okay? Maybe he knows he's been rumbled and he's having the guy watched. By our fluteplayer pal, say. Anyway—'

'So Lepidus just happens already to have secured the services of a man who is, fortunately in the light of subsequent events, not only a proficient murderer but also a professional fluteplayer?'

'Uh, yeah.' I was beginning to feel out of my depth. 'Okay, well, maybe not by the fluteplayer. Anyway—'

'And how does he come by the fluteplayer in any case? His son or daughter having contacts among Rome's low life I can understand, but not Lepidus Senior. His character – at least as expressed through his public persona – is all wrong.'

Gods! I didn't deserve this; it was only a theory, after all, and I didn't really believe it myself. I just didn't have anything better to offer at the present moment. '*Anyway*.' I froze her out with a look. 'The guy realises that he has to nip the leak in the bud—'

'Leaks don't have buds, Marcus. Don't mix your metaphors.'

'So he arranges for Cornelia, as the weak link, to be zeroed by our fluteplayer, who is no doubt one of his very extensive body of dependent clients. However, that still leaves him with the problem of the—'

'His own niece? And a Vestal?' Perilla sniffed. 'Corvinus, I told you, Marcus Lepidus Senior is one of the most respected men in Rome. You know that yourself. Now stop talking nonsense, please. What else did you find out?'

I sighed and gave up the unequal struggle. Yeah, well, maybe I had been spouting pure moonshine at that. The lady was right: once you actually put the thing into words, possible though it might be as a theory it stank. 'Not all that much. Some murky details of the daughter's love life, plus ditto for Aemilia, but neither seem to have much mileage to them. We're stymied, Perilla. Barring Lepidus there's no one with even the hint of a motive. My best bet at present would be the senior consul, but that's only because the guy has male fluteplayer connections. What reasons Galba would have for zeroing a Vestal I just can't begin to guess.'

'I should hope not,' Perilla said primly.

'We need to find the actual murderer. This phantom fluteplayer bastard. And unless Lippillus can come up with—'

'Why not ask your flutegirl friend to help?'

I stared at her. 'What?'

'Surely it's self-evident, Marcus. If you're looking for a fluteplayer then you should ask a fluteplayer.'

'Jupiter, you think I haven't done that? Aegle's already

told me she didn't know who the guy was! Nor did any of
the other girls!'

'I'm not talking about the man at the rites, I'm talking
about the consul's friend. Aegle might be able to track him
down for you. If the two turn out to be one and the same,
unlikely as that may seem, then well and good. If not then
there's no harm done, is there?'

Feminine logic; brilliant! Sure, I should've thought of it
myself, but it takes a woman to spot the obvious, and *pace*
Perilla I didn't believe there could be two professional
male fluteplayers in Rome connected with this business,
even though we still had the hurdle to get over of why,
make-up notwithstanding, the guy hadn't been recognised.
It beat going through Celer, too: I didn't know how many
male fluteplayers there were in the city, but I didn't fancy
checking them all out. I got up off the couch, dumped the
wine and gave her a proper kiss.

'Thanks, lady,' I said. 'I'll catch you later.'

On the way out, just for the hell of it, I told Bathyllus
I was going to see my banker and watched the bastard's
eyes cross.

I was lucky on two counts: the day had faired up enough to
make walking a possibility, and when I got to the tenement
in Suburan Street Aegle was at home.

'Hey, Purple-striper!' she said when she opened the door
and stood aside for me to pass. 'You'll be getting me a
reputation if you're not careful.'

'Sorry.' I hung my cloak on the peg.

'Oh, that's okay.' She followed me into the sitting-room.
'It was a compliment. Around here being screwed by one of
the nobility's a social plus. Or would be if it ever happened.
Shift that stuff off the trunk and sit down.'

I moved the pile of dirty washing on to the floor. Lying on top of it was a scrappy book-roll that looked like a generation or two of mice had lived off it exclusively. I glanced at the title-label: Meleager's *Garland*. Well, that text didn't need any more abridgement, that was sure.

'Some light reading?' I said.

She picked the thing up and laid it carefully on the window-sill. 'Don't patronise me, Corvinus,' she said. 'What I do in my own time's my own business.' She sat down on the room's only stool. 'So. You know who killed Thalia yet?'

'No.' I parked myself on the clothes chest. 'I was hoping you might help me find him.'

'I've given you all the help I can. Or do you still not believe me?'

'Oh, I believe you.'

'You'd better. We stick together, us girls, I told you that. We have to because we're all we've got. Your Vestal's one thing, Thalia's another. She was family.' Her birthmark flushed and her lips tightened. 'If I or any of us can nail that bastard then we'll do it.'

'Fine. So pin your ugly ears back, sister. I want to find a fluteboy pal of the senior consul's.'

She looked at me sideways. 'Of Galba's? And pal as in "pal"?'

'Yeah.'

She whistled. 'Mothers, you're fishing in deep water! You think he's the one that did it?'

'I don't know. Maybe. You know who he is offhand?'

'No. I'll tell you now, though, he isn't anyone on the circuit. One of the lads gets to screw a consul, you hear about it. Strictly within the family, of course, but there aren't many secrets among fluteplayers. Not that big, anyway.' Her brow furrowed. 'He could be from out of town; from Ostia or Veii. Naples, even.'

'No, I'd bet this guy was local. If he's the killer, which I think he is. Or at least he's resident in Rome.'

'You want me to put the word out?'

'Sure.'

'You've got it.' She shifted on her stool. 'One bit of advice? Professional viewpoint?'

'Yeah. Go ahead.'

'This business, you don't get freelancers, not the way we operate. Boys or girls. Slots aren't exactly easy to set up on your own, and in any case anyone stealing the cherries out of the cake is going to be very noticeable very quick. Me, I'm laid back about these things but others aren't. Try to muscle in without going through proper channels and you'll find yourself being talked to seriously down a dark alleyway some night, maybe have your fingers broken or your lip slit. Ignore the warning and you'll end up breathing Tiber.'

'So?'

'What I'm saying is there are no outsiders. I may not be able to recognise every fluteplayer in the city, but there were eleven of us at that party barring the ringer. One of us should've known her.' She paused. 'Him. Whatever. None of us did. If the guy had stuck around we might've asked questions later, but covering for Thalia and getting through the slot was more important at the time than the whys and wherefores. We took him – her – at her own valuation. Call it a truce, if you like.' I nodded. 'So professionally your "fake" didn't exist: he/she was a real fluteplayer, only not a known one. Given what I've said, that leaves you with a hybrid. Someone who's professional standard but not a pro in the literal sense. You with me?'

This was fascinating. I should've turned Aegle loose on the case before. 'All the way, lady,' I said. 'Go on.'

'You get them now and again, in the big families. Home-bred slaves who show some talent for the pipes, who the master trains up for purely domestic consumption. Parties. Banquets. Quiet evenings by the pool before bedtime. I think your murderer's one of these. Maybe he's still a slave, maybe he's got his cap, makes no difference to the skill. You understand me?'

'Yeah.' Jupiter! 'You mean he could be part of the Galba household? Or maybe one of the guy's freedmen?' I'd suggested that aspect of things to Perilla re Lepidus, but I hadn't thought of Galba. Maybe I should've.

'It's possible. Just an idea. But if the killer and your consul's stud are the same person it might add up where doing the job's concerned.'

My brain was humming. It would make sense, a lot of sense: the guy would know the ins and outs of the house itself without being told, for a start. As Aegle said, it would mean there was a strong, ready-made link between him and Galba that went beyond the sexual: slave to master or client to patron. It still didn't explain why the senior consul should want Cornelia dead, but the mechanics of the business were working out like a dream.

'Leave it with me,' Aegle said. 'If the guy's a player – and he is – someone'll know him.'

'One problem,' I said. 'The slot was in the Galba house itself. Surely – given the fact that he went there to commit murder – he was taking a hell of a risk? If he was one of the household the other servants would've recognised him.'

'Not as big a risk as all that. Remember the house was closed to men. If he was the ringer, the servants wouldn't be expecting to see him or any other man there after sunset, especially among the paid musicians. And his disguise was perfect. That guy was a *woman*, Corvinus; butch, sure, but female as they come. At least on the surface.' Aegle grinned. 'Also they may have fed us well enough but they sure as hell didn't wait on us. The slaves had enough to do keeping the silk-mantled brigade's plates full without bothering about the band. We were left to our own devices. Me, I helped myself whenever a tray passed, so I might've got noticed, but I'd bet the last thing on that guy's mind was eating.'

Yeah. Fair point. I stood up. 'Okay. Thanks, sister. If you get something Celer knows where to find me.'

She shook her head. 'Uh-uh. I don't want to bring Celer into this. The boys and girls are safe, but I wouldn't put it past that bastard to split.'

Fair enough; and I didn't trust Celer more than half myself. I gave her my address. Then I went back home to wait.

22

I waited for three full days. Which isn't to say, of course, that I stayed in twiddling my thumbs or washing my hair. There wasn't much I could do as far as the case was concerned, sure, except to check with Lippillus whether he'd got any change out of the other residents of Thalia's tenement (he hadn't), but with all this murder and mayhem my private life had taken a back seat and there was plenty to do that didn't involve sleuthing. For a start, I called in at the city judges' offices with a dinner invite for Gaius Secundus and his wife. I felt guilty as hell about Secundus. Like I said, we'd been close friends as kids and the Murena favour was the second time I'd traded on the friendship without giving anything back, which isn't the Roman way. The least I owed Gaius was a good dinner.

Then there was the Winter Festival shopping. Jupiter, I hate that, but with less than ten days to go it had to be done. I gritted my teeth and did the rounds of the markets, the Saepta and the chichi shops on Broad Street, the Argiletum and Iugarius. The Winter Festival, of course, is really for the slaves — it's the only holiday the poor buggers get, barring a day for the Festival of the Matrons and another in August for the inauguration of Diana's temple — but everyone gets a present nowadays, and I knew Perilla had already stashed mine (a sharp new mantle; that lady's nothing if not an improver, and she gives me one every year) at the bottom of a spare-room clothes chest. For Perilla I got a couple of rolls of Carneades's philosophical lectures (don't ask) which she'd go into ecstasies over and, as an afterthought, a cut-price edition of Meleager's Menippean satires for Aegle. Mother got perfume, like I give her every year, and I already had Priscus's little goody: a ring I'd picked up in Athens with the head of one of the Seleucid kings on it. Meton was easy: he'd been dropping heavy hints about a new omelette pan ever since we'd got back. So was Lysias: the guy's belt-mad, and I found him a Spanish one with gilded studs. Alexis was more difficult, but I had a sneaking suspicion the kid was blossoming in the romance department so he netted a snappy tunic and a flask of good hair-oil. Bathyllus . . .

I spent a lot of time and thought over Bathyllus's present. The little guy isn't easy to buy for; he's got enough hernia supports already to equip a legion's artillery division, and as for patent hair-growing remedies he's tried them all without so much as a sprouting follicle. Finally, on a Gallic stall in Cattlemarket Square, I found the very thing: a pair of woollen long johns à la the Divine Augustus that would've stopped anything short of a direct hit from a siege bolt. When he was out of a January dawn buffing up the paving stones outside our front door Bathyllus would just love these to bits.

I'd just stowed them away in the study with the other presents – it was just short of lunch-time – when the little bald-head himself shimmered in.

'You have a visitor, sir,' he said. 'A woman.' Sniff.

'Yeah?' I closed the lid of the chest before he caught a pre-Festival glimpse of the winter woollies. 'Merciful gods! One of them, eh? She got her castanets and a rose between her teeth or has she left them at home?'

Not a flicker. Maybe the woollies were a mistake after all: that guy's impervious to everything the world can throw at him, sarcasm especially.

'That I couldn't say, sir,' he said. 'However, she is waiting outside. In the lobby.'

And he'd probably checked the floor mosaic in case she scuffed it with her plebeian sandals while he was gone, too. I'd noticed the terminology: *woman*, not *lady*. Where maintaining the social distances is concerned Bathyllus could give a dowager lessons. I sighed.

'Okay, little guy. Wheel her through.'

It was Aegle, of course, complete with flute-case. 'Hi, Purple-striper,' she said as she took her cloak off. 'Nice place.'

Bathyllus made a sort of strangled choking noise. Yeah, well, he couldn't see many visitors in just a gilded G-string and bra. 'I'll leave you in private, then, shall I, sir?' he said.

'You do that.' I kept my face straight. 'Go and adjust your truss, sunshine.'

He sniffed and left.

Aegle had laid the flute-case against the wall and settled herself on the couch.

I grinned and poured us each a cup of wine. 'You want me to tell the slaves to beef up the hypocaust, lady?' I said.

She laughed. 'Hey, I'm sorry. I had an all-night slot at a house on Caelimontan Road and it wasn't worth going home to change. You mind?'

'I don't. My head slave might need major corrective surgery, but at least he'll go into it happy.'

'That wasn't how it looked from here.' She sipped her wine. 'I've found your fluteboy for you.'

Hey! 'No kidding?' I took the stool next to the desk.

'His name's Scorpus. It was like I thought, the guy's one of Galba's freedmen. Got his discharge about a year ago. He runs a second-hand furniture business in the Remuria, just up from the Naevian Gate.'

My skin prickled. 'He does *what*?'

'Runs a furniture business. Galba bought him into it. He must've given hell of a satisfaction in his tootling days, because it's a proper going concern and that bastard's close enough to skin a flint.'

'Hang on, Aegle,' I said. 'This is important. You're telling me this Scorpus is a used furniture dealer?'

'Sure. Like I said, fluteplaying's a closed shop. And it doesn't exactly pay. Used furniture's big business, especially in the Aventine district where people can't afford fancy prices for new. He's coining it hand over fist, my informant tells me.'

Shit; Alexis's pal Melissa had said that Aemilia's bit of rough was a second-hand furniture salesman. Added that this guy had family connections with the Galbas, that didn't leave any room for coincidence. I'd been chasing the wrong hare. 'You seen him?'

'No. I thought if you're not busy we could do that together.'

'Sure we could.' I sank my wine in one and stood up. 'We'll go round there now.'

'You mind if I have something to eat first? I haven't had anything today and I'm starved.'

'Uh, yeah. Right.' I crossed over to the door and yelled, 'Hey, Bathyllus!'

He was there in two shakes of a G-string tassel, radiating prime disapproval. 'Yes, sir. At your orders, sir.'

'Cut the crap and bring the lady some lunch, sunshine.' I looked at Aegle. 'Ah ...'

'Just bread will do fine. And some greens if you've got them,' she said.

'Greens, madam.' You could've used the guy's tone to ice fruit juice. 'Yes, madam. Certainly, madam.'

'Get Meton to make up a tray,' I said. 'That cold pork and cumin from yesterday and the bean stew. Plus anything else he's got going.'

'Yes, sir. Cold pork, sir.' He glanced at Aegle's legs, stretched out and visible in their full lovely length. She grinned back at him and winked. 'At once, sir.' He left with a final sniff.

'Your major-domo doesn't like me,' Aegle said when he'd gone.

'Oh, Bathyllus is okay. He just isn't human, that's all.' I opened the presents chest and brought out the Meleager. 'By the way, I got this for you. It was for the Festival but you may as well have it now.'

She took the roll like it was made of cobwebs and looked at the title. 'The *Satires*! Corvinus, this must've cost—'

'It's a bargain-basement copy. Fourth-hand and two of the roller horns are missing. Besides, one of the careful owners spilled ink all over the last page so you'll never know whodunnit. So no big deal, lady.'

She'd gone very quiet. 'Thanks,' she said.

'What for? If this Scorpus of yours is the guy we want you deserve the old hack's complete works in the gold leaf edition.'

'I told you. Finding him wasn't a favour. We all owed it to Thalia. And I don't get many presents, certainly not books.' Her fingers brushed the paper. 'I'm grateful.'

'Yeah. Well.' I refilled my cup: if we weren't going straight out I might as well have another one while I waited. 'Who was your informant, by the way?'

She set the scroll down. 'One of the boys. He played up at the Galba place eighteen months back when Scorpus was laid up with a poisoned hand and the guy gave him a few tips. Not musical ones.'

'Uh-huh. He meet the lady of the house, at all? Galba's wife Aemilia?'

'No. It was an all-male dinner.' Aegle hesitated. 'You think she was the one who arranged it, don't you? The murder, I mean.'

'Maybe.' Jupiter, the lady was quick!

'She and Scorpus . . . ?' She made a circle with her thumb and index finger, then slipped the other middle finger through.

I grunted. 'Uh, yeah,' I said. 'Yeah. That's how it looks, anyway.'

'Hey!' She laughed. 'Don't look so shocked, Corvinus! It isn't as rare as you think. If you men can screw any good-looking slave that takes your fancy why shouldn't the women? Especially if they're going short otherwise. Happens all the time, only they keep quiet about it. And the boys aren't going to talk, are they?'

My mouth must've been hanging open, because I found myself closing it. Gods! This was seditious stuff! She hadn't batted an eyelid, either. 'Uh, no,' I said. 'No, I don't suppose they are.'

'So.' She stretched out on the couch. I noticed she'd painted her toenails. 'Scorpus had an in with the mistress as well as the master. To coin a phrase.' Ouch. 'But why should she want a Vestal dead?'

I'd been asking myself the same question, and I didn't have an answer. 'Search me, sister. Still, it fits. Celer tells me Aemilia would have a list of the girls at the rite.'

'Yeah. Only the names, though, not the addresses. And if her tame fluteboy was Scorpus then how did he get in touch with Thalia?'

That brought me up short. Hell. I hadn't thought of that. The lady was right: Scorpus might have the technical qualifications, but he wasn't on the circuit, which meant he wouldn't automatically have the contacts. We still had that hurdle to get over. 'Fair point. You have any ideas yourself?'

She considered. 'If I were you I'd have another word with Celer. That bugger would sell his grandmother for the asking, and he probably has, but he's no hero.'

'Right. Good suggestion.' There was a knock on the door: Bathyllus with the tray. Fast work, but then he had a vested interest. 'Fine, little guy. Just put it down.'

He did; carefully and with eyes averted. Evidently we had a five-star, gold-plated huff situation here. Jupiter! Minions!

'Will there be anything else, sir?' he said.

'No, that about covers it.' He sniffed and straightened. 'Oh, one thing more. We'll need the litter. Tell the lardballs ten minutes.' I looked at Aegle. 'That be okay?'

'Make it fifteen, Bathyllus.' She was already tucking in. *Insouciant*, I think, is the word. I really liked Aegle. There weren't many people who could out-snub Bathyllus.

He exited, out-snubbed and fizzing.

Starved was right; the tray looked pretty empty by the time the lady was through with it. That last lunch I'd seen her picking at in the Suburan cookshop must've been a one-off, or maybe she was just making full use of the opportunity. We left the dishes for the little sourpuss to clear away and set off for the Remuria.

23

The Remuria got its name because it was the part of the Aventine where Romulus's brother was standing when he spied his vultures. The place has changed in the last eight hundred years, and not for the better: if the old guy came back now he wouldn't see the sky for tenements, he'd find the vultures walking around in tunics, and there'd be a hell of a lot more than six of them. In fact, from the looks of the lean, mean, corn-dole-fed faces we passed I wondered if maybe we should've brought a back-up team. Certainly if things turned rough the litter slaves would be no help. After the climb up from Circus Valley the lardballs were so knackered they couldn't've handled a brace of determined three-year-olds.

We got lost a few times, but finally an old guy who could've been Nestor's grandfather if the Pylos royal family had gone in for nicking the tiles off temple roofs pointed us down a rubbish-strewn alleyway between two anonymous blocks of flats. Sure enough, it ended in a walled yard with a heavy gate. There was nothing to show who owned the place – I doubted if one in ten of the locals could've read a sign anyway – but the yard was heaped with furniture under a makeshift roofing of sailcloth. Most of it seemed to be basic stuff: iron bedsteads, stools, basin brackets. Cheap quality, nothing too big or too fancy, or even too intact. Yeah, that made sense: in the Remuria most of the punters would be strapped for space and cash, and who worried about a collapsing bed when the real problem was a collapsing bedroom?

Aegle had been right about it being a going concern, though: I counted four men, three of them loading a wagon while the other scratched his balls to one side. Obviously the man in charge. I got out of the litter and went up to him.

'This place belong to a guy called Scorpus, pal?' I asked.

'Yeah.' He was leering at Aegle, who'd come out behind me. She was wearing her cloak, but it only covered her to the knees.

'You know where I can find him?'

'He's out buying.' He turned his head away and spat into the mud to one side. 'Property by the Naevian Gate.'

Down the hill a bit, to the south-west. 'Uh-huh,' I said. 'You care to be more explicit?'

He considered. 'Family Mucius Trupho,' he said at last. 'Only the guy's dead. Sale of effects. Third tenement before the gate, first floor left.'

'Thanks.' I turned back for the litter.

'Hey, sister!' the guy yelled. 'You a flutegirl? Want to give us a tune on your pipe before you go?'

'Screw you,' Aegle snapped over her shoulder as we climbed in.

'Sure.' He chuckled. 'Any time.'

We leaned back against the cushions and the lardballs took the strain. Aegle's birthmark was flushing scarlet and her lips were set.

'I'm sorry about that,' I said.

'No problem, Corvinus.' She grinned suddenly. 'I could eat that bastard for breakfast and spit out the pips. It just gets a bit wearisome sometimes, you know?'

Yeah; right. I gave the guys their directions and then ducked my head back in. We headed down for the Naevian.

*   *   *

Even without the slimeball's exact directions we wouldn't've had any difficulty finding the right address. The furnishings for sale — such as there were of them — had been brought down the tenement steps and were laid out in the street for potential purchasers to finger over. Most of the neighbourhood had turned out, too, whether they were buying or not: when there're no chariot races or games scheduled, in the Remuria you make your own entertainment. I noticed, though, that there were three hard-looking guys standing around on the fringes and keeping their eyes peeled. From the facial similarity, they had to be family, probably Trupho's sons: even something as big as a bedstead can grow legs and walk on the Aventine if you leave it unattended for more than five minutes, and they were obviously keeping tabs on their property until the cash had changed hands. When the lads put us down I climbed out, Aegle behind me, and walked up to the nearest.

'Excuse me, friend,' I said politely. 'Is there a guy called Scorpus here, do you know? Used furniture dealer?'

'Sure.' The guy pointed. 'That's him with Ma.'

I looked, then looked again just in case, but there was no mistake. The man talking to the wizened crone who was probably no older than forty was six six in his sandals, built like a trireme and black as the inside of the Tullianum at midnight. Disguised or not, fluteplayer or not, if Scorpus could pass as any sort of female for more than two consecutive seconds to anyone who wasn't purblind and a congenital idiot then I'd eat my mantle.

Bugger. So much for that angle. I didn't even bother to ask Aegle if she recognised him; I just steered her back into the litter and told the boys to take us home.

We were both pretty quiet on the way back.

'Hey, come on, now, Corvinus,' Aegle said eventually. 'It's not the end of the world.'

'You want to bet?' I snarled. 'That guy was my best shot. In fact he was my only shot. With him out Aemilia goes too, and Galba, for what he was worth, and they leave fuck all behind them.'

'It can't be as bad as that.'

Cheery optimism I could do without. It just made matters worse. 'Is that right now?' I said. 'You like to estimate how many other unaffiliated male fluteplayers there are in the city? Ones that don't have their sandals made in a boatyard and can wear a short skirt and padded halter without looking like something out of a drag version of a titanomachy?'

She giggled. 'He certainly looked a stud, though. I can understand why Aemilia dropped her pants for him. Even Galba.'

True; but then I wasn't in the mood to see the funny side of things, not yet, not by a long chalk. And I hadn't been kidding; I'd expected a lot from Scorpus. 'Cut it out, lady,' I said. 'We're in trouble. You're the professional consultant; where do we go from here?'

She looked out through the curtains. 'Well, I'm not sure about you, Corvinus, but I'm headed for a slot this evening at a broad-striper's house down Tusculan Road. Some of us have to work. You can drop me off at the intersection.'

'Jupiter, sister, it's not halfway through the afternoon yet! If you don't want to go all the way back to the Subura then come home with me and I'll get Lysias to take you in the coach.'

She looked at me sideways. 'You'd really do that, wouldn't you?' she said.

'Sure I would. No problem.'

'Yeah.' She gave a small sigh. 'Well, I suppose you would, at that. Uh-uh. Thanks but no thanks. I've got a friend living down that way. I'll call in in passing, kill the time there.'

I didn't believe her for a minute, but there wouldn't've been any point arguing. If I'd learned anything about Aegle in our short acquaintance it was that she was some independent-minded lady. 'Two slots in two days,' I said. 'That's not bad going, is it?'

She shrugged. 'It happens sometimes. Although for me not often enough. This one's just a fill-in for Harmodia.'

'Yeah?' I was making conversation; anything not to have to think about the case. Or lack of one. 'Who's Harmodia?'

'The girl whose place Thalia took at the rites.'

Oh, yeah; the one who'd gone sick. 'She's not back yet?'

'She called in at the clubhouse a couple of days after the ceremony, but only for the news. Her throat was still swollen. She wanted to sign off until the Festival. Celer was livid because she's pretty popular, but there was nothing he could do. We're sharing her slots out between us.'

Something brushed my spine. 'She, uh, missing out on a lot of work, then?'

'Sure. Harmodia's popular, like I said. The punters ask for her by name.'

'Popular enough to take the best part of a month off and not feel the pinch?'

Aegle laughed. 'We're none of us earning that much, Corvinus. And Celer isn't someone to cross. Still, it's her decision.'

I remembered what Celer had said about the girls shacking up temporarily with some well-heeled client. 'She wouldn't be malingering, would she?' I said. 'Caught herself a rich boyfriend and be taking a pre-Festival break?'

'No.' Again I got the odd sideways look. 'No, not Harmodia.'

The tingle was getting stronger. Why it was there, I didn't know, but you learn not to ignore these things. 'You happen to know where she lives?'

'Sure. In Transtiber, near the Cestian Bridge. But why?'

'You free tomorrow? Could you show me?'

'If you like.' She frowned. 'What's your interest in Harmodia?'

'I don't know.' I didn't; not exactly. 'Maybe none. Just humour me. So when's the best time to catch her in?'

'One time's as good as another. Not evenings, though.'

'Okay. We'll call it mid-morning. I'll pick you up at your place.'

'Fine. But don't bring the litter. It makes me seasick, and I'd rather get wet.'

'Yeah. Yeah, right.'

I dropped her at the junction with Tusculan and the lads turned left and began the slow climb to the Caelian. I was almost whistling.

Maybe optimism wasn't such a bad thing after all. At least it was a possible line of enquiry. And after the Scorpus let-down the gods knew I needed a break.

24

Transtiber I don't know all that well. It's a little world of
its own; or maybe not so little, and not just one world.
Like the name implies it takes in the whole far bank of
the river, from Vatican Field in the north to the southern
slopes of the Janiculan. The full length of the city, that's
to say. The full social spectrum, too. Up on the Janiculan
or on Vatican Hill itself you're in rich urban villa country:
mansions with the number of bedrooms well into double
figures and a dining-room for each season of the year. The
fat-cat belt, new money mostly but lots of it: government
contractors, owners of shipping lines, guys who've cornered
the market in grain or wine or oil or whatever else the city
uses in bulk. Spanish racehorse breeders who need a little
place to hang their mantles when they do business in Rome.
Even the occasional politician who's managed to salt away
enough kickbacks to buy himself some clean country air.

At the other end of the scale there're the tenements,
crowded into the low-lying land in the bulge of the river
next to the bridges and sandwiched north and south by
the big warehouse areas. This part's one of the poorest in
Rome. Most other places, ground- and first-floor property
makes at least some claim to respectability. In Transtiber
after the rains go to bed any lower than the second storey
and you can wake up to find eels in your blanket. That's
if you wake up at all. Still, one thing the locals share with
their fat-cat colleagues up the hill is exclusivity: rich or poor,

they're Transtiberines first, Romans (in the city sense, at least) second and nowhere. For Transtibbies, Rome stops at the bridges. Cross the Sublician or the Cestian and you're in another town.

Harmodia's tenement was on a corner site next to an oil-seller's. It looked in better repair than most, although that wasn't saying much: if I'd been the oil guy I'd've had a permanent crick in my neck from checking for falling masonry.

'That's her flat up there.' Aegle pointed. 'Second floor, third window from the right. She isn't in, though.'

'Yeah? And just how do you know that, lady?' The shutters were open; it was a beautiful December morning, with not a cloud in the sky.

'She keeps birds in a cage on the ledge. When she's out she leaves them with a neighbour. That's them, in the window next door.'

Yeah; I could see the little fluffballs. Hear them, too. You'd've thought this was spring rather than close to the Winter Festival.

We went up. For a tenement it wasn't too bad; there were none of the personal smells you'd get on an ordinary city stairway, and not so much as a scribble on the walls. That's another thing about Transtiber, or maybe the same thing: poor or not, the place is more like a big village than an urban slum. The locals take a pride in their property like wouldn't happen in the Subura or Circus Valley.

Aegle knocked on the door just to make sure. There was no answer. I thought of Thalia's place, but I wasn't really worried: the girl had been alive and kicking seven days ago, at least, when she'd called in at the guildhouse, and Aegle's point about the birds showed there was nothing unusual about the housekeeping arrangements. Still, it looked like we'd made another wasted journey, which was a bugger.

'We'll ask Aquillia,' Aegle said.

'She the neighbour?'

'Yeah.' She went to the door opposite and knocked on that. 'She should know.'

At least we struck lucky this time. Aquillia turned out to be a real butterball: a little middle-aged Spanish dumpling as far from Thalia's Mother Nemesis as you can get. She ushered us in, set down the bowl of ground chickpeas she'd been making into rissoles on the table and wiped her hands on a cloth. A clean cloth, I noticed, which went with the rest of the room. Obviously Aquillia was the houseproud type.

'She's staying at her mother's for a while, dear,' she said. 'Girlfriend trouble.'

I glanced at Aegle. Uh-huh; so that explained why she'd turned down my suggestion of the rich toyboy. 'She been gone long?' I said.

'Six or seven days, sir.' Aquillia gave me an assessing look, but she hadn't hesitated. 'She said she wouldn't be back until after the Festival.'

'Uh-huh. You happen to know where the mother lives?'

'In the city, down by Pottery Mountain.' Yeah; I'd got her: way downriver, beyond the Aventine and near Ostian Road. Pottery Mountain was just that: a huge scrapheap built up over the years from the city's empty oil and wine jars, ferried there on barges and unloaded by municipal slaves. 'She runs the family pastry business in Bakers' Market.'

Six or seven days. So she'd left at the time of her visit to the guildhouse, which was two days after the first murder. It fitted. The back of my neck prickled. 'Uh, what kind of girlfriend trouble would that be, now?' I said.

Aquillia shook her head firmly. 'No, sir,' she said. 'You ask her yourself about that, if you really want to know.'

'It's okay, Aquillia,' Aegle said. 'Corvinus here's a friend. And it's important.' She glanced at me. 'Right?'

'Yeah.' The prickle was becoming a full-blown itch. 'I think it might be very important.'

Aquillia looked from one of us to the other. 'She's in some sort of trouble?'

'Nothing that's her fault,' I said. 'But she may be, yeah. I'm sorry, lady, but this once you're going to have to break your rule.'

Aquillia grunted and looked at Aegle again. Aegle nodded. 'All right,' she said. 'I'm saying nothing against Harmy, mind. She was bad news, that one, the worst. I told Harmy from the beginning: "You drop her, girl, before she drops you hard." Thank the gods she saw sense while she still could. She's a good girl, Harmy. I don't like to see her hurt.'

'You know this girlfriend's name?'

'She called herself Myrrhine.'

I caught Aegle's eye but she shook her head. 'Means nothing,' she said. 'No one I know. What did she look like, Aquillia?'

'Biggish woman; woman, not girl: mid-, maybe late twenties. Not tall but well-built. Broad shoulders, muscular arms. Face had pockmarks all over.'

Aegle was looking excited. 'She have very short nails?' she said. 'Short to the quick, like she bit them?'

'That's her.'

'Yeah. Right.' Aegle turned to me. 'You've got your flutegirl, Corvinus.'

Jupiter! I stared at her. 'You sure?'

'Hundred per cent. I noticed the nails while she was playing. We all have short nails, you need them for the pipes, but these'd been chewed. And the pockmarks explain the heavy make-up.'

Shit; the killer had been a woman after all.

'She played the flute, all right,' Aquillia was saying. 'That was how Harmy and her got friendly. They met in a cookshop in the Subura.'

'Maenalus's?' That was Aegle again.

'That's the name. Harmy says she uses it a lot while she's working.'

'It's where a lot of the girls hang out,' Aegle told me. 'Just up the road from the guildhouse.'

'Who made the running, Aquillia?' I asked. Then, when the woman's brow furrowed: 'Did Harmy start the conversation or was it this Myrrhine?'

'That I don't know, sir, but I'd guess Myrrhine. Harmy's a quiet girl. She don't talk much.'

Uh-huh. Things were beginning to take shape. 'And when did this happen?'

'The day before the kalends.' Four before the murder in other words. We'd got our killer for sure. 'Myrrhine moved in the next day. That was when the trouble started.'

'Trouble?'

'The woman was a bitch.' The word, out of character, came out quiet and deliberate. 'The morning of the third day Harmy came to me crying.'

'Yeah?' I pricked up my ears. The third day would be the day of the murder. 'She explain why?'

'She'd been bad for a while with her throat. It'd got worse, seemingly, and she'd had to give up her place playing at the rites of the Good Goddess to another girl.'

'Thalia,' Aegle said.

'That was her.' Aquillia nodded. 'Anyway, that morning she'd told Myrrhine. They had words. Myrrhine punched her, loosened a tooth and almost broke the poor girl's jaw. Then she left.'

Yeah, well: it didn't take much to see what had been going on here. Loose tooth or not, Harmodia had been lucky; Jupiter, had that girl been lucky!

'And she didn't come back,' I said. It was a statement, not a question: if the bitch had done then we'd've had another corpse on our hands. That was certain as tomorrow's sunrise.

'Not for three days.' Aquillia's lips set. 'I told Harmy: "You go to your mother's now, girl; you leave that woman to us, to me and my Aulus, we'll handle her." She wouldn't, the silly girl, not at first; you know how they are at that age, sir, they haven't the sense they were born with. Only two days later she came round with her birds to say she'd changed her mind.' Yeah; that'd be after she'd had the news at the guildhouse and tumbled to what was going on. Kid or not, Harmodia wasn't stupid. 'She was just in time, too. The woman came back that night and tried to get in but the door was locked and we had the key. I sent Aulus out, and he said the language you wouldn't believe. Aulus's been a stevedore down at the docks for fifteen years and he'd never heard the like. It took him all his time to get rid of her.' She paused. 'That Myrrhine's evil, sir. And I don't use the word lightly.'

Yeah; I'd go for that assessment. And stevedore or not, Aulus had been pretty lucky himself not to end up with his throat slashed; in view of which I wondered if the guy hadn't glossed over the details a bit where his wife's sensibilities were concerned. If so, personally I didn't blame him. 'One more question, Aquillia,' I said. 'You happen to know where this Myrrhine lived before she moved in here? Or even where she might be now?'

'No. And I don't think Harmy does either.'

Well, we'd have to see about that. Certainly our next job was to talk to the girl herself.

'Okay,' I said, getting up. 'Thanks for your help, mother. Harmy's lucky in her neighbours.'

The woman reddened. 'She's only nineteen, sir,' she said. 'Aulus and me, we had a daughter of our own once, but she died. I don't need thanks.'

'Even so, unless I'm wrong you saved the kid's life. Literally.' Out of the corner of my eye, I caught Aegle giving me a sharp look. 'Last thing. If Myrrhine calls round again, or anyone else for that matter, you play dumb, right? And tell the local Watch. Mention my name' – I gave it to her in full, plus the address – 'give the guy in charge Myrrhine's description and ask him to get his lads to keep an eye out for her, pick her up if they can.'

Aquillia frowned. 'You don't know the Watch around here, sir,' she said. 'It wouldn't do a lot of good, believe me. As for the rest of it, whatever happens across the river in this neighbourhood we look after our own. If the woman makes any more trouble there won't be a third time. My Aulus'll see to that.'

Ouch; that had the quiet sound of a promise, not a threat. Dumpling or not, the lady had a core that was pure steel. You don't mess with Transtibbies.

'Fine,' I said. 'Just take care, you and Aulus both. And let me know, right?'

'Where to now?' Aegle said as we left the building. 'Pottery Mountain?'

'Yeah.'

I was looking around carefully, but I couldn't see any sign of a homicidal fluteplayer in the vicinity. Even so

– and call it paranoia if you like – I wasn't taking any chances: if Harmodia had lived this long it was because her new girlfriend didn't know where she was, and the logical thing for Myrrhine to do in that case was to stake out the girl's flat and wait for her to come back. And if Myrrhine was watching then it made getting to Harmodia without running the risk of taking the bitch with us in the form of a tail a real bugger.

Being where we were, and going where we were going, of course, the solution was obvious. And that was unfortunate . . .

Yeah, well, there was no way round it; walking was out anyway, and, besides, Pottery Mountain was a long way off. Bite the strap, Corvinus.

I turned back to Aegle.

'Hey,' I said. 'Litters make you seasick, right?'

'Right.'

'Fine. You want the good news or the bad news?'

'Come on, Corvinus, stop messing! What is this?'

'Just answer the question, sister.'

'Okay,' she said cautiously. 'The good news.'

I grinned. 'We're not taking a litter.'

25

I hate boats. Sea boats are the absolute pits, but river boats I can live without as well. I don't think Aegle was too keen on them either, although by the time we'd cleared the tip of the island she'd gone the colour of a bad mussel and wasn't communicating much. At least the skiff or the punt or whatever the hell it was that we'd hired at the Cestian was fast, and we were travelling with the current: even in winter when the river's high the Tiber's no place to be for longer than you can help, not if you like to do your breathing through your nose. I noticed that the guy who owned the thing and was propelling us downriver breathed with his mouth. Probably an old seadog's trick, like never pissing into the wind.

He dropped us at a wharf just upstream of the mountain itself. I asked directions from a couple of guys fishing – Jupiter knew what they expected to catch, and why: this far down, below the exits for the city's drains, the water looked like soup – and we headed off for Bakers' Market.

Aegle was a better colour now, but she was still looking pretty queasy. 'You think this Myrrhine would really have killed Harmodia?' she said as we walked past the long line of state granaries: this is corn country, the main unloading stretch for the grain barges ferrying the city's life-blood from the big transports down at Ostia.

'Sure she would. That was why she came back.'

'But why kill her at all?'

'Use your head, lady!' I said. 'Harmodia was the first victim; or she should have been, rather. It was a set-up. For the mechanics of Cornelia's murder to work Myrrhine needed an in with one of the girls playing at the rites. She stakes out that cookshop near the guildhouse you mentioned . . .'

'Maenalus's.'

'Right. Once she's found her mark she makes friends with her; the idea being when the time comes she zeroes the girl and takes her place.'

'So Thalia died instead.' Aegle was looking sick, and it wasn't sea-sickness now. 'Because she was standing in.'

'Yeah. That sore throat saved the girl's life. Myrrhine'd set the scam up nicely, only it went down the tubes at the last minute when Harmodia told her she'd cancelled out. She had to cut her losses there and then and go for the replacement.'

'Why didn't she kill Harmodia anyway?'

'She couldn't run the risk of being caught. Also she'd other fish to fry. Besides, Harmodia was no threat, she didn't know nothing from nowhere. Later, after the murder, things were different, especially since Thalia was dead too. Harmodia would've been a fool if she hadn't put two and two together. If she'd still been around when Myrrhine came calling the girl would've died. Myrrhine had to kill her to shut her mouth.'

'That's horrible.'

'Sure it's horrible. The kid can just thank Aquillia and her husband that it didn't happen.'

Aegle went very quiet after that, and she looked even sicker.

We were getting close. I could see Bakers' Market up ahead; smell it, too, a combination of fresh bread, herbs and spices. The street trade in sweet and savoury buns, bread-rings and honey cake, like every other trade in Rome, is run by families who've been in the business for generations, and most of them had set up here to be near the corn supply and save on freight charges. Harmodia's mother'd belong to one of these. Jupiter knew why the girl had gone for a fluteplayer rather than sticking with the family trade, but you get these mavericks at every level. Look at me. If I'd stuck with tradition and done things the way Dad wanted me to I'd've had my broad stripe by now, maybe even made city judge, and be spending my time hobnobbing with slick bastards like Nomentanus and buttering up sleazeballs like Galba. Yeah, well; it's nice to get something right now and again.

I'd forgotten to ask Aquillia for the mother's name, but Aegle knew it anyway so we found the particular bakery no bother: a small concern in an alleyway off the main square. There was a slim, dark-haired girl inside, pulling a tray of hot bread-rings from the oven.

'Hi, Harmy,' Aegle said.

The girl almost dropped the tray. 'Aegle!'

'Yeah. How's it going?'

Harmodia didn't answer, just brushed a lock of hair out of her eyes and looked at me. I noticed she had a purple bruise on her jaw.

'Who's this?' she said.

'A friend. Marcus Corvinus. He wants to ask you a few questions.'

I thought she was going to run: her eyes slid left and right like she was deciding which way offered the better chance.

'No hassle, sister,' I said gently. 'Only we have to talk about your pal Myrrhine.'

Harmodia set the tray down on the big stone table that

took up most of the floor space. Her hands were shaking. 'She didn't tell me nothing,' she said. 'I swear she didn't.'

'It's okay.' Aegle moved forward and gave the other girl a hug. 'Corvinus knows you weren't involved.'

'Is Thalia all right?'

My spine went cold. Shit; of course, she wouldn't know. 'No,' Aegle said softly. 'Thalia's dead.'

The girl gave a sort of whimper and her hands went up to her face. Aegle led her to a bench and sat her down. I waited.

Finally she straightened. I'd expected she'd be crying, but her cheeks were dry. Well, you had to be tough to be a flutegirl. Slip of a thing or not, Harmy was no shrinking violet.

'Okay, Corvinus,' she said. 'Tell me how much you know already and I'll help all I can.'

I kept my voice neutral. 'Myrrhine used you as an in to the rites of the Good Goddess so she could murder the Vestal. She left you the morning of the rite after you'd told her you'd cancelled out. Then when you reported in at the guildhouse and found out what had happened you made the connection, panicked and ran. That's it, sister, all there is. No big deal, and all perfectly understandable.' Sure, I'd left Thalia out, but that was intentional: the kid had to have given Myrrhine Thalia's name and address, but she'd be feeling guilty enough already without me throwing in my penny's worth.

She glanced away and nodded. 'Yeah.' Her voice was dead. 'That about covers it.'

'You care to fill in some of the gaps for me, maybe?' I said. 'Like who this Myrrhine is?'

'I don't know much about her. We met at Maenalus's and got talking. She said she'd been a player once down

Capua way and asked about slots in Rome. She'd heard about the rites of the Goddess, and I told her I was playing at them.'

'Uh-huh.'

'After that we ... got quite friendly. One thing led to another and I invited her home.'

'She volunteer any other information about herself?'

'No. I asked her where she lived, but she said the let'd fallen through and she was between places. I thought maybe that was part of the come-on, but I was interested myself by then so it was a plus rather than anything else so I didn't push.'

Bugger. 'She didn't give any clues? Let anything slip? Nothing at all?'

'No.'

'Think, Harmy!' Aegle squeezed the girl's shoulders.

Harmodia frowned. 'There was one thing. It probably isn't important, though.'

'Yeah?' I said.

'Just before we left Maenalus's a fat guy came in. Really fat; a waddler. We'd split a whole jug of wine and we were at the giggly stage. I said to Myrrhine, "You ever see anything like that before?" and she said, "Sure. The Hippo at the Crocodile would make two of him."'

'"The Hippo at the Crocodile"?'

'Yeah. Just that. These words, like it was a man and a place. I asked her to tell me more but she just laughed and changed the subject.'

Well, it was something, but nothing much. The Crocodile sounded like a club — aka cathouse — but there were hundreds of these joints in the city, some with a life span shorter than a mayfly's, and it could be any- where; maybe not even in Rome. If it even mattered.

Still, I shelved it for later consideration. 'Anything else, sister?'

'We weren't together for very long. And she was more . . . physical than a talker.' Harmodia dropped her eyes. 'The only other thing that might help was the business on our way home that first day.'

'Yeah? What business was that?'

'We were going along Iugarius. There was a priest coming towards us; you know, one of those easterners from the Great Mother's Temple, they look like long-haired women. Myrrhine took one look, grabbed my arm and pulled me across to the other pavement.'

'She give any reason?'

'She didn't want to, but I insisted.' Harmodia tried a small smile. 'We were both pretty drunk, Corvinus. She'd made me bang into a guy in the road selling pendants and he wasn't too pleased. Neither was I. When we got to the other side I asked her what she thought she was doing.'

'And?'

'You want me to quote?'

'Sure. Go ahead.'

'She said, "These fuckers are the dregs. Just breathing the same air they do makes me sick to my stomach."'

Ouch. 'Odd.'

'I asked her why, but she wouldn't say anything else. And that's about all I can tell you. We did talk over the next few days, sure, but on her side it was mostly questions. A lot of them were about the rite; what went on, who'd be there, that sort of stuff. Now I know why, but then it just sounded like she was interested professionally. Any questions I asked about her and her background she just wouldn't answer. I don't even know how she came to learn the flute.'

I sighed; hell, I'd expected more, a lot more. It may not've been a completely wasted journey, but it was the next thing to it. Our phantom fluteplayer was as phantom as ever. 'Okay, lady,' I said. 'Grilling over. What are your plans now, exactly?'

She glanced back at the oven. 'I'll stay here until after the Festival at least. Maybe for good. Mum's snowed under; it's one of her busiest times, my sister's having a baby and she's had to look after the stall herself. Anyway, I'm not going back home until Myrrhine's caught.'

'Yeah. That's what I was going to recommend myself.'

She was quiet for a long time. Then she said, 'Has she been round since? Myrrhine?'

'Once.' I was cautious. 'Your neighbour's husband sent her away with a flea in her ear.'

'Good. I never want to see her again.' She shuddered, then looked at Aegle. 'I'm sorry about Thalia. Really sorry. If there's anything I can do ...'

Aegle hugged her again. 'Hey, don't worry,' she said. 'It's not your fault.'

'But it is. You know it is. It should be me that's dead.'

Smart girl. And she was quite right. What could we say? We left.

26

We had a very late lunch in a cookshop in Bakers' Square itself. Neither of us fancied the long walk into town, nor a litter, let alone another boat trip, but by the time we'd finished the sun was in its last quadrant so we walked as far as the Ostian Gate and picked up a public carriage from the rank. I took Aegle back to the Subura – she was pretty subdued all the way – and then gave the guy his orders for the Caelian.

So; what had we got? On the plus side, the murders were solved, at least as far as having the name of the killer was concerned. That was about it. Sure, I could go to Camillus tomorrow and give him Myrrhine's name and description for the various Watch divisions, but I wasn't under any illusions how effective that would be. The Watch was stretched as it was, and the city's a big place. If she knew we had her tagged, Myrrhine could disappear into somewhere like the Subura or the Aventine tenement district and the chances of finding her would be as close to zero as made no difference. I'd half thought of playing it very dirty, using Harmodia as bait to bring her back to the flat in Transtiber, but I'd put that idea aside as soon as it came: I could be wrong about Myrrhine staking the building, and anyway it was far too risky for the kid. The bitch had killed three times already, we couldn't cover all the angles and if I ended up responsible for a fourth corpse I'd never forgive myself. So no bear traps, not unless we were desperate. And we'd a way to go yet before that happened.

The Crocodile and a foreign priest. The first, although it sounded the more promising, was actually the weaker lead of the two. If it was a lead at all. Like I say, Rome's full of cathouses with weird names, like the Jumping Gaul or the Three Ones; at least the less salubrious districts are. The Crocodile could be anywhere. Or nowhere, for that matter. The best shot I could give it was to ask Lippillus. If I struck really lucky he might know of it himself, because where Rome is concerned the guy's knowledge is encyclopaedic. Failing that I could get him to put the word out round the other regions, although that was a clear second-best: Watch commanders aren't all as efficient as that shit-smart dwarf, and some of them — I suspected including the guy responsible for Transtiber — are only in the job for the backhanders they get from the local night-time entrepreneurs. They would either not know, not care or ask for a non-returnable upfront contribution to the widows' and orphans' fund. Probably all three.

The priest angle was a far better bet. Sure, to kill a Vestal in the first place argued that our pal Myrrhine didn't have the normal inbuilt horror of divine retribution, and she might just turn out to be a nut with a pathological hatred of anything to do with religion, but I doubted it: that you don't get all that often, especially with people of Myrrhine's class. On the other hand, the incident had happened. So why?

The obvious explanation was that she was afraid of being recognised.

The fact that the guy was a priest of the Great Mother made the theory even more attractive. Cybele's been in Rome a long time — she was invited in from Asia by the state two hundred years back to help tip the divine scales against Hannibal — but the authorities have always handled her with kid gloves. Sensible. Religions from the mystic east and Romans — at least the pukkah variety — are like oil and water, they don't mix, and whatever theological street-cred it has any cult that appeals primarily to women, involves orgiastic rites and asks its priests to dress up in flowing robes and lop their own wollocks off while chewing suspect substances isn't going to go down a bomb with the staid city fathers. As a result, Cybele has only ever had one temple in Rome, on the Palatine where it's nice and visible, and her priests are strictly non-citizen: Asiatics, not even Greeks. If Myrrhine had been a devotee at some time — and being slave- or freedwoman-class made that a fair possibility — then that meant the Palatine set-up was the only game in town: she'd know them and, more important for my purposes, they would know her. QED.

It was too late to go calling today, but Cybele's temple was my logical next step.

I just made dinner. Sure, with the Festival — and the omelette pan — on the horizon Meton wasn't likely to throw a serious wobbler, but it was as well not to tempt fate. Not that I was too hungry: the cookshop I'd taken Aegle to was offering lung stew with garlic, which you don't see that often, and I'd pigged out. Still, I could pick, and with Meton it was being there on time that counted.

Perilla was already in the dining-room.

'Hi, lady.' I kissed her and settled down on the couch. 'Good day?'

'Not bad, Marcus. How was your flutegirl?'

'Which one?' Bathyllus was serving the hors-d'oeuvres. He gave me a sniff in passing and I grinned. 'There're three of them now.'

'Three?'

'Sure. Aegle, Harmodia – the kid whose place Thalia took – and the killer.'

Perilla set down her cup of fruit juice. 'I thought the killer was a man,' she said.

'That was yesterday, lady. There've been developments.'

'Corvinus, unlikely as it is that you're suggesting some form of outré hermaphrodism at work that is how it sounds. Now perhaps you'd like to explain a little more clearly.'

I explained.

'You mean the rites weren't profaned after all?' she said when I'd finished. 'You've had Torquata repeat them for no reason?'

'Ah.' Shit, I hadn't thought of that aspect. 'Well, anyone can make a mistake.'

'Perhaps. But you don't know Junia Torquata, dear. When she finds out she will kill you. Probably very slowly. I doubt if Nomentanus will be too happy either.'

Yeah, well; that guy's unhappiness I could live with. I snitched an olive from Bathyllus's passing tray. 'Forget the rites, Perilla. As far as the murders are concerned we're getting there. The next stop's Cybele's temple.' I told her Harmodia's priest story.

'It certainly makes sense.' Perilla selected a pickled radish from the bowl on the table. 'Especially if the woman is a fluteplayer. The cult of Cybele does tend to use its own devotees for the ceremonies rather than professionals.'

'Yeah?' I poured myself some wine. 'Is that so, now?'

'So I'm told, at any rate. You've still no idea who could be behind the original murder?'

'Uh-uh.' I shook my head; that was the real bugger. The identity of the killer was one thing, but we still didn't have so much as a smell of the person responsible. Let alone a motive. 'He – or she – had to have some connection with Myrrhine to make it happen. Also, of course, they had to feel threatened in some way.'

'Unless it was a simple revenge killing. Perhaps your Myrrhine had a personal grudge against Cornelia, or even Vestals in general. After all, the second murder – Thalia's – was ... I suppose you might call it an operational one, to facilitate the first. Why should there be anyone else involved at all?'

'No, that won't wash, Perilla.' I reached for another olive. 'You're forgetting young Lepidus. He felt he was responsible for Cornelia's death. He must've had some reason to think that. Besides, how would Myrrhine have known the layout of the Galba place in advance? And she had to, to make the whole thing work.'

'I thought you said that she'd questioned your other flutegirl – Harmodia, was it? – about the details of the rites? Including, presumably, the venue itself?'

'Sure. But the Galba house was only this year's venue. It changes every year, with the consul. Or the consul's wife, rather.'

'Had Harmodia been there before? On another occasion? Did you ask her that?'

'Uh ... no.' Hell; this was slipping away from me here. Whether I liked it or not, the lady had a point.

'As for Lepidus, what he thought and what the reality of the situation was could well be two different things. He was obviously not the most balanced of young men. He could have been fantasising.'

'Yeah? And what about Niobe, then? Sure, we've cleared the matter of the note up, but her death was no fantasy.'

'Hmm.' Perilla frowned. 'Yes, well, I suppose that does

present a difficulty. It couldn't have been coincidence, could it? An unconnected killing?'

'Come on, lady!'

'Of course, Niobe was Cornelia's slave. The grudge could extend to her.'

I laughed. Say what you will, Perilla's a fighter. 'You believe that?' I said.

Perilla ducked her head. 'No. Perhaps not. But I do think that you're looking for needless complications. Catching the actual murderer would be success enough. I'm sure Camillus would agree, for one.'

Yeah; that was certainly true. The deputy chief priest had never liked my idea that one of the upper classes was involved. He'd go for Perilla's theory with open arms, Niobe or not. 'Okay,' I said. 'I've had a hard day. Truce; sleuthing over for the evening.' I shelled an egg and dipped it in the fish pickle. 'So tell me: what's been happening on the domestic front?'

'Gaius Secundus and his wife sent round to say they'd be delighted to come for dinner. I've suggested the day after tomorrow.'

'Fine. Wear your biggest earrings.'

She stared at me. '*What?*'

'Just do it, lady. Furia Gemella will, and I don't want you outgunned. You told Meton?'

'Of course. He was delighted. He suggested wild boar with myrtle and cumin. And perhaps a duck stuffed with dried plums and apricots.'

'Great.' We didn't give dinner parties all that often – that was one of Meton's pet grouses – but when we did the guy pulled out all the stops. And his fruit-stuffed duck was a minor culinary miracle. 'Anything else in train?'

'The clock. It's been making peculiar noises all day.'

Oh, hell. 'What kind of noises?'

'Digestive.'

Gods! That thing was more trouble than Armenia! 'Perilla,' I said, 'search your soul, lady. Just how much do you really want a flatulent superintelligent sundial?'

'It isn't a sundial, Marcus, it's a clepsydra.'

'Whatever.'

'And it isn't intelligent.'

'You want to bet? That bastard's smart. Burping's just the next stage in its campaign of psychological intimidation. Get rid of it now or we'll both regret it.'

'Oh, Marcus!'

'Believe me.'

There was a squeaking noise; not the clock, Bathyllus with the main course. I thought it might be the little guy's hernia appliance, but it was the trolley wheels. Another of these clever-clever Greek gizmos: if Jupiter had wanted us to use trolleys he wouldn't've given us the tray. Ah, well; you couldn't stop progress. At least we hadn't got as far as a revolving ceiling that buried you in rose petals or squirted you with perfume yet, although no doubt some over-sophisticated bugger would get round to inventing that sooner or later.

'Dinner is served, sir,' Bathyllus said. 'Enjoy your meal.'

I lifted the dish covers: poached bluegill with rosemary and mint, pork liver with bacon slices and leeks in a raisin sauce. Yeah, well; life could be a lot worse. Maybe I was hungry after all.

Mind you, we should've been having bulls' testicles in cinnamon and nutmeg. With a visit to Cybele's temple in prospect, that might've been more appropriate.

27

The Temple of Cybele's pretty impressive, if you like the fancy ornate Graeco-Asian style, which I don't. Mind you, when it comes to temples I'm not exactly turned on by the grand Etrusco-Roman style or the harsh clean-cut simplicity of Doric, either. If you want an architectural grand tour then tough. As far as I'm concerned a temple is a temple is a temple. And incense gets right up my nose.

I grabbed a passing acolyte in the porch and sent him scurrying for the duty priest. That turned out to be a fat Syrian with more rings on his fingers and bells on his toes than you can shake a stick at and hair smeared with unguent that smelled like a goat with serious personal hygiene problems. More ungulant than unguent, in other words. I liked the saffron robes, though; very fetching.

'Yes, sir?' he said. 'How can I help you?' Polite, for an acolyte.

I gave him my name. 'I'm looking for a woman called Myrrhine, pal,' I said.

He didn't exactly clap hand to forehead and stagger backwards, but the little beady eyes buried in the rolls of flesh blinked.

'Myrrhine?' he said.

'Yeah. You know her?'

He fizzed. 'I think you'd better talk to the archigallus, sir,' he said at last.

Uh-huh; this sounded promising. The name had definitely

registered. And the chief priest himself, eh? Incidentally, I've always thought the title was on the unfortunate side, given these guys' physical condition; at least if you took the second bit of the word as Latin, not Greek. Under the circumstances 'First Cock' has a kind of ironic ring to it.

He took me by the shoulder – it was like being mugged by a bolster – and led me into the temple proper. I'd never been inside the place before, naturally, but I had to admit I was impressed. The goddess at the far end was forty feet high if she was an inch, seated on a throne with two lions flanking her, and the three pairs of jewelled eyes followed us all the way, glinting through a fug of incense that had me coughing. The fat guy gave her a perfunctory bow and ducked through a curtained door just short of the Holy of Holies.

'If you'll wait here, sir, I'll see if the Lord Attis is free to receive you.'

'Uh, yeah; yeah, you do that,' I said. Attis; the Living God on Earth. Jupiter, these guys were something else! The hairs on the back of my neck prickled. It wasn't often I got to talk to a real live god, even if he was self-appointed.

God or not, he kept a pretty seedy antechamber. There were a couple of pegs with robes hanging on them and a pile of dirty dishes on a table in the corner. Despite the incense fumes that drifted in from the temple proper next door the place smelled of old socks. I kicked my heels in silence for a good five minutes, trying not to breathe too deeply.

The priest came padding back.

'The lord will see you now,' he said. 'Follow me.'

I'd expected a study like Camillus's, but I was shown into a room that could've doubled as a whore's boudoir. Given that the whore had a thing about eastern art. Jupiter knew where they'd collected all this stuff from, but it was as full of overblown furniture and recherché knick-knacks as a Saepta curio shop.

The archigallus was lying on a damasked couch. If I'd thought the first guy was fat this one looked like a beached whale. The priesthood of Cybele obviously liked their home-grown divinities on the large side. Maybe the appointments went by weight.

'Valerius Corvinus.' He held out a plump hand. I took it. No bones; it was like holding a bag full of warm porridge. Scented warm porridge. 'Sit down, please. I'm told you were asking about Myrrhine.'

'Yeah.' I pulled up a stool ornamented with gilded cats.

'May I know why?' The voice was like warm porridge too.

'I think she may have killed a few people,' I said. 'Including a Vestal.'

'Ah.' No surprise; not a whisker. It could've been a by-product of omniscience, mind you. 'Yes. Of course. I have heard about that. Dreadful; simply dreadful.'

'She's one of your devotees?'

'Was,' he said quickly; too quickly. 'We haven't seen Myrrhine in the temple for quite some time.'

'Uh-huh. But you know who she is?' That got me a long stare that had nothing of the divine *ataraxia* in it. I was beginning to feel slightly pissed off. 'Come on, lord! I mention her name to a guy at the door and he blanches to his toenails and brings me straight here, no questions asked. How many of your flock merit the full five-star treatment of an introduction to the boss?'

He smiled. 'Very few. Nor does the archigallus know every woman who comes to worship the Mother by name. You're quite right, Valerius Corvinus; I know exactly who Myrrhine is. However as you'll see an enquiry about her does demand a certain amount of ... indulgence on your part. And a certain degree of reticence on mine.'

'Okay.' I folded my arms. 'Consider yourself indulged, lord. So who is she?'

He shifted his bulk on the couch. The woodwork creaked. 'She is — was — the slave of a gentleman named Gaius Considius Proculus. I can't remember his address offhand, but he lives, I think, on the Pincian near the Flaminian Gate. Not that that will help you much because she's no longer there. Of her current whereabouts you know as much as I do. Or as he does.'

'He freed her?'

'Not exactly.' I was still getting that considering look. 'Myrrhine is a Thracian, from Perinthus on the Propontis. She was brought up as a devotee of Bendis who has, as you're no doubt aware, close similarities to our own Lady Cybele. Her parents sold her to a slave merchant as a very young child and she was bought by Proculus who was then attached to the governor's staff in Athens. Since she showed a certain aptitude for music, he had her trained as a flutegirl.'

Full-scale biographies I could do without. 'Could we get to the point, please, sir?'

'Indulgence, Corvinus.' He hadn't raised his voice. 'This is all relevant. You asked; let me answer.'

Fair comment. I said nothing.

'When Proculus returned to Rome he brought the girl with him. At a certain stage — she was, I think, sixteen at the time — she became, with her master's permission, one of our devotees. Eventually, one of our most fervent devotees. Her fluteplaying skills made her a most welcome addition to our ranks, and she performed regularly in the rites of the Megalensia. The temple — we — became her second family, perhaps her first. This is important.'

'Uh-huh. So what went wrong?'

I might as well not have spoken; the guy looked straight through me. Oh, yeah; indulgence.

'Twelve years passed. I mean, from the beginning. During that time the girl – or woman, now, rather – had changed, become more withdrawn.' He hesitated. 'It is not our policy, Valerius Corvinus, to interfere between master and slave. Although the cult is long-established and widespread in Rome, we are still tolerated rather than respected. We cannot – dare not – take sides. You must know that slaves, female slaves especially, are required to perform certain services for their masters which may be repugnant to us but are none of our concern.'

Yeah; I was beginning to get his drift. 'You mean Proculus raped her.'

'You do not "rape" a slave,' the archigallus said gently. 'Slaves, according to your Roman law, are property, not people.' Ouch; he was right, though. And I knew guys who thought less of their butlers than their fruit dishes. 'Let us say he used her sexually. Had been using her, over a considerable period, perhaps since he first acquired her. There was, I repeat, nothing we could do. He was quite within his rights. That brings us up to last year. Myrrhine ran away. After, I'm afraid, having stabbed Proculus's head slave and abstracted certain valuable items of silverware.'

Jupiter! I sat back. We weren't talking petty here: under the law runaway slaves get pretty short shrift: when a society's built on slavery you can't afford just to shrug and go out for a replacement, or it would be happening all the time. Runaways who use violence and take a slice of the master's property with them are right beyond the pale. Forget branding on the face and a spell at the treadmill; all they can expect if they're caught – and they usually are, eventually — is to be nailed to a plank and hung up for the crows.

'She came to us demanding sanctuary. Not asking, note, demanding, as a right. Of course we had to refuse. She was held while the authorities were contacted; or at least an attempt was made to hold her.' Again, the archigallus hesitated. 'She became abusive. Finally she drew a knife and fatally wounded two of our acolytes. In the temple itself, if you can believe that. She escaped as a consequence, and we haven't seen her since.'

I sat back. Shit. No wonder the guy remembered her. And no wonder she'd pulled Harmodia across the street when she'd seen a priest of Cybele coming towards her. An exit like that wouldn't be forgotten easy.

'Where did she get the knife?' I said.

'She always carried one. She had a fascination with knives, even as a girl.'

Yeah, that figured. I'd bet she looked after them, too. Harmodia hadn't mentioned that aspect of things, but maybe their acquaintance had been too short or the bitch hadn't wanted to arouse her suspicions. Waking up to see your partner carefully stropping a knife blade is enough to give anyone second thoughts about continuing a relationship. 'And she didn't get in touch again?'

'No. We informed the Religious Officer' — that would be one of the Board of Fifteen responsible for overseeing foreign cults — 'and buried our dead. I hadn't thought about Myrrhine since, until Hermodotus told me you were asking for her.'

Well, I'd got my information, and it all fitted. We weren't any closer to motive, though; or associates. 'She have any contact with the dead Vestal at all? Cornelia?' I asked.

'Not that I'm aware of. And it's most unlikely.'

'What about other Romans? Members of the upper classes, I mean?'

The archigallus smiled. 'I told you, Corvinus, and in any case you must know yourself: our cult is not one that is attractive to the Roman establishment, certainly not to the aristocracy. Again I have to say no.'

Bugger; well, that was that. I stood up. 'Thank you for giving me your time, archigallus.'

'You're very welcome. I'm sorry about Myrrhine. She was, as I said, a valuable member of the cult; perhaps, had circumstances been otherwise, she might even eventually have become a priestess, although of course not here in Rome.'

Jupiter! Still, where these whacky mystery cults were concerned maybe a fascination with sharp instruments and a readiness to carve up anyone who got in your way wasn't an impediment to a religious career. And who was I to judge?

I left.

28

It was still only mid-morning when I left the Temple of Cybele, and a lovely day for walking. I came down off the Palatine into the Septimontium and headed towards the Public Ponds district. If I was lucky I'd catch Lippillus at the Watch House; maybe, if he wasn't too busy, split a lunch-time jug. I'd got Thalia's murderer for him, sure, and he'd want the name, at least; but I could also pick his brains about the Crocodile. If we could find that, then maybe – just maybe – we might find the woman herself. It was worth a try, anyway.

The gods were smiling: he was in, beavering his way through a small mountain of paperwork. From what I could see of him behind it he didn't look too happy.

'Hey, Lippillus.' I sat down on the bench next to his desk. 'How's it going?'

His head came up. Unhappy was right: the guy had that frayed-at-the-edges look that suggested late nights, early mornings and not much free time in between. That made sense: being a Watch commander these report-conscious days is no joke, and if you liked to stay personally at the investigative cutting edge, which Lippillus did, it meant holding down what amounted to two jobs.

'Oh, hi, Corvinus.' He tossed a wax tablet on top of the pile and picked up another. 'Sorry, I've been meaning to get in touch. No luck on your flutegirl. I've had one of my best men knocking on every door of the tenement, but no one saw nothing, Watchman. Par for the course.'

'The killer's name was Myrrhine. She's a Thracian. Runaway slave, belonged to a guy called Considius Proculus.'

He stared at me. 'You found her?'

'No. Not the lady herself. But I've got a description. Maybe some sort of a lead as well.'

'Yeah?' He grinned. It took years off him. 'That's great! Any time you want a job with the Watch, pal, just ask. What kind of lead?'

'You happen to've heard of somewhere called the Croco-dile?'

'The Hippo's place? Sure.'

It was my turn to stare. 'You know it?'

'I should do. My lads are round there breaking up brawls three, four times a month regular. Or picking up the pieces, rather. It's a cathouse this side of the Raudusculan Gate, specialises in the rougher end of the market. We'd've closed it down long ago, but the punters would just move somewhere else and give us the same headaches, and at least the Hippo cooperates.'

The Raudusculan was where the Ostian Road passed through the old city wall, in the valley between the two main peaks of the Aventine, west of the Remuria. Right on the edge of Lippillus's patch, in other words. I'd been lucky right enough.

'Can you take me there?' I said.

That got me another grin. 'Corvinus, believe me, if it meant getting away from these bloody reports I'd take you all the way to Capua. You've got it. That where you think this Myrrhine hangs out?'

'Could be. She mentioned the name, that's all.'

'Fine.' He paused. 'You want a couple of the lads as well? For back-up?'

I hadn't thought of that, but it might be an idea: if

we did find Myrrhine then I didn't fancy taking her on single-handed, even with Lippillus there. Like Aquillia had said, that bitch was evil, and if she was as handy with a knife and as ready to use it as past events suggested then now was no time for heroics. 'Yeah,' I said. 'If they're free.'

'Fair enough.' He got up and went to the door. 'Hey, Faustus! Chilo! In here a minute!'

The two guys who had been propping up the outside desk when I'd arrived shooting the breeze with the clerk looked up and lumbered over. Yeah; that would just about do it where back-up was concerned. Either one of them could've punched out a rhino.

Lippillus made the introductions and explained the situation – standing, he came up to about the shorter guy's chest – and we set off for the Crocodile.

The place was a real dive, I could see that from the outside: a ramshackle two-storey building in a rubbish-strewn street of tenements backing on to the old wall itself. Some hack with more imagination than talent had painted the eponymous reptile on the wall beside the door, but the paint had flaked away over time until even the least critical of art lovers – who probably didn't feature much anyway as a class among the club's clientèle – wouldn't've recognised it for what it was unless they'd known in advance. Still, it showed we were dealing with an old-established firm here. That was nice; longevity always inspires confidence.

Lippillus pushed open the door and we went in. There were three customers drinking at the counter, but they took one look at us and suddenly decided they had pressing business elsewhere. I noticed they gave Faustus and Chilo a wide berth, walking very carefully like they were tiptoeing on eggs. I didn't blame them.

That left a trio of hard-eyed girls, obviously employees taking an early lunch break, and behind the bar the fattest guy I'd ever seen who just had to be the Hippo.

'Hi, Hippo,' Lippillus said. He hadn't even glanced at the punters while they made their exit. 'How are things?'

The fat guy smiled. Or at least rearranged the mounds of flab that made up his face. Jupiter, he was gross: three hundred pounds, at least, and every ounce of it blubber. 'Watch Commander!' he said. 'A delight to see you! A jug of our best wine, a few pieces of cheese and an olive or two. On the house, of course.'

Lippillus looked at me. I shrugged, he nodded and we went up to the counter with the two squaddies in close attendance.

The Hippo was filling a jug from a flask. He glanced over his shoulder at me. 'We don't see many purple-stripers in this part of the Aventine, sir,' he said. 'If you don't mind my saying so.'

'This is Marcus Valerius Corvinus, Hippo.' Lippillus took four cups from the pile on the counter, inspected them, swapped one for a fifth and set them out. 'He's a good friend of mine and he wants to ask you some questions.'

'Any friend of yours is always most welcome at the Crocodile, Commander. You know that.' The fat guy poured for us then cut a huge wedge from the cheese on the bar counter. I noticed, though, that the phoney bonhomie had gone up a notch, if that was possible: 'questions' was obviously a word that made our cheery pal nervous.

I tasted the wine. Considering the place, I'd been expecting rotgut, but it wasn't bad. Not top-of-the-range stuff, sure, nor even second — either would've been pushing things — but good for its class. Very good. 'Corfinian?' I said.

The Hippo was ladling olives. He straightened and gave

me a look that could've been respect but was probably wind. 'Close, sir,' he said. 'Very close indeed. It's from Sulmo. My cousin's farm.'

'Nice.'

He put the plates of cheese and olives in front of us. I tried a bit of the cheese, and it wasn't bad, either. Just goes to show, you can't trust first impressions. I could get to like this place.

Maybe it was telepathy. The girls along the bar had been giving me the eye over their bread and pickles since we'd come in. Now one of them – a stacked Mauretanian with shoulders that could've been smoothed ebony – called out, 'Hey! Purple-striper!'

I turned. 'Yeah?'

The Hippo was glaring at her but the other girls were sniggering.

'You want some dessert after that, you just say, okay? Real genuine purple-stripe dessert.'

'Maybe another time,' I said. 'I've got dinner to think of.'

Trite, sure, but I'd got her range. The girl laughed.

'Just remember I've had practice and I'm a good cook,' she said. 'The best.'

'Cut it out, Phoebe!' the Hippo snapped. The sniggering stopped like magic and the girls got suddenly interested in their plates. A mound of blubber the guy might be, but he clearly had the edge on his staff.

I turned away. Okay, fun over, time for business. 'You know a woman called Myrrhine, Hippo?' I said.

It was like throwing a stone into a pool: I could feel the silence spreading. If the girls had been quiet before they were like mice now. Mice with large ears. You could've heard a pickle drop.

'Maybe,' the Hippo said finally.

'Come on.' Lippillus hadn't so much as looked up from his wine and his voice was quiet, but the fat guy flinched.

'Yeah. Yeah, okay, I know Myrrhine,' he said quickly. He picked up a cloth and ran it over the counter, just to show how calm he wasn't. 'So?'

'Don't get smart, Hippo,' Lippillus murmured. 'Please. Now really is not the time.'

The Hippo was beginning to sweat; not a pleasant sight. 'That lady's bad news, Commander,' he said. 'Crispa here'll tell you.'

The girl on the far end of the trio shook her long hair away from her face — if she was a natural blonde I'd eat my sandals — and lifted her top lip. Two front teeth were missing. 'That was Myrrhine did that,' she said. 'The woman's a maniac.'

'She was only in here a couple of times.' The Hippo put the cloth down. 'First with a girl we don't have any more, but there was no problem. The second was with Crispa.'

'She wanted me to—' Crispa explained in detail just exactly what Myrrhine's requirements had been. Big Faustus, drinking quietly at the other end of the counter, choked on his wine. 'I told her to fuck off, I wasn't doing anything like that, not for nobody. So she hit me.'

'We got her out of the room,' the Hippo said. 'Then she pulled a knife. Luckily we'd a couple of regulars in here drinking. I had them throw her out and told her not to come back.'

'When was this?' I asked.

'Two months ago, maybe three.'

Bugger. 'And you haven't seen her since, right?'

The Hippo chuckled. It was like seeing a mound of jelly hit by an earthquake.

'Sure I've seen her,' he said. 'Practically every day. She has a room in one of the tenements up the road.'

29

'I want her alive, okay?' I said. 'That isn't negotiable.'

Chilo, the smaller of the two squaddies – meaning he was only half a head taller than me and twice the width – hefted his watchman's club. 'Sure,' he said. 'No problems.'

'Don't get cocky.' Lippillus was looking across the street at the tenement building the Hippo had directed us to. 'She's armed, she's dangerous and woman or not she's no pushover. Only just remember we end up with a stiff and you two'll be eligible for the Great Mother's priesthood yourselves. Right?'

Chilo grinned. 'Right, Commander,' he said.

'I'm not joking, Watchman.'

The grin disappeared. The other guy, Faustus, nodded quickly. 'Got you, sir,' he said.

'Fine.' Lippillus turned to me. 'Okay, Corvinus. She's your find. You have the shout. How do you want to play it?'

I'd been wondering that myself. We knew the flat number – top floor, first door on the left – but not whether the lady was in or out. Or, if she was in, if she'd spotted us already from the window. There were too many dodgy factors to risk playing smart.

'We go up and knock,' I said. 'Then we take it from there and play it as it comes.'

Lippillus grinned. 'Good plan, Scipio,' he said.

I gave him the finger. 'Right. Let's go.'

It was the usual seedy tenement; in fact, seedier than

most since the tenants didn't seem even to have the energy to lug their garbage out into the street before they dumped it, so the smell on the staircase was something else. We got up to the top floor with no more excitement than a brush with a stray dog scavenging among the bones and vegetable peelings, and Faustus banged on the door. No answer. Three more bangs and the door opposite opened. A wizened old guy put his head out. If I'd seen him on the stairs I would've taken him for a less savoury piece of the garbage.

'What . . . ?' he said.

Which was as far as he got before Chilo snarled 'Watch!' at him and he ducked back in.

I reached past Faustus and tried the handle. Locked. So. The lady was out.

'Okay,' I said to Lippillus. 'You're the expert here, pal. What do we do now? Go down again and hang around till she gets back?'

But Lippillus was fumbling in his belt-pouch. He brought out a lock-pick. About five seconds later the door was open.

'Uh-uh,' he said. 'We wait for her in comfort. Except for Faustus.'

I was happy to go along: I might have the shout, but Lippillus and the other guys obviously knew what they were doing and they'd done it before. Faustus went downstairs to keep watch across the street. If Myrrhine showed up he'd give us a wave when she was safely inside the building then follow her up to cut off the only possible escape route.

The operative word was *if*. I hoped that the woman wasn't staking out Harmodia's flat after all, because if she was then we were in for a hell of a long wait.

Lippillus relocked the door with his pick while I took a look round. Which didn't involve much more than what the phrase literally means. As far as Lippillus's waiting in comfort went, you could forget it. There was only the one room, and that was standard for an under-the-tiles let in this part of town, i.e. poky as hell, cold as an Aventine landlord's heart and with about as many amenities as a rabbit hutch minus the straw. It was neat, though: not a speck of dust. A houseproud killer, right? The thin mattress on the floor had a clean blanket lying on top, carefully folded, and beside the window was an old clothes chest that may've been a prayer away from kindling but actually showed signs of having been polished. That was all. Except, of course, for the lady's collection of knives.

They lay on top of the chest, five of them with space for a sixth, arranged in a tidy row from big to small along with a well-used whetstone, a cup of water and a leather strop. I picked one up and tested it with my thumb. Cheap quality, with a plain wood and leather grip like the knife that'd killed Cornelia; only, like the murder weapon, it had an edge you could've split a hair on.

The missing sixth was the one we'd have to worry about.

'Nice hobby.' Lippillus was standing behind me.

'Yeah.' I put the knife down. 'Well, that puts the lid on it. If there was any doubt, which there wasn't. She's our killer.'

Chilo had settled his big shoulders against the wall that formed an angle with the window, just far enough back to keep an eye on the street below without being seen himself. The top of his head brushed the beam that supported the tiles above us. He looked like he could stand there for ever. I just hoped he wouldn't have to.

'Okay, Marcus.' Lippillus sat down on the mattress with his back to the wall. 'While we're waiting for your girlfriend to show you can tell me just what the hell's going on. After that, we're down to swapping jokes.'

It was more than halfway through the afternoon before Chilo, still watching, made a quick sideways movement with his hand and we knew we were in business.

The party walls in these places are pretty thin: we could hear the sound of footsteps coming up the stairs clearly, long before the rattle of the key in the lock. In that room, there was nowhere to hide; we'd just have to rely on the element of surprise. Chilo flattened himself against the wall next to the door jamb on the opening side while Lippillus and me took the front, in full view. With any luck, Myrrhine would be so busy worrying about us that she wouldn't see the guy who really mattered until it was too late.

There was a pause, a long one. Then the door opened slowly.

Too slowly.

Maybe it was a sixth sense; it had to be, because I'd take my oath that none of the three of us had so much as breathed with the bitch outside, let alone made any kind of noise. Whatever the reason, when Chilo went for her round the jamb she stepped back quickly like she was expecting it and punched him once, hard, in the chest. He gave a sort of grunt, dropped his club and slipped to his knees. I could see the woman's hand clearly now, the one she'd punched him with, and it had something that wasn't a key in it. There was blood there, too. Shit.

I yelled and jumped for her, but Chilo was in the way, sprawled across the threshold, and my foot caught against his leg, spinning me round. The woman drew her hand back and Lippillus shouted a warning, but there wasn't a lot I could do except grab for her knife arm and hope my fingers connected.

I missed and went sprawling on my back with Myrrhine standing over me.

Footsteps hammered on the stairs. She paused, glanced sideways, then at Lippillus, and her eyes widened. I swear she shrugged. Reversing the knife, she put the point beneath her own throat and shoved . . .

Suddenly there was blood everywhere.

Faustus and Lippillus got to her at the same moment, pinning her against the door, but I could see she was a dead weight already and the knife-hilt, with no hand to support it now and no blade visible, was sticking out from under her chin. Jupiter, that thing had been sharp! I pulled myself to my feet and slumped against the jamb.

'You okay, Corvinus?' Lippillus said over his shoulder.

'Yeah.' All I felt was sick. That and grateful that Myrrhine hadn't had time for herself and me both. 'Check up on Chilo.'

Lippillus left Faustus holding the body and bent over the fallen Watchman. He was down there for a long time before he shook his head.

Well, I'd got my fourth corpse after all. And a complimentary fifth. The bitch had gone out with a bang.

She'd taken what she knew with her, too.

30

I left Lippillus to clear up the mess. 'Mess' was what it was: another guy dead, Myrrhine dead and the case shot to hell. Not that it was anyone's fault, we couldn't've played it any more carefully than we did, but that only made things worse. I still felt guilty; about Chilo, especially. The guy had a wife and a young son. I asked.

I'd nowhere else to go now, either: with no Myrrhine to question, the trail to whoever was backing her – if anyone was – wasn't just cold, it didn't exist. Any theories I might have had were either disproved or didn't admit of proof one way or the other. I didn't even have the ghost of a suspect any more, not one with any sort of credible motive anyway, real or theoretical. In short, we were five-star, no-nonsense, totally and irrevocably buggered.

I don't think I've ever felt so miserable.

I broke the bad news to Perilla and we had a quiet postmortem dinner while she tried to cheer me up. At the dessert stage Bathyllus made some sniffy comment about cathouses and I snarled at him, really snarled, which is something I never do: baiting the little guy is one thing, but he and I both know it's a game and we're happy just to score points off each other with no real blood spilled on either side. He apologised, which is a thing *he* never does, and that made me feel worse.

The next morning I went round to Camillus's to give

him what might well amount to the final update, but he was out of Rome on business and wouldn't be back for two days. So much for reporting in; Jupiter, I even missed when I was throwing in the sponge! I spent the afternoon getting quietly stewed in one of my favourite wineshops off Market Square, racking my brains – or what passed for them – trying to think of some avenue I hadn't been down or some alley that I'd ignored. There weren't any. Nothing, zero, zilch all the way; what you saw was what you'd got.

The day was as far gone as I was before I called quits and staggered off home pissed as a newt. Or at least half pissed as a half newt ...

Perilla was in the atrium, and furious. Oddly enough, she was furious wearing her best mantle and an uncustomary pair of earrings. That ought to have given me a hint, but it didn't.

'Corvinus, where on earth have you been?' she snapped. 'Secundus and Furia Gemella will be here in half an hour!'

I goggled at her. Then the penny dropped. Shit! The dinner party! I'd forgotten about it completely! 'Uh, yeah,' I said. 'Yeah, right ...'

Bathyllus materialised from nowhere, like he does. 'The baths are hot, sir,' he said. 'Perhaps you'd care to bathe while I lay out a fresh tunic and mantle?' Stiff as hell; the little guy hadn't got over his chewing yet. But at least he was talking to me. And being helpful.

'Yeah, okay, Bathyllus,' I said. 'Great. Thanks, sunshine.'

'Don't mention it, sir.'

I padded off towards the bath suite, shaking my head to clear it. The walk from Market Square to the Caelian had used up some of the wine, sure, but I was still a good jug short of cold sober; no way to start a dinner party, especially not with Gaius Secundus who could sink them as fast as I could. And not with that wife of his, either, for different reasons: I'd only met Furia Gemella once, and that years ago for about two minutes, but even on that short acquaintance I'd guess the lady wouldn't take kindly to her host being boneless before the evening got started.

The bath worked wonders, especially the cold plunge at the end, and by the time I was dried off and freshly mantled I could've said 'Livillan Lanuvium' with the best of them. I was feeling a lot brighter, too. Dinner parties – Mother's excepted, of course – I enjoy.

Secundus and his wife had already arrived. Perilla had got them into the dining-room and settled with their pre-dinner drinks, and Bathyllus had served the less complicated hors d'oeuvres.

'Hey, Gaius,' I said. 'I'm sorry I'm late. How's the boy?'

I saw Furia Gemella wince. She was still the same curvy little half-pint I remembered, although the curves had filled out drastically over the years and she'd added an extra chin. I'd been right about the earrings, too. The archigallus could've used the ones she was wearing for rattles.

'You've met Gemella, Marcus, haven't you?' Secundus said.

'Yeah.' I stretched out beside Perilla: there being only the four of us we were only using two of the couches. It was cosier that way, anyway. 'Last time I saw her she was carrying a bowl of soup.'

That got me a glare from the lady, although Secundus grinned. There was a long and painful silence. Ouch; we were off to a bad start here. Maybe I wasn't going to enjoy this particular dinner party after all.

Bathyllus came round with the top-ups and filled my cup. We were having Falernian: Secundus liked a good wine, and

I had the impression Furia Gemella's tastes would run to the traditional.

Well, maybe not altogether. 'That is a simply *marvellous* clepsydra you have in the atrium, Perilla dear,' she said brightly. 'Is it from Amphytrio's?'

'That's right.' Perilla gave her a smile; her company smile, I noticed. Perilla was finding Furia Gemella wearing too. 'We've only had it since the beginning of the month but it's become almost one of the family already. Hasn't it, Marcus?'

Like the fucking family dog that pisses all over the furniture, I thought, but I didn't say anything, just nodded.

'Really? How nice!' Gemella beamed. 'I've been trying to persuade Gaius to buy us one for ages. They are so chic! And of course beautifully made. I don't know why every house doesn't have one. I love the little titan with the hammer, don't you?'

Oh, Jupiter! And we were in for at least three hours of this! I sighed and signalled to Bathyllus to bring on the starters proper.

At least Meton had done us proud: besides the usual eggs, olives, raw vegetables and fish pickle dip we'd got chicken-liver and onion patties, small Lucanian sausages, seafood dumplings and truffles in a coriander wine sauce. Furia Gemella's eyes lit up. Yeah; I could see where these curves had gone now. And where the double chin came from.

'Oh, lovely!' she said, and dug in.

Well, that was her out of it hopefully for the next ten or fifteen minutes. I turned to Secundus. 'So,' I said, 'how's the new job going, pal?'

'The Treasury?' He helped himself to a sausage. 'It's okay. Boring, but someone's got to do it. And at least I don't have to move much. With this leg of mine I'd find it hard to get around.'

'Don't complain, Gaius.' That was Gemella, between mouthfuls. 'If it hadn't been for your leg we'd never have met.'

'Nor we would, dear.' Was that a wince? Maybe there was hope for the poor bastard after all. I stifled a grin. 'I never thought, though, Marcus, that I'd end up pushing a pen. Especially when I got to be a city judge. With soldiering out, the law would've been a good second-best. At least you're dealing with people rather than figures. Or you get a commission like Gracchus's that gives you something really useful to do that you can enjoy at the same time.'

I shelled an egg and reached for the fish pickle. 'Who's Gracchus?'

'Jupiter!' Secundus laughed. 'You never go near Market Square, pal? The emperor's commission on loans. Gracchus is one of the other city judges. He's heading it. Rubbing these broad-striper bastards' noses in their own' – he caught Furia Gemella's sharply applied eye and paused – 'greed.'

'Oh, yeah.' I dipped the egg. 'Your colleague Nomentanus told me about that.'

'With his teeth clenched, no doubt.' Secundus was still chuckling.

'No. Not at all. He seemed pretty cheerful about it, as a matter of fact.'

Secundus was staring at me. 'Nomentanus? *Cheerful?*'

'Sure.' The back of my neck prickled slightly. 'There any reason he shouldn't be?'

'Yeah. You could say so. A good million reasons, in fact. Marcus, Nomentanus is in the manure up to his eyebrows. He's so far in hock he couldn't dig himself out with a spade.'

The prickle had grown to a definite itch, and Perilla was looking at me with wide eyes. Meanwhile, Furia Gemella had found the truffles.

'Hang on, pal,' I said. 'Cut the jokes, okay? This is important. I got the impression from talking to the guy that a) he wasn't in the loans scam business himself and b) he was loaded.'

'No to both.' Secundus took a swallow of wine. 'I'm Treasury, remember? I get the inside edge. Nomentanus is one of the biggies; when the bill for repayments hits his mat it'll have six figures. And after what he spent on running for city judge, not to mention Board of Fifteen member before that, he hasn't got the price of a bath. And I'm not giving you privileged information here. Anyone else on Market Square would tell you the same.'

My spine had gone very cold. Oh, gods; dear sweet gods! 'Nomentanus is a Board of Fifteen member?'

'Sure. He has been for the past three years.'

I lay back, brain spinning. Shit! I'd got my link! The Board of Fifteen were responsible for watchdogging foreign cults in Rome. When Myrrhine had knifed the archigallus's two acolytes a year back he'd naturally reported the incident — with, presumably, full details of name and description — to the Board of Fifteen officer who had Cybele as his particular patch. No prizes for guessing now which officer that had been, although I could check to make sure. And if Myrrhine was one of the temple's foremost devotees, with two previous years of the job under his belt one got you ten that Nomentanus knew her already.

Sextius Nomentanus, eh? Jupiter! It couldn't be a coincidence; no way, nohow, never. Between the loans business and the religious officer angle I'd got the bugger six ways from nothing!

'Marcus, what is this?' Secundus had set down his wine cup. 'What did I say?'

'Nothing you need worry about, pal,' I said. I'd known Secundus for a long time and, nice guy though he was, he wasn't Rome's brightest. How the Treasury was running these days Juno the Warner herself only knew, but then the man at the top was only a figurehead anyway: the permanent staff did the real work. 'It has to do with the case I'm on at the moment.'

'The dead Vestal?'

'Yeah. Yeah, that's right.'

'You don't think *Nomentanus* killed her, do you?' That was Gemella; quicker on the uptake than Gaius, but then that wouldn't be difficult. Obviously the prospect of talking scandal had finally won over the truffles and she was looking at me with huge baby-brown eyes. 'Oh, how dreadful!'

'No, Gemella,' I said carefully. 'That was a runaway slave called Myrrhine. She shoved a knife through her throat yesterday in an Aventine tenement. I was there at the time, in fact, and my laundrymaid's still trying to get the bloodstains out of my third-best mantle.'

'Really?' Gemella blanched and patted her lips with her napkin. 'Fascinating. Ah ... if you'll excuse me a moment.' She got up quickly and made for the door, napkin pressed to her mouth, followed closely — after a sideways glare at me — by Perilla. The clepsydra basin would be nearest, but no doubt Perilla would handle things. I'd pay later, mind you, when the lady got me alone, but it'd be worth it all the same. Meanwhile I could do a little capitalising. I turned back to Secundus.

'You wouldn't know whether Nomentanus had a rich elderly aunt stashed away somewhere, would you, Gaius?' I said. 'A childless aunt. Or maybe an uncle.'

Furia Gemella's sudden exit hadn't fazed him; in fact, he was looking a lot more relaxed than he had done up to then. I didn't blame him: it would've had the same effect on me if I'd been married to the lady. 'Uh-uh,' he said. 'Not that I'm aware of, anyway. Why do you ask?'

'Because the guy wasn't putting it on. He had no reason to, for a start, not with me; quite the reverse, in fact. He just couldn't help crowing, that's all. And if he really was loaded and could laugh off the prospect of a six-figure fine, not to mention a little expense like recelebrating the rites of the Good Goddess, then the money must've come from somewhere. More than that, it must've come sudden and there must've been a hell of a lot of it. The only legal way for that to happen is a legacy. Some well-heeled relative with no other family dropping off the perch.'

'If Gaius Nomentanus had had a rich aunt, Marcus, then we'd all have heard of her long ago.' Secundus grinned. 'Believe me. He's that kind of bastard.'

'Yeah. I thought that might be the case.' I hefted the wine jug and filled Secundus's cup. 'Drink up, pal. The night's young and there's plenty more.'

So; that was that; scratch legal. Still, we weren't home and dry yet, not by a long chalk. Nomentanus might be our man, but the problem was if he hadn't come by the money legally then where had he got it? *Why* he'd got it, sure, that was obvious: the guy had been paid for services rendered. Like recruiting Myrrhine, for example. Only that left the question of who had done the paying. And, again, why. Like I'd said to Secundus, we were talking a hell of a lot of gravy here: a million in silver, which was what Secundus had implied that Nomentanus would owe the Treasury at minimum, was enough to qualify someone for the broad stripe. Parting with a sum like that would've made a serious dent in anyone's bank balance, yet Nomentanus could shrug it off. So what he was getting – and consequently what his employer was paying – was obviously a lot more.

And the mirror-image of that was what the *employer* was getting was worth the fee. At least to him.

What the hell was going on?

31

Secundus and Gemella left early. Gemella made the excuse that their youngest kid had colic, but she'd been pretty tight-lipped the rest of the meal and Secundus looked sheepish, so I took that with a pinch of salt. We saw them to their carriage and went back to the dining-room to finish off the fruit and nuts.

'Well,' I said, 'if you're expecting a return invitation don't hold your breath.'

'Marcus, sometimes I despair of you.' Perilla settled down on the couch beside me. 'Your behaviour was dreadful, and quite deliberate.'

I grinned; she wasn't angry, not really. I could tell by the lack of snap. 'Come on, lady!' I said. 'That bit of vicarious seaminess made the woman's evening. She'll have great fun for the next month slagging me off to her pals at the honey-wine klatsch.'

'That is beside the point.'

I filled my wine cup: Secundus had knocked as decent a hole in the Falernian as he dared with his wife's beady eye on him, but there was still a lot left. More than there should've been. I felt sorry as hell for Gaius Secundus. 'She make it to the plumbing, by the way?'

Perilla's lip was trembling. 'Just,' she said.

'That's good.'

'She also asked me how I could stay married to you.'

'Yeah? And?'

'I told her we all had our little crosses to bear. She seemed to like that.'

I laughed and kissed her. 'You can take those earrings off now,' I said.

She did. Things got interesting for a moment, then she drew back.

'What was that business about Nomentanus?' she said.

I gave her a blow-by-blow account of our barber's-chair chat, plus what Secundus had told me while she'd been out watching Gemella lose her starters. 'He's our link, lady. As a religious officer he'd know Myrrhine and the kind of woman she was through the temple. When the time came for Cornelia's murder she'd be the perfect person to recruit.'

'But if Myrrhine was on the run then how did he know where to find her?'

'Yeah.' I frowned. 'That's the bugger. We've got one end of the tie-in but not the other. Still, it must've happened somehow. And the loans bail-out is a clincher.'

Perilla bit thoughtfully into one of Meton's cinnamon tartlets. There weren't all that many of them left: righteous indignation hadn't take the edge off Furia Gemella's appetite any. 'A million sesterces is a great deal of money,' she said. 'Who could afford an amount like that?'

'Any one of the real fat-cat families. The Crassi. The Luculli.' I paused. 'The Lepidi.'

She put the tartlet down and stared at me. 'Oh, no! *Not* Aemilius Lepidus again! Marcus, I thought we'd been through that!'

'He's becoming a better bet by the minute, lady.' I took a swallow of wine. 'The guy's seriously loaded, which is the sine qua non here. Parting with a million would make him wince, sure, but it wouldn't break him, not by a long way.

And if you discount the probity factor, which could be pure whitewash and probably is where these senatorial bastards are concerned, he's the only one who comes close to fitting the bill in other respects.'

'What about the daughter?'

'Not with that amount of money involved, Perilla. She's family, sure, but a million plus is big gravy. Raising that kind of cash would mean selling property. Even if Lepida had her own private fortune – which she might – old Lepidus is the legal head of the house. She'd have to go through him for a signature because he holds the purse-strings. And indulgent father or not he's going to be pretty suspicious if she tells him she's a million or two short on the housekeeping this month and can she please sell a few tenements to take up the slack.'

'Hmm.' Perilla rested her chin on her hands. 'Very well. Why Lepidus?'

'The same reasons I gave you before. Theory, rather. The guy's stepped out of line somewhere in a big way and his son finds out. Young Marcus confides in Cornelia and Lepidus has her zeroed for the sake of safety.'

'Through the agency of Sextius Nomentanus. How?'

'How what, lady?'

'How does Aemilius Lepidus pick on Nomentanus to act as go-between? He can't know, surely, that Nomentanus has the perfect contact in Myrrhine. Nor indeed that he would be sufficiently venal to consider becoming involved in the murder of a Vestal.'

I sank a mouthful of Falernian. 'Jupiter, Perilla, I don't know. The venal bit, sure, no hassle: Lepidus is a leading member of the Senate; he'd have his finger on the pulse, so he'd be aware of the guy's circumstances. Also he's no slouch when it comes to assessing character. But as far as the rest goes you've got me.'

'There you are, then.'

'There I am nothing. The circumstantial evidence adds up. He admits — because he couldn't do otherwise — that he wrote the note that got Niobe killed, and he has the nerve and the brains to risk a double bluff. Also if he's the guy ultimately responsible for Cornelia's death then it explains his son's message to me.'

'"There are worse crimes than murder."'

'Right. Cornelia was practically the guy's daughter. Or at least she'd been his ward. Killing her — even at second hand — would go beyond simple murder. Certainly in young Lepidus's book.'

'But, Marcus, it was Lepidus himself who told you what his son had said.'

'So?'

'Don't be intentionally obtuse, dear. If Lepidus were responsible he wouldn't have done that, surely. In fact, it would be an extremely foolish thing to do.'

'Double bluff again, lady. We don't know who else knew about the message. If Lepidus hadn't delivered it and it'd come out later I might've smelled a rat. This way the guy comes across clean.'

Perilla sighed. 'That's all very well, but there's nothing you can prove, is there?'

'Sure there is. There's the money. If Nomentanus has suddenly come into a fortune then he has to be able to account for it. Even if Lepidus didn't pay him directly — which would be stupid, and Lepidus, at least, isn't stupid — then the transfer has to have left a trail. It's only a question of backtracking.'

'So in the first instance you go to Nomentanus, accuse him of being a paid assassin, and ask to see his accounts.'

'Jupiter, Perilla!'

'But Marcus, what alternative do you have?'

'We do this officially. I go to Camillus, explain the situation and ask him to set up an investigation of the guy's finances. Under the circumstances he'll do it, sure he will: at other times a phoney inheritance might slip past the board with no more than a raised eyebrow or two, but if there's a good chance it's payment for the murder of a Vestal the authorities'll take the bastard's accounts apart with tweezers and a scalpel.'

'Aemilius Lepidus is a very influential man. If he were involved then he'd have any investigation stopped, surely. Or at least compromised from its inception.'

'He wouldn't dare, Perilla. Any attempted monkey business would be an automatic admission of guilt. And if I ask Camillus to use imperial auditors instead of senatorial he'll have even less chance. These guys are sharp, they're mean as rabid ferrets, and because they're only responsible to the Wart they can tell any interfering broad-striper, including Aemilius Lepidus, to go and play in the sandpit.'

'Well, I must admit it does sound promising.' Perilla kissed me gravely. 'Let's leave it for the night. Now. Do you really want any of these tartlets or shall we get Meton to shelve them for tomorrow?'

Uh-huh; a proposition, if I ever heard one. I grinned. 'Shelve them, lady. Shelve them by all means.'

'Good.' She kissed me again and got off the couch. 'In that case I think we should just go to bed.'

Fine by me. Absolutely fine. I finished the wine at a gulp and followed her upstairs.

Afterwards I lay awake with Perilla asleep in the crook of my arm. The link between Myrrhine and Nomentanus was still bugging me. Perilla had been right, of course: knowing that the woman would make the perfect killer was only the half of it. By the time Cornelia's murder was on the cards, Myrrhine had been gone a year, squirrelled away on the Aventine. So how the hell had Nomentanus known where to find her, especially at what must've been short notice? An intermediary was possible, sure; but I doubted that Myrrhine had any friends at the temple, certainly not anyone she'd let into the secret of where she was holed up. Proculus's house was out for the same reason: sure, she could've had friends there, but a killing and a theft were pretty big disincentives for any of her fellow slaves to keep up what could turn out to be a dangerous acquaintance if she was ever caught. Besides, she'd struck me as a loner: *withdrawn*, the archigallus had said, even before she did her runner. For anyone in her past life to have known about the Aventine tenement would've meant she'd made overtures herself, and that just didn't sit right: I couldn't envisage Myrrhine, having made her break for freedom, putting herself in the power of any former acquaintance, friend or not, who might choose to cash in by splitting on her. Also, how would Nomentanus have known who to approach?

Okay. So that horse wouldn't run and we were left with Nomentanus himself. Could the guy have caught sight of her by accident, maybe, any time in that intervening year and recognised her? But surely, if he had, he would've blown the whistle. And she would've been careful to keep away from the better parts of town where there was more of a chance that she'd be spotted. Which was why, no doubt, she'd chosen the part of the Aventine down by the Raudusculan Gate. That wasn't exactly an area where you saw many—

Shit. I stopped. It was possible; sure it was. It had to be something like that, anyway, and checking wouldn't be too difficult. Furthermore, if I was right then we'd got the guy by the balls and all we had to do was pull.

Enough for the night; more than enough. I eased Perilla off my arm, turned over and went to sleep.

32

I got to the Crocodile about mid-morning. The same punters who'd sloped off when I'd walked in with Lippillus and the Watchmen two days before were drinking at the counter, but this time all the reaction I got was a long hard stare from the nearest. Yeah, well; it was nice to think you weren't a threat to anyone's simple pleasures.

'Hi, Hippo,' I said. 'Remember me?'

'The wine buff.' The fat man beamed. 'Of course, sir. What can I get you?'

'Another cup of that Sulmonian'd do nicely, pal. And a word with your girl Phoebe if she's around.'

The beam broadened. 'Phoebe's with a customer at present, sir, but if you'd care to wait I'm sure she'd be delighted to accommodate you.'

'Fine. Fine.' I took out a copper coin and laid it on the counter.

'That's not necessary, sir.' The Hippo put the full wine cup in front of me. 'On the house. As I told the Watch commander, any friend of his is welcome at the Crocodile.'

The punter with the stare hawked loudly and spat. It could've been coincidence, sure, but it sounded like a comment to me. Still, I'd had worse; I gave him the benefit of the doubt, my best smile and a friendly nod. Just then the door opened and another customer came in, a heavy-shouldered, youngish guy with an unshaven chin and a workman's tunic. He ordered his wine with a grunt, paid for it and took it over to one of the far tables without giving me or the other punters so much as a glance. Yeah, well: it was a friendly place, the Raudusculan, full of happy smiling faces. Maybe it was my aftershave.

The Hippo picked up a cloth and wiped the counter in front of me.

'Terrible thing, sir,' he said. 'That Watchman being knifed. Gives the place a bad name.'

'Yeah.' I sipped my wine. 'Lippillus was telling me what a nice, orderly, law-abiding part of the city this is.'

My pal the punter sniggered into his cup. The Hippo gave him a glare. 'Shut it, Antistius!' he said, then turned back to me. 'I told you Myrrhine was a bad one, sir. The street's better off without her.'

'She here long?'

'A year, give or take. Kept herself to herself most of the time. But then most people around here do.'

Yeah; I'd believe that. Half this part of the district was probably keeping a low profile in case it got noticed. 'No visitors? Men friends?'

A pause. 'You saw, sir. With Crispa. And the other girl I told you about. She wasn't that way inclined.'

'Uh-uh; I don't necessarily mean sexual. Maybe just an acquaintance.' I held his eyes. 'Could be a purple-striper. One of your customers, perhaps.'

The Hippo's jowls wobbled. The guy definitely wasn't smiling now. 'Purple-striper?' he said. 'Myrrhine? Oh, no, sir! And what would a purple-striper with any sense be doing around here? Saving your presence, of course.'

'Phoebe seemed to imply different. That she'd had a certain amount of purple-striper experience. I was just wondering whether her guy and mine could be the same person.'

'Oh, you don't want to pay any attention to Phoebe, sir.' There was a bead of sweat on the Hippo's forehead. 'It was only a come-on. Believe me.'

Yeah. And I was Cleopatra's grandmother. Hell. This was going to be difficult ...

'If you're asking about Myrrhine's friend, squire, then maybe I can help you.'

I glanced round. Antistius the Spitting Punter was looking at me in an expectant kind of way. He rattled his cup on the counter.

''Course, I'd need something to oil my throat with first,' he added.

Okay! And I can take a subtle hint when it's given. Maybe I wouldn't have to wait for Phoebe after all, which might be a good thing because I had the distinct impression from the Hippo's general demeanour that he hadn't liked the turn the conversation was taking one little bit. I pulled another coin from the purse in my mantle fold. 'Have a drink on me, pal?' I said.

'That's uncommon decent of you, consul.'

I grinned in spite of myself. For a parody of a plummy upper-class accent it wasn't bad; overtones of my Uncle Cotta, in fact, when the old guy was pissed and putting it on.

'What kind of friend would that be, now?' I said.

The Hippo took the coin this time and topped up the guy's cup. He didn't look too happy as Antistius left his two silent mates to their pie-eyed ruminations and came over to where I was standing. If looks could kill my new informant would've been hamburger.

'Not a purple-striper,' he said. 'Plain mantle. You're right about him being a customer, though. I've seen him in here quite a few times, in fact.' He glanced at the

Hippo, eyebrows raised like he was waiting for confirmation.

If so it didn't come. 'Have you, indeed?' the Hippo said. You could've used his tone for slicing beets.

'Yeah.' The guy swallowed half the cupful straight down and grinned at him. 'Real gent. You know who I mean.' No reaction. 'Oh, come off it, Hippo, you know the fancy bugger as well as I do!'

'How do you know he was a friend of Myrrhine's, pal?' I said to break the deadlock.

He sank the rest of the wine, set the cup down and fixed me with his eye. Yeah, well. I reached into my purse. I had the idea that when the Hippo poured this time he'd sooner the stuff was neat rat poison, but he didn't interfere.

'I live in the same tenement she did.' Half that cup went the same way as the first. 'Third floor. They passed me once on the stairs.'

'Yeah?' The hairs on my neck prickled. 'When was this exactly?'

'Maybe half a month back. Thereabouts, anyway. Can't say I fancied her myself, but there's no accounting for taste.'

'That's the last taste you get in here anyway, Titus Antistius.' The Hippo was polishing the counter like his life depended on it. 'I'll tell you that now, boy!'

'Come on, Hippo!' Antistius didn't seem too worried. 'You don't mind me talking, surely? Especially since you're such a great pal of the Watch. Besides, the consul here's putting money in your pocket.' He drained the cup and set it down with exaggerated care like it was made of glass.

Shit. The purse again. 'Fill it up, Hippo,' I said. Then to Antistius: 'You like to describe the guy?'

'Sure. Medium height, thin mouth, eyes close together. Smooth type, a real lady-killer, well-groomed. Looked like he kept himself in good shape.' He winked at the Hippo. 'He'd have to with Phoebe, isn't that right?'

The fat man grunted; a defeated sort of grunt.

Yeah; that was Nomentanus, okay. To the life. The plain mantle didn't make any odds, either. If the guy was slumming it he wouldn't want to be too obvious. I turned back to the Hippo.

'Right, sunshine,' I said. 'Forget the fan-dance. Just for the sake of completeness I need a name. You can tell me or the Watch commander when he drops by again. Which will be about an hour after I leave. Only I guarantee he won't be asking so nicely. Get me?'

'Sextus.' The Hippo's face was grey. 'That's the only name the bugger ever gave me. What he tells Phoebe I don't know and I don't care.'

That put the lid on. Sextus – first name – for Sextius, middle; not very imaginative, my pal Nomentanus. But then there wasn't really any need. I took out a silver piece and laid it on the counter.

'Thanks, pal,' I said to Antistius. 'A present from the Senate and people of Rome. You've been a great help. Buy yourself the jug.'

I left.

Okay; so we had a viable scenario here. Nomentanus had known Myrrhine at the temple and had been the man the archigallus had called in when she knifed two of his staff. Some time over the next twelve months, he'd seen and recognised her outside the Crocodile; a coincidence, sure, but not a huge one given the guy's obvious propensity for low-life sex and a desire on both their parts to keep away from the more popular areas of the city. On his side that was as natural as it was on hers: tomcatting isn't illegal, but some of these selection committees are pretty strait-laced, and for a religious officer and city judge with his eyes on the consulship to be seen brothel-crawling doesn't do his career chances much good. Which explained why he hadn't shopped the woman, too: giving the authorities the goods on Myrrhine would've raised some nasty questions, like what a paragon of the establishment was doing down at the RAudusculan in the first place. And he'd be blowing his own cover at the same time. The game just wasn't worth the candle.

Then of course the Cornelia business had come up . . .

That was the bit I stuck at. Sure, the mechanics of it were clear enough thanks to my drinking pal: Nomentanus had made himself known to Myrrhine and they'd arranged things between them. But I still didn't know how he'd got the commission, who had given him it and why. Getting the answers to these questions would be a long hard slog. Even with Camillus on the team putting the screws on the bastard from above, with the woman herself dead I'd only got circumstantial evidence and Antistius's word that the two had been in league. Like I say, tomcatting's no crime and so long as he paid his bill the guy's sex life was his own concern. If I simply faced him with what I'd got at the moment he'd throw me out on my ear and laugh while he did it. I had to have more.

Like, for example, a link with Aemilius Lepidus. That guy was involved; he had to be because he was the only one who fitted. But he and Nomentanus were chalk and cheese, character-wise. Lepidus – on the face of it, anyway – was one of the oldest and most highly respected senators in Rome, whereas Nomentanus was a brash young pusher. Sure, like I'd said to Perilla, Lepidus would have his finger on the pulse, he'd know that Nomentanus was on the make, potentially anyway; but that's a hell of a long way from having the nerve to approach the guy cold re zeroing a Vestal. If it had been the daughter, now . . .

I stopped. I'd been walking up Ostia Incline towards the Circus. There's a lot of traffic that way, tunics rather than mantles, and one of them – a big, beefy guy carrying half a cartload of onions on a string like they were a party garland – slammed into my back. I picked myself up and apologised. He went off muttering.

Hang on, now. I'd dismissed Lepida because, like I said, she wouldn't have the financial clout to sub Nomentanus over the loans business. On the other hand, put that to one side temporarily and she was perfect. She was Nomentanus's type, for a start: young, a go-getter and without a moral bone in her body. More important, if they were working together then boyfriend-poaching aside it would explain her sudden interest in Aemilia – for which read the layout of the Galba household – and why she'd dropped that lady like a hot brick after she'd got what she wanted. And there was one last thing. Alexis's girlfriend Melissa had said that Lepida had a broad-striper steady she was keeping on a string. If the guy turned out to be Nomentanus then we were laughing.

Okay; assume he did. How would it work?

The father and the daughter were in it together; they had to be, for the financial angle to fit. Same scenario as before, or maybe with the variation that it was Lepida who'd stepped out of line rather than the old man. Yeah; that would make a lot more sense: that lady was wild, and whatever the reason behind this business was it had to be major. Exile, at best. Leave that for the present. Fine. So.

It's the lady who makes the running. She's in a jam, her brother's found out somehow, he's gone crying to Cornelia and he makes the mistake of telling his sister. Or she finds out some other way that the secret's out; that aspect of things didn't really matter. The brother she can handle – he's family, he won't split – but Cornelia's an unknown quantity. They've never liked each other and Cornelia's too much the goody-goody to be trusted. Lepida talks it over with her boyfriend Nomentanus, maybe makes a few promises, like for example she'll marry him if he does what she wants. Nomentanus is no fool: sure, he'll help – he's got the perfect plan all lined up and waiting to go in any case – but he wants more. The guy's broke, and in a few months he's going to be hit with a bill that would make anyone's eyes water. So he says, Fine; you go to Daddy, explain the situation – maybe not in detail, just that you need a million or two in cash to get you out of a hole. Call it a dowry.

Lepidus jumps at it; well, maybe not *jumps* exactly, but the guy's killing two birds with one stone here: he saves the family honour and at the same time he gets his hell-cat of a daughter off his hands. He doesn't, of course, know about the Vestal until it's too late. By that time, naturally, he's in it himself up to his aristocratic ears. He can't blow the whistle on Nomentanus and his daughter, even if he wants to, because he's an accomplice before the fact; after, as well, because to save his own neck he's had to connive towards Niobe's death into the bargain . . .

There are worse crimes than murder. His son had known, sure he had, even though he stopped short of accusing his father to his face. Why Lepidus had passed that on to me – barring the explanation I'd given Perilla – I didn't know. Conscience, maybe. Lepidus couldn't tell me the truth, sure, but at bottom he was an honest man, I'd bet on that. Not that it made him any the less guilty.

It all fitted; subject to the tie-in between Nomentanus and Lepida existing, of course. And proving that – or, if I was unlucky, disproving it – all depended on Alexis.

33

I despatched the guy on his secret mission straight away, together with his Winter Festival outfit, a snazzy gilt brooch for Melissa and a few quiet words of advice. We were halfway through a late breakfast before he showed up the next morning.

'Hey, Alexis!' I said. 'How did it go, pal?'

Not that I needed to ask: he looked dead on his feet and totally happy. Mission accomplished; at least on Alexis's side. And, I suspected, on Melissa's.

'Marvellous, sir,' he said. Beamed.

'Yeah, well, apart from that.' I glanced at Perilla, who was grinning. 'You don't want to hear this, lady. Bribery, seduction, abuse of privilege, suborning of the household staff ...'

'I'm sure it was in a good cause, Marcus.'

'Uh-huh. The best. So.' I turned back to Alexis. 'Your girlfriend have time to give you the guy's name, sunshine?'

'Yes, sir.'

I kept my fingers crossed. 'Sextius Nomentanus?'

'Yes, sir.'

Bull's-eye! I gave a whoop. Jupiter, I'd got the bastard! In fact, I'd got all three of them together. There were still the whys and wherefores, mind, but these could wait. Now I was sure of my ground I could make my report to Furius Camillus and let him take it from here. Which reminded me: Camillus might well be back now, or at least his head slave would know when he was expected.

'You feel up to another walk across town?' I asked Alexis.

'Yes, sir.' He was still beaming. Walk, nothing: I'd've bet the guy could've floated. 'Where to, sir?'

'The King's House. Fix me up a meeting with the acting chief priest asap.'

'Right away, sir.' He left as if Cupid were twanging away at his heels. Well, if nothing else I'd brightened up one small life.

'You've really solved it, Marcus?' Perilla said, honeying a sesame bun.

'Yeah.' I stretched out. 'Two days before the Festival, too. Perfect timing.'

'So what will happen now?'

'That's up to Camillus. Or rather, the Senate; maybe even the emperor. One thing we can be sure of: they won't sweep it under the carpet, not with a Vestal dead.'

'Hmm.' Perilla bit into her bun. 'I can understand Nomentanus and Lepida, but not the father. You're sure about Aemilius Lepidus? Absolutely certain?'

'Sure I am, lady. Like I said, the money's a clincher. With gravy like that involved, Lepidus had to be part of it.'

'He just seems most unlikely, that's all. In terms of character.'

'Come on, Perilla! I took you through the theory. The guy needn't've known what he was getting himself into at the start. And by the time he did know there wasn't anything he could do about it.'

'Yes. I understand that.' She was frowning. 'On the other hand, you did say that during your first interview with him he was prepared to swear that he knew nothing about the secret his son had shared with Cornelia. Surely by the time he spoke to you that had to be untrue. If he didn't yet know for certain, he must at least have had an inkling of what was going on, and I just don't think, being the man he is, that he would have volunteered to perjure himself simply for the sake of putting you off the scent.'

'He didn't offer to swear he knew nothing of the secret, lady; he said he'd take his oath that his son hadn't told him anything about it at their final interview. Which may have been the case, because both father and son already knew where they stood.'

'Very well.' Perilla was still looking doubtful. 'You're probably right. Still, it strikes me as mean. And I cannot, honestly, see a man like Aemilius Lepidus descending to a piece of sophistic trickery.'

Yeah; that aspect of it had been worrying me, too, and not just that: Lepidus had *felt* real. Still, he was a clever guy, and I couldn't forget that Augustus had tipped him as emperor material. You didn't get to be emperor without being capable of wearing two faces at once when necessary. Look at the Wart.

Well, the case was over and I'd done my best. Now it was up to Camillus and the lawyers. Besides, the Festival was in two days, and even sleuths need a break.

Alexis came floating back to say Camillus was home and he'd be delighted to see me whenever. I headed off for the King's House.

The Jupiter look-alike showed me through to the guy's study. He was on his own – no Junia Torquata this time – working at his desk, but he waved me to the reading couch, put the book-rolls in their boxes and sat back down in his chair.

'So, Corvinus,' he said. 'How are things going? Any further forward?'

'The case is solved, sir.'

Camillus's eyebrows went up. 'Really?'

'The actual killer was a woman called Myrrhine. She—'

'A woman?' The eyebrows went up another notch. 'But the last time we talked you were very certain that the fluteplayer was a man in disguise.'

'Yeah.' I swallowed. 'Yeah, I know I was. I made a mistake. I'm, uh, sorry about that.'

'I'm sure you are.' He was looking at me with definite amusement. 'Will you tell the chief Vestal or shall I?'

'Uh ... maybe it would be better coming from you, sir.'

'Yes,' he said drily. 'And perhaps the news ought to be broken gently to Sextius Nomentanus as well, under the circumstances.'

'That's not such a problem.' I kept my voice neutral. 'I think Nomentanus knows already.'

'Does he, now? Well, it certainly saves me a rather awkward—'

'Nomentanus knows, sir, because he was the guy behind the murders. Or at least one of three people responsible.'

Camillus sat back. 'He was *what*?' he said.

'There's no doubt. None whatsoever. He has definite links with Myrrhine going back two years or more. Also, he seems to have come into a great deal of money recently.' I explained about the loans business, and Camillus's face grew graver.

'Yes,' he said. 'Yes, that certainly makes a lot of sense. Well done; well done indeed. Your friend Secundus was perfectly correct: Nomentanus's financial circumstances are extremely straitened, or should be. I told you that before, or implied it at any rate, when the question of paying for the recelebration of the rites came up.' Hell; so he had; I'd forgotten that. 'Also, he is as his colleague told you one of the worst offenders under the terms of the new law. You will of course have your investigative commission. An imperial one, as you suggest. That I guarantee.' He frowned. 'Not that I'm totally happy with your findings. I don't personally like the man and never have, but he is one of our most senior magistrates. You can prove the accusation?'

'Sure. Like I say, he had connections with the killer and he was actually seen with her. It all fits, right down the line.'

'Then there's no more to be said. It's a matter for the senior city judge.' Camillus paused. 'You mentioned that he was one of three.'

'Yeah.' I hesitated: this was going to be the really tough part. 'The other two are Aemilius Lepidus and his daughter.'

I thought the guy was going to stand up, but he didn't. His mouth formed a hard line. The silence lengthened.

'Valerius Corvinus,' Camillus said quietly. 'Have you taken leave of your senses?'

I'd been afraid this might happen, especially after the conversation with Perilla, but there wasn't a lot I could do except go in swinging. 'Uh-uh.' I shook my head slowly. 'Like I said with Nomentanus, it all fits. Sure, proving it depends on the findings of the commission, but I'm convinced in my own mind. Completely convinced. Lepida was the driving force – she was the one recruited Nomentanus – but the father had to be involved.'

'But, Corvinus, Aemilius Lepidus is one of the most highly respected men in Rome.' The deputy chief priest was still speaking quietly, like he was explaining to an idiot why two and two made four. 'He is also, I must tell you, one of my oldest and closest friends and the most honourable man I know. *Consistently* honourable. There is no way – and I mean *no* way, Valerius Corvinus — that Lepidus would associate himself with a crime of this nature. Or indeed of any nature. I'm sorry, but whatever proof you think you have you are wrong. Totally and utterly.'

Jupiter! I took a deep breath. 'Look, sir. If Nomentanus did get that money — and I admit that's something we still have to prove — then it must've come from somewhere. The connection with the man's daughter is proven fact. Lepidus had a motive; in fact he's the only person in this whole set-up, barring the daughter herself, who did.'

'What motive could Aemilius Lepidus possibly have for engineering the death of a Vestal?'

'Saving the family honour. I'm not saying the guy was in on it from the first, only that by the time he knew what was going on it was too late to back out. He—'

'That would make no difference!' Camillus's hand slammed down on the desk; hard, and so suddenly and unexpectedly that I jumped. Our eyes locked for a good half-minute. Then he passed the hand over his face. 'My apologies, Corvinus. That was unforgivably rude of me, and unmerited on your part. However, I stand by the words. Believe me, the moment Aemilius Lepidus became aware that he had involved himself in a crime, especially one of this magnitude, he would feel himself compelled to report it to the authorities. Whether his daughter was concerned or not. That, I can assure you, is a simple, absolute fact based on a lifetime's knowledge. I'm sorry, but I can only repeat: however sure you are, you are nevertheless totally and utterly wrong.'

Deadlock. Well, there wasn't much more to be said. I'd got the guy's promise that he'd set up a commission to investigate Nomentanus's accounts. All I could hope for was that the proof would be there; that, at least, Camillus would have to accept, and I'd done my bit to my own satisfaction, if not to his. Not that I bore the guy any ill-will; he'd given me the truth as he saw it, and the responsibility for any prosecution lay ultimately with him and the chief city judge. I stood up. 'Yeah. Okay,' I said. 'Let's leave it at that, then. At least the killer herself is dead, so I've achieved that much.'

Camillus bowed his head for a moment, then looked up again. 'Please don't think I'm ungrateful, Corvinus,' he said. 'You really do have my congratulations. Nomentanus I am willing to accept, subject to further proof, of course. Lepida also. Knowing the woman's character and past as I do, her guilt would come as no surprise. But not her father.'

'Yeah,' I said. My mouth felt bitter. 'Right.'

Camillus paused. 'This Myrrhine, incidentally. You told me very little about her, and I should have asked for more. She's dead, you say?'

'Yeah. She killed herself before we could get to her. And one of the Public Ponds Watch.'

'Another corpse.' The eyes closed momentarily. 'She was a colleague of the dead flutegirl? What was her name – Thalia?'

'No. She was a slave, attached to Cybele's temple. That was how Nomentanus knew her.'

'Of course.' He nodded. 'The Board of Fifteen connection. You really have been extremely busy, Corvinus. And extremely thorough. So the woman was a temple slave?'

'No. Only a devotee. She belonged to a guy called Considius Proculus. She ran out on him about a year back and knifed one of the other staff, plus subsequently a couple of the temple priests. She was hiding out in a tenement near . . .'

I tailed off because Camillus had stopped listening. He was staring at me.

'*Gaius* Considius Proculus?' he said.

There was a catch in his voice. Something cold touched my neck. 'Yeah,' I said. 'Yeah, that's right. You know him?'

Camillus's face was expressionless. 'No,' he said. 'No, not personally. Perhaps it's a coincidence, young man — these things happen — but Gaius Proculus was arrested and executed five days ago. By order of the emperor.'

34

'Perilla, what the fuck is going on?'

'Calm down, Marcus.' The lady set the poem she'd been working on when I'd come in on the ledge of the ornamental pool. 'And don't swear, please. It isn't necessary.'

'According to Camillus, this Proculus guy is sitting peacefully at home with friends celebrating his birthday – his fucking *birthday*, for the gods' sake! – when Macro's goons force their way in and arrest him for treason. An hour later he's being garrotted in the fucking Mamertine—'

'Marcus!'

'With no fucking trial and no fucking chance to defend himself. And I'll fucking swear if I want to swear!' I kicked the couch leg.

'Marcus, you're being childish. Stop it.'

I took a deep breath and held it, then exhaled. 'Yeah,' I said. 'Sorry, lady. But put yourself in my shoes, right? I thought the case was tied up with a nice neat bow round and then this happens. Where do you think that leaves me?'

'Very angry. Yes, I can see that. Still, it's no excuse for bad language.'

Fair point. I threw myself down on the couch. 'Okay. So let's go back to the original question. Expurgated this time. What is going on?'

'Perhaps nothing. It could be coincidence.'

'No coincidence. That sort I don't believe in. And the order was official, too: the Wart's signature was on the document. One of Camillus's broad-striper mates was there at the time and he made the officer in charge show him it.'

'Then the man obviously had committed treason.'

I laughed. 'Perilla, come on, okay? You know what "treason" means as a charge as well as I do; just the word, with no details. Especially if there's no explanation, no trial and a quick execution. The guy was stitched up. The question is why, and who by?'

'If the emperor signed the order himself, then . . .'

'The Wart's on Capri. Sure, he probably did sign it, but one gets you ten it wasn't his order. Most of the stuff over the imperial signature these days comes from Gaius and Macro.'

'Hmm.' Perilla put her chin on her hands. 'What did Proculus say when he was arrested?'

'According to Camillus's pal he didn't have a clue about the reason. Genuinely.' I reached for the wine jug on the table beside me and poured myself a reviving belt of Setinian. 'Nor did Camillus himself. That smells. Whatever is going on here it stinks to high heaven.'

'Very well. If you think there's a connection with the murders then what is it?'

'Jupiter knows.' I took a swallow of the wine. 'But we're in a whole new ball game now. A political ball game. Proculus had nothing to do with Cornelia's death; he couldn't have had. The only link the guy had was that he—' I stopped. 'Oh, Jupiter! Jupiter best and greatest!'

'Marcus?' Perilla's voice was sharp. 'Marcus, what's the matter?'

I waved her down. Sweet gods! Political was right! And it made sense; at least, some sort of sense . . .

It explained how I could be wrong about Lepidus, too.

'Marcus, will you *please* tell me what the matter is.'

'We know what Nomentanus got out of arranging Cornelia's murder. We never asked about Myrrhine.'

Perilla made a huffing noise and reached for her notebook and stylus. 'Look,' she said, 'if you're going to be infuriatingly Delphic over this then—'

'Nomentanus got himself off the hook over the loans business because whoever hired him picked up the tab. Myrrhine wanted something different. And it wasn't money.'

'So what was it? A pardon and her freedom?'

'Uh-uh. Something less personal. Or rather personal in a different way.'

'Marcus—'

'She wanted Considius Proculus's head. It all hangs together,' I said as I refilled the wine cup. 'And it means we're talking top level here. Absolute top. We have to be, because there's no way Nomentanus or Lepida — or even Aemilius Lepidus himself — could swing an execution order with the Wart's signature on it. The same goes for Nomentanus's cash bail-out. Sure, the Lepidi could manage a million or two at a squeeze, but there ain't many families who could match them. Barring the Caesars themselves, naturally.'

The lady had put the wax tablet down again. 'Marcus, you're saying that the *emperor* is behind this?'

'Tiberius? No way, never, not the Wart. Gaius, now . . .'

'For heaven's sake! Why should Prince Gaius pay to have a Vestal killed?'

'Why I don't know. Or not exactly, rather, because we're back to young Marcus Lepidus's secret. The kid was one of the prince's circle of pals, remember, and he could've seen or heard something he wasn't supposed to. That I'd believe, no problem: that bastard must have enough skeletons in his closet to fill a boneyard.'

'But a *Vestal*! Marcus, he's our next emperor!'

'I've met the guy, lady. You haven't. He's ten tiles short of a watertight roof and he's got an ego the size of the Capitol and a code of ethics you could drive a cart through. Killing a Vestal wouldn't lose him much sleep. Believe me.'

Perilla was quiet for a long time. 'All right,' she said. 'How would it work?'

'Practically? With Gaius pulling the strings?' I sipped my wine. 'No sweat, none at all. He's on Capri himself, of course, but his buddy Macro's in Rome. Very much so. Macro may be a prime bastard but he's no thickhead, he's the de facto imperial rep and he knows his way around. He'd have the lowdown on Nomentanus, for a start, and because the guy's obviously crooked as a Suburan dice match the recruitment pitch would be easy-peasy.'

'I thought you said that Lepida was the moving force.'

'Uh-uh.' I shook my head. 'Not if the secret wasn't hers. It has to be our pal the city judge. Lepida was involved, sure, but only as the second-stringer: Nomentanus would need inside information to pass on to Myrrhine, and his girlfriend's the obvious source.'

'You think she'd give him it? For the asking, as it were? She wouldn't profit personally in any way, would she?'

'Perilla, that bitch would do it just for the kick it gave her.' I stretched out on the couch. 'I doubt if she had any more motive than that. Our sweet little Lepida is not a very nice person. The word "rotten" springs to mind.'

'So.'. Perilla was frowning. 'Prince Gaius – through Sertorius Macro – recruits Nomentanus, who in his turn enlists the services of Myrrhine and Lepida. Nomentanus's reward is purely financial: enough money to clear him of his up-and-coming debt to the Treasury with possibly a substantial sum over and above. Myrrhine's price is the death of her former owner who persistently raped her as a child.'

'Yeah. Plus, in Nomentanus's case, a better-than-average chance at the consulship in a few years' time. Having an emperor-elect in your pocket is pretty powerful clout in career terms. I'd say he made a fairly good deal.'

'If he lives to collect on it.'

I nodded. 'Personally, lady, I wouldn't take any bets. Playing footsie with Gaius Caesar isn't exactly conducive to a long life. But then I get the impression the guy hasn't got all that much between the ears, not where planning for the future's concerned. I doubt if he thought that far ahead; or maybe he thinks he's covered his back somehow.'

'Hmm.' Perilla played with a lock of her hair. 'One thing puzzles me. Cornelia was killed, and Niobe, of course, but not young Marcus Lepidus himself. If the murders were intended as a cover-up then why not him?'

'They'd've got round to it. Cornelia was the weak link, she had to go first. Lepidus was Gaius's pal; he wouldn't't've told, not in a hurry, anyway. And by the time his mouth was the only one left to be shut he was dead anyway.'

'All right. So what about motive? I mean Prince Gaius's motive? You said it yourself: a million in silver and a senator executed is a high price for safeguarding one secret. You've no idea what it could have been?'

Yeah; that was the real bummer, and we couldn't get past it. I took a swallow of wine. 'Search me, Perilla. Like I say, the loopy bastard must have enough dirty underwear in his basket to keep a laundry going a year. But whatever it is, this one's big. Maybe he's planning to knock the Wart off his perch before his time.'

'Unlikely. Tiberius can't last all that much longer in any case, and apart from Gemellus he's the only member of the imperial house left. Besides, as you said he virtually controls the state through Macro already. What would he gain?'

Not a lot; added to which – although I'd never told even
Perilla this – thanks to the Wart's tame astrologer Gaius
knew for a certainty that his name would be the next on
the imperial decrees. An assassination plot at this stage just
wouldn't be worth the trouble. The same went for poisoning
Gemellus's porridge: the kid hadn't even put on his adult
mantle yet, he was a sickly wisp of a thing, and when the
Wart popped his clogs one got you ten his Uncle Gaius
would chew him up at a sitting without breaking sweat.

'Excuse me, sir. Madam.'

I looked round. Bathyllus had oozed in on my blind
side.

'Yeah, little guy?'

'Meton asks me to intimate that lunch will be served in
five minutes.'

'Fine.' The Call of the Chef. Well, we'd just have to leave
it at that for the moment. I emptied my cup, picked up the
jug and followed him through to the dining-room.

There are worse crimes than murder . . .

That was the key; sure it was. The problem was, I didn't
know what lock it fitted.

I still wasn't any further forward by bedtime; if indeed there
was anywhere else to go. Sure, I wasn't dumb: if Gaius and
Macro were behind this – and I'd bet a year's income to a
poke in the eye that they were – then I wasn't going to
make much headway in any case. I'd had brushes with the
imperials before, and I knew my chances of getting any of
the dirt to stick where it belonged were about as good as
an oyster's were of making consul. Still, I'd've liked to solve
the case for my own satisfaction, even if the bastards did go
unnailed. Camillus might be interested, too.

I went to sleep with my brain still buzzing. I don't usually

dream — or at least if I do I can never remember the details —
but this one was a beaut, clear as crystal. I was back in Athens,
with Perilla, at one of these highbrow plays of hers where the
villain gets it in the neck in the final act after the chorus have
spent two hours explaining in tedious detail why he or she has
it coming. We were up in the top tiers with the fruit-and-nut
brigade, looking down at the stage. There were two actors,
one in a young man's mask. the other in a woman's. Maybe
it was the distance — it seemed a hundred yards, easy — or
maybe it was because the crowd on the benches around us
were making so much noise, but I couldn't hear what was
going on, let alone recognise which play it was. I began to
get bored, and I shifted around on my cushion until Perilla
poked me in the ribs with her elbow.

'Sit still, Marcus!' she said. 'How can they murder anyone
properly with you fidgeting about?'

'Who's the guy?' I said.

'Corvinus, don't you know *anything* about Greek drama,
for heaven's sake? Orestes, of course. And the woman is his
sister-in-law Lepida.'

'Uh . . . right. Right. Thanks, lady.' I tried to concentrate,
but the old man at the end of the row had stood up, slipped
on a pair of clogs and was tap-dancing down the staircase
towards the priests' seats. I recognised the Wart. Orestes
stopped speaking and turned to stare at him.

'Really, Grandfather!' he snapped. 'This isn't necessary! I
only had them murdered, after all. You'd think you cared.'

Just then they swung a god from a crane above the stage;
only it wasn't a god, it was young Marcus Lepidus. He was
wearing a tutu, like the hour marker on the water clock, only
instead of holding a pointer he had a sword in his belly and
his guts were spilling out. He held up his hand, and the three
raised their faces to look at him. Drops of blood fell from

the gaping wound on to the masks. The whole theatre was
suddenly silent; I could even hear the creaking of the rope.
Lepidus opened his mouth and cleared his throat.

'Listen carefully, Marcus,' Perilla whispered. 'It's the
solution. The god always has the last word.'

I bent forwards, all ears.

'There are worse crimes,' Lepidus intoned, 'than murder.'

I woke in a cold sweat. It was worth it, though, because I
knew now what young Lepidus's secret had been.

35

Next day I paid my really final visit to Furius Camillus at the King's House where he had his office. I'd just given my name to the clerk on the outer desk when the acting chief priest's door opened and a guy in military uniform came out. He gave me a quick, sour glance and carried on walking without so much as a nod. Yeah, well, I wasn't crying. Sertorius Macro's path and mine had crossed briefly a couple of years back when Sejanus was chopped, but on that occasion we hadn't exactly forged the bonds of a lasting friendship. Now he had Sejanus's old job as commander of Praetorians, a political no-hoper like me was beneath the great man's notice. Also, of course, I'd spent the past half-month doing my best to bugger up his carefully orchestrated bit of whitewashing; unwittingly, sure, but these things are bound to rankle. No wonder the bastard had cut me dead.

'You can go in now, sir,' the clerk said.

I tapped on the door and pushed it open. Furius Camillus looked up from his desk. He didn't look happy, to put it mildly; in fact, if he'd been a younger man, or a less self-controlled one, I had the distinct impression he'd've been busting up the furniture.

'Ah. Corvinus,' he said. 'Come in, my dear chap. Close the door and take a seat. I was just going to send for you. There've been ... developments.'

Angry or not, the guy sounded embarrassed. I thought I knew why, too. I pulled up a chair.

'Don't tell me,' I said. 'Your application for an investigative commission into Sextius Nomentanus's finances has been refused and you have orders to drop the case down a very deep hole.'

He blinked. 'Correct,' he said. 'In both particulars. Corvinus, I am bitterly sorry. Not to say ashamed.'

Well, it was all I could've realistically expected. I'd been through this before, and there was no point getting angry myself, certainly not with Camillus. 'That's okay,' I said wearily. 'It happens. Sertorius Macro, right?'

'Indeed.' Camillus spoke through gritted teeth. 'Gods, I hate that bloody man! What the hell right has he to—'

'He was the guy behind Nomentanus. Or rather, his boss Prince Gaius was.'

Camillus sat motionless for a good half-minute, staring at me. Finally, he nodded.

'Yes,' he said. 'Yes, I see. That would explain it.' Then, simply: 'Why?'

'Gaius was responsible for the deaths – ostensibly suicides – three months ago of his own mother and brother. Macro had orders from him not to let the fact go public.'

'Sweet gods!' The deputy chief priest's face went the colour of milk. 'You're sure?'

I shrugged. 'I've no proof, if that's what you mean, and I'm never likely to have; but, yeah, I'm sure. It's the only explanation that makes sense. Certainly Gaius was behind the murders, whatever his reasons were.'

'Gaius himself? Not Macro?' There was a hint of quiet desperation in the tone that I recognised: like a drowning man reaching for a life raft he knows probably isn't there but feels he should make the attempt anyway. Macro as a villain was one thing, but taking in the idea that Rome's next political master was a parricide – let alone living with it – wouldn't come easy to someone like Camillus.

'Uh-uh.' I shook my head. 'Macro might have the clout to stop an investigation here at Rome, but the rest of it – the money angle and the fake treason rap that nailed Proculus – are out of his league. He's no Sejanus, not yet, much as he'd like to be. It has to be Gaius.'

'Not necessarily.' The initial shock over, Camillus had gone very quiet and stiff. Now he cleared his throat. From his impersonal, clinical tone we could've been discussing a fine point of ancient liturgical practice. Understandable: this conversation wasn't just verging on treason, it was over the edge and halfway beyond. 'Oh, no one genuinely believes that Agrippina and Drusus starved themselves willingly; their deaths were too convenient and too close together for coincidence, especially in conjunction with Asinius Gallus's.' He paused. His eyes stared past me at the far wall. 'However, the consensus of opinion is that all three ... fatalities ... originated in a direct order from the emperor.'

'Tiberius had years to get rid of Agrippina and Drusus.' I could've added that the Wart had good reason, too, especially in the lady's case, but Camillus wouldn't know that. 'He didn't. Why do it now?'

'To secure the succession.' Camillus was looking more uncomfortable than ever. It was to the guy's credit that we were having this conversation at all; me, I've got no hang-ups about airing the dirty linen of politics, but even the best broad-striper spends most of his life tiptoeing round the washing-basket. The line between hypocrisy and self-preservation is pretty thin at that level. 'Agrippina and Drusus were the last of the Julian family, and Gallus was their last major supporter.'

'Yeah, right,' I said. 'So if our next emperor's a Julian

himself – which Gaius is – then why kill them at all? The crown prince's own mother and brother? That's some coronation present.'

Camillus blinked and sat back. 'Put like that,' he said, 'it does seem a little ... anomalous. Your alternative explanation, please.'

'Okay.' I'd thought about this on the way over; in fact, I'd thought of nothing else since I'd woken up with the pieces of the puzzle neatly assembled. Sure, I hadn't covered all the angles and never would, things being as they were, but it held together. And the way things had panned out it had to be right, in outline at least. 'First of all, look at it from Gaius's point of view. He may be a Julian by birth, but he's Tiberius's grandson by adoption. He's crossed over the fence and the family's an embarrassment, especially his mother who's hated the Wart for years. And an elder brother would just be a complication. If Gaius is to establish his credentials as Tiberius's successor – *Tiberius's* – then they're better off dead.'

Camillus was still looking at the wall somewhere to the side of my left ear. 'That,' he said, 'if we're speaking dispassionately, as I assume we are, would be an equally strong reason for the emperor himself to have them killed. As I said, to ensure the stability and ease of the succession.'

'Granted. All I'm saying at this point is that in theory Gaius has as much motive for wanting the pair of them dead as Tiberius. Fair?'

Camillus hesitated. 'Yes,' he said finally, like he was dragging the word up with a hook. 'Fair.'

'Fine. Now we get down to character. In your honest opinion, is Gaius Caesar congenitally capable of engineering the deaths of his own mother and brother?'

Camillus was silent for a long time. Then instead of

answering the question he murmured, so softly that I had to lean forward to catch the words, '"There are worse crimes than murder."'

I said nothing.

'That was what young Lepidus meant, wasn't it, Corvinus? That Gaius was not simply a murderer but a parricide?'

'Yeah,' I said quietly. 'Yeah, I think so.'

'Sweet holy Jupiter!' The guy was looking ill. 'So Lepidus knew?'

'He knew. How he found out I'm not sure, nor how Gaius – or Macro, rather – knew that he knew. Cornelia was easier. Macro must've had Lepidus watched. Then it was just a case of creating an opportunity.'

'And of course when Cornelia was murdered the boy realised that he had been the cause of her death. The innocent cause. And that he was powerless even to bring her killers to justice.' The chief priest closed his eyes briefly. 'No wonder he committed suicide. He was a good Roman. Corvinus, this is horrible. What can we do?'

'Nothing.' I felt pretty gut-sick myself. 'Tiberius may even have known about Agrippina and Drusus from the start.' Yeah, I'd bet he had, at that: the Wart didn't miss a trick, he was a cold-blooded bastard where political necessities were concerned and he wasn't in any doubt about his grandson's character. He wouldn't mind taking the rap, either: the tough old bugger was used to being slandered, and the deaths of two more relatives added by popular opinion to his score would be like water off a duck's back. Still, that didn't make Gaius's crime any less. Anything but. 'File and forget, Camillus. Put it down to dirty politics.'

Camillus half smiled. '"Dirty politics",' he said. 'A good phrase. The two words seem to go together more and more naturally these days.' He stood up; stiffly, like the old man he wasn't. 'I've lived too long, Valerius Corvinus. Much too long.'

I didn't say anything, but I knew what he meant. Maybe we all had.

'Well, you've fulfilled your task, young man.' Camillus suddenly took to straightening the objects on his desk, aimlessly, like he needed to feel his hands busy with something, but his voice was brisker. 'You're right, of course; there is nothing to be done, in Gaius's case at least, especially if he had the emperor's . . . cognisance.' His mouth twisted as if the word hurt him. 'The same, unfortunately, goes for Macro. For the present, at any rate.'

Yeah. I thought that that would be the verdict. Not that it made swallowing it any easier, mind. I kept my expression blank.

'As for those more directly involved, Sextius Nomentanus and Lepida,' Camillus cleared his throat again, 'I hold myself to my promise. Leave them to me, and to friends like Lucius Arruntius. Aemilius Lepidus is a sick man, he won't last much longer and losing both a son and a daughter before he dies would hit him hard, but in Lepida's case punishment is only deferred.' He looked at me directly; hard and cold. 'They'll pay, Corvinus, both of them, one way or another, you have my oath on that. I owe it both to Cornelia and the boy. Not to mention my own conscience.'

'Yeah. Right,' I said. I got up.

'You have plans for the Festival?' He followed me to the door.

'No. Not really.' I felt empty.

'Nor have I. I think a quiet few days are in order. The past month has been very tiring.' He hesitated. 'My thanks again, young man. Remember, the fault isn't yours. You did your best.'

'Yeah.' Some best: five innocent deaths, counting Chilo the Watchman's, and I was walking away from them. It was getting to be a habit. 'Have a good Festival, Camillus.'

What else could I do? I went home.

36

Not straight home; I took in Renatius's wineshop off Market Square — the place I'd got stewed in the afternoon of the dinner party with Gaius Secundus — and set about drowning my sorrows. Or some of them, anyway. At least I couldn't fault the weather: by some freak it was almost as warm as March, and most of the outside tables were taken by guys from the Square and the government buildings round about it catching an early lunch. I grabbed the last free bench and ordered up a jug of Spoletan — Renatius was an Umbrian, and proud of it — plus some bread, cheese and olives to fill in the corners.

Yeah, well; that was that, then. Like Camillus had said, I'd done my best and it wasn't my fault we were screwed; certainly if Gaius and Macro were involved there wasn't much point taking things any further, not to mention dangerous to try. It rankled, sure, and the incompleteness left a bad taste in my mouth, but I'd been through this scenario before a couple of times and I was getting pretty philosophical about it. There ain't no sense in bucking the system; especially when the system can roll over and squash you like a beetle without even noticing.

I felt bad about all the deaths, though. Camillus had said that Nomentanus and Lepida would pay, and I trusted him, but the promise of payment in the abstract wasn't exactly satisfying. Call me a ghoul if you like, but I wanted blood, and I wanted it now.

Wants don't get. And at least the case was solved before the Festival; just in time, too, because the next day was the first of the three. I stretched out my legs, sank half the wine in my cup and began to feel better: Renatius's Spoletan is good stuff, and he doesn't overdo the water, either. Hell; what was I beefing about? Spoiled case or not, this was my first Winter Festival in Rome for ten years. I could go down to the Festival Market in Argonauts' Porch with the other punters and buy the candles, the clay dolls and the sticky animals no one ever got round to eating, do the usual holiday things. Who needed sleuthing, anyway?

'Hey, Corvinus!'

I looked up. Gaius Secundus was limping towards me with a candelabrum under his arm.

'Hey, Secundus.' I made space on the bench and signalled to the waiter. 'Last-minute Festival shopping?'

'Yeah.' He parked himself and set the thing down. 'Present for Gemella.'

'Uh-huh.' I took a closer look and grinned. Whoever had sold him it had seen the guy coming. *Rampant cupids* was the phrase that sprang to mind, and the artist seemed to have a penchant for grapes. Having that on the table when you were eating would be a sure-fire way to indigestion. 'She'll love it.'

He shot me a look that was pure old-Gaius and laughed. 'Actually, yeah, she will,' he said. 'It'll go perfectly with the other five. What're you doing down the Square, anyway? Besides getting pissed and sneering at expensive artwork?'

'Unfinished business.' I sipped my wine. 'With the chief priest.'

His face sobered. 'The Vestal murder?'

'Yeah.'

'I thought you'd solved it. The runaway slave.'

'That's right.' I didn't want to go into details; certainly not the finer ones. Luckily the waiter came over at that point and I ordered a plate of sliced sausage and a second cup. 'So how's life with you?'

He helped himself to a piece of my cheese. 'Not bad. You still interested in Sextius Nomentanus, by the way?'

I played it careful. 'Uh-uh. Not any more, pal. The guy's a dead-end.'

Secundus chuckled. 'He's that, all right. Or was that a joke? You knew already?'

'Knew what?'

'He was found on the Aventine early this morning. Near the Rudusculan Gate.'

I set my cup down. 'Nomentanus is dead?'

'They don't come deader. Knife through the heart.' He mopped a scrap of bread in the olive oil. 'The Watch think he was tomcatting and got himself mugged. He was wearing a plain mantle, but luckily the local Watch commander recognised him.'

That would be Lippillus, and it didn't surprise me: Lippillus recognised everyone, and a city judge would be as easy to place as his own grandmother. Shit, though! While Secundus started in on the olives I leaned back and thought things through.

It couldn't've been Camillus's doing, that was certain. And not Macro's, either. Sure, like I'd said to Perilla the guy might well have been booked for a seat on the Ferry, but if Macro had ordered his ticket punched he wouldn't've bothered putting the brakes on Camillus's investigative commission: auditing stops at the grave in this city, and slamming down the shutters on a dead man's accounts would've been pointless. Not to mention eyebrow-raising. Which left the simple, straightforward Watch explanation of an Aventine hug. That was likely enough not to strain anyone's credulity, because knifings in the Raudusculan were two a penny; still, my skin prickled. I'd wanted blood, and I'd got it.

Maybe there was such a thing as divine justice after all.

Lippillus himself was waiting for me when I got in, perched on a couch in the atrium with his short legs swinging like the disreputable dwarf he was. Perilla was feeding him Meton's dried-apple cake. I held up a hand before he could speak.

'Yeah, I know, pal,' I said. 'I heard already. Sextius Nomentanus, right?'

Lippillus swallowed a mouthful of sponge. 'The lads found him tucked in an alleyway next the Crocodile. Neat job: one punch, between the ribs. He probably didn't have time to blink.'

'Marcus, if you two are going to talk anatomical details I think I'll go elsewhere.' Perilla got up. 'Besides, I have work to do.'

I grinned. 'Yeah, okay, lady. Catch you later.' When she'd gone I turned back to Lippillus. 'How did you make the connection? With me, I mean? Nomentanus was after your time.'

'The Hippo said you'd been in asking about him. I thought maybe you'd like to be kept informed.' He paused. 'Also that you might be able to help finger the guy who did it.'

'Uh-huh.' Well, the first bit didn't surprise me: Lippillus could add up faster than an abacus, and the Crocodile would be a logical starting point. The second I wasn't so sure about, especially under the circumstances. My sympathies were all with the killer. 'So what happened exactly?'

'Exactly, I don't know.' He reached over to the wine

jug on the table and poured for both of us. 'Nor does
the Hippo.'

'Genuinely?'

'Yeah. I knew it might be important so I leaned on him
a little.' Ouch. 'Nomentanus was seeing one of the girls on
a regular basis—'

'Phoebe.'

'Right. He went upstairs, came down half an hour later,
had a drink – it must've been about an hour after sunset –
and left. That was the last the fat guy saw of him.'

'He was alone?'

'Yeah. The Hippo says he thinks one of the other
customers – not a regular – may've left at his back but
he can't be sure. The place was full at the time.'

I took a swallow of wine. 'He remember anything about
the customer?'

'No. Not much. Big guy in his twenties, rough type,
maybe a carter. You get a lot of carters in the wineshops
by the gates.'

'Not after sunset you don't.' Sunset was when the carts
moved out to make their deliveries. 'And carters tend to stick
together. They've got their own favourite watering-holes.'

Lippillus grinned. 'You sure you don't want a Watch job,
Corvinus?' he said. I gave him the finger. 'Okay. So not a
carter. That sort of thing, though.'

'He been in before?'

'The Hippo couldn't swear to it either way. It's possible, the guy looked familiar, but like I said the place
was packed and he didn't have the time to notice him
properly.'

I sighed. Yeah, well; it was suspicious, sure. Still, a solo
mantle in the Raudusculan – plain or striped – would be a
prime target for an enterprising knifeman after a fat purse,

and conspiracy theory didn't necessarily apply. Besides, who-ever the guy was who'd zeroed the bastard, vested pecuniary interest or not, he deserved Rome's congratulations and a pension. 'So that's that, then,' I said.

'Maybe. Nomentanus was a city judge. On the other hand the powers-that-be aren't exactly screaming for action.' Lippillus gave me a quizzical glance over his wine cup. 'And that's strange, Corvinus. These two things just don't go together. Unless of course besides being seen as a damn fool to go tomcatting alone on the Aventine after sunset the guy's blotted his copybook in other ways.'

There'd been half a question in his voice. I answered it; I owed him that much.

'He was Myrrhine's boss.'

Lippillus set his cup down and stared at me. Then he whistled softly. 'Uh-huh,' he said. 'Even so, murderer or not, for a city judge not to get automatic five-star treatment we have to be talking political here. Right?'

Jupiter, the guy was smart! 'Yeah,' I said. 'We are.'

'Political enough to scrub the investigation altogether?'

'Easy. Twice over. And if you try to push things, Decimus, you'll be slapped down so hard your head'll ring. From both sides, senatorial and imperial.' I held his look. 'I'll tell you something else: this time it's got my vote. The bastard deserved everything he got and more. How he died is secondary.'

'Fine,' Lippillus said equably. 'Keep your hair on. I'm just thinking aloud here.' Gods! *Thinking aloud* was right: I could almost hear the guy's brain chug. 'Senatorial I can understand, but not imperial. You mean the Wart? Or Gaius and Macro?'

This was getting too close for comfort. I could just tell him the whole story, sure, but that sort of knowledge was dangerous. We'd got corpses enough already. 'Lippillus,' I said, 'watch my lips, okay? Cut it out now, please. You just do not want to know. Believe me.'

I might as well've been talking to the wall. He picked up his wine cup again and sipped slowly.

'Gaius and Macro, then,' he said. 'So what particular dirty laundry are those two beauties kicking under the bed?'

Oh, shit. Well, what the hell; he'd probably work it out anyway in another couple of chugs. It was sickening: solving the case had taken me half a month's hard grind and here he was with the basics in two minutes flat. 'Hang on, pal,' I said. 'You like to hear a scenario? A totally fictitious, totally hypothetical scenario with absolutely no bearing on the real situation whatsoever, in this world or any other?'

'Yeah.' He was grinning. 'I'll settle for that. Tell me.'

I told him. The whole boiling. By the time I'd finished he wasn't grinning any more.

'There isn't anything you can do?' he said.

'Not a thing. And even if there were, I doubt if I'd do it. The Wart'll carry the can like he always does. What's another bit of mud? Whereas when he hangs his mantle up at least Gaius'll start fresh.'

'Screw fresh. The bastard's rotten to the core. In the old days mother-killers got the Rock, whoever they were. Now if their last name's Caesar we put it down to political expediency.' Lippillus got up. He was angry as hell. 'You were right; I didn't want to know. Now that I do, as a Watchman I feel just that much dirtier.'

'How do you think I feel?'

Lippillus grunted. 'You're lucky, Corvinus. You were born one of the great and good. Me, my dad worked a hammer at the cattle market. Where wading through shit's concerned, you've got the family edge.'

Ouch. The guy had a point, though: purple-stripers take in the murky ground rules of politics with their mother's milk. If I couldn't sympathise with the cover-up, at least I could understand the whys and wherefores. Lippillus had a cleaner mind than I did; he couldn't do either.

We walked to the door in silence.

'Have a good Winter Festival, Decimus,' I said.

The frown lifted; not altogether, but enough. We shook hands, which is something we don't often do.

'Yeah. Yeah, Marcus,' he said. 'You too.'

37

I like the Winter Festival. Partly it's the anarchist in me, partly it's the pure pleasure of seeing the happy smiling faces of the slaves when they wake up on a Winter Festival morning to the knowledge that for three whole days they don't have to take any nonsense from the bastards in the mantles. Or that's the theory at any rate. Licensed anarchy and role reversal for three days a year may sound a peachy way to keep the wheels of society oiled, but there's always the morning-after effect. Any silly bugger stupid enough to use the family's best Corinthian vase as a spittoon or feel the mistress up while she's passing him the turnips at dinner is just asking to be clobbered the moment things get back to normal.

Every household has its own little ceremonies. Me and Perilla, we start the day off in the atrium giving out the presents and the cash, after which the guys and girls are free to do what they want until dinner-time. Kitchen staff excepted, for obvious reasons: if we tried to muscle in on the cooking side of things Meton would throw a fit. Besides, Perilla can't boil an egg without burning it, and you can carry equality too far.

So there we were, up and brushed, bright-eyed and bushy-tailed. I'd got my new mantle – not on, because everyone slops around at the Festival – and Perilla had her book-rolls. Bathyllus went into quiet ecstasies over his long johns. I'd bought Alexis a belt like Lysias's to go with his sharp new courting tunic, and Meton had gone back to the kitchen clutching his omelette pan. The various minions and skivvies had their little chinking bags, I'd broken out the sticky animals and that was the heady excitement over for another year. The atrium began to empty. Finally there were only us and Bathyllus left.

'You got any plans for the day, little guy?' I said.

'Yes, sir. I thought I might pay a visit to a friend near the Querquetulan Gate.'

'Uh-huh.' I grinned. 'Good idea, sunshine. You can show her your new thermal leggings.'

Bathyllus coloured. '*He* is a retired schoolmaster from Ephesus, sir, an expert on Pindar and most respectable. We used to play draughts together on the first day of the Winter Festival regularly, until you and the mistress went abroad.'

'Uh, yeah.' I wiped the grin off. After all, it was a holiday, and Bathyllus-baiting was out of order for the duration. 'Yeah, right. Have a nice time, Bathyllus.'

'Thank you, sir. You too.' He left.

Now we were alone I grabbed Perilla round the waist, lifted her up and held on while I planted a Festival smacker between nose and chin. 'How about you, lady?' I said. 'It's a beautiful morning. You fancy a walk?'

'If you like, Marcus. Where to?'

'I thought Sallust Gardens.'

'Mmm.' She gave me a return peck and smiled. 'All right. If you just put me down and stop messing up my mantle I'll—'

Something went *urgleurgleurgle*.

I stiffened. 'Uh ... was that your stomach, lady?' I said cautiously.

'No, dear. I thought it was yours.'

Urgleurgle.

Uh-huh. I set her down slowly and carefully. I didn't want to turn round; I *really* didn't want to—

Urgleurgleting!

'Oh, shit,' I said. I turned and looked at the clock . . .

I could see the pointer rising from here; fast and steady. From the looks of things, if our pal in the tutu and her friend the jolly titan had their way this was going to be the shortest Winter Festival on record.

'Marcus . . .' Perilla said.

Urgleurgleurgleting!

We both watched in fascination. I'd been right to be wary of that thing. The cunning bastard had bided its time until the house was empty. Now it was ready to make its move.

'Don't panic, lady,' I murmured. Then I yelled, '*Bathyllus!*'

Urgleurgle . . .

Pause. *Long* pause. We held our breaths.

'There, Marcus,' Perilla said finally. 'It's—'

. . . ting!

Urgleurgle . . .

The bugger was playing with us. I broke out into a sweat.

'Marcus!' Perilla was really alarmed now. 'Can't you do something?'

'Not a lot.' I went over and looked up at the cistern. Perilla joined me. There was a good five gallons of water in there, and normally it'd stay put, but on this occasion I wasn't taking any bets.

. . . urgleurgleURGLEURGLE . . .

'Oh, fuck!' I said.

'*Marcus!*'

. . . URGLEURGLEURGLETING! TING! TING! . . .

Clunk.

Silence. A *waiting* silence. I didn't like the sound of this.

I stepped carefully to one side, my eyes on the clock. 'Uh, Perilla,' I murmured. 'No sudden moves, right? But if I were you I'd get out of the ...'

TINKLETINKLETINKLEPSSSSSSSSS ...

Too late, and with the contents of a whole cistern behind them the cupids were doing it out of full bladders. The overflow cleared the basin in two seconds flat, hit the tiles in a wave and kept coming. Perilla squealed and jumped back clutching the hem of her mantle while the cistern cheerfully emptied itself all over the atrium floor.

Bastard! Clever, conniving bastard!

'Having problems, sir?'

I looked round. Bathyllus had oozed in like a water-rat, his sandals making little plashing noises in the spreading pool round the now-empty clock.

'What does it look like, pal?' I snapped. 'Get half a dozen skivvies in here with mops and buckets!'

'Skivvies, sir? Mops?' He sniffed. '*Buckets?*'

Oh, hell; the Festival! Cunning was right! 'Look, little guy, never mind tradition, this is an emergency, okay? Bring anyone who's around, even Meton. Your draughts can wait.'

'Very well, sir.' Another sniff. 'I'll see what I can do.'

He squelched off.

The atrium – or that corner of it, at least – was like something out of the flooding of the Nile. I paddled over to my couch and took off my sodden sandals. Perilla was doing the same.

'That monster goes back, lady,' I growled. 'First thing tomorrow morning.'

'It's the Festival, Marcus. All the shops are closed for three days.'

'Fuck.'

'Don't swear, dear. And don't be silly. It's just a little teething trouble; you can expect that with any new machine. The engineer will—'

'Perilla, watch my lips.' I glared at the clock and it sneered back at me. 'This is final. Either that thing goes or I do. It's alive, it's smarter than both of us and it hates us.'

'Nonsense!'

'How else would you describe something that waits for the perfect psychological moment and then pisses all over your living-room floor? Jupiter, even a Gallic wolfhound wouldn't do this much damage. For a parallel you'd need to go the length of a fucking elephant.'

Perilla was wringing out the edge of her mantle. 'Marcus, dear, you're needlessly anthropomorphising. It's only a machine. And please don't swear; I've already told you.'

'Listen, lady. If we don't send it back then I'll personally fucking anthropomorphise the brute with a sledgehammer and a hacksaw. And that's a promise.'

'Very well. If you're sure.'

'Sure I'm sure.'

The mop-and-bucket gang trailed in: Bathyllus, Meton and two vegetable-peelers. They didn't look happy. Meton especially. Gods! Come dinner-time we were all going to suffer, I could tell that now. Scratch the special Winter Festival meal; it was going to be omelettes all round, with no afters, and lucky to get them. No one was going to tell me this wasn't planned. 'Right,' I said. 'Thanks, pals. Just—'

Knock knock knock.

The front door. I'd bet the clever bastard had engineered that as well somehow. Bugger. This was all horribly familiar. Still, it couldn't be what's-her-name the stringy Vestal back. I doubted if we were on her Winter Festival visiting list. I just hoped it wasn't Mother; that was all I needed.

'Shall I get that also, sir, or do you think you can manage?'
Bathyllus, and sarky as hell.

'No, that's okay, sunshine. I'll do it.' I padded through
to the lobby and opened up.

Aegle was standing on the step with a covered plate in
her hand. Beside her was a big, well-muscled guy I half
recognised but couldn't place.

'Happy Winter Festival, Corvinus,' she said. 'We're not
disturbing you, are we?'

Behind me I could hear the clanking of mops and buckets.
'Uh, no.' I stepped back. 'No, come in.'

'That's okay, we're not stopping.' She handed me the
plate. 'I brought you some sticky animals from Harmodia's
mum's stall. A Festival present. And this is Thalia's brother
Phrixus. He wanted to meet you.'

Phrixus held out a hand the size of a spade, and I suddenly
remembered: the customer in the Crocodile, who'd come in
after me the time I'd asked about Nomentanus and sat
quietly drinking his wine while I was talking to my thirsty
punter friend. The last piece of the puzzle slipped into place.
Our eyes met as we shook, and I knew he knew that I knew;
also that it was why the guy had come.

'Happy Festival, Phrixus,' I said.

'And to you, sir.' The voice was quiet with just a touch
of wariness. Smart, too, with good vowels. Rough hands
and working tunic or not, Phrixus was no uneducated
bonehead.

'You, uh, sure you wouldn't like a cup of wine?' I said.
'On the house this time.'

The corner of his mouth lifted and the wariness left his
face. 'Oh, I'm not much for wine, sir,' he said carefully. 'Or
wineshops. Just now and then, when I'm working.'

'Is that so, now?' I said. I closed the door behind us and

motioned them towards the stone bench that ran the length of the lobby wall. 'What work do you do exactly?'

'I run a transport business. Three carts, out of the Tiburtine Gate.'

'Not the Raudusculan?' I kept my voice neutral.

'No.' His smile was more relaxed now. 'I've been down there two or three times, but it's not an area I know well. In fact, if I hadn't been tagging along behind a friend the first time I visited I might never've found where I needed to go.' He paused. 'And I'd've hated that to happen. I really would.'

'Meaning the last time you managed okay on your own?'

'I got what I wanted done, sure.'

'Uh-huh.' I sucked a tooth. 'Debt collecting, would that be?'

'That's right.' His eyes held mine. 'You have a problem with that?'

I shook my head slowly. 'Not me, pal. I'm all in favour of people paying what they owe.'

Aegle had been looking from one of us to the other. 'Corvinus?' she said. 'Phrixus? What is this?'

'Just a friendly conversation, lady,' I said. 'Shooting the breeze, that's all.'

'Yeah, sure, and I'm Cleopatra.'

I grinned and handed her back the plate. 'Okay, Cleo, why don't you have one of Harmodia's mother's sticky hippos and close your ears for a minute?' I turned back to Phrixus. 'Ah ... this debt collection, friend. You missed out on the first instalment, right? Why would that be, now?'

He shrugged. 'I was around. I just didn't have a chance to collect, that's all. Too many other creditors muscling in. It was no big deal. So long as the transaction got made it didn't matter who made it.'

'And the, uh, debt itself? How did you find out about that?'

'Aegle here told me.' Aegle looked up at him and opened her mouth to speak but closed it again. Phrixus ignored her. 'She gave me your . . .' He paused; his lips twitched. 'She gave me the address of that friend I mentioned.'

Ouch. 'You mean the purblind, unobservant bastard you followed twice to the Raudusculan without his knowing you were behind him?' I said.

He grinned. 'Yeah. That's the one.'

'So you just hung around outside his front door from first light on and stuck with him when he came out, right?'

'Uh-huh. Easy.' He patted his stomach. 'Good for the waistline, too. You get flabby working the carts.'

Hell! And I hadn't had so much as a prickle! I was losing my touch! Still, it'd all turned out for the best, so maybe that was why my sixth sense hadn't kicked in with the usual warning.

Aegle had put the plate down on the bench beside her. 'Look, you two,' she said. 'Cut it out, okay? You're talking about Myrrhine's death, aren't you?'

I let her have my blankest stare while Phrixus carried on grinning.

'What gave you that idea?' I said.

She flushed. 'I'm not stupid, Corvinus, so don't patronise me. Are you saying there was someone else involved in the murders besides Myrrhine? And that Phrixus here killed him?'

'As a matter of fact there was.' I kept my face straight. 'Myrrhine was recruited by one of the city judges, a guy called Sextius Nomentanus, and yes, by pure coincidence Nomentanus is dead. About Phrixus killing him I don't

know.' I glanced at the big guy. 'That name ring any bells
with you, pal?' I said.

Phrixus shook his head slowly. 'First time I've heard it,'
he said. 'And I don't remember killing anyone with purple
on his mantle, either. That's the gods' own truth.'

I turned back to the girl. 'There you are. Satisfied?'

'No.' She shrugged. 'Evidently you are, though.' I didn't
speak. 'So how did he die?'

'Who knows? Coincidence, like I said. Or call it divine
retribution if you like.' Being careful not to look at Phrixus,
I took one of the sticky animals. It could've been a horse,
or maybe a goat: Harmodia's mother was no artist. 'That's
the way the Watch are viewing it, anyway. As just another
Aventine mugging. Case closed.'

Phrixus stood up. 'We won't take up any more of
your time, Valerius Corvinus,' he said. 'It's been nice
meeting you.'

'Likewise.' I could still hear the clanking of buckets. 'A
real pleasure. Uh ... one last thing, pal.'

'Yes?'

'You ... uh ... take small commissions? Like moving
articles of furniture?'

'Sure.' He frowned. 'Such as?'

'There's something I want delivered to an acquaintance of mine, name of Furia Gemella. A water clock.
One of these big marble bastards. I know it's the Festival, but ...'

'No problem.' The frown lifted. 'I'll bring the cart round
myself. After sunset today do you?'

'That'd be perfect.' I held out my hand and we shook
again. 'Nice meeting you, friend. Have a good Festival.'

They left. I grinned and went back inside to pick up
Perilla for our jaunt to the Sallust Gardens.

Case closed. Definitely, this time. Yeah, and a lot more satisfyingly than I'd thought it would be, in more ways than one. The clock would go well with Gemella's set of candelabra. And the lady would just love the cupids.

AUTHOR'S NOTE

The story is set in December AD 33. The prominent 'Julian' Asinius Gallus, Drusus Caesar and Agrippina did indeed die in this year, all from starvation, after a long term of imprisonment in separate locations and within weeks of each other. It is also interesting — from my point of view — that the deaths coincided more or less with Gaius's own marriage to Junia Claudilla, who had connections with the imperial family; with the marriages, likewise arranged, of his two sisters; and with Gaius's virtual establishment as Tiberius's de facto successor.

Tacitus, of course — being Tacitus — puts the blame squarely on Tiberius. In the case of both Drusus and Agrippina, he cites a campaign on the emperor's part to blacken the characters of the dead Julians, alleging persistent treason and, in Agrippina's case, adultery with Gallus. Also interestingly from my conspiracy-theory novelist's viewpoint, the historian reports the Senate's shock that Tiberius should make public Drusus's slanderous attack on his own person, as reported verbatim to them by (significantly) an officer of Macro's Praetorians, which included the wish that the emperor might suffer divine punishment for killing so many members of his family. The Senate, Tacitus says (*Annals*, VI, 24), 'were both horrified and amazed that [Tiberius], who had once been so clever and secretive at concealing his crimes, had become so confident that he had stripped away the very walls [of Drusus's prison] and shown his grandson thrashed by a centurion, beaten by slaves, and begging in vain for life's basic necessities.'

Damning stuff, and a neat bit of constructive propaganda, possibly, on the part of Gaius and Macro: another handful of mud thrown at the old regime which would set it nicely in contrast with its up-and-coming replacement. Certainly it would make sense in the context of my fictional framework, with Macro – Tiberius's mouthpiece at Rome – carefully engineering matters so that the blame falls on the emperor while his real patron Gaius goes unsuspected.

Whatever the truth may be, I would stress yet again that the story per se, in common with all the Corvinus stories, is a work of fiction, not of fact; in the case of *Last Rites*, specifically, there was no murder of a Vestal in AD 33, nor is Sextius Nomentanus a historical figure. As with *Ovid*, *Germanicus* and *Sejanus* – the other 'political' Corvinus books – I hope that readers who know something of the background will find the underlying theory plausible and even thought-provoking in terms of real history, but – and very importantly – it must be kept in mind that being a novelist I can and do create links and invent motives for which no objective proof exists, even where the people and incidents themselves are real; which practice, of course, is complete anathema to the academic historian. Thus to view the stories in any way as 'history' would be dangerous in the extreme.

That aside, the reader may be interested in the actual, historical fates of some of the characters. Galba became – very briefly – emperor on Nero's death in AD 69. He was killed while attempting to escape during an insurrection by the Prætorians fomented by his equally short-lived successor Salvius Otho. Macro survived into Gaius's principate as his major supporter but was forced into suicide by him the following year, AD 38. Marcus Aemilius Lepidus Senior died in the course of the year of the story's setting, although Tacitus does not give a precise date. I have implied a terminal illness, but held back the death for reasons of plot and also to link it (through Furius Camillus's promise to Corvinus) with his daughter Lepida's death three years later. She had lived, Tacitus says, 'detested [for her immoralities], but escaped punishment while her father was alive', a comment which was the origin of the part she plays in my story. After Lepidus Senior's death she was prosecuted for adultery: the names of the prosecutors are not given. The charge being proved beyond doubt, she committed suicide.

Latin names, where the characters actually existed, are always a problem. I turned the confusion of the two Marci Aemilii Lepidi – father and son – to use in the plot, but had to separate out the two women, Aemilia (Galba's wife) and Lepida. Both, in reality, had the same name, Aemilia Lepida. Obviously this would have caused difficulties both for me and for the reader; hence my (purely arbitrary) division of the single name between them.

Another area of potential difficulty, or rather of difference between the Roman world and ours, is that of the priesthood. We tend to think of a priest as a person with a religious vocation who fills a role clearly marked off – in its essence, anyway – from the secular. The Romans did not; at least where the state religion was concerned (mystery religions such as that of the Great Mother Cybele were another matter, as was the priesthood of Jupiter, which was governed by archaic taboos). Roman priests did not, in any sense, 'represent' the gods, still less preach a code of moral values to a laical flock: their function was more administrative, to see to it that the rites and sacrifices of the religious year were properly conducted and, in certain cases, to prescribe ad hoc ceremonies on the authority of a written compendium of past precedents. Because of this, there was nothing at all anomalous to Roman eyes in a priest *simultaneously* holding both a priesthood and a secular magistracy, nor did he necessarily even have to be religiously inclined: to give a priest the title of 'Reverend' or similar – or for a priest to expect it – would, to a Roman, make no sense at all. Thus although in Roman terms Nomentanus would be a 'priest' – his title in Latin translates as 'one of the Fifteen responsible for conducting the necessary rites' – I have avoided the word where he is concerned and used the invented phrase 'religious officer', which emphasises his administrative function.

The reader might also be interested in the custom of the Winter Festival ('Saturnalia' in Latin). This took place over three days, from 17 to 19 December, and has definite similarities to our own Christmas; or rather to the medieval festival characterised by the Lord of Misrule. During this period the normal rules governing society were relaxed, suspended or even reversed; for example, slaves ate in the dining-room before the family meal and the party-mantle ('synthesis') plus freedman's cap replaced the toga as ordinary outdoor day-dress for upper-class citizens – at least, on the first day. Gifts were exchanged, and also candles and clay dolls, which served the same function as our Christmas cards. There was a great deal of gambling (not strictly legal at other times) and people played games. On the first day, dice were thrown to determine the 'King' – who could be a slave – and for the duration of the Festival his instructions had to be obeyed by all on pain of forfeits.

*   *   *

Finally, the clock. The smart-as-paint Greeks were fully capable of producing a water clock ('clepsydra' – literally 'water-stealer') of the kind I've described, although I have gone over the top a bit with the duck-valves: the differing length of the Roman hour throughout the year was catered for – as I imply in the text – by adding and removing wax to vary the flow of water. The clock's origins, however, owe a lot to the new all-singing, all-dancing computer which we've just acquired although, like Corvinus, I view it as too smart for its own good and continue to use my steam-driven Amstrad PCW8256 for writing. It hasn't, as yet, shown any signs of megalomania, let alone incontinence, but I'm keeping tabs on it.

My thanks, as always, to the staff of Carnoustie library for getting me books; to my wife Rona, ditto; and to Roy Pinkerton and his colleagues of Edinburgh University's Classics Department for fielding the occasional awkward technical question.